The Song Itself

A Gnostic Remembrance

Authored Anonymously

**Translated
by**

Yäq Cuartz

TheSongItself.net

Published by TheSongItself, Jacob Curtis

ISBN 978-0-6151-6920-0

TheSongItself.net

Translator's Preface

Fortune shined upon me the day I found this mysterious autobiography in our city's central library. It was without barcode, ISBN or Dewey decimal designation. At the time, I was perusing books on woodworking. I planned to build a bridal gazebo for my now ex-fiancé (an investment in a mail-order bride will not pay off, I must warn the reader; if one chooses this form of matrimony, keep her away from hot-dog venders—they are a randy and unscrupulous lot). The codex stood betwixt Mrs. Ann Tinomy's The Art of Luthiery: A Discourse on the Foundations of the Techne of Song and her sumptuously illustrated tome titled Carving Crazy Cats: The Weekend Whittler's Guide to Wacky Statues of Bastet (a book that is filled with both practical carving techniques and stories concerning the Egyptian feline goddess; I encourage all to pick it up at their leisure). The manuscript was enclosed within a weathered and deteriorating goatskin cover—stitched to form a small briefcase-like satchel. Geometrical shapes (intersecting circles and triangles) were etched on this cover. It looked much like those other Gnostic codices found by a certain Egyptian farmer while he was digging for guano in the Nag Hammadi Valley. Upon opening the book, I found it was written in a language resembling Greek. I took it from the shelves and hid it in my coat, so captivated by its enigmatic script and binding.

After some investigation, I discovered that the codex was written in several languages, some ancient and others of a more modern pedigree. Most of the manuscript, I have come to learn, was written in a particularly old form of Greek. There were, however, also chapters in the Egyptian language of Coptic, the Semitic language of Biblical Aramaic, and the climactic final chapters were written in Pig Latin. Many English words were also utilized, especially where purely modern ideas or devices were described.

I showed this codex to a professor of linguistics and ancient languages who was, at the time, lecturing at the local university. He enlightened me to the nature of the scripts. When I attempted to enlist his help in its translation, he informed me, "I would refuse to disgrace a fire with this bastardization of noble tongues," adding with a snort, "even if I were freezing to death." He was explaining, as I understood him, that his reverence for the work would compel him to die of hypothermia before destroying such a masterpiece. He would not translate the codex. I think he was quite distraught at lacking the mental and spiritual fortitude necessary to translate such a magnificent opus, for he fell into hyperbole, saying it was "the worst Greek" he had ever seen (and he even personalized the attack, conveying something about my profoundly vexing and obtuse nature).

After taking my proposed collaboration to other scholars, and receiving similarly reactive responses, I set upon the task of translation alone. I intensely studied the codex's ancient forms of communication. After feeling fairly comfortable with these scripts, the call of translation seized me. Although I feel that this current translation is quite 'literal', I have taken some minor editorial liberties. Realizing that many of our anonymous protagonist's sentences lack either verb or noun (and sometimes both), I illuminated these fragments with the most appropriate words. I have attempted to add only a few short chapters of my own creation (to better express the author's intentions), and have merely dismissed a few paragraphs and one chapter from this version.

Translation is an arduous and introspective process requiring spiritual stamina and mental focus, especially for the newcomer. It is my sincerest hope that I have accurately rendered the words of the original into a form that the English-speaking world may appreciate and digest. This translation has been a labor of love and has brought me, personally, to an exhilarating stage of spiritual and intellectual growth. I beg of you, dear reader, to breathe in the profound truths of this document, allow it to dwell within you—making the words part of your innermost being as I have done. For me, this manuscript is more than just a collection of interesting characters and dilemmas, but a document of divine wisdom.

This manuscript holds within its pages the allegory of human resurrection on a sublime level. Works, such as this one, resound with the humbling, esoteric chime of human recognition. Like this memoir, there are certain few works that simultaneously embrace and ridicule the mysteries of man's fate. This book delves into one human being's redemption. It is full of self-inflicted suffering and banal epiphany. I believe it to be a factual account, despite the fact that our protagonist is obviously liberal with the truth, that inconsistencies dominate the pages, and that supernatural phenomena linger behind every word. It is a story of inner struggle and redemption through experiential knowledge.

Interestingly, the entire drama unfolds before a Gnostic backdrop. This term does not qualify a single sect of individuals or a homogeneous philosophy; only through the systemization of common themes have we, moderns, ascribed these various groups, some archaic and some more recent, with a single title. Although academics continue to bicker about the definition of Gnosticism and the common threads that draw together this complex of devotees, it seems clear that the two dominant ideas of all these groups are *experiential knowledge* and some form of denial of the physical world. Our protagonist, too, journeys through a world where this type of gnosis is distilled.

I hope, dear reader, that you find this historical document as enlightening and amusing as I do.

Yäq "Oudeís" Cuartz
Portland, Oregon
February 2003

To the Reader
(From the Author)

Please don't place too much trust in my words, for I tend to deceive both myself and my fellows. At the same time, allow me some bit of confidence; my intention is not to mislead (understand "intention" with a certain ambiguity). Think of me as "friend" and as "other", but do not place me in an embrace—proximity compels me to lie. Above all, relinquish your judgment and disgust until you've heard the entire song, until you've hummed every word and your fingers have touched every page. I encourage you to roll the stone over in hand and sculpt it with the flesh of your palm, but wait before flinging it at your sexless messenger, wait until you've reached the tonic of this etude.

Yes, I am now forced to confess that I brought the book—the ancient hymnal. Yes, I knew before I arrived what I possessed and to whom I brought it. But I forgot; you must believe me. I forgot it all within the inferno—at the beginning.

This book sings my remembering, just as I sang my remembering. I have written it so that you too may sing it. The written word, however, like musical notation, compels us to cognitive sloth (just ask Phaedrus). Our society fails to regard memory as a virtue. Instead, we think that memory is not necessary in a civilization where writing is so ubiquitous. But I warn, and I jot down my story simultaneously, memory is the foundation of knowledge. Memory should not be denied; we are obliged to remember, despite Time's sedulous work to the contrary. When my song ends, try to hum it back to yourself or transpose it to the clavichord, but remember the song. It is not only my song but also a reflection of the Song Itself. Thank you.

"Or have we not known that all of this overture is from the Song Itself that there is need to learn?"
—Plato's <u>The Republic</u>, 531D

1.

Promethean Nightmare

Rain's tapping woke me from a visionless dream. I heard no sound at all. Overhead, the ovum moon flooded the half-sleeping world with light through a passing window in the clouds. I walked aimlessly through the wet streets. The heavy air of the evening hung motionless and cold, promulgating only silence and the sulfuric stench of fire.

I turned and beheld a fury of earthly apparitions accompanying this unnatural silence. Fire trucks flung their red and yellow warnings across the building facades, the swirling lights looked like demons spiraling around the buildings. Tentacles of flame flailed angrily from a third-story window as firefighters aimed their water cannons at the blaze and erected ladders skyward. A huge black column of smoke rose up like a brawny genie answering a misguided wish. Apartment dwellers, evacuated from slumber, stood in slippers—their arms clutching their shivering bodies as they gazed at the inferno that was home. A pale man convulsed in the street, contorted with epileptic shock; his parted robe revealed his tensed white muscles. A little girl in pink pajamas, clutching a worn teddy bear, buried her sobbing face into the comfort of her mother's midriff. And within this nightmare, I knew the horror of history had been incinerated by misguided justice, but would soon be resurrected from the ashes.

I walked toward the chaos of fire and smoke, caught within a surreal silence, passing anxious police officers unreeling yellow caution tape and stepping over canvas hoses taut with flowing water, to the double doors of the building. Not a soul attempted to stop me from entering, nor did anyone seem to acknowledge my presence as I made my way past the smoke stained faces and the heavy black hats of the firemen. I felt like an unnoticed child captured in a nightmare.

One of the large doors was propped open bidding my entry. They stood ten feet high, adorned with intricately wrought stained glass in art-nouveau style. Their translucent images sparkled with color. These doors seemed wholly out of place; two slight and naked nymphs, beautifully rendered in flowing lead line and brilliant color, reposed within a framework of slithering green foliage while a large white moon floated effortlessly between them on their fingertips. This pagan scene graced both doors, and I passed through their watchful color then under the stone, bas-relief sign bearing the structure's name: The First Aeon.

The marble floor of the foyer lay burdened with plump hoses trailing through the dark hallways and up the stairwells. Firefighters wielding axes and lugging breathing apparatuses scrambled in the halls as I moved effortlessly to the third floor. This hallway was filled with smoke and darkness. It was void of light. I followed my fingers along the wall, feeling my way along the pealing wallpaper. This realm was vacant of firefighters; the smoke must have been too intense and the heat too overpowering for even their skill and equipment.

Finally, I found my fingers blindly tracing the rounded engraving of 3-3-3. This place burned with an incestuous familiarity. As I stood in front of that apartment door, shrouded in the object of arson, I felt an unholy seething in my stomach. It fought, writhing with agitation. My entrails ached as I placed my hand on the scalding doorknob; this malignant fetus erupted in a frenzy of spasms. Unaware of my own actions, I kicked the door with an unbeknownst force; it shattered in a brittle hail of debris. Its splinters and remnants, accompanied by the newly found oxygen, added fuel to the room's combustion. A bright ball of flame from this deadly mix exploded into being as I rushed into the room. My irises violently overtook my pupils, imprisoning them to mere pinholes from the eruption of light. The walls of the room bled with fiery paint. The furniture burned from within, illuminated by internal incineration. The floorboards glowed with fire's consumption. Stacks and stacks of books stood around the walls like fiery sentinels witnessing the furious episode. The light of flame was devouring the whole room. The inferno sucked every ounce of atmosphere from the place leaving only a dead Tartarosian light.

Then, I saw her lying on the ground, her thin arms loosely pulling her knees into her chest. Little dots of crimson clung to her angelic skin and had splattered themselves on her azure nightgown. Her chest heaved sporadically, and she coughed under the toxic vacuum of smoke and heat. The youth's eyes were shut tight in an attempt to battle this nightmare, filling her face with wrinkled anxiety. Yet, within this unnatural scene, a piece of my soul grasped hold of a foul pleasure. I gazed at her young body, with its sensuous curves and archetypal beauty—the innocence of her naked toes and the fluid contour of ankle stretching into calf. Her thick hair, the color of fertile earth, fanned out around her head highlighting her aquiline beauty. She laid there—feminine purity. Beneath her nightgown, her soft breasts and erect nipples, stimulated by the ferocity of the events imprisoning her, unknowingly taunted my senses. Time had evaporated, the flames of this sonorousless world bathing statically on this carnal object. My eyes followed those perfect toes to hills of pink heel and milky calf, and then made the assent atop the knee with perception spreading through the round hedonism of the thigh, the gentle furrows of her gown stopping any further visual straying. The nest in my stomach churned. I buckled over, wrenched with pain and self-disgust.

As I lifted the suffocating cherubim into my arms, I caught sight of a round shadow in the room's corner. Substance crept into this form, as I squinted through the accumulating smoke. It took on the shape of a man in unnatural position. The figure lay contorted with a roll of pale fat spilling out of a fleece bathrobe and over its boxer shorts. A pool of blood and small pink and white chunks of organic matter formed a material halo around the head. The face was masked in a gruesome collage of bloody holes and ruptured flesh. I could see no weapon within its reach—no implement within the proximity of suicide. This scene burned fiercely of murder.

I shook the sight from my mind and clutched the young, but dying, girl close to my chest. She felt weightless in my arms. Her warm and fading breath touched my check. Her heart pounded against my body as she fought the toxic world. This beating seemed to rattle my own body, as if her soul was seeking sanctuary in my sinful cavity. How I wished I were pure enough to give her spirit safe harbor.

I raced through the lightless atmosphere. Time raged once more. Heat and flame penetrated every pore of my body. The whole building ached with the disease of fire. I felt the oak flooring begin to buckle as I raced down the stairs. I sprinted through the oppressive heat of the foyer and then burst into the cool night.

I left my girl to the earthly care of the street. The firemen had exited the building; perhaps it was too dangerous even for those who were trained in the suppression of Prometheus' gift. I watched as the ravenous flames, like hungry worms, twisted their way through the wood and brick. Standing there, calmly absorbing the images, I was only abstractly conscious of a past. The elements of this scene clung to my memory with familiarity, yet I could not (or perhaps refused to) recognize the reality of my history. The feelings were like those with which one is infused during the activity of sleep, where one is met with a paradox of emotion. The dreamer has a casual acceptance that this dream environment is a place she has traversed previously, yet another entity of the soul knows that this is no region it has been. This slumbering wanderer may think to herself, "This is my house," although her vision of the place is like nothing she has encountered—perhaps much larger or in a different style. Her soul is in conflict, not knowing whether to believe the feeling of the place or to believe the visual data.

As I walked from the inferno, the raindrops gained weight and tempo. The sky gathered strength and aided the firefighters in their smothering. They were now preparing for a second assault on the building. All of them had evacuated the structure. Flames and smoke poured from several windows and the roof. Paramedics were loading an elderly woman into an ambulance. Three teenagers stood pointing at the collapsed body of the young woman whom I had saved as a second ambulance jolted to a stop. A robust police officer sat on a curb holding a bloody piece of gauze to his temple. The epileptic stood coughing and wiping his brow. The little girl, who had previously taken refuge in her mother's stability, was now sleeping—wrapped in a thick blanket, her mother tenderly brushing her hair with her fingertips. Everyone was oblivious to the gathering storm. Instead, they were immersed in the repercussions of fire.

My mind stumbled into questions of fiery specters and rain. Nothing brought answers, but the world expanded as the silence gave way to a single woody tone. This harbinger soared down, penetrating the ether of silence with its breadthless power. My sense of hearing was restored by the distinctive hum of a clarinet.

The Music of the Pleroma and the Psychopomp

And with that single note, the world blossomed into sound. The gutters, clogged with debris and overcome with water, overflowed with a second ferocious splashing of rain like the rattling of snare drums. The storm drains, overburdened by their task of expelling the weather, backed up and were belching like a myriad of tubas playing in different keys. Cars and trucks barreled through the flooded streets, creating foamy wakes of water, oil and refuse in shrill and sweeping tones. The wind squealed through the trees' branches like oboes in high register. A truck sat idling—the strokes of its engine clanked in consistent time. There was the viola wail of a street bike and the trumpet blast of an angry car horn. A young couple, clad in raincoats, ran together; the fingers of their four hands were entwined around an umbrella. Their feet rhythmically scattered puddles over the sidewalk. The howl of a rain-drenched cat shivered through the amplification of his alley. I was captive within the auditory confusion of water: spattering, splashing, tapping, gurgling, and whooshing in its fall to earth. A clarinet, free from this cacophony, floated above—an unaffected, crisp solo over the chaos of sound. I followed it.

As I gained distance from the inferno, my skin bristled from the evening's dank air. I shivered—my hands in the pockets of my pants and arms tight against my sides. The rain had gained strength, as the clouds remained a looming reminder of the nature of this place with only two seasons: spring and fall. This city was forever under the facet of rain: either the tepid rain of spring or fall's cold precipitation. The rain had mingled with the oils of my forehead. My hair was plastered against my head, as if I had just stepped from the tub. I was hardly dressed appropriately for this November weather, wearing only cotton garments now heavy from the evening's showers.

I tried to recall what had led me out of doors with such ill-suited clothing, but life—up to the vivid thrall of fire—was itself only wet ash and embers. Like the apartment building, the complex of my memory lay in smoking ruin leaving only a drenched façade. All that had come before this moment had been incinerated. I was left with only the calcified and soaked remains of recent events: the dead man, the girl, the rain, the silence and the flames.

As my mind rummaged through the charred corridors of memory, my body was only a block away from the music's source. I walked slowly to the band. A crowd crescented the musicians, some stood wearing trench coats glazed with rain, others wore parkas glistening with the slick phosphorous radiance of the street lamps. The group made four: a double-bass player, drummer, guitarist and clarinetist. The empty branches of deciduous trees and brick multi-storied buildings framed them like an improvised amphitheater. The whole city stood around this eclectic quartet.

I examined the band, engrossed by this out-of-place occurrence, and forgot my own shivering. The bass player towered over them all. He stood six-and-a-half feet tall. His thin fingers, knobby joints protruding, gripped the neck of his instrument, as he gazed silently at the clarinetist. A cloud of condensed breath wafted from his mouth. He was draped in a long tan trench coat. His jaw was clenched angular and rigid. His whole body contradicted the meandering soliloquy of the clarinet. He was tensed and focused, as if ready to spring at a moment's notice. His eyes were slits behind his wire-rimmed glasses, and his thin lips were pulled taut over his teeth.

The drummer sat relaxed, scratching at his head with one of his sticks. He wore a black beret over his straight black hair. An enigmatic bronze emblem was pinned to his hat. His thick lids gently hid the portals to his soul as he stretched with meditative ease. Heavy jowls and olive complexioned flesh hung from his face, masked in serene expression. He was of great contrast to the green and lanky Teutonic beast of a bass-man—instead, sitting round, Mediterranean and leaving middle age.

The guitarist was perched on his amplifier tapping the pale spruce top of his guitar. The cord of the amp trailed like a tail across the street and into a near-by business. He nodded his head to the hidden rhythm of the clarinet. A cigarette dangled from his lips and jittered with excitement. He was a white man in his mid-thirties. Short brown hair shot from his head in all directions like a confused nimbus, and his goatee stood twisting from his chin in defiance of gravity. He tapped his foot to the apparition of time. The little man wore an emerald raincoat that was stained in various shades—tokens of many past events. This guitarist

14

possessed a narrow face whose most prominent features were a Romanesque nose and dark, sleepy eyes.

Then I turned my attention to the clarinet player. His flesh was as black as the grenadilla wood of his instrument. His belly inflated and deflated as he gave life to the dark serpent in his mouth. He swayed with his long and elegant river of song. His shoulder-length dreadlocks accentuated the harmonic motion as he leaned easily into his notes. Only his complete focus and a thin linen robe, tied under the armpits, defended him from the elements. The unblemished purity of his attire danced gingerly around him in the wind.

...And then a cymbal rolled; its volume mounted evenly though the streets, until, with cosmic crescendo, broke, and the music poured as if from the firmament. The cool-headed tones of the clarinet mingled with the clouds and fire of the night. The bottomless tones of a double bass became the black sky on which the clarinet danced with the reflecting maiden of night. A bashful guitar twirled with seventh chords along this musical ecliptic. Slowly, the six-string found his place among the nocturnal singers and began echoing in thirds and fifths the sauntering melody of the woody stick. The two swung innocently, twirling together upon aeons of innocence. Then, as if realizing themselves, becoming conscious of their strength and their fury—their immortal disgust—they loomed and spread. It became like Genesis and Ragnarok simultaneously, as bass drum and cymbals thunderously resounded. The simplicity of echoed melodies began gaining speed and discord. Wrathful sound swept through the streets. With frenzied chromatic power, the guitar and woodwind, amplified and angry, struck the city relentlessly. Augmented and diminished chords scorched the ears. The bass rolled out wave upon wave of cosmic sentence, shaking bone and planet and Time all at once. Modulating in half-steps higher and higher, the clarinet shrieked, curdling the blood with understanding. The guitarist beat his instrument, generating piercing wails of feedback. This universal requiem was clad in sonic vengeance. It was the sonorous revenge upon creator and created, and yet, in its omnipotent horror it possessed majesty and beauty. These chords and this atonal epiphany rushed through the clouded night, over blacktopped progress with the intensity of blue-white flame, consuming spiritual perversity, cleansing and purifying the audience via temporal-spatial annihilation. The scale of the sound, the balanced power of every purifying, punishing, awe-inspiring note culminated, conveying a primordial meaning beyond the limits of the starry sphere or the concrete tombs.

My heart pounded against my chest. Every muscle of my body was tense. The world was sanctified in sound. The inferno receded, giving way to tones and rhythms of dark revelation. The pace slowed. Space crept between the notes, each clear, distinct from its brethren in noble melodic minor. The clarinet sang prophesy under the new sky. Clouds gave way to the redemption of moon and the Song Itself. The tyrants of night gazed down from their celestial home and the ovum moon echoed light from missing Helios.

I opened my eyes and saw the band of musicians, the five and eight-storied brick and concrete buildings, the sparkling black streets, the red and yellow schools of leaves floating down curb grates, and all the bystanders trying to snap their fingers and tap their toes to the nocturnal jazz etude—a pretext of being untouched by the judgmental music. The musical group set a less avant-garde course by playing a swing song. The music lost its rapturous intensity, and, with this loosening, the players relaxed—dropping their shoulders, grinning with closed eyes and nodding their heads to the accentuated rhythm of the high-hat. Swaying back and forth with the Two and the Four, the bass player plucked the sinuous stings of his instrument in articulate, bouncing arpeggios, giving the song a strolling feel. His fingers ambled with ease and fluidity up and down the fingerboard. The drummer's sticks skipped along the taught head of the snare and the golden crown of the ride cymbal. His beret and corpulent face bobbed with the syncopated thumps of the bass drum. The guitarist strummed out clean, full chords on every beat; his left hand gingerly striking a pose and then

16

moving to the next chord and then the next. He was exact in his refined movements, yet his tone was warm and calm.

The clarinetist eased himself down onto the wet grass. He stretched his arms out from his body and allowed his head to dangle and roll in arcs. He seemed to be gathering his strength for this wholly new musical endeavor. Then I saw his eyes. I recoiled at the abominable sight—stark white orbs. They stared through my heart as if a chilly wind was blowing through my chest. The complete absence of color contrasted the lightless background of his flesh. These eyes were not severely cataracted; they were like nothing I had ever seen, just perfect white spheres—no iris or pupil. It was as if those spheres were suspended within a black void and their perception was directed entirely at me. He leaned his clarinet against a wide oak while still staring at me, as his gnarled dreadlocks, like slowly closing drapes, fell gently over his face and hid the objects of my anxiety.

A rotund Latino lady in her mid-forties stepped from the crowd of onlookers and gracefully entered the domain of the musicians. She bent over picking up a microphone, then began to hum and snap her fingers to the beat. Her round and pert figure pulsed with life; her penetrating smile pushed her full and gravity-defying cheeks from her face. She bobbed with the gentle waves of sound. Her humming evolved into *la-la-ing*, beautifully abstract, and then she burst into language—although the words themselves seemed to only skip on top of the surface of her deep tenor swells.

"Ain't got no time for matchin' socks, and life's too short for smokin' rocks. Ain't got no mind for red-light stoppin', and life too cruel for all the bomb dropping... Mayonnaise..."

Two teenage girls in quilted camouflage coats took hands and began to dance. They swung in exaggeration and glee, doing pirouettes and a periodic jitterbug. The clarinetist smiled and nodded his head with approval. The guitarist winked at the young ladies, who, in turn, blew him kisses with playful sensuality as they held each other breast to breast. Other couples joined the kinetic festivities: a middle aged pair in evening dress, poised and elegant, box-stepped stoically; an elderly couple, barely swaying to the music, grinned with tenderness at each other; two adolescent skate-boarders pretended to play their boards like rock guitars while grimacing and shaking their heads in double-time; two winos stood from their intoxicated repose arm-in-arm and rocked back and forth with the rhythm. The park pulsed with the ambling music. Within a few minutes, all of the threatening tension of the first song had evaporated into a communal swing.

  With this change, I relaxed, finding a seat of newspaper below an alder. My mind was suddenly free of the evening's strife. I sat with my arms gently crossed, resting on my knees. My head was crooked back against the stability of the tree. The clouds were disintegrating into the blackness of space; even some stars began to show through the gloom of sky. The moon hung at its zenith dominating the cosmos above. She was a great barren goddess, always in harmonic flux—so unchanging in her periodicity. My eyelids began to shut out her light. The struggles of the evening must have taken a huge toll. The world slowly lost its light, becoming only oscillating sound. The soft tenor words of a new song washed over my ears, "…Two days till midnight, eight minutes to the sun. In two hours I'll be in Memphis, then my journey's done…" Then, even the music faded from my consciousness. I fell into a profound sleep—the type of being that is utterly liberated from the processes of mind. It is as close to the negation of being that one can obtain without completely integrating oneself into the Abyss. From one of these naps, suspended in the nothing, one often awakes perfectly refreshed and ready to tackle waking events, yet this was not my fate. Instead, I think I may have left part of myself in that vacuum. Or perhaps I merely visited what I had left previously, that part of myself that I had lost before ascending the stairs of the inferno. It is difficult to determine whether the former or later holds more truth, because I am not who I was then. After retracing my steps, to proclaim truth in the present would be an abortion

18

of words. Nothing is what it was then; I have looked at it, digested it, and now know only imagination and song.

My dream of nothing receded, slowly taking on form and substance until it burned with image and sound. The little goateed guitarist was playing solo as I opened my eyes. Jazz no longer captivated the ears of the audience, but a fast country song. His thumb struck out oscillating bass notes while his other fingers played the melody. He sang in a queer, nasally tone:

Oh Barbelo, Barbelo,
Ya lonely little girl,
Barbelo, Barbelo,
Ya frightened little chile.

Ya made love ta yar innocence,
Pregnant with dissonance,
Wanderin' through the lightless night
Bound by abstract fright.

Ya bore witness ta yar shame,
Forsakin' yar own son's name.
Through error and tragedy,
Ya made the world a parody.

My eyes were completely open, although I could feel they were still puffy and red with sleep's remnants. I pressed my hands to them in an attempt to squeeze out the remaining sleep. The minstrel sang on:

Barbelo, Barbelo,
My illustrious mother,
Barbelo, Barbelo,
My serpentine lover.

Yar infamous son
Said he was the only one.
He gathered all the fools

And made ya sing the blues

Oh ya know the Stranger exists
Somewhere beyond these mists
Beyond all this error
Beyond all this terror.

Oh Barbelo, Barbelo
Wake up, wake up, wake up
Wake up...open your eyes
And deny these skies.

The bass drum began accompanying the guitarist's rhythmic thumb, accenting the upbeat. Gradually the tempo slowed to a toll. They continued this as a duo for several bars until the bass player, too, began smacking out the same rhythm. The tension mounted, as it had when I first came upon this group, but now it possessed the tension of structure and uniformity behind it, rather than the abstraction of free form. Then the clarinetist began echoing the haunting melody of the guitar. The two danced in unison. They played only in a pentatonic minor. They never strayed from the simple, hypnotizing melody. Then, simultaneously, they stopped. The crowd was silent. The moon was on its descent behind the buildings. A few seconds elapsed before onlookers awoke from their trance and answered the silence with sober applause.

I struggled to my feet. My bones groaned reluctantly at the chore of standing. In gaining my posture, I glanced down at the newspaper that had been my seat. Its headline drew in the present strife of the world: "Bloody Battle in Afghanistan," written in bold letters over a picture of long-faced American soldiers trudging over an arid mountainside. For all the madness and song of the evening, the rest of the world continued on its grand course, unstable and bloody. The headline also fit the chaos of the evening, as though it foretold of surreal events and (presently yet unrealized) ideological mayhem.

I overheard the clarinetist breathe inaudible words to someone behind my back. Then the green-coated guitarist tapped me on my shoulder.

"Hey, kiddo," he said, his voice was confident, although somewhat high-pitched and raspy. His arms came up to hug me, but stopped short when he saw my confusion.

His face had an emerald tinge from the light reflecting off of his raincoat. A cigarette dangled from his lips, fluttering while he talked, "I'd been thinkin' ya went back down south, down on back ta ol' San Fran-Cisco." He pronounced his words with exaggeration and playfulness.

"Do I know you?" I questioned, utterly confused, for I could not place his face.

"Sure, sure. We caught up with each other a few days ago, when ya were luggin' 'round that satchel."

I had no recollection of what he was talking about. I felt confused and a bit paranoid at his collegial demeanor. These feelings got the better of me and, with voice too loud, I asked, "Who are you?"

The little man smiled slyly, as if he had been hoping for an opportunity to answer such a rude question. He suddenly pushed me to the ground. The roughly five-and-a-half feet tall guitarist loomed over me. I could feel the wet earth seep into my clothing as I gazed up at him in shock.

His expression had completely changed; his voice grew deep and wide, his face contorted in anger: "I am the Thrice Great Guide." With a slow dramatic arch of his arm, he strummed a distorted chord from his guitar. "I am the harmonic messenger of the Nada, the winged messiah of the crossroads, guide to the underworld. I am your advocate and your judge." The sound of the music echoed through the streets, bolstering his wrathful voice. "Through me you will go to sleep and awake in the valley of History. With me you will sing the Song Itself." His fingers hammered out harmonics along the neck of his instrument, the notes cascading over his speech. "I am the liar and the saint, wise man and thief." He smacked the strings with a malevolent blow. "I have brought you the Word and the fire by which to read it. Through me you will love the world and agonize in leaving it. It is I who will show you what you already know but fear to remember. I am the immortal one, the thrice-great psychopomp, the inventor of tone. I'm Epi, and don't forget it, ya lil' shit."

Behind him, the band members played something akin to carnival music—full of staccato, accented upbeat and disjointed chromatics. Once the "Messenger" was finished with his diatribe, the whole band and a few of the bystanders began laughing, quite proud of Epi's prank.

He bent down and extended his hand to me. In my ignorance and discomfort, I grabbed it, as if to pretend I was at ease with the joke played at my expense. I regained my footing, and the prankster held my body close to his, gleefully patting me on the back.

"Ya're a good ol' kid," he proudly announced. "That's what ya are. No denyin' it. Ya can take a good laugh, that's why ol' Epi likes ya." He flicked his cigarette into a puddle and it immediately sizzled out. "Ol' Epi likes ya, that's why he does that shit, but ya gotta be more friendly, and stop playin' this shit—'Who are you?' Yar' memory can't be that bad. Don't give poor ol' Epi that kind a grief, life's too tough even without that shit. So, what'd ya think a the gig? Did ya like? Maybe a bit too much at the beginnin'. Honestly, what'd ya think?" The members of the group were fixed upon me for an answer, except the clarinet player; he was disassembling his instrument and methodically placing the sections in its case.

Still shaken by the joke and the brashness of the guitarist, I answered with a quivering voice, "Ah, I liked it. You guys sounded really tight. It was very good." I waited nervously for their response.

"Thanks, but loosen up, we ain't gonna bite ya." Epi snarled and snapped his teeth together.

"Leave child alone, you push too hard," the drummer mumbled from behind his trap set, shaking his head.

"Ya seem pretty shaken up. What's wrong, ya forgotten what ya was doin' here?" Epi asked.

I looked at all of the faces self-consciously. Most of the crowd had dispersed, only the band and the two girls in camouflage remained. "Yes."

"Then ya're in a world a shit," the green guitarist stated. "Let's go ta my place and get this here thing figgered out." He turned to look at the two girls and shouted, "Can ya guys help ol' Zosimos git the kit in the van, thankya." Looking back at me he growled, "Grab my amp, I'll get the ax an the cord. We'll take this crap ta the shop."

I walked over to the amplifier and took the handle. As I began carrying it toward the door, which the Epi was entering, I felt a strange sensation on the back of my neck like a warning of some impending danger. A paranoid vision shot through my mind of a man—a silhouette of a man— staring at me from behind. Although I did not turn around at that moment, his shadowy form filled my mind's eye, standing with his hands in his pockets just out of reach of the street lamp's light. To turn and see him would have been to endow him with existence. He stood like a specter along the path that I had just walked. His unseen presence consumed me with fear. The putrid being in my stomach struggled violently, reacting to the shadow. I gagged, dropping the heavy piece of equipment and turned toward the figure dominating my mind only to find that it had vanished.

"Ya're the worst roadie ever in the history a music," Epi spat. "Be careful, those things ain't cheap."

"Come on, y'obviously need some coffee. It's only a bit past one." He patted me on my back and made his way through a lightless doorway. I lugged the heavy piece of equipment to the open door of the "shop" and waited for a moment anticipating the "pop" of a light switch, the hum of electricity through a filament, and the unnatural glow of a bulb, instead I heard Epi's brazen voice within the darkness, "What the hell ya waitin' fer? Y'ain't getting' no invitation from God, and I ain't gettin' any younger. Get yar ass in 'ere, I want a cup a joe."

Trismegistus

I was compelled to follow his voice, as if all other possibilities were nonexistent. Not a thought in my mind opposed it. I was an automaton trailing him, whether out of social graces, fear or just a hopeless sense that I had no other options. I felt utterly alien within this environment I had been led. His voice echoed though the building, bouncing off of unseen objects in the collage of shadow and opaque forms. The space seemed to expand and contract according to his voice—sometimes wide and expansive, other times claustrophobic and cluttered. Once I would feel confident in my estimations of this environment, I would immediately recognize my ignorance by knocking my shin against some immovable metal object.

"Over here," he shouted. "Wrong way, chica!"

Finally I saw his face illuminated by the flame of a lighter as he drew deeply on a cigarette.

"Ya can set it here," he said. "Follow me."

I tried to trace the sound of his footsteps as he continued through the darkness. The air was heavy and wet; it held the odors of mildew and freshly cut wood.

His trudging ceased, and I heard the shrill squeals of a metal gate being pulled back. "Get in the elevator, we're goin' up," he panted, as he pulled me into the lift. "First floor: toaster-ovens, moonlight and women's lingerie," he cackled as the contraption hummed and clanked under our weight.

Windows of yellow light passed us as we ascended.

"Ya know what this buildin's called?" he asked. "The Pronoia Hotel," he chuckled at his own wisdom. "'Ya know what it means, kiddo?"

I turned to look at him with an expression of ignorance as we passed another illuminated window.

"Ya don't, do ya, well ya sure will. Yep, I got a pretty good feelin' a that. Ya sure-as-flies-love-shit will, ol' chile."

I waited in vain for an explanation of the name and the meaning of his knowing condescension, but it did not come.

The elevator stammered to a halt, and Epi, with the full weight of his body, pulled the gate open and flooded the small cell with light.

"This's it, the eighth floor, refrigerators, vacuum-cleaners and things that go bump in the night," he proclaimed.

My guide led me through the musty, green hallway. The building must have been a labor of love when it was first erected at the turn of the century; thick, elaborately carved moldings, richly patinaed with age, adorned every doorway and the joints of ceiling and wall. The walls were chest high with wainscoting that was covered with the nicks, scrapes and gouges of disrepair and time. The smell of smoke, urine and cooked fish hung in the air. The hay-day of this building had long past. I got the sense that it now functioned only as a tomb for souls unaware of their own deaths, the ghosts still cooking food, smoking cigarettes and going to work out of the habits of a prior life.

"This's the place," he announced as he fumbled for his keys, unlocked the door and ushered me inside.

A wave of stale cigarette smoke and rotting debris hit me. The walls were the jaundiced color of Epi's teeth, as if they too were stained with coffee and smoke. Raw wooden planks of various colors and lengths lay scattered throughout the room. Ashtrays, toppling with butts, sat in every spare space; there must have been at least six in the living room alone. Cups ringed inside with stains from evaporated coffee littered the apartment. Books, several hundred, some open face down, some open face up, some standing on the legs of their covers, some used as coasters, some shoved into the cushions of the couch, some contorted in all types of disregarded positions were strewn throughout the room.

And then there were the guitars, beautiful instruments shining and newly-polished, hanging on simple hooks from the walls: a green electric guitar with gentle inviting curves, the grain springing out at the eye like tiger stripes; a parlor-sized steel-string with gleaming chocolate sides, and a simple classical guitar that gave the on-looker a sense of tone without even making a sound. These instruments, so perfect and obviously loved, boldly contrasted the disorder of the rest of the room.

"Enough of yar google-eyin' this dump, let's have a cup a joe," he chided, and smacked his hands together as he walked into the kitchen, stepping on and around various types of debris.

"This coffee's a bit cold, but nothin' a microwave can't fix," he shouted from the kitchen. As he warmed our drinks, I stood silently gawking at the room, the clutter, the beauty and the contradiction of this man.

Uncomfortable with the silence, yet recalling the acrimonious response the last time I spoke, I timidly reported, "These are beautiful instruments, quite striking."

"Thanks. Glad ya like 'em. 'Can't remember if ya said ya still played?"

"I don't think so."

"Yeah, didn't think ya did."

He stepped from the kitchen with steaming cups in either hand.

"He set my cup on an open faced book. "Have a seat," he offered, pointing to the couch.

The springs moaned as I sunk into the piece of furniture.

"It's the only one I didn't make myself," he announced proudly.

"Only what?" I asked, shyly looking up from the steaming cup.

"Why, the only piece of furniture," he stated with aplomb.

I looked around the room searching for the pieces of furniture. I had not been conscious of any when I had first entered the apartment, probably due to the overwhelming amount of clutter. In addition to a couch and coffee table, I was able to discern two cherry glass-doored bookcases, a massive oak Morris chair and two finely oiled end tables.

"I made 'em all," he said, as he began thumping a pack of cigarettes on the coffee table. He ripped into the pack, scattering the cellophane and foil onto the floor, then he threw a cigarette into his mouth from the level of his belly and lit it—all in one fluid motion.

"They are all very nice."

"Ol' Epi made the guitars too, or do ya not remember that either," he said, grinning with skepticism. "Out a curiosity, what all do ya recall, anyway?"

"I don't want to talk about it," I spoke into my coffee mug.

"Ya mean ya don't want ta talk, or ya don't want ta talk 'bout recallin'," he pressured.

"I don't want to talk about anything at all," I raised my voice defensively and felt my face blush. "I'm sorry. I haven't felt like myself this evening, in fact, I'm not sure … I apologize, I don't know what has come over me. I need to be honest; I don't recognize you, and I don't know…" I took another sip of the bitter coffee in order to regain my composure.

Epi narrowed his eyes, looking me over carefully for a few awkward minutes. My muscles were taut with the suspense that this unpredictable man created. A knowing and condescending smile slithered across his face, the same one that I had seen so many times already this evening, yet this smile held a greater depth of knowledge; a sparkle shown in his eyes and a sliver of teeth was reveled between his lips. There was a knowing dualism in his look. I was struck by his resemblance to an icon I had seen, although Epi was smiling. This sixth-century image called "Christ Pantocater" had held my attention when I had seen it. It was only after some contemplation that I had realized that there were really two faces of the icon, one half holding the beneficent eye of mercy and the other infused with the stern rigidity of justice. The two halves mingled and compelled the paradoxical feelings of salvation and fear.

"Somethin' tells me yar not goin' back to the hotel despite yar need fer some rest. Get off yar ass," he said as he shooed me off of the couch. He pulled the cushions off of it and pulled out the hide-a-bed. All kinds of rubbish had found a home in the mattress: cigarette butts, books, candy wrappers, sticky coins, straws, a flat-head screwdriver, and a wide assortment of filth. I did not know what to make of his offer.

"Drink yar coffee and get some shut-eye. Ya need it." He threw some sheets at me that were speckled with small, round burns and ominous stains.

"Don't mind the cat, she won't hurt ya, not ta say that she's harmless. Nor'll she wake ya when she comes home, she's very conscientious."

He exited to his bedroom after refilling his cup in the kitchen, however this time he failed to heat it.

I fell to sleep quickly.

2.

The Magical Cat

I woke staring at the yellowed ceiling and feeling the oppressive weight of cigarette smoke on my lungs. Vacant thoughts poured through my head: *I better get going to work; I must be late because the sun is already up; which city am I in today?* Slowly the events of the evening—the fire, the moon, the stirring music—all trickled into my consciousness. They flowed slowly and filled my recollection drop by drop until I remembered where I was sleeping.

A phlegmy cough from the other room shocked me into sitting; that odd little guitarist, Epi, was rummaging around the kitchen. A swirling gray cloud of smoke lit by the rays of the morning sun was the beacon of his presence.

"There ya go, honey," Epi crooned with affection. "Hope ya like yar breakfast, Stinker; it's lamb and rice, all organic like usual. Only the best fer Epi's ol' friend."

Naturally, without thought, I reached for an open pack of cigarettes sitting on the coffee table and lit one. It tasted stale and bitter. "Ya're awake, uh? Ya want some grub? Or how 'bout a cup-a-joe?" I then heard the familiar click of the microwave door and its hum of work. I wondered if he ever *brewed* coffee or whether he just recycled what was left in some cup he had left neglected the week prior. He walked out of the kitchen holding two mugs and a hotdog sandwich. "This should cure any pangs in yar stomach," he stated, thrusting the meal at me with pharmacological assurance. "Wash that sucker down with a good ol' cup-a-joe." The coffee spilled over the sides and onto a book as he set it on the coffee table.

"So, how did ya sleep?"

I took the sandwich from him. The cold pink dogs poked their unappetizing heads from between the bread slices. "I guess pretty well," I yawned. "I mean, I don't even remember sleeping, only closing my eyes and waking up."

"Good, very, very good. That's what I like ta hear— a Lucretian rest," he proclaimed proudly, nodding his head as if he had some role in the endeavor of sleep. "But now ya're awake, right?"

"Yes," I answered, feeling a bit anxious at his question.

"Ya positive?"

"Yes, I am positive," I replied indignantly.

"Now ya don't have ta get all in a tizzy, I'm just makin' sure, 'cause all kinds a folks're walkin' 'round like they're all awake, but they ain't. Anyway, how's the grub?"

"I'm sorry, thank you. I appreciate the food and also your generosity for letting me sleep here last night. I've been feeling sort of..." I paused to frame my words without jeopardizing myself, "I've been feeling a little out of sorts, as of late, and thank you for your hospitality."

He gave me a wink as a large, gray tabby with celadon eyes strutted from the kitchen, hopped to the oak chair and began to lick herself. Epi watched my eyes follow the cat. Epi's face lit with excitement and that, now familiar, sly smile emerged.

"A magical cat has taken up residence with yar old, eccentric frien' Epi." He picked the cat up, sat down in the armchair, and placed the compliant animal on his lap. He spoke of their meeting, and immediate recognition of kinship, as if it was yesterday. He leaned back, relaxing his shoulders and grinning at the opportunity of recounting the scenario. The cat appeared less engaged, arching her back in callisthenic parabolas. "Yep, she's a kinetic disciple a Appolonius," he said, pointing to the posturing animal on his lap. "Pistis is what keeps ol' Epi sane..."

"Oh yeah, the beginnin'," he began, "that was quite a day. That was a day much like yesterday, full a fire trucks, smoke and *murder*." he winked. "But that was 'bout ten years 'go, yep it was. That was the day the batty bitch, who was living 'bove the 'Taste a Cairo', made a life changin' decision (and a death decision, I'd like ta add). Yep, that loony took a gallon a diesel and made herself inta a molotov cocktail. The whole damn thing was quite a hootenanny. She chose ta incinerate herself on her fourth-story balcony. Everybody showed up fer the spectacle, 'seemed like the whole damn city came ta watch. First, ya had the people that were just walkin' by, then ya had all the cops, followin' them ya got both the media and the fire trucks. The waves a spectators built until the fuckin' melodrama crescendoed with the evil witch lightin' a cigarette and *poof*, it was then 'bout water and the six o'clock news." At this point Epi had increased the pace and volume of his speech, slapping his leg with excitement.

"Kiddo, ya need some background on this alchemical hag. She was not one a those typical crazies ya might pretend not ta see on the street corner pushin' a shoppin' cart overloaded with the tin cans, plastic bags and rusty trinkets a'a life spent in a mental hell. Nope, she was a tad more up-scale (only in the financial sense, mind ya) and a shit load more diabolic tha' that. She read tarot cards and cast curses fer a livin'. Failin' investment bankers and egocentric unrequited lovers were 'er only patrons—only the desperate backstabbin' portion a society. She was no good witch a the west; she was one a 'em mean and nasty witches, like the one that tried ta gobble up glucose lovin' Hansel and Grettel. She was an evil bitch, ta put it mildly.

"Anyway, this curse-castin' crone had this cat. At the time, Pistis wasn't much ta look at; ya really had ta look deep, but when ya did, she had this inner beauty that's hard ta describe. But this poor ol' feline was trapped, imprisoned if ya will, in some kinda conjurer's incantation, 'cause if she could a taken off, she would a. This ol' cat couldn't leave the cunt's tomb a'an apartment. Ya look at that cat and ya saw oppression, plain and simple. She was a forced familiar, stolen from a lovin' home, compelled ta'a life in malignant darkness."

Epi's face became red and swollen with emotion. "Poor kitty," he continued, reaching for a used napkin to wipe potential tears, "poor, poor li'l kitty. She developed a rash that stemmed from her physical and spiritual incarceration." He stroked the cat's furry cheeks, and she purred lovingly in response, nuzzled her face against Epi's nose and curled into a ball.

"Now that skanky cauldron-stirrin' cock-sucker finally broke. Snortin'all them fumes from boilin' newt's eyes and Turk thumbs finally threw 'er over the edge. She musta poured over all a her spells and manuals a the black arts and found somethin' really rich. Whatever the shit was, she ended up on 'er balcony drenched in diesel and screamin' ta heaven, hell and all a us in-between 'bout our insignificance compared ta 'er omnipotence. I swear ta ya, friend, I saw 'er head twist three-sixty, then she started jabberin' in tongues. It was some kinda witchy prelude ta 'er self-pyrofication. But I'll tell ya, ain't nothin' like a li'l self-immolation ta get a day goin'," Epi winked. "I still remember it like it was yest-er-day; I was held entranced by the event till she lit the cigarette and the flames engulfed 'er instantaneously. *Poof*!" He clapped his hands, "then she lost the tiny bit a composure she had (screamin' and flailin' 'er arms 'bout)," Epi demonstrated this process, and I felt sorry for his neighbors who were forced by his volume to hear his recounting, "...and I was released. I ran inta the buildin', pushin' through all the cops and fire dudes and kicked in 'er fuckin' door. It was like I was on a mission from God. I grabbed that cat by the scruff a her neck, and she was emancipated from the evil hag."

At this point in the adventure, Epi caught his breath as though he had just raced up those three flights of stairs and saved his furry comrade. His eyes possessed the tired but heroic glimmer of a man proud of his noble endeavor. "Yep, I saved ol' Pistis. She's been with me ever since. I mean, there was that time she got hit by the ice-cream truck, and I thought she had traveled ta the Kitty-Elysian Fields, but that was 'fore I truly understood what she was all 'bout."

He took another sip of his coffee and lit another cigarette. "Well I had done gone an buried ol' Pistis. Ya see, I picked up what I thought was her lifeless carcass (in fact, I had ta use a small shovel ta collect all a it), and I buried the damn thing with great ceremony an sorrow. But, by the time I'd patted the earth down an shed a few tears an come back ta my place, there she was, ol' Pistis purrin' away fer some food like nothin' ever transpired." Again, Epi attempted to hold back his watery emotions, but their force overcame him. "She'd come back, my meowin' companion."

"Ya see, she's a magical cat. Not the magic a the ol' smelly Paraceleus worshipin' bitch, but a more refined, more pure, more holy type a conjurin'. She first arrived in this fair city in the eighteen hundreds, when the Indians still called it the 'Valley a Death'. Ya know, one a the head honchos a ol' Stump Village was a guy by the name a Pettyfatale, ya've seen the streets and buildin's and shit that's named after 'im. Well, he was set on makin' this place more than just a dot on a map, but a bustlin' modern metropolis tha' would make 'im rich. Along with his grandiose dreams, he brought a Jewish accountant and part-time manservant named Hoeb. Well, ol' Hoeb's kin had a long history in the Rabbinical arts, and his great-grandfather was perhaps one a the greatest Kabalistic rabbis that the world's ever seen. The reason I brin' this up is 'cause Hoeb's great-grandfather *made* this cat. Yep, I understand why ya're lookin' at me that way, I didn't believe it at first either, but that's right, Epi never lies," he chuckled to himself devilishly. "Ol' Rabbi Hokhma, Hoeb's great-grandpappy, fashioned our much beloved Pistis out a clay. Now, ol' man Hokhma didn't plan at first ta be sculptin' a cat. No-siree, he was hopin' ta bringin' his lovely little girl back from the land a no return. Ya see, she had died a tuberculosis, this was back when that shit would take ya out. With her death, he lost it, or ta put it more eloquently, Elvis had left the buildin' (if ya catch my meanin'). So, the once wise (and sane) Hokhma, consumed by the loss a his only child ta God's hand, went 'bout makin' 'er himself. Now, I'm not gonna go inta details a the whole process, fer no other reason but 'cause I don't understand any a it," he licked his lips and winked, "but Hokhma acquired some magical clay, the same shit that Adam was made out a, or somethin' like that. He then started moldin' and sculptin' and kneadin' and wackin' the stuff, but he realized that there wasn't enough ta make a physical replica a his darlin' daughter. He must a despaired and paced the floor a his cold Prague apartment. And then, *click*, a light switch must a been flipped (even though I know they didn't have light switches way back in the day, 'cause hombre was Old-School, really Old-School). Any-who, he'd decided ta make this Kabalistic effigy in the likeness a'a cat. Yep, 'cause his daughter loved cats. In fact, she would rescue 'em from the nasty, wet Prague alleys and give 'em love. So he fixed himself a cat. After he'd done all a his sculptin', he said a prayer, placed both the name a his daughter and the name a God in the cat's mouth and then, with his rabbinical CPR trainin', breathed life inta the inanimate object. Presto-change-o-transmutation-abracadabra, ya've got beautiful ol' Pistis, or what she was called way back when, ya see I renamed her; she was called Melog, but I didn't think it reflected 'er inner beauty."

Epi stretched his limbs in an effort to continue his journey through history. He lit another cigarette, took another sip of coffee, and suddenly beat his chest like Tarzan to build strength for the rest of journey to the present. "Now ya see, Hokhma had another child 'fore he finally kicked the bucket. Melog passed through the hands a her creator's son and then through the hands a his son, Hoeb. Ya see, as great families often go, the blood thins and becomes wicked and corrupt. That's what happened in this case. By the time all those noble, though a bit loco, Hokhma genes gotta Hoeb, they had grown mighty fucked-up. Hoeb was a whorin', opium-addicted, bitter, self-indulgin' cut-throat. Dude was fucked. And, as soon as he'd brought Pistis ta the West Coast, she hit the ground a-runnin'. She found kind and generous families ta stay with till that ageless and evil witch cast her spell and the rest is history."

The cat purred and nuzzled Epi, as if she had approved of his rendering of the story. "Do ya want another cup-a-joe?" he asked pointing to my empty cup and looking concerned. I shook my head and attempted to extinguish my cigarette in one of the heaping ashtrays. "Well, I sure do," he said making his way to the kitchen.

"I want ta add somethin' very important ta all a this; she's a damn special beast. And I only use the word beast in reference ta her physical appearance," he shouted. "She's got the *divine spark*."

The microwave clicked on once again. Once again, I wondered from where he was getting his coffee.

"Like a human, but even greater than most humans. I'll explain all that ta ya some other time, we've got time."

He sat back down in the chair with a new cup of coffee and Pistis jumped back into his lap, curling herself into a ball and closing her eyes. "Ya know, or I guess ya don't know," he continued, "that we've conversations." He nodded affirmatively. "We chatter 'bout all sorts a things, but usually spiritual things, and I don't mean no Age a Aquarius crystal worshippin' shit either. No, I mean… yar not ready fer that. Anyway, nobody believes me, but… let's go down ta the café and get some real vittles. Actually, ya go down and pick me up a burger and meet me in the shop."

I was no longer afraid of this enigmatic and foul little man, in fact, I found myself quite amused by him. The feeling that I had met him before, which came upon me the previous night, was now even greater. Every gesture that he made tickled my memory with vague recollection. Although he was bullish and arrogant, I felt confidence in him, as though he knew me better than I knew myself. It seemed like he was more genuine in his concern for me than I could ever be for myself. Following his directive came naturally; I was relieved that I had some direction, no matter how mundane it appeared.

I hoisted myself off of the hide-a-bed. My clothes, which I had slept in, were marked with wrinkles and things acquired from spending the night in the dirty accommodations.

"It's right next ta the shop. Ya know where it is," he spoke through a smile.

Café Zoe

I walked down the eight flights of stairs to the street level. The cup of coffee that Epi had given me had, to my amazement, settled my stomach and more; I could feel life trickle back into my limbs and a calm sweep through my body. My mind was far from the events of the previous night, and I set out on my simple mission of obtaining lunch for my host. In my refreshed state, I caught myself delighted by those things which people usually walk past: the sheen of sunlight on the foyer's marble floor, thin fissures of age on the ceiling tiles, a spider suspended in his web between the wooden telephone booth and the juncture of wall and ceiling, a wadded napkin with lipstick traces in the corner, a wide strip of duct tape holding the sign for the fire-evacuation plan in place. I felt as though I was seeing with fresh eyes; all these mundane things captured my attention. In my awe of the trivial, I nearly walked right through the leaded glass doors of the building's main entrance. This act broke me from my trance and forced me to look outside. I stared through the beveled panes of glass that hung in the web of leading; the world was awash in rainbow light. I pushed the heavy doors open and stepped into the uncommonly warm and bright November day.

The sun, although low in the sky, was at its noon zenith. I looked at my wrist to determine the time, but found that I must have removed my watch before falling asleep and had forgotten to put it back on when I woke. I suddenly felt a ting of anxiety at not having a timepiece; without a watch, actions of the rest of my contemporaries seemed displaced.

The café was only a few steps away, within the same building in which I had slept. On the other side of the apartments' entrance, I saw the sign for Epi's shop: "From Tree to Song", in green elaborately carved letters, and "Hermes Epithymos: Luthier, Liar and Psychopomp," in smaller letters underneath.

The name of the cafe was painted in thin yellow script on its doors: Café Zoe. I entered the small shop, immediately besieged by the buttery scent of muffins, croissants and scones, and, over those savory smells floated the earthy aroma of coffee. This was not the bitter, nearly toxic smell that lingered above Epi's brew; instead it was smooth and welcoming. Each wall of the café shown with a different color, bright and inviting. An eccentric assortment of pictures adorned the walls: a pastel flower still-life, a John Wayne portrait on velvet, a crude, nouveau-medieval woodcut of the crucifixion, a misty landscape of a forested mountain, a Renaissance print of a bearded man in exotic robes holding a lute and caduceus with flames harmlessly circling him, a Daliesque oil painting of a robust, naked Eve handing a pear to an emaciated Adam while a winged serpent gazed from a tree—the whole time the world around them was melting with surrealism. A mural of five planets, the sun and the moon revolving around the earth was painted on the ceiling. It included a sign pointing to the earth reading, "You Are Here"—the whole mural rendered in simple but vibrant colors and thick lines. The floor, too, held a mural of similar style, but the theme was quite different: flames and brimstone, skeleton devils and tortured naked figures, and another sign, reading: "You Are Here, Too." I walked around the patrons sitting on this hellish scene of pain and evil as they read, sipped coffee and nibbled on bakery items.

Arriving at the counter I was greeted by a young woman, "Hello, how can I help you?" She had a sparkle to her speech. I looked at her awkwardly, trying to remember what I had come for. She possessed narrow birdlike features and large round eyes that dominated her face. Her hair draped to her shoulders in subtle waves of shining black. She was beautiful, although not the type of emaciated and aloof beauty one may find on Parisian fashion runways, but a more rarified type of optimistic and cherubic beauty.

"Are you OK?" she asked politely, confused at my silence.

"Yes," I stammered, "Thank you. I'll get a hamburger, please."

"I'm sorry, we don't serve hamburgers."

"Oh," I said, looking around the room embarrassed.

"That's Epi's friend," a rough voice shouted from across the room in an accent foreign to me, "I saw with Epi last night after music." These words came from the rotund drummer I had seen the previous night.

The young woman's affect immediately became more personal; she stared into my eyes as if she had suddenly remembered my face, "Oh, yeah, sure. One burger coming right up. You can wait over there with Zosimos, and I'll bring it over to you." I pulled some money out of my pocket, and she held my hand back, "If it's for Epi, you don't need to pay," she said, giving my hand a slight squeeze.

"Thank you," I responded, feeling my heart rate increase in tempo at her gentle touch. I rubbed my hand where the shadow of her touch still lingered, then I sat down with the drummer.

"How are you," he barked, the "r" encumbering his tongue.

"Well."

"That is what like to hear, you are well," he said. It was difficult to sense whether he was smiling or frowning, his features were being pulled down by their own flabby weight. His eyes were mere slits under the oppression of his thick lids. "I like hear that people are well, it makes happy," he reiterated. I imagined that he must have been smiling underneath his flesh. "I am Zosimos, you heard play drums last night."

"Yes, I enjoyed listening to you—all of you."

"Thank you very much, but I don't always play drums, my favorite instrument is piano. I will play for you," he said warmly, "You like Scriabin?"

"I think so," I said hesitantly.

"You know," he responded, acknowledging my polite ignorance, (he began moving his hands up and down in the air as if to play the piano and humming an unrecognizable melody), "it is very good. You will like ...

"Eva, she is very pretty girl, do you think?" he said pointing to the girl behind the counter. I nodded shyly. "She paints—very talent. You should talk to her. I can tell she is your kind. I know these things," Zosimos winked and pointed to his temple. "Very talent girl, she has zest for life, spark..." He continued mumbling incomprehensibly for a number of minutes, as if he was talking to himself. A few words did get through his jumble of syllables: "book," "Sophia," "fire," "memory"... Finally, sense broke upon my ears, "Epi, you stay with Epi last night, this is right?" He took a sip from his cup and uttered more words thickly draped in his accent; they were undecipherable. My understanding of his words resumed with, "He is good man, makes many of jokes—bad jokes," he laughed, "but very wise—virtuous man," he nodded sternly, and his nod sent his jowls into subtle tremors.

"Yes, I agree,"

"You know him long?"

"Not long, I don't think."

"Not long," he repeated, nodding into his mug.

"Virtue?" I said unconsciously, "you don't hear that word used very often."

I had pricked his attention with that seemingly simple statement. "NO! Never hear it anymore. Very little virtue left," he spoke firmly while shaking his head. "Very little virtue left, only *nice*," he winced, showing his teeth with effort. "*Nice*, only mediocre, means not make trouble." He was disgusted by the word's scarcity. Zosimos spat his words out from his fat lips, "No one have balls, if do, are no good is what people think. This place have no integrity, why no one is virtuous, only *nice*. If you are *nice*, then you no spine. All this 'I'm OK, you OK—humbug. No, you not OK, you spineless. I tell you this, because you to know, not like others; they have their *nice*, we have virtue." I nodded diplomatically more focused on the gestures of his thick finger and shaking jowls. "Let me tell," he said regaining his composure, "Epi is virtuous man; he is trickster, but he virtuous man. He is not nice, you know, but he true and old. He not look old, but he much old than I. He have much wisdom, you listen to him, but it like..." he stopped and looked at the ceiling, thinking of an appropriate analogy, "it like listening to symphony; there many notes, and you listen one strain for hours, but you missing symphony itself. You know my meaning?"

We both looked up as the young woman handed me a box, dark stains of grease were seeping through its bottom. "Thank you," I said looking into her eyes.

"You say that a lot, it's kind of cute," she winked and walked into the back of the establishment. Her thin hips rocked rhythmically as she went into the back of the café.

"I think she like you," Zosimos said with an elbow nudge. "You are lucky, she is very pretty, she new here." I felt blood flood my cheeks as I got up nervously to leave the situation.

"Good bye, my friend. I play piano for you," he laughed and waved his thick hand as I hurried out the door.

I walked with my head down in embarrassment those few steps to Epi's shop. Staring through the window, I saw Epi's ghostly form at his bench working a piece of rich mahogany with a spoke shave, the thin, sparkling pieces of wood curling slowing around his feet. He was engrossed in his work, but looked up eagerly when I opened the door.

Epi's Muse

Through Epi's hands, wood found a second life, and in the company of a true musician, these common boards would find a life divine. From this primordial chaos of spring clamps, chisels, saws, smoothing planes, hot irons, plywood forms, sharpening stones, spoke shaves, jackplanes, calipers, knives, drills, rasps, and scrapers, the creator gave breath to the dead wood.

The shop was organized in such a manner that only an initiate in Epi's mysteries could possibly find anything for which he or she was looking. Only Epi held the esoteric knowledge of this divine order. I later learned that our luthier could close his eyes and, in seconds, find any tool or board in the shop at anyone's random behest. The catalogue within his mind worked like no other, scattered yet retaining everything.

"Oh, ya brought my cow-wich!" with eyes focused on his lunch. He set down the spoke shave and grabbed the box out of my hand. "Greasy wonder," he dramatically moaned. His expression changed as a revelation shattered his focus, "Nothin' fer yaself? Ya've gotta eat or ya'll shrivel up ta'a piece a baked dog shit."

"I'm not hungry. The hotdog sandwich filled me up," I said as Pistis nuzzled her face on my hand. I had not seen her and jerked my hand back with surprise. The cat, unperturbed by my spasm, began sniffing the hamburger's box.

"Loosen up an have a seat," he said as he pulled a stool up to his massive workbench. "Now I'm not bein' rude or inconsiderate fer grubbin' this ol' steer down in front a ya, 'cause ya had yar chance. Ya could a grabbed yar own grub, ya see."

"No, don't worry about me, I'm OK," I spoke, then thinking about Zosimos' lecture on virtue.

"So, whatcha think a the ol' shop? 'Hasn't changed much since ya was a kid." he garbled his words with a mouth full of hamburger.

"It's quite impressive," looking around the room. Guitars stood in front of the large window at the front of the shop, gleaming in the unusual November sun. A six-foot tall bandsaw towered in the corner, as if guarding all that took place in the work area. Epi's maple workbench, its four-inch thick top—scared and pockmarked from years of abuse—stood in the center of the room like a massive gravitational body stabilizing the whole. Richly finished cherry cabinets with half-open dovetailed drawers and a-jar glass doors, that would have been more appropriate in a gourmet chef's kitchen than a workshop, overflowed with tools and other equipment. I recognized the rod-iron gate of the elevator in the back of the shop. A pornographic poster hung on one of two doors in the back of the studio. The postered door was bolted and locked shut. Depicted on the poster was a thin yet sensuous young woman without clothing, revealing herself in a squatting position and staring straight at the front door of the business. This "shy" girl looked through the entire area with a wanton smile, biting her pinky finger. She revealed no shame as she greeted everyone who entered Epi's lair.

"She's a pretty one, huh? I'd bet ya'd like a piece a that naughty little wench," he growled, noticing my scanning eyes stop at the picture. "That's my little Barbie (and I don't mean no plastic doll). Ya can't have her, she's mine, ya see," he joked as he plunged his teeth into the hamburger. "She's my muse," he said, spitting pieces of bun and meat as he spoke. "She's one hot mama, yes siree."

"Yes, she's very beautiful, but not exactly subtle," I laughed.

"Well, not in some ways, but if ya look long and hard (sorry fer the pun), ya'll see a hell a'a lot more than what a glance will gi'ya. Think a her as one a'em Buddhist man-da-las. Sometime ya should come down 'ere (and that's spelled C-O-M-E, not the other way)," he chuckled, slapping his knee, "come down 'ere and meditate, tryin' to truly absorb the picture. Maybe ya'll reach enlightenment." He whacked me on the back, unconsciously smearing ketchup all over my back.' "Anywho, that's fer another time. Ya still haven't answered ol' Epi's question, what do ya think a this place?"

"The guitars are gorgeous. Feels sort of funny that they're in the same room as Barb," I grinned, "I mean, the guitars are sort of regal."

"So, ya're warmin' up ta ol' Epi, are ya? I'm glad ya're jokin' and I'm glad ya like his axes, but," he said, pointing back at the picture, "how do ya know she's not the forgotten Queen a Heaven?"

"I suppose I don't."

"Many things in this godforsaken world are not what they appear. Ya gotta step beyond yarself, live in two places at once, and embrace the 'yes' and the 'no', otherwise, yar just fucked. Fucked. Fucked. Fucked," he smashed his hand down on the bench to add emphasis to his words. "Don't think ya know somethin' when ya don't." His eyes then narrowed and his tone became sharper, "And don't play no fuckin' games with yarself, cause, ya ain't the only one ya'll hurt."

I sat quietly. Although he was quite strange and base, I did not want to upset him. In fact, my fear of him had been rekindled.

"I'm just fuckin' witch ya," his affect transformed back to his more typical jovial style. "Don't get all funky on ol' Epi, he's just pullin' yar chain, that's all." With this comment, I received another slap on the back, feeling too hard to be entirely playful. "Ya look a tad bit pale, kiddo. Let's get some more vittles in ya," he mumbled as he pulled me toward the front door.

As he brought me out and back to the café, I pondered as to how this brash and hedonistic man was virtuous. I attempted to don my most polite and engaged face, but my feelings were somewhere else; I had little trust in him. I hated that I feared him. I hated that I had no other options than to allow him to drag me around, order me about and spout ridiculous vulgarities at me.

A Latte, a Ball of Wax, and God Man

When Epi and I got to the café, Zosimos and the lanky bass-player, whom I had seen the previous night, were sitting at a table in the afternoon sun. Epi pulled two more chairs over to their table, and we sat down.

"Fuckin' gorgeous day, ain't it?" Epi announced to the group, staring wide-eyed at the sun, "Just fuckin' beautiful, no other words fer it, I'll tell ya."

"Very nice day, but worries me," Zosimos complained.

"Ya've always got a burr in yar britches, ya Egyptian sodomite!" retorted the luthier. "Ya ain't never just appreciatin' what is."

"And think," Zosimos said through what was probably a grimacing expression, "think I say good about you to child."

"Good things? I thought ya were against lyin'," Epi stated sarcastically.

"Stupid luthier," Zosimos laughed, "let me be. Leave games for children, too old wrestle about."

I was soon brought a tuna sandwich on a square orange plate and a foamy latte. My nostrils bristled with excitement, the heavenly aroma out did by ten fold the stale and watery brew Epi gave me that morning. I devoured the sandwich then nursed my coffee while the others talked. This afternoon was bright and warm with a gentle, cleansing breeze. Sparrows hopped and chirped, picking the ground around our table of any crumbs. The park, where the music had been played, stretched out before us; a brick walkway ran in between wide strips of green grass and under ancient trees. The radiant sunrays warmed my face as I examined the "Old Church" beyond the park; its spires stood nearly six stories tall topped with copper crucifixes tarnished green and brown from the elements. Zosimos continued to mumble, and Epi continued to answer him with sarcasm and a wide, playful grin. The bass player listened attentively.

"This true, this true, I saying. These therapist unearthing 'repressed memories' in clients," Zosimos stated firmly. "Found people has experienced all type of atrocities. Thing like incest, murder, satanic rituals—terrible thing. And when I saying to you, you must understand, these thousand and thousand of people saying this, normal, respectable people."

"Like yarself?" Epi joked.

"No, I mean yes, normal people: housewife, accountant, contractor, nurse. During therapy they recount most awful deed."

"Ya know what Freud would call that stuff?"

"No."

"Fantasies," Epi chuckled at himself.

"Well, you may be joke, but you not far off truth."

"I never am," Epi interjected confidently.

"No real. Upon investigation, most claim, deep seed memories, shown unreliable. The patient believes thing happened, therapist believes patient—everyone convinced. truth was different. One think, if people correct in beliefs, how many undocument murder there been, how many instance of incest, how many cult of Satan. It unthinkable. Mind are soft, like piece of wax," Zosimos said, pretending to squeeze a ball of wax in his thick fingers. "What dream become truth. What truth become dream. Mind very malleable. This, I think, very important."

"Memory can sure fuck with ya, no denyin' that, ol' man," Epi acknowledged.

The bass player quietly jotted something down on a small notebook that he had brought from his pocket.

"Immortalizing the ramblings, ey Glaucon?" Epi remarked.

"Yep, I sure am. This will make some great stuff in my novel," he said without looking up from his scribbling, "You guys give me some of the best material."

Epi looked at him slyly, "Well, ol' Zosimos and I want part a the royalties when that sucker's published."

I relinquished my silence, "What's your novel about?"

Eager to talk about his creation, Glaucon said, "Oh, gosh, it's about a lot of things. It's about music and love and the pain of life, but more importantly," he pointed to the drummer, "(I got this part from Zosimos) it's about the immortal soul—the God Man."

"He's got from me. I done extensive research on religion," said Zosimos proudly.

"He's a stinkin' Coptic Priest, if ya ask me," interrupted Epi pointing to Zosimos.

Rolling his eyes at his friend's comment, he resumed, "I done much research, but research not everything; I lived— lived well. I suffer and I rejoice. I been married four times, but I no children. I made pilgrimage to sacred place, but, most important, I seen the god within self." He tapped his chest. "You see, within us is divinity, this our soul. We human being, descendent of Adam. Because of this, we in image of divine. Everyone," he spoke emphatically, "everyone, you see, homeless men drink from bag over there and investment banker rushed to meeting, all have piece of god inside. Son of Man…"

Zosimos' speech on the divine nature of the soul was cut short by a banana-yellow Ford pickup speeding by. Once it had just passed the group, a man in the bed of the truck pulled down his pants to reveal his extremely white posterior and howled, "Ball licker!" No one saw his face, only his ghost-white buttocks; his face would forever be cloaked behind the luminosity of his behind.

A defensive silence fell over the group, as if one of us had been judged by the passing 'mooner'. Epi broke the silence with laughter and knee slaps, "He's sure got yar number, ya ol' prophetic nut-case. Get it, *Nut* case?" He pointed accusingly to Zosimos.

"Yes, I understand," Zosimos spoke, resigned to the fact that his friend was so crass. "As I saying, all of us possess Spirit. Spirit is alien in world of appearance; it not from material world. No, it not. It a fallen *spark of light*." He spoke methodically now, articulating every syllable in order to be clearly understood (a feat quite out of character for this Egyptian who seemed to love to mangle the English language). "This spark foreign to world of corruption. When descended to material world, forgot itself, and becames corrupt. It difficult to imagine, but Epi who helped lead me to many my conclusion on nature of soul," rolling his eyes.

Epi smiled like a proud father, "I'm getting' another cup a joe, anybody else want nothin'?"

"I come with you, my friend," said Zosimos, struggling to raise himself from his chair. Epi helped him from the seat, and they both entered Zoe's.

Glaucon looked around to make certain that no one was listening to what he was about to say, "My book is a modern version of <u>Moby Dick</u>. The ship, you know, the Pequod, it's an SUV. The driver, Ahab, is a mad Vietnam vet bent on finding and blowing up Bigfoot, who claims ate his leg. Ishmael and Queequeg are hitchhikers whom Ahab entangles within his self-destructive scheme. It's going to be the next great American novel, I can feel it. It's gonna be better than <u>On the Road</u>." He looked eagerly for my approval. Glaucon was one of those utopian intellectuals, still receptive to grand ideas. He believed the ideal could be attained. Gluacon gorged upon ideas of beauty and rebellion with a profound appetite due to the tapeworm of innocence. "It's the human search for meaning—the metaphor of the orphan, like Zosimos was saying."

"It sounds very interesting. I would love to take a look at the manuscript, if you don't mind," I said politely.

"Would you? I could use some constructive criticism."

"Certainly. It would be my pleasure."

"It's not quite coherent enough for you yet, but soon, give it a couple more months, and it'll be ready," he said enthusiastically.

"I look forward to it."

"You are going to be in town for a while, right?" he asked.

"I think so," I responded.

"Good, besides, Epi has taken an interest in you, that doesn't happen very often. You should feel sort of honored."

"What do you mean, 'taken an interest' in me?" I asked.

"Oh, don't get the wrong idea or anything, but he knows a lot of stuff. He's a real curiosity, sort of a local philosopher. He's a real smart guy. Anyway, I've got to get back to work."

"What do you do?" I asked, as he got up from the table and threw a black bag over his shoulder.

"I'm a bike messenger."

He waved goodbye as he rode down the street on his ten-speed. I reached into my pocket for a pack of cigarettes and realized that I had a cell phone in my coat. After withdrawing and lighting a cigarette, I took the phone from my pocket. I did not recall owning a phone. Perhaps this would be of some use, if I wished to gather the past.

The bell of the "Old Church" rang out loudly with a single toll as Epi and Zosimos stepped from Zoe's Café. "You are pig," said Zosimos smiling.

"No, 'you are pig', my friend," Epi mocked Zosimos' accent.

He changed his expression, "So Glaucon didn't hear what happened last night?"

"No", Zosimos said looking down at the ground.

"Let's not bring it up."

The Egyptian nodded.

They sat back down at the table and resumed their taunting, maked misogynistic jokes (despite my presence) and talked about what they would eat for dinner. I listened to the two eccentrics jabber while I watched the passers-by.

Separatia and Conjunctia

Epi had gone back to his workshop and Zosimos had left to the library to do some research. I was left with my coffee, my thoughts and the cell phone. The phone hung heavily in my pocket, and as I thought about its weight, the parasite in my stomach rolled over uneasily. Someone was practicing a Bach fugue on the organ in the "Old Church"; the geometric tones marched from the building like a brigade of tonal soldiers. These regimental notes ascended and descended ionic stairways in fast-step. The organist halted their march in mid-step, only to re-tread the measure in practice. It was a methodical and relentless learning, constantly forcing his soldiers on the march. The organist rallied the troops, compelling his notes to weave in and out of each other, and, if any were to collide, they would start back at the beginning of the phrase.

I took the phone from my pocket and set it on the table. I half-heartedly debated with myself whether I should turn on the electronic device and check the messages or leave it on the table and take the first bus out of town. I picked it back up and pressed the "on" button. It beeped, joining the tonal infantry, and its screen filled with spots, then illuminated with the number of the phone itself. This was my number, a sort of numeric name.

I jumped from my seat, startled by unexpected lips against my cheek—light and wet. I fumbled to hide the phone in my pocket before looking to see who had committed the transgression. The imprint of the lips clung to my face, and my hand immediately went to touch it.

"You gonna call somebody," a transparent female voice asked. I turned around and saw the pair of teenage girls, still in their camouflage coats, whom I had seen dancing the prior night. "Who you gonna call?" one asked playfully. "You gonna call your sister?" One of the young ladies stood in front of me as the other stood behind me rubbing my shoulders provocatively and without my consent.

Their scent filled my nostrils. They smelled sweet and heavy, a mingling of body odor, dirt and oranges. Her fingertips dug into my triceps.

"You gonna call your friend Epi? He's our friend too. The both of us took your place when you ran away," one of the girls said, as she sat on my lap.

"Pardon me!" I shouted, standing up and thus throwing the girl off. She pouted melodramatically as she ran her fingers through my hair. Her fingers sent uninvited swells of arousal and anxiety through my limbs.

"Are you scared of us, pretty one? We mean no harm," they spoke with feigned innocence. "We don't want to scare nobody. We're friends of Epi too. We don't mean no harm. We just want to be your friend."

An old man, who had been reading in the park, looked up from his newspaper to watch the scene. My stomach shook uneasily, and I felt my hands tremble slightly. "Who are you?" I asked rudely.

"I'm Separatia."

"And I'm Conjunctia."

"We're Epi's friends," they stated in unison, their voices ringing a discordant major seventh. They couldn't have been more than twenty years old. Their faces were pert and round. Their chubby bodies seemed to move without the chains of gravity. They nearly looked like twins, the impression further validated by their identical coats and similar straight, blond hair. Although they were no longer touching me, they stood within inches, penetrating my boundary of comfort. I could smell the warmth of their breath, simultaneously repellant and sexual. "We want to be your friend too," they cooed.

"Who are you?" I questioned.

"Give us a cigarette, and we'll tell you."

"Are you ladies old enough to smoke?"

"Oh yeah, we're both twenty-one. We're legal," they giggled simultaneously.

"OK," I said, as one of them reached into my pocket without my permission. She pulled two cigarettes from the pack and gave one to her partner. My face flushed.

"Thanks, cutie. Are you scared of us anymore? We don't mean any harm."

"No, I'm not scared of you girls," I stated as I sat back down, attempting to dispel any appearance of anxiety. The man in the park looked back down at his newspaper. The girls took the vacated seats of Epi and Zosimos, and sat with their legs wide apart and hands fidgeting in front of them.

"We help old Epi in his shop. He takes care of us real good. He's real nice. We live in one of the back rooms," they chattered in and out of each other. "Epi calls us his Sibyls. That's our pet name, you know. We're like his kids, sorta. He takes care of us real good. We like to play with him." They spoke with confidence and freedom. "We like Epi a whole bunch, and we want to be your friend too." They stuck their tongues out at me and, turning to each other, as if the whole scenario was choreographed, kissed each other with closed eyes and force. Although I felt confused and taken aback, blood rushed into my genitals. I looked on in disgust and sexual fascination. "Don't mind us, sexy, we just do what we want. We're the yin and yang, the up and the down, the love and the hate. We don't mean to scare you, cutie. Do you think you could be our friend?"

I hated myself for feeling so uncomfortable around them. Why should I recoil at their freedom and ease? "Yes, I will be your friend. Yes, why not?"

They jumped from their seats with glee. They hugged each other while still jumping up and down and chanted, "We have a new friend. We have a new friend," like excited elementary school children.

Despite their childishness and their all too astute social awareness, they possessed an inexorable amount of life. They danced about for some time. I watched them, their yellow hair accentuating their movements as they skipped together across the street causing cars to screech to a halt. Their bright blue eyes boasted of a passion for living that compelled one's respect, even within the perversity of their display. I caught myself smiling along with them as they bounded hand in hand. The Sibyls seemed to be something like a mixture of playful sprites and tempting sirens. They possessed a dichotomy of innocence and unabashed sensuality. After a few minutes of their gala, they ran back to my table and plopped themselves down, suddenly sitting rigid with fingers interlaced on their laps and knees together as if none of their histrionics had taken place.

"Thank you for being our friend," stated one.

"We really like you," the other added.

"Good," I nodded stoically. "I'm sure I will enjoy our friendship as well."

They looked at each other and laughed, as if some joke had been made of which I was unaware. Looking back at me, they requested, "Ask us a question. We will answer any question."

"OK," I looked up into the vibrant blue sky, thinking of a good question. "All right, I've got one," I said playfully. "What type of things do you help Epi with in the shop?"

"That's an easy one. We true the Trees of Life and Knowledge," they giggled.

"What do you mean?"

"We square rough sawn boards with the sharpest and heaviest hand planes."

"Epi makes the planes himself," interjected the other. "They are more perfect and beautiful than his guitars. They have to be, 'cause they prepare the wood to sing."

"We are not the last to plane the wood, no, Epi must breath life into it. He is the messenger and creator."

"That's very interesting," I said, thinking instead, 'What has the dirty old luthier been filling these poor kids full of?' "So you've learned quite a bit from the old man?"

"Oh yes, but you don't have to condescend."

This response caught me off guard. They had seen through my words. I did not know what to say. I blushed.

They giggled. "We saw you last night."

"What?" I coughed.

"Yes, we saw you when no one else noticed. It was a nice thing to do for that girl, she would have died otherwise."

I was completely taken off guard. "What are you talking about?" I asked deceitfully.

"You know, sexy. The police found a body. Did you kill him? Had he done something to you?"

"The police found a body?" I questioned obtusely.

"You saw the body, cutie. We know you saw the body. It was arson and murder. We know you saw the body." Their affect had changed from playfulness to solemnity. They craned their heads toward me. "Did you kill him, cutie? We will protect you. We saw you. Did you start the fire? Why did you save the girl? But you saved the gun first. She was a little girl like us. Did you know him? Did you think he was a bad man? We saw you when no one else noticed."

Their questions burned. I felt trapped within their words. Then I spoke up firmly, trying to regain my composure, "You will answer my questions, you said. Then tell me where the girl is. Is she dead?"

"She is not dead. She is at Providence Hospital in the intensive care ward. She is not dead, you saved her life, but she is not conscious. She will die; we all die. She can't breath on her own. They have a machine making her breath." They paused, smiling, then whispered, "We won't tell on you. 'Cause you're our friend, and we like you. You're cute.

"It'll burn, and you'll remember. You'll sing and save, for not a second, but you'll have to remember. The questions we asked, we know the answers. We hid the weapon." They jumped from their seats giggling and ran off through the park on their toes.

The organ continued to direct its tonal troops in geometric formation over the backdrop of traffic and bustling city.   It struck me as out of place, although everything seemed out of place. I had difficulty determining what was out of place and what was not. My 'ball of wax' was melting and twisting in the warm hands of fate. Life and memory had dissolved. The perfect system of Bach betrayed the incomprehensibility of the past, just as Euclid's geometry somehow betrays what we know of physical reality—ask any carpenter. The organ disbanded its soldiers to silent leave. I decided to go talk with Epi.

Ecclesiastical Honing

I attempted to shake off the dismaying interaction with the girls.   Epi was bent over rummaging through a drawer. He stood up with a plane in his hands, a gorgeous plane of polished metal and fertile-earth colored wood. I could sense its mass by merely looking at it.

"All is vanity!" Epi shouted as I entered the shop, proceeding to laugh in his characteristic manner. "Nothin' better than a holy fool spittin' proverbs. Is that a proverb too? If it ain't, it is now," he chuckled. "Oh, rivers runnin' to the sea, dusty winds, nothin' new, time ta be born, and all that shit. Ol' Dave's kid 'a bit of a loon, if ya ask me. He was sort a righteous and sort a right, and, at the same time, not too righteous or right. 'Ain't nothin' wrong with some contradictions. Contradictions won't get ya edited out a the Big Book, and I'm not talkin' 'bout any a that AA business. Ya see," Epi continued, as he scratched himself inappropriately with the tool, "too few contradictions makes Jack a dull boy."   I grimaced at the mad luthier, not understanding from where his flood of words was coming. It was as though he was just continuing a conversation he was having with himself before I entered the room. "Ya know, Dave's son should a done more jabberin' 'bout fellin' sticks and fuckin' whores. Everybody likes fuckin' allegories. Randy proverbs woulda got the modern reader's attention.

Ya know, Ol' Tarantino really coulda helped the Preacher out, addin' some shotgun blasts, some drippin' prostitutes an some hopped-up bank robbers."

Epi set the plane on the bench and disassembled the iron from the bed. "Ya see, I've been thinkin' 'bout the kid fer some millennia now, and if all is vanity, then what the fuck? I mean, what the fuck? So fuckin' what? Every shit-suckler that's graced the surface and the bowels of the earth know that it's all vanity. We forget it all, and we're all forgotten—big fuckin' woop-tee-do. No shit Sherlock! Oh, I better write that one down," Epi mocked in a high-pitched squeal. "So scribble, scribble, scribble, jot, jot, jot. And where are all my books, shit, ya gotta go inta some esoteric chat-room and down load the shit ta get at 'em. And Davie's kid got into the Old Testament. Fuck him. That's why I calls 'em the Great Unwashed." Epi roared at his own vagrant words. I stood watching with arms akimbo. "I find my vindication in toil, alright. I'll show 'em vanity. I'll fuck 'em all. Who's dead, kid? Who's gone ta Sheol, huh? I'll show ya how dangerous splittin' logs is. I'll show ya. Sure, they made a song out a your words, but I *am* a song. What did they play it on, huh? Mortal fucker!"

After Epi had sufficiently stomped the floor, he began laughing and patting me on the back, "You're a good one. That's right. A bit forgetful, but that's alright. Don't let no one tell ya otherwise, OK? Now we got some business ta attend ta. That biblical fagot got somethin' right, a blunt iron takes too much strength. And it ain't everybody possesses a Herculean physique like yours truly." Epi said this as he rolled up his sleeve and pointed to his bicep. "So here's somethin' dandy. This ain't no mambi-pambi hand plane. It ain't yar mamma's freakin' smoother, NO! This here is six-and-a-half pounds a tool-perfection. It's brass and steel and rosewood. The iron ain't no modern drop-forged, no-edge-holdin' piece a shit; it's over an eighth a an inch thick an two-an-three-quarters wide. It's one hand-forged bad ass mother-fucker, I'll tell ya." Epi stroked the plane in his hands. "The rosewood infill's straight from

Brazil and's been polished by my palm's toil. Some fool may say, 'but wait Epi, it sure looks an awful lot like a Norris A6: the king of all planes, the plane of planes, the plane by which all planes are judged.' But I heartily laugh at that statement and say, 'I must vehemently scold ya fer your ignorance and short sightedness. This is not a Norris or Spires or any a those noble (but unperfected) British planes a the turn a the century; No, this's the archetype, the Adamas, the Aleph, the numero uno. This divine smoother's better and before all the others. None other can touch it when it comes ta smoothin' a board and leavin' a polished and perfect sheen, even on the gnarliest of figured woods. Not a Bedrock 604 and a-half, not Matheson or Preston or Record or whatever can live up ta the prototype a all—the original smoother-o-light (although she's heavier than a son-bitch), the alpha and the omega. Recently, others have attempted ta forge the perfect hand plane; they have done some good work, but have failed ta create such perfection as I have. This plane that's before ya's the *shiz-nit*, mother-fucker. This here smoother can draw a continuous shaving that's lighter than nitrogen an more transparent than the President's incompetence. This bitch never chatters, 'cause her ass is too fuckin' heavy. Her iron's bedded at fifty degrees. Her steel sole is lapped perfectly fuckin' flat; they don't make a measuring gauge that could show any error a her sole."

Epi caught his breath by lighting a cigarette. He then took three whetstones from his bench, a bottle of kerosene, a vile of black polish and a leather strop. Epi handed me the iron. The mass of the piece of metal was impressive and cold. "She's meaner than Scylla," he continued. "She's eaten more Arkansas than the last commander-n-chief. No pansy-ass shit-sharpener can hone this here blade. This thick and hard-ass iron ain't fer the faint a heart. And don't even think 'bout askin' 'er fer mercy, 'cause she ain't gonna give it. Ya better off prayin' 'er fer some big-ass dollop a patience."

"You want me to sharpen this iron?" I asked timidly. It did feel like a daunting task, in a strange metaphysical way (especially after Epi's tirade on its difficulty).

"Sure as shit ya're gonna do it," Epi replied. "It's good medicine fer ya. Ya're all fucked-up in the head, ta put it mildly. Ya needs some good old-fashioned tedious toilin'. There're times in this fucked-up existence when questions're the game ta be played, but there're other times when folks need ta quiet the mind and thinly smile. This is one a 'em fuckin' times fer ya, kiddo. Now take this little piece a *techne* perfection, and get-a honin'." Epi's air changed from reprimanding to pedagogical, "Now remember, hold 'er steady and don't forget ta lap the back a the iron. Ya're in luck, she only needs a bit, and she don't need ta be re-ground." Epi left through the back door. I heard an engine wheeze and stammer into a hum, then trail away to silence.

The hand plane was quite impressive. The brass sides sparked with yellow brilliance. I picked the plane up, and even without her iron, lever cap and cap iron, she possessed a daunting amount of weight. The tote radiated warmth into my hand; this plane felt like a warm-blooded being, rather than metal and dead wood. It exuded an aura— both fearsome and sublime. As I picked it off of the bench, a "thin smile" creased my face.

The whetstones lay in beautiful walnut boxes, dovetailed and patinaed by oxygen and light. I arranged them as to grit from left to right, thumbing them to determine their place in line. Then, after shooting the stones with lubricant, I began honing. First, I lapped the back on the coarsest stone. Then I guided the bevel over the stone in even figure-eights, allowing the iron's own weight to press against the stone without any force provided by me. Once a burr had risen across the back of the edge, I moved to the next stone and began the processes again. I was utterly focused on the task at hand. It was as if the world beyond the oilstones had never existed. The task was simple. Oil, mixed with stone and metallic dust, crept into the prints of my fingers, accentuating all the contours of my fingerprints with bold darkness. The iron, being so hard and large, took a significant amount of time to hone, but only patience, not strength, was needed for the task. I had finally reached the strop when Epi returned.

"How's it goin'?" he blurted, startling me from the trance.

"Fine," I replied distantly.

"I knew ya'd remember how ta do it."

Yes, I did remember how to do it. The act of recollection stunned me for a moment.

"Ya see, ya gotta wait fer death 'fore ya completely forget," Epi laughted. He set a paper bag onto the workbench. A loaf of bread, completely crushed by unconsciousness, and several packages of turkey-dogs peered over the rim of the sack.

"Le' me see," grabbing the blade from my hands. He gently ran his thumb perpendicularly over the edge. "Not fuckin' bad at all. Ya're an ol' pro," he congratulated and slapped me on the back. "Now ya probably know, but this whole honin' process has quite a number a different cults. Every decent craftsman has 'is or 'er own dogma concernin' the sharpenin' a irons. They all swear by some different idol: oilstones, water stones, diamond, ceramic, sandpaper or combinations a these. Then they got different lubricants, strops, methods a moving the iron over the abrasive, even frightening contraptions that cost more than a table saw. It's like a mythos a sharpenin' fer 'em. They initiate their acolytes ta the mysteries like it was some fuckin' religion. 'The best method', 'the best stone'—it all reeks a alchemy, if ya ask ol' Epi. Like they've all got some *Lapis Philosophorum*. Ya see, all a this," he pointed to all the instruments around the shop, "all a this starts with the sharp iron and a stick."

Epi screwed the cap iron to the cutting iron and then placed them back in the bed. All of his motions were fluid and precise so as not to defile the newly honed blade on any metal. Finally, he tightened the lever cap and set the plane in my hands. May arms, still supple from my meditation, gave several inches to gravity.

"Go ahead, give 'er a spin, or rather, a push," Epi joked. He threw a four-quarter inch board of maple on the bench and tightened the piece of wood between a bench dog and his tail vice. "Come on, give 'er a try; ya can't hurt nothin'."

With my fingers, I timidly felt the tongue of the blade sticking out of the sole; it was barely apparent to the touch. "This board's pretty flat, so ya don't need much iron," Epi encouraged. I placed the plane on the board. My right hand snaked around the tote and my left firmly gripped the knob. The rosewood felt mellow and good. Then, I pushed the plane evenly across the wood. I was delighted as the ribbon of wood rose through the throat in a gentle spiral.

"There ya go," Epi shouted. "Ya're a carpenter again. See, ya remember. It hasn't been that long."

"Now, 'fore ya go ta bed ('cause ya really look like shit and need some more rest)," Epi said, as he took the plane out of my hands, "wouldn't ya say that the whole honing thin' was pretty cathartic?"

I nodded.

"Ya know, the preacher's even more cynical than ol' Epi. Maybe 'cause the dead bastard's mortal," Epi giggled. "Maybe 'cause his god's a real asshole. Take god out a the picture, or demote him (or some shit) and what does it sound like Davy's son is sayin'?" Epi paused as if his enigmatic words meant something to me.

"Anywho, before ya nod off ta Never-Never-Land, I gots a few more seeds ta plant. As I said before, 'All is vanity,' even honin' irons. The sleep a'a laborer is sweet, even though ya're fuckin' stiff when ya wake back up (at least I am)," pointing to his crouch. "Sorrow beats laughter any day, 'cause the mournful countenance makes yar heart happy (and I ain't referrin' ta no Spanish knight). Shit happens. There's no end ta scribblin' books. And, last but not least, hombre must exert more strength if she's usin' a blunt iron. And get ya ta a nunnery and go ta bed. P.S., don't be readin' no Ecclesiastes!" Epi slapped me on the ass, and I left the shop for the hide-a-bed.

3.

Beyond Phenomenology

I slept through the remainder of the afternoon and the evening, as Epi had encouraged. The sleep, however, was not entirely restful; I was continually jarred from slumber by muscular spasms of the hands. My dreams were taken up by honing irons—nocturnal figure-eights of steel on stone. These dreams bled into the physical world with my hands duplicating the actions of their mental cousins. Here, the physical and the psychic met, tearing me from sleep. It occurred only four or fives times that night, but the stammers seem to draw light on the day's conversations.

When I awoke, Epi had left a hotdog sandwich, a cold cup of coffee (which he may have warmed for me, but time had consumed some of its caloric) and a note. The note, written on the back of an over-due electric bill, was polka dotted with coffee stains and a large brown ring—testifying to its use as a coaster or perhaps that muddy circle was Epi's seal. Epi's penmanship was poor, the letters, at first glance, appeared perfectly indecipherable; he had not printed or used cursive, instead he used some other individualized form of writing that held little communicative value. I attempted to interpret the note while I ate the sandwich and sipped the cold brew. By the time only a crusted corner of the meal remained, I had translated the note: "Everything one needs in life is on this table. Yours Truly, Epi." I scanned the table, thinking that he may have meant items other than the sandwich and the coffee. The table top contained a half-pack of cigarettes, a few pieces of foil chewing-gum wrappers, a ball of tissue that held some type of dried body fluid inside, an over-piled ashtray, a book published in the 1930s on the Rosette Stone, a three-quarter inch chisel, a cracked guitar pick and a mostly spent book of matches (not to mention assorted filth).

I drank little of the coffee, preferring to spit it back into the cup. With the desire for a more tasty 'cup-a-joe', I left for the coffee shop. Zosimos was sitting outside the establishment rolling a cigarette. "My friend," he spoke through his flesh, "it good to see you."

"I'll be right out," I politely said, as I entered Zoe's.

The clock on the wall read seven A.M. Eva stood behind the counter with a chipper grin. "How are you," she asked.

"I'm doing well. Yourself?"

"Very good. I love that its dark when I wake up," she interjected.

"Do you?"

"Yeah, you can't tell if it's morning or night. Everything is quieter because few are out. I like being the only person awake." Her smile grew larger, and she squinted mischievously.

I grinned too, "I enjoy being alone; there's no one to judge your actions."

"That's an interesting way to look at it."

"What do you like about being quietly and solely awake?" I pressed.

"Oh, I guess I just feel special, like I'm the only one witnessing these colors and these sounds. Maybe I'm a little egotistical, but that's my reason and I'm stickin' with it," she giggled, masking her self-conscious laughter with her thin fingers.

"Good enough for me."

She handed me a latte that she had been fixing during our awkward conversation. "I hope this is what you wanted. It's my favorite," she said.

"It looks absolutely perfect," I said without looking at it.

"Enjoy!"

I went outside and sat down by Zosimos. He was licking a fat cigarette he had just rolled. His tongue was dispersing a heavy coating of saliva on to the paper, soaking it though. Then he handed it to me.

"This for you, my friend, pure Turkish tobacco." I thanked him reluctantly. "This very good tobacco. Most people smoke in pipe, but who need for pipe? It very sweet and moist. Very good tobacco, you like very much." He reached into his pocket for a box of matches. Zosimos struck one and then another, unsuccessfully attempting to shelter the flame from the light breeze. Finally, I got my lighter out and lit it myself. The cigarette produced dense and powerful smoke. It felt like inhaling mercury. I began thinking how his yellowing tongue had just violated the object that was now in my mouth, but out of manners, I continued to smoke it, taking a light puff without inhaling.

"You like?" he asked with animation.

"Yes, thank you. It's very good," I lied, barely touching the end to my lips, but always left with a mouthful of bitter brown worms with every drag.

Attempting to turn the conversation, I pointed to Zosimos' black beret, "What does the metal insignia mean?"

"This," he jumped at the opportunity, "this my family crest. You see, it focal point is the caduceus. Do you know what is?"

The symbol to which he referred was a slender rod braided by two serpents. "It has something to do with medicine, doesn't it?" I asked.

"Yes. Very correct," he approvingly replied. His jowls began shivering with excitement. He started to giggle with my insight so joyously that his whole body shook. The kinetic energy of his mirth launched the cherry of his cigarette into the hood of a passer-by. This caused him to howl with glee. He slowly regained his composure and re-lit his cigarette (with my help).

"So," he continued, "my family been in medicine for many century." His accent began doing havoc on his meaning. "I am *fernimoocologist*."

I was completely unable to ascertain the meaning of his last word. "A phenomenologist?" I tried to clarify.

He shook his head, "No, a *fernomacoligist*!"

Still, unable to understand him, I asked, "A phrenologist?"

"No, a *fermacologist*."

Getting frustrated, I raised my voice, as if my volume would somehow enlighten me to his meaning, "A philologist?"

"No, no, no. Like medicine, a *fermicololgis*... Oh, I can't say it anymore!" he spat with frustration and crossed his arms as if I had disgraced him.

Humbly I tried again, "A pharmacologist?"

"Yes!" he yelled joyously, "that is what I been saying. My father was apothecary."

"I see. So did you work for a pharmaceutical company?" I asked, happy that we had come to terms.

"Oh yes. I did. I was shining star. I make important drugs for world—many live saver and misery ceaser," he proudly stated. "I also write many treatises on property of chemicals, but I also write on spiritual property of universe."

"That sounds very interesting."

"It very interesting, but now I teaching culinary chemistry to kids who developmentally delayed."

I began thinking about these poor children who have to deal with this man's incomprehensible speech. Zosimos began a long diatribe about the importance of food and the soul and the different chemical properties of foods. Most of his speech was utterly mangled in his muddled manner of talking, so I will not reproduce the mismatched syllables here. His eyes oscillated inside of his head as he spoke, as if oblivious to any interlocutor. His cigarette, being rolled so loosely, continued to go out and he, in turn, continued to light it. I nodded frequently to show my attention, although I understood little.

"But really, I love writing," he used as a segue, "although most it has been destroy."

"Most of your writing?" I asked feigning concern.

"Yes, it very bad, very bad indeed. It a huge loss to world; it very good writing. I wrote about many important issue, but people not ready, if ever be ready." Zosimos' jaundiced eyes became glassy as he spoke, "I do not know if ever be ready. They burn almost every thing, except my last book: <u>On Last Letter</u>."

"Was it about the letter Z?" I interrupted.

"No, no. It on letter Omega, but that not exact what about. But Christian fundamentalists destroy my only copies of other books. I attempt to publish lifetime work myself—how you say—vanity press? What I say is books were at publisher and burned all down. My only copies were destroying. Ignorant people, evil and wicked. I told people about my books, and they call me *haroteek.*"

"Herwick? Isn't that a type of sheep?" I asked. "Why would they call you that?"

"No, no! *harrowtick.*"

"A heretic?"

"Yes, yes. This is it. Their minds too small for my idea. It plight of great man that they met with adversary. You must know, I have vision in sleep."

"Like dreams?" I asked.

"Yes, but not just dreams, but vision. It as if I see beyond this physical…how you say—this *reelum?*"

"Realm?"

"Yes, thank god you got it this time. This *reelum* not most real. No, this not case. There more real *reelums* than this. I have vision of scene, character and occurrence symbolize different compound, element and process. Vision have led me breakthroughs for *faremarcology.* But at one day I realize there further truth to vision. Vision foretold truth concern spiritual correspondence. You understand, place we live, not city, but world, it poor representative of more real world. But with correct correspondence of thing in world, one become closer to other—arrive at spiritual insight.

"There many factor: word, molecule, temperature, process, tone, etc. These many factor of spiritual insight or knowledge. It taken me lifetime for understand just few of thing." Zosimos had become very animated again; he was pulling at the rings on his fingers as he spoke.

"You hear of conservation of matter?" he asked.

"Yes."

"I speaking of you in layman term so for you better understanding what I say to you. Conservation of matter mean nothing be complete destroy. So no essence ever annihilate. This, some think, law of nature. This true law. But many not understand this also true of spiritual thing also. Your soul not be destroyed. So see, we learn from world is carried to more real world. World ordered by natural law, but real world more perfect—more real—and it perfectly order by law. It reason is our key to heaven; we know perfection through knowledge, all else suffering."

"That is very interesting, Zosimos," I nodded.

"Yes. It very interesting, but more than interesting; it true. You have an undestroyables soul and capacity to know god. This what all people possesses. There been others like me, those who sought god through nature. Many of them called alchemist, but most them care nothing in changing lead to gold. History spoken slander; lead to gold only metaphors for spiritual journey. Yes, distilled chemical and combined molecule, but these act were done not in monetary gain (most of time) but in spiritual knowledge."

"Yes," I said watching my long and happily extinguished cigarette.

"Reason key for door, but one must experiences world, run sand through one fingers, combine acid and base," he smiled. " Some calls this Hermetic or Gnostic, but whatever calls it, this how one come to know God. Distill spirit!" As the climax to his soliloquy, Zosimos accidentally pulled off one of his rings, and it was flung into the street. His fervor for the alchemical content had caused the ring to be projected nearly twenty feet, projected by the gunpowder of his excited testimony.

Zosimos got up and scrambled over to the ring. He reached it right before the tire of a Honda Civic did. The car, with the bereted alchemist in its path, skidded to a halt. The driver coolly laid on the horn until Zosimos got out of his path. The shriek of the horn damaged any serenity the park possessed; everyone stared at the driver, who sat motionless at the wheel, the meat of his hand on its focus. The old man flipped the driver the bird, and the car finally moved on. "Fooking cook-sooker," Zosimos shouted, as if to add insult to injury to the few people sitting under the peaceful darkness of the morning trees.

Demiurge of Sound

I walked into Epi's shop after the near fatal ring episode. Epi greeted me with a toothy grin imprisoning a cigarette; his teeth were like a guillotine that had not accomplished its purpose, instead only squeezing the life out of its victim. "Howdy, *compadre*!" shouted Epi. "This's the third day a the rest a yar life (or somethin' like that). Today yar eyes will be opened ta fashionin', ta creation, ta the process a the gods, ta becomin' a god, i.e., ta makin' a lute!" he said in his exaggerated style. He waved his hands in the air, bowed and stepped to one side as if a curtain had been drawn open to reveal his shop. "This here is the primordial chaos from which yar fashionin'll begin. With these blades," he said pointing to the rack of chisels, "and with boards like these here ones," he motioned to a stack of wood in the corner, "ya'll become a god. Ya'll partake a the act a creation." The tabby cat on his bench let go an apathetic 'meow' to heighten the melodrama. "What I'm sayin' is that ya're gonna make a geeter, whether ya wants ta or not. I know a bit about medicinals and this here's the anodyne fer ya—gettin' those fingers inta creatin'."

I must have given him a vacant stare, because his brow revealed his frustration. "Get yar ass over here. Ya gotta learn the art a fashionin' lutes, and by lutes I don't mean banjos and violas, but acoustic guitars." Epi took my hand and pulled me to the bench. "Sit here," he demanded. I climbed onto the bench and sat amongst the shavings and the chips. "Now close yar eyes." I did as he requested. "Now listen." I heard the luthier scramble across the floor to the front of the shop, then a loud thump followed by scurrying; finally I heard the warm hum of a guitar, each string being plucked independently towards one of higher pitch. The sound was neither loud nor soft. The independent voices of the strings merged to a single oval tone, causing me to take a slow, deep breath. Another thud and scrapping. This was followed by a different, but similar sound. Again, each string began independent of the others. Each tone held more power and edge than the first set of notes. The whole was more voluminous, filling the entire room with its ringing presence. "Which one do ya prefer?" Epi asked.

"They are so different I can't choose," I hedged with my eyes still closed.

"Damnit!" Epi gruffed. "Ya gotta choose."

"I choose the latter."

"'Ain't got no ladders here, Jacob," he joked. "OK, then, open them apertures." I opened my eyes. Epi held a stunning guitar in his hands. The guitar's surface seemed to collect all of the light in the room and draw the eye away from everything else. "This here, as ya may know, is a steel string guitar, rather than the gut stringed one I played prior," Epi informed. "They's both damn fine instruments, but very different beings. So ya're gonna build a steel stringed box. This is a good start, more tension seems yar style, but very good. Now there's some questions that ya gotta wrestle with." Epi sat on the floor and began to finger-pick some type of hillbilly jig while he spoke. "Now do ya want ta pluck with yar fingers or do ya wants ta pick with a pick? What kinda music do ya want ta play? Do ya want volume or somethin' more subtle? Ya gonna be usin' light or heavy strings? 'Gonna be usin' a slide? What's your momma's maiden name? How pretty do ya want the geeter? What type a wood do ya what the air to be pushin' through? What color is yar panties? Mellow or sharp highs, soothing basses, more middlin tones? What kinda tension ya want on those strings? How many strings ya want? What kinda wood ya want reflectin' the waves?..." Epi continued for a few minutes with his parade of tongue-in-cheek questions. The entire time he played a silly, bouncing song with swinging bass line as his cigarette danced on his lips to the music. Then, the music stopped.

"I don't know?"

"OK, OK. I realize that 'em's a heap a questions. So we'll try one at a time. First, da ya want ta play with a pick or them worthless things hangin' off yar wrists?"

"Both."

"That can be done. Next, do ya need a shit load a loudness?"

"I don't think so."

"Super. Do ya want a more mellow sound or do ya want somethin' a bit brighter. And with this question..." he stopped in mid sentence and scrambled to get some wood. "If ya go a bit mellower, but still with tones a integrity, ya can use this fine, fine wood which I get illegally." He held up a board that had rich browns and blacks and shades of crimson woven through it. "This here's Brazilian Rosewood. It don't come easy and don't tell no G-man I got it, they'd joke me up faster than if I mowed down a whole gaggle a nuns in my pickup ('cause that ain't no federal offence, ya see, lessen theys thought I was some type of serial mower). Or," he held up a piece of wood that gleamed with pale tiger stripes, "do ya want somethin' a bit more vibrant, more glitzy, but less graceful? Neither one's *better* than the other, just matters yar preference."

"I don't want to break the law..."

"That surprises me," Epi smiled. "So ya choose flamed maple. A good choice," he nodded. Epi continued to ask questions and I continued to respond with feeble answers. He showed patience. He showed me different body styles of guitars and even put a few guitars in my hands so that I could get a feel for them. He talked of finishes, fingerboards, scale length and countless other aspects of the instrument. This process took an hour. By the end of the planning he, with miniscule help from myself (despite Epi, at one point, placing a pencil in my hand and guiding it across a large sheet of paper) ended up with a full scale drawing of a six-string 'OM' style, flamed maple body, spruce topped, mahogany necked, steel-stringed guitar with ebony fretboard and bridge, mother of pearl fret position inlay, white plastic binding, 25.4 inch scale length, and abalone rosette whose back and sides would be dyed green to set it apart from its pure white sound-board (although many of Epi's guitars had an element of emerald to them). "It'll be a damn fine instrument, I tell ya," Epi said humbly as he looked at the plans. "Great for finger-pickin' ragtime," he added. With all of his questions, I had never once mentioned anything concerning ragtime music.

"Now, ya're gonna be a brand-spankin' new artificer a sound. I know, whether ya yarself do or not, that ya're up fer the task. Ya gots ta have some shit present in yar mind before ya go fashionin' and artificin'," Epi said in seriousness. "There's been written 'bout an hombre who made shit, that after he made his business he got all frustrated and tore up every thin' he made (excludin' two a every type). Then he got all regretful and promised he never tear shit up again. But then he soon told everybody that he would eventually tear shit up again (but that was in the sequel). If ya ask ol' Epi, he was one confused bastard. But ya can learn somethin' from it: don't get all frustrated and do stupid stuff. Ya gotta love the things ya make, even if they don't come out so hot. And if they're real shitty, do away with 'em once and fer all. Don't be all wishy-washy."

Epi picked up a coffee mug from his bench and took a hard swig. It must have been stone cold, since it had been sitting there the entire time he had been questioning me. He appeared not to mind its lack of heat. "No matter how much ya plan yar fashionin', there's gonna be stuff ya don't expect. The fella I was talkin' 'bout was a bit false with himself, thinkin' that he knew everythin'. Nobody's omnipotent, ain't nobody. Now remember, above all be patient. Don't get all wrathful and vengeful at yar creation, 'cause it's yar ignorance and yar fuck-up that brought it inta being," Epi said pointing at my chest, filling me with more self-awareness than I was comfortable. "There's aspects a makin' shit that ya got little control over, but most a the fuck-ups are 'cause ya didn't foresee it and didn't know. That ain't the wood's fault." The cat meowed acknowledging the statement's truth. "Use patience. Don't get yar drawers all knotted up over some problem and rush through it, but don't get so full a anxiety that ya don't do shit atall. Just keep goin'. If ya fuck up, ya fuck up; it ain't the end a the world," Epi winked. "But do everythin' ya can not ta fuck it up. Ignorance ain't no good excuse."

The luthier lit a cigarette and then continued, "I've got some reading material for ya." He handed me two book-matched spruce boards. "This's what ya gotta read and study. Decipher the grain, study it 'fore ya dig in with a chisel or saw. This's what ya gotta know and understand. It don't take ignorance as an excuse, it'll just split under the tension a the strings or the fibers'll tear out if'n ya plane it the wrong way, these here'll be the diaphragm to project the voice. Bla, bla, bla, we ain't gonna get inta no more a this meta-esoteric shit, fer now. Let's get workin' that cellulose."

He then snatched the boards from my hands before I could "read" them, and, in their stead, placed a one inch by three inch by twenty-six inch piece of mahogany. It was a rough sawn board, brown with a hint of pink and long, shallow pores, the traces of the saw streaked its surfaces. After explaining the process of cutting and rough carving the neck (an explanation that was all too meager for my practical understanding), he turned to leave and get a sandwich. I was abandoned holding this short board from some Latin American country that I had never visited. The board felt alien and strange. It was as if I was to communicate with it in some language that I had never heard. I imagined that it must be horrified at being in such fearful and ignorant claws. But I followed Epi's dictate; I would make a neck.

Epi stopped himself as he was leaving, "Oh yeah," he said turning around, "I gots some cheat notes fer ya." He handed me a huge leather-bound notebook. It held no index or table of contents. The papers enclosed were made of various types of material, from modern typing paper to ancient papyrus. "If ya ever get inta a bind, refer ta the tomb, I means tome—same difference," articulating the B. Epi left.

The pages of the book were inscribed with diagrams and undecipherable writings. It was a sort of esoteric handbook on building guitars, that much I understood.

The mahogany became my focus. I planed, then measured for flatness with a straight edge, then planed some more. Then I carefully cut the wood at an angle six-inches from the end. This would eventually be the head of the guitar. I thinned this piece down, shore up the sawn edges, and, using one of Epi's jigs and some clamps, glued it back onto the board from which it was cut, but in an inverse manner. The neck was taking shape—I had the back angle of the guitar's head.

Epi had come back, now humming behind me. He sorted through his boards and stacked wood. This stack would be the guitar that I would build. I would be its reluctant artificer. The wood was beautiful: black ebony, gleaming maple, colorless spruce, red mahogany. As the pile took shape, with boards of different colors, textures, gain patterns and dimensions, I felt excitement. I wanted to create, to be an artificer. I wanted to sculpt with those shining steel chisels and to plane with the heavy iron. The material began calling me to shape it and give to it new life.

"Will ya be a beneficent or malignant demiurge?" Epi asked coyly. I looked up from my work with doe eyes. "You don't know until ya're done, do ya?" He laughed as if he held some secret to which I was not yet aware.

The next hour was spent planing the edges of both the spruce boards that would become the soundboard and the maple boards that would be the back. The edges of respective boards had to create perfect seams. Epi helped significantly, constantly holding the boards together against a bright shop light, "Not yet, ol' Epi can see a bit a light through this here juncture; its mockin' ya." He would hand them back to me for further truing. After several repeated examinations, he silently nodded his approval. We ran a bead of glue down the edges and placed the boards into jigs for clamping. "They'll be great," Epi affirmed. "This here today's been an ass-spankin'ly good start!

"Now, ya need ta get some grub and coffee inta ya. Go up and fix yarself some grub, I'll be up in a bit," Epi suggested.

I did as he recommended; I went up to the apartment and fixed a sandwich, using the sole residents of his refrigerator: hotdogs, relish and white bread. However, I did not have any coffee. I was tired already, and wanted to sleep. The slow fashioning of the day had worn me out, and it was much later than I had thought it was. Time seemed to have compressed as I had worked on the neck and joined the boards, as if it was playing some strange trick. The meditative act of focused activity had kept my stomach settled. This was good.

After consuming my meal, I went back down to the shop. Epi thrust a broom and dust pan into my hands. "Ya gotta keep it orderly—an important rule, I tell ya," Epi demanded. "If it ain't clean, then who knows what kinda shit can creep inta yar fashionin'. Keep the damn wanderer out, kiddo." After these pedagogical words, the luthier journeyed upstairs.

I swept up the dust and the shavings. The errant particles hung in the air, highlighting the slanted twilight rays of the sun.

The Smoking Buddha?

The sun lit the skyscrapers; their glass and steel exoskeletons burst into a spectacular fire of reds and yellows as the sun began its twilight descent behind the hills in the west. Clouds, as if chasing the sun, began a western migration over the city. These two forces, one bright and eternally consistent, the other an unpredictable element of nature, created a spectacle of contrast: the falling golden disk radiating light, painting the city with long strokes of red and purple from the west, and the dark charcoal blanket smothering the fire from the east. The city clung to life in the middle ground, between the stark shadows of cloud and building, and the beaming wonder that had warmed the unusual day. Wind swept into the city, stirring the chatter of leaves and birds, as a preamble to the coming darkness. The human inhabitants, too, were affected by the change in light—staring out the windows of their offices to watch the covers of night descend at five o'clock, all of them dreading the sunless journey home.

My anxious questions of the previous day, summoned by the nymphs, had slowly lost their strength with meticulous labor. The seven flights of stairs to Epi's apartment were the final chapter of the day's emotional soothing.

I quietly pushed the door open and walked into the smoke filled room. Epi sat tapping the side of his coffee mug. It sounded somewhat rhythmic, but just as I thought I had captured the tempo, I realized that I never had it at all. Done with his fashioning for the day, he was participating in his evening ritual (his constant waking ritual also), sipping a lukewarm cup of coffee and chain-smoking cigarettes. His callused and scared hands appeared to be always engaged, either working wood, strumming his guitars or busy with cigarette and coffee cup. And even when his hands were not occupied with a cigarette, a cigarette was burning near by— his ever-present incense. Smoke was this fool-saint's toxic halo. He reeked of its malignant odor. You could smell him a mile away. It lived in his clothes, his hair, his apartment; it seemed to infest his whole life. He must have noticed my wincing stare at his clouds of burnt tobacco. He must have sensed my disgust with that filthy shroud. He never hesitated to acknowledge and confront anything I did or thought. There was an emotional awareness and unflinchingly direct quality about him. Perhaps that was what I respected most about this luthier.

His eyes narrowed to slits, and his ears moved back on his head. A smile slithered across his face. One of his arduous monologues was the punishment for my disapproving thoughts and petulant look.

"Ya know, ya got a lot a work done taday—lots a work." He spoke slowly, and the cup tapping ceased as he eased back in his chair. "After getting a lot a work done—an I mean a lot, a whole heap a work done—I just love ta sit back, with a cup a joe an a death-cicle, and just contemplate the meaninglessness a all the day's toil. I'm talkin' 'bout all the sweat that I filled that mean ol' bucket a Time with. Ya get my meaning?"

He took a sip of his coffee, his eyes not leaving my repentful gaze. I was in for it; I was going to get some long, incoherent lecture. Perhaps he would speak concerning the nature of Love, or blasphemize the Catholic Saints. Regardless of his content, the ultimate question in my mind was: how long will this madman jabber? As usual, I was sure I would listen silently, I would nod affirmatively at his sideways notions and 'yes' him toward silence. And so I followed the script with head nodding and OK's.

"When I use that putrid word *Time*, I don't want ya ta think that Epi's saying it exists, at least not inherently, but what other words does he have ta signify the illusion? Time is a fickle little cock-sucker and should not be spoken a lightly..." He meandered on, concerning the whorish nature of Time, and then invalidated her existence altogether through talk of antinomies, digital clocks and metaphors of gonorrhea. Epi finally wore himself out on the subject. Just as his eyes dimmed with the discourse and he reached for another cigarette, he was infused with a second wind, "...Anyway, ya were eye-ballin' my *cigarro* cloud. These ol'things are my gurus. This cigarette helps me slither inta these super-deep thoughts, these thoughts concerning the nature a man and Time itself and all that other profound shit." He paused and began tapping his cup again, this time, however, those annoying ceramic dings were slow and methodical, space filled their gaps, and they dripped on my mind like Chinese water torture.

"Ya see, smokin' may be bad fer the body, but it sure is a boon ta the soul. I've been smokin' these stink-sticks fer ages (ever since they been invented), and let me tell ya, they have became a magic carpet ta the land a 'Enlightenment.'" Epi rubbed his hands together and stretched his shoulders in large circles as if preparing for an athletic feat. These preparatory calisthenics were accomplished as the half-smoldering cigarette jittered on his lips, and his eyes squinted through the smoke.

"So ya see, chica, what I'm talkin' 'bout's Nirvani, and I don't mean that shit-strummin' rock-n-roll conglomerate a whinin' pussies. No, I mean somethin' closer to satori, prajna intuition, the destruction a concepts and shit—that state a spiritual transcendence sought by so many folks, yet reached by so few. Yeah, I'm testifying 'bout that beautiful spot where the universe offers up a clarity way outa the reach a Being and that whore-ghost, Time, and all that bullshit day-ta-day and year-ta-year, yar-nose-ta-the-grindstone kind a crap that traps us in a little cell without us knowin' it. The *Cell*," He screamed these last two words, and the object of his dialogue flew from his mouth as if in protest to this diatribe. It landed on his thigh still burning. He jolted up from the couch in reaction and began furiously brushing both legs. Then, realizing that he had merely moved the smoldering object from his precious body to his precious, filth-stained rug, he began stomping. The rug—red, blue and green arabesques intricately woven in a harmony of color—showed black-spotted evidence that this "dropping" occurred with some frequency. Once Epi was certain that the fire was out, he grabbed another smoke, matches appearing almost magically, and lit the cigarette with a practiced motion.

"Where was I? Yes-Yes, the Cell." A pause followed where he eyed me ominously to build suspense and foreshadow his next statements. "This Cell, ya see, this is that dark place where most people live their whole lives—without realizing it, ya know. It sure is dark, fat black rats gnawing at yar toes, the walls moist with mold and etched by yar predecessors with tired lines markin' out the days and decades that they rotted there before ya, cold rustin' iron bars forged in Hades adornin' the door and miniscule window, the screams a yar fellow inmates echoin' down the hallway. It sure is a nasty place ta be. It's those damn Kantian antinomies, Time and Space, that are the jailers. Very bad place, I say ta ya. And what put us there: our death grip on concepts. It's either stranglin' our motivation ta act or, perhaps worse, acting against our true interest. Ya see what I'm sayin'? In that dungeon a misperception, we experience only sufferin'. Sure, every once and awhile the warden, who we call Fate or Chance, and yeah, that slut a the dice, she throws us a measly little crust a bread that makes us think, 'Hey bro, this ain't so bad,' but then the next day some drunken fuck in his big ol' Lincoln Continental mows down our whole family and all a our friends as they're goin' inta Church ta praise the Lord-our-God fer all a his divine benevolence while we're standin' on the other side a the street thinkin' 'bout kittens and lollipops before we see our kin's bodies, in bloody discombobulation, get smeared down the street against the fuckin' bumper. Ya catch my meaning here?"

I added a wince to my usual nod.

"Ya see," he resumed, "We've gotta step back and put it all in perspective, or we'll go mad in the prison a Life. And I can tell ya're askin', 'How do I step back, wise ol' Epi? How do I take the pain away and see that concepts are concepts, and my gaolers are empty wind?' Well, I'm 'bout ta explain it all. Now I'm not sayin' that ya simply want ta be one with the All and stop there—merely meltin' the concepts so the whole damn universe is one bubblin' meltin' pot of crap. Besides, why the hell do ya want ta be one with ignorance or nipple rings or Ebola virus or crappy shit like that? But we'll get ta that part a bit later."

He leaned forward and slammed his hand on the coffee table. "Ya've gotta get some enlightenment. E-N-L-I-T-E-N-M-E-N-T: enlightenment. And ya can't buy it durin' some freakin' blue light special. Ya've gotta go within," he said hitting his fist against his chest. "Put yar miner's helmet on, ya know, the one with the little light on top, 'cause it's a-time ta go diggin'. I'm talkin' 'bout soul-shovelin', kiddo. I'm talkin' 'bout delvin' deep in a big-ol' abyss a shit. Get out-a-the-way, here comes Epi with the shit-shovel a knowin'." He smacked his hands together, pleased with himself.

"Now I'm getting ta the part 'bout the *papiros*, so just bear with me fer a bit longer; I'll show ya the yellow brick road ta that city called Transcendin'-All-this-Shit. So, let's make like ol' Aristotle and shatter everythin' into categories. What're all the elements a smokin'? First off, ya've got the smoker, that's the little world. Next, ya've inhalin' and exhalin', which is breathin', i.e., the verb involved in smokin'. Then ya've got the fire, the tobacco and all that atmosphere, in other words, the physical element other than the dude smokin'." As he spoke these statements, he pedagogically numbered all these facts on his fingers. "Keep in mind," he continued, "breathing is a very important part a any meditative practice. Breathing is the communion between that microcosm a the individual (our first element a the process) with the macrocosm (the third element), or what we could call the Universe. The smoke itself is sorta the mediator between the two worlds; it allows us ta *see* our inherent connection with the rest a the world (I shy away from the word 'oneness' here, ya see).

"Let me explain in greater depth. We inhale the fire and oxygen and energy a the Cosmos," he took a drag of his cigarette. The tip flooded with crimson. Then, exhaling smoke from his mouth, "We respire the contents a our communion back inta the earthly void. Ya see, we're hopelessly bound ta the Universe. We've gotta breathe in order ta remain alive, at least in the common sense a the word, and, when smokin', we highlight that biblical act a breath. When we're a-inhalin' and a-exhalin' while we're working on a fucked up carburetor, we don't see the communion; we don't truly experience that being-bound to the All, we're too consumed by the problem at hand. And so by just smokin', by itself, we get the divine perspective and oceanic feelin'. It shouldn't feel good; there's coughin' and your blood pressure goes up. But it's reality—you see what is real and what isn't.

"Aristotle evaporates as his categories melt back together, makin' 'em meaningless. Man, when I'm suckin' on *die zigarette*, it's like framin' the Nothing. It's that kind a sublime awareness that only truly profound souls have access ta, meanin' smokers. The burnin' a organic matter is not only a metaphor capturin' the process a organic decay, or oxidation, but it's also a metaphor concernin' *une destruction organigue* on a spiritual level. What I'm sayin', is there's a conflagration a the soul, where the spiritual part a us's consumed by Universal Fire. Smokin' can be *spirituel*. But it don't come fer free, and I'm not talkin' 'bout those tax stamps on the bottom a every pack, nor am I spoutin' 'bout the price on yar physical well-bein'. Ya've gotta do some serious work."

He stared at me hard with those dark eyes. "I'm revealin' the mysteries here, pay attention. Ya've gotta do one beautiful, destructive thin'."

He sat back, crossed his legs and closed his eyes with his cigarette dangling from his lips. "Ya've gotta only be smokin'. Only smokin' and nothin' else. Ya've gotta focus, havin' that intellectual and spiritual understandin' that ya're part a the All and that same All is part a ya. When ya're there, within the bosom a that momentless moment, ya're one with all the shit. Ya realize Time's only time, that it's in your mind and not reality inherent. She's only some marketin' ploy by some malevolent and confused fucker upstairs. But, unfortunately, you and all the shit are entangled, includin' all the shit that's not true, but smokin's been pointin' that out." He remained silent for a few seconds, pretending to be in a deep meditative trance.

His eyes then shot open, and he resumed his usual melodramatic style. "I'm not sayin' that any ol' jackass, just because he's got a fuckin' cancer rod hangin' from the chops is the Buddha. Moral of the story, 'don't be a prisoner, chile, a some bullshit conjurin' bastard. And with mindful and diligent practice, one can see that prison a concepts and reach celestial enlightenment—like me. Then the question becomes what you do with all that enlightenment. For another time." With these concluding comments and a devilish wink, he extinguished his cigarette with a gentle twist of the wrist.

Epi began laughing and slapping his thigh with malicious amusement. He was slapping it right where the cigarette had burned his blue jeans. I just smiled and joined him in his fiery ritual.

"So, ya're gonna crash here again ta night, I take it?"

"If you don't mind, Epi."

"Shut the fuck up," he spat, "don't give me that shit, kiddo, a course ya can stay here, as long as ya don't give me any more shit." He pointed to the mounds of trash in the room, "Ya see, I got plenty a shit, and I haven't even dealt with it. I ain't got no energy fer yar B.S." He switched gears quickly with a smile and gave me a pat on the back. "Goin' back down ta the shop. Ya get some shut-eye, ya look like crap and we're getting up hours before the sun comes round here; we gotta go fellin'." He winked and closed the door.

I found sleep quickly.

A Dream of Genesis

Silence and darkness enveloped me. Sweat clung to my body. The walls of the room no longer hung with guitars, nor were they lined with bookshelves, instead, I saw no physical walls at all; absolute darkness, the void, imprisoned me. My heart hammered my ribcage. My sense of space played tricks on me; at one moment I felt tightly trapped, as if I was in a tomb, at the next moment, I had the sense of endless space. The only element of stability present was the hard, dusty ground under my feet.

I saw the ghostly flicker of candlelight stretching across my arms from behind like ubiquitous hands clutching me. My stomach seethed with pain. Slowly I turned my head. A silhouette of a man stood with a yellow candle floating behind him so that I could not make out any of his features. His form was daunting, at least seven feet tall draped in a hooded robe. He held a book outstretched. The angle of the light allowed me to see the book's battered hide cover, scared by antiquity; one of its corners was black from a singeing. Strange geometric shapes adorned the cover, stitched with flaming thread. The impression of the animal's spine, whose flesh now made the cover, stretched horizontally around the codex culminating in a thong, which at one time was the animal's tail, but now secured the cover closed with a bronze buckle. I took the book from the phantom's hands. Its weight was nearly more than I could bear, and I struggled with its heft. The shadow swept his pale hand over the book, endowing it with powers of levitation. It hovered in front of me, its clasp opened itself and the hide cover parted to reveal thick papyrus pages with black, unintelligible calligraphy. I felt, not heard, the words of the messenger upon my flesh; these transparent waves of words permeated my skin and muscle, reverberated down my spine, giving voice to the spirit: "Read the codex, for in it you will find the knowledge of the beginning and the end, for it is the Song of Genesis and Resurrection; through it you will become like Enoch and bear witness to the Truth."

I looked back down at the meaningless words in frustration. Then, from their mysterious script—this forgotten language, like the words of the messenger—rumbled with voice through my core like the tremors from the low registers of a great organ shaking a cathedral:

In the beginning the Universe was the primal abyss, it was the Nothing, and this Nothing had neither thought nor light, for it was before the Word of the Light. This is the Nothing that can not be thought, for it is beyond the Thought and the Light; it is the great Stranger. Framed in the Nothing, Sophia had a thought, and this thought was of herself, for she was the Light, and this thought was the realization of her light and herself. She is the one without a shadow, for she is the Light that thought itself in the Nothing. Sophia was the origin and birth of the Light and of the Great Tragedy, for she suffered despite the Light that opposed the Nothing. Her thought became the Tragedy, for she thought herself and she thought outside herself and thought the Nothing that framed her being. She wept as she thought the Nothing, for the Nothing was of no consolation. She wept, for her only partner was the Nothing, which framed her, and she knew not her origin. She was alone with the Nothing, from which she thought herself. This was her solitude. Sophia, in her great loneliness, that was her thought, embraced the abyss of the Nothing, which she called father, and she gave birth to Error.

Error was the great abortion. She called Error Jaldabaoth, and she turned from him in shame, for she saw that her son was an abortion and she turned her back to him. Through his mother, he had a divine spark, but this spark could not reveal itself, for his father was the Nothing, the great darkness, the abyss. In his ignorance Jaldaboath proclaimed, "I am God. I am the only god. I am a jealous god." He then saw his shadow, which he called chaos, and from half of his shadow, he formed the seven archons. He told the archons, who were his children, "I am God. I am the only god. I am a jealous god. You are my children, for I have created you from my shadow. For this, you must worship me and call me the only god and the god of wrath." And he placed them each in one of the seven realms of his shadow, which is chaos. These seven realms are the seven spheres of Heaven. This heaven he called his dominion and called himself king. These are the seven archons. They ruled the seven heavens of chaos. This chaos knew not of the light, for it is the absence of the light, the shadow of the demiurge. Sleep overtook the craftsman of the heavens, for he was heavy with toil. He fashioned himself a footstool, which he called Earth and placed it at the center of the spheres. Jaldaboath spread himself across the cosmos and slept. As he slept he had a dream. He dreamt of the light of his mother and was confused, for he was ignorant. He dreamt of a man of light, Adaman, who was loved by the Light. Jaldaboath awoke in a jealous rage and proclaimed, "I am the only god. I am a jealous god. I am the god of wrath. Archons, make for me a man in the form of the man of light whom I saw in my dream, and I will rule over him as I rule over you. Once he is here, we will kill him and the love of the Light will be mine. So the archons set out to make the image of the man of light. They placed him on Jaldaboath's footstool, but the man they had formed did not move, for he had no spirit. Jaldaboath raged, for it meant Nothing to rule over a man who did not move.

At this time the archon of the last sphere of heaven, which was called Moon, thought herself and became beautiful. Then she thought her father, and she was more beautiful still. Then she thought her father's origins, and she came to knowledge, for through the thought of the Light she became radiant. In her knowledge, she hated her father, who was ignorant. Sophia saw that the Moon hated the Demiurge, and went to help her. Sophia told the Moon that, by begetting Jaldaboath, she had given him some of her spirit, the divine spark. Sophia asked the Moon to tell Jaldaboath, who was the tyrant, to breathe into the nostrils of

Adaman in order to animate Adaman. The Moon told her father, who was Jaldaboath, that he should blow into Adaman's nostrils in order to animate him. Jaldaboath did this and, in so doing, lost his spirit. Adaman stood up and walked about on the footstool. Jaldaboath saw that he had given his spirit to Adaman. He saw, too, that Adaman now had more intelligence than Jaldaboath, and Jaldaboath was full of wrath. In fear of Adaman's intelligence and spirit, he cut Adaman in half, so that he would be separate from himself, thus creating male and female. The male half was called Adam and the female half he called Eve. Then, Jaldaboath took vengeance on his beautiful daughter and her radiance, so he defiled her, and her beauty withered. From her brutal defilement, she bled and she became barren. This blood fell to earth, some of it mingled with the seed of her father creating plants and animals, some of it mingled with the Light, which she thought and created two trees, the tree of knowledge and the tree of life.

Jaldaboath saw the power of the trees and feared them. He went to Adam and Eve and said, "I am god. I am the only god. Do not eat of the tree of knowledge lest you will die." Sophia saw that the spirit that she unwillingly passed to her son Jaldaboath, which is the divine spark, was now within Adam and Eve. Because of this, she called them son and daughter and loved them. Sophia, out of love for her son and daughter, took the form of a serpent and sat in the tree of knowledge, calling Eve. Sophia said to Eve, "The god of wrath says, 'You shall not eat of any tree in the garden?'" and Eve told the serpent, that was Sophia, "We may eat of any of the trees of the garden; but God said, 'You shall not eat of the fruit of the tree which is in the midst of the garden, neither shall you touch it, lest you die.'" The serpent said to the woman, "You will not die, for I am your mother, who is Sophia, and your soul is a divine spark, which can not be destroyed. Eat the fruit of the tree and your eyes will be opened. Now you are asleep, but once you have eaten of the tree, you will be awake, for you will have knowledge." Eve ate of the fruit and brought it to her husband and he ate of the fruit, and their eyes were opened.

In fear of God, who was Jaldaboath, they hid themselves. Jaldaboath came to the garden, not seeing the man and woman, he shouted, "Where are you?" and Adam said, "I am here. I hid myself, for I was afraid, because I am naked." "Who told you that you were naked, have you eaten of the tree of knowledge which I commanded you not to eat?" asked Jaldaboath. The man said, "It is Eve who gave me the fruit of the tree, and I ate." The tyrant asked, "What is this that you have done?" Eve responded, "The serpent beguiled me, and I ate." But Jaldaboath looked around the garden and saw no serpent, for the serpent, who was Sophia, had gone back to the pleroma. The lord of the cosmos, who is Jaldaboath, was afraid that the man and the woman would begin to think and hate him and overpower him, as did his daughter, the Moon. Fearing this, he said, "I shall clothe you with thought and matter and be your protector, for I am the only god." After saying this, he took a piece of earth, which was dust, creating two tombs, which he called bodies, and put the spirit of Adam in one and Eve in the other. Then he created disease, hunger and pain, to make them forget the knowledge that they had gained from the tree, and make them think that their spirits would die if their bodies disintegrated. The tyrant said to Eve, "I will greatly multiply your pain in child bearing; in pain you shall bring forth children, yet your desire shall be for your husband, and he shall rule over you." Then he said to Adam, "Because you have listened to the voice of your wife, and have eaten of the tree of which I commanded you, 'You shall not eat of it,' cursed is the ground because of you; in toil you shall eat of it all the days of your life; thorns and thistles it shall bring forth to you; and you shall eat the plants of the field. In the sweat of your face you shall eat bread till you return to the ground from out of it you were taken; you are dust, and to dust you shall return." Finally he drove them out of the garden in order that they may not eat of the Tree of Life and become like gods.

After reading the words from the ancient text, I looked up from the codex. The boundless darkness no longer enveloped me, instead, the shallow-light of the kitchen's filament bulb spread around into the living room. My host stood before me, holding out a cup of coffee for my consumption. "Ya look like ya must a slept pretty sound. I thought ya was dead and gone and left poor ol' Epi to his lonesome."

I took the mug and drank.

4.

Dualism, Paradox and the Trees

"Come on, kid, we're on a journey O-destruction," Epi slapped me on the shoulder. "Finish that cup a coffee an we'll get goin'."

I downed my coffee and pulled my jacket on, which, like the rest of my clothes, had become quite wrinkled and rank smelling. Epi rolled his eyes and pointed to my garments, "Those some nasty shit. Here's some fresher and more appropriate clothin'. Business casual don't quite fit what we're 'bout ta do." He handed me a plaid wool shirt and a pair of much abused coveralls. I put the clothes on and followed the old luthier.

Before leaving the building, Epi stopped at his shop to grab a chainsaw. "This is my engine a negation, girlie. Ain't she a beauty?" He held the saw up at eye-level giving me opportunity to examine it. The piece of equipment reeked of gasoline. Every crevice of the device was filled with a mixture of oil and sawdust. "She's done fell many beautiful specimens a conifer. This baby's killed 'em all." His eyes twinkled with pride. "Maybe I'll let ya fell a few yarself one a these days; there ain't nothin' like negatin' nature."

Once our luthier had his implement of destruction, we exited the shop and stood in the parking lot. The streets glistened with rain, and the calming tap of precipitation surrounded us. The rain had amplified all the smells of the city, both pleasant and noxious: the cleansing smell of grass, the crisp odor of cloud, the acidic smell of carbon monoxide and the sour bite of decaying garbage.

Epi pointed to a green late 1960s Chevy pickup, "This here's my rig. She's a fuckin' demon, I'll tell ya. She may only get five miles ta the gallon, but we've been through hell tagether, and I ain't usin' no metaphor."

I seated myself in the cab and took my place beside my friend. The cloth seats were splattered with black stains and streaks of brown soil. The truck held the same fragrance as Epi's apartment, smoke and rancid food. Paper coffee cups, the crumpled remnants of fast food meals, crushed cigarette boxes and the tiny thin flakes of cigarette ash were strewn on the seat and on the floor (I hated to think what sort of horrors lived behind the seat). Epi placed the chainsaw in the bed and got behind the wheel. He cranked the ignition and pumped the gas; the beast of a truck coughed and groaned under the pressured whine of the starter motor and then erupted into a tremendous growl waking all of the neighbors.

"Let there be life!" Epi shouted with pleasure, as if he had been unsure if this contraption was going to start. "She sounds good!" he squealed, still pumping the gas. "That's right baby, it's all good." He eased his valiant steed out of the parking lot and rumbled slowly down the deserted streets to the freeway on-ramp.

A man was sitting on a blue milk crate at the mouth of the freeway entrance ramp, the only soul we saw at that hour. "Look at that fat fuck," screamed Epi. The man was enormous. A great roll of flesh spilled out from his all-too-tight shirt. One could see every ripple of fat beneath the rain soaked and transparent shirt. It was stretched so tightly over his immense girth that one could see its very fibers slowly giving way under the strain. He held a cardboard sign that read, "Out of work porn star hungry for love."

"That is one poor fat bastard," Epi howled.

"Yes, very grotesque," I affirmed, but some part of me ached at the sight of this poor man, not in disgust, but with empathy. He testified to an emptiness and longing to which I could relate.

"I'm all fer porn," Epi snickered, "but that's some sick shit. At least the poor fuck knows what he wants, he just don't know how ta get it, and this early with nobody 'round."

We pulled onto the freeway, the engine moaned under the pressure of Epi's foot. The dial arms of the instrument panel bounced as we sped down the highway. Epi rolled down the window, and I followed his lead. The fresh air of the morning flooded the cabin, whipping the trash into a frenzy. Some of the debris escaped through the windows, other pieces continued to chatter with the flurry of speed and air. Epi commented on the flying garbage, "It's the great trash exodus. It sure beats actually cleanin'." I looked backed and saw our trail of papers and containers bounding along the dimly lit highway behind us.

Epi turned on the radio. Without looking at the road, Epi fine-tuned the dials until the soft hum of a bass could be heard beneath the wind. "All right, daddy-o, it's ol' Mr. Davis. This is a great song, simple yet profound. Ya know which one this is?" he said, turning to look at me. I could barely hear it through the tempest of air. I shrugged my shoulders. "Damn, kiddo, ya got some learning ta do. This is *So What*. It's fuckin' beautiful!" He began to tap the meat of his hand against the steering wheel. "It's fuckin' beautiful," he said with his eyes closed. My mind was not on the music, instead, I was playing out scenarios of highway crashes that I had seen on the local news; driving with Epi, I realized, was truly an opportunity for Fate to intervene horrifically.

Epi placed a cigarette into his mouth and lit it with a jittering cigarette lighter, nearly putting it in his eye. He then spoke with calm, "So, we're goin' ta paradise and gonna cut down the Tree a Life. Damn thing never did nobody no damn good anyway. Then, once we've sawed it up good, we're gonna take its twin, that bitch bark Tree a Knowledge, but not taday. We'll saw that one up good too. Then, ya know what we're gonna do with that shit?" He looked at me through the corner of his eye. "We're gonna build us some guitars, like the one ya're makin'. That's damn right, we're gonna build us some heavenly lyres whose harmony will stretched beyond mind and touch the Goddess a Light." My ears perked up with his mention of a 'Goddess of Light'. "The warm tones a our instruments will release the divine spark up ta its place back in the Pleroma. Ya done started the process, and I'll show ya every part."

I was shocked by what was coming out of Epi's mouth. These things were from my dream. "What did you say? The Goddess of Light? Where did you get that idea?" I questioned.

"You've seen the testament to ol' Epi's nasty habit a perusin' antique books, or should I say antiquated," he chuckled. "Yeah, I read my fair share. Ya're a chile a letters yarself, at least ya tote 'em 'round. I thought ya'd pick up on that ol' Gnostic shit." He smiled as though he knew something that was still hidden to me. "Yep, I dig that wacky religious shit, if ya know what I'm sayin'. It's pretty groovy and all, but playin' an buildin' *geeters* is my true religion."

"What is Gnosis?" I timidly asked.

"Gnosis, it's a whole bunch a shit all rolled up inta one convenient and flaky academic term. In Greek it mean 'knowledge', but now a days people throw the poor battered word around like it's a whole lot a nothin'. Most use it ta mean the folks who figure that god isn't such a nice guy after all, and is just a bastard. In fact, they thought he was a down right mean and ignorant hombre. See, those knowers thought that the physical body a'a man was not a temple, as some fucks think, but a portable tomb—a walkin' sepulcher, if ya like. They thought that the only decent thing 'bout somebody was their divine spark, which had fallen from the true heaven, which they called the Pleroma. This divine spark was not from god, at least not from the creator god, but from that beautiful land-o-light that was beyond god and his evil friends. Now, if ya start readin' the Bible with their theory lodged in yar head, ya start seein' the document in a whole new light; Yahweh becomes a tyrannical, unjust, jealous demiurge and the serpent in the Tree a Knowledge becomes the savior. The whole thin' makes life look even more fucked than it feels," he shouted slapping his knee with approval. "Now this Gnosis stuff is chock full a dualistic shit, fer the most part. Ya got darkness verses light, ya got ignorance verses knowledge, ya got the evil demiurge verses the ultimate unknown deity, ya got man, with both his divine spark verses his bodily material shit, but at root a it all, ya got the Divine Tragedy. I'm not talkin' about some Dante sequel either, no, I'm talkin' 'bout divinity trapped cause a its own failure, that's what I'm talkin' 'bout.

"But ya gotta remember somethin', this dualism shit ain't nothin' new, it always been there. Fer instance, ya got that nutty Iranian, Zoroaster, who had a good god and a bad god. They eventually go ta fisticuffs ta mark the eschatology. Then, ya got those crazy Indians, and I don't mean the ones with war paint. They've got the whole 'Being verses Becoming' thing down pat. And don't forget ol' Plato, with his fuckin' 'forms' and then all their transitory shit (though some argue ol'Plato ain't a dualist, but I've seen his pistols). You get my meaning, kid? Do ya see how people are trapped? Do ya feel the power a the 'caught-between'? And then I ask ya," Epi's eyes grew large and shot a terrified look at me, "How's the Nothin'? Ya hear me? How's it trapped in yar ignorance? Ya like it? Ya like yar nice little coffin? Ya need some fuckin' air holes, I got an auger in the back? I ask again, how's the Nothin'?" Epi then howled with laughter and hit his forehead on the steering wheel, utterly consumed with himself.

I just watched him. I had become very accustomed to his eccentricities and twisted diatribes, but now I was caught. I was caught between Epi's ability to creep into my dreams and his crass, condescending demeanor. He too was dualistic; he was a sort of divine messenger and the basest of earthly men.

"I love fuckin' with folks, I really do, but I like ya a lot, ya see. Ya're all right, even if ya're a little fucked up yarself. Maybe that's why I like ya, 'cause yar pretty fucked up, like yar ol' friend Epi, but in a different way," he cackled this as he put his arm around my shoulder in an attempt at camaraderie.

"Now ya see, there're dualisms everywhere, and I love 'em. Take the guitar, fer instance. Ya know the most important part a the guitar is the soundboard. From the soundboard all sound passes inta the Pleroma." He elbowed me in the ribs. "Without it, the strings would be pretty dim and nobody could hear a fuckin' thin', but the soundboard makes it sing, it gives the string breath, it endows the string—and the guitarist, fer that matter—to break from the shadow a matter, inta the divine regions a spirit. Ya get my meaning? Anyway, I'm getting' ta the paradox. The soundboard needs ta be as supple and thin as possible; the thinner it is, the more it will move with the harmony a the stings, therefore the more air it will push through it. Ya see, ya want the soundboard ta move with the oscillations a the strings, but on the other hand, it needs ta be strong and have integrity. If it's too weak it will buckle under the tension. The strings hold over a hundred pounds a force within 'em. Ya get my meanin'? This's the paradox, ain't she a doosy? The spark, ya know, is in the strings."

I nodded in affirmation.

The truck had turned off the highway and was bounding over the inconsistent surface of an abandoned logging road. The chainsaw beat against the bed.

"Now, kiddo," Epi continued, "We're gonna do somethin' that many would find sacrilegious and even blasphemous, we're gonna do some negatin'. But ya've gotta understand somethin' first. The trees we see're like images in a pool a water a the real trees. I don't mean ta get all platonic on yar ass, but this is how I want ya ta think 'bout it, at least fer right now. Now this tree we're gonna do some hackin' on, it's only a likeness a the real tree, which's the Tree a Life. We're gonna chop this earthly tree down so that it can participate in the divine Song a Life. By us killin' it and buildin' guitars from its guts, we'll be givin' it a second life—we'll be resurrectin' it and lettin' it ascend ta its primal origins. It'll give birth ta its ethereal voice that'll call ta its mother. It'll transcend its earthly tomb and partake a the divine song. We'll bring the Trees a Life and Knowledge back tagether and let 'em sing together. It's about song and minglin'—the softwood and hardwood, the yin and the yang—all that shit. The process'll bring ya back. Ya see what I'm sayin', 'cause this is the shit? We're retakin' the world from the fuckin' demiurge! That's what I'm sayin'! We're sendin' the trees back to mama while we dwell with song!"

He scratched his head, "See here, ya got these two woods—soft and hard. They get tagether, like fuckin', like Adam and Eve or Bert and Ernie, they're paired. They gotta become one again. One is deciduous (fallin' apart when it gets cold), the other ain't. They're trees, but they're different. One bears fruit, and one don't. They long ta sing. Ya throw a bit a metal inta 'em (the strings I mean), which has been tempered by fire (the light), and ya got yar song. Life plus knowledge equals a damn good tune. The voice soars, and we, too, participate in the beauty."

Epi looked over to me. His brow suddenly furrowed. It seemed to me that this was quite atypical for Epi, he rarely showed a consciousness that stepped beyond his own being, but there was a great deal about Epi and his breadth of consciousness of which I was still unaware. Silence accompanied his concerned gaze, and the truck appeared to drive itself, for looking at the road was of no concern to the luthier. Then, Epi asked, "So, what's got ya'll out a sorts?"

I was not sure how to answer. The dream that I had had was too personal, I neither wanted him to mock it nor to verify it as something important. "I had a dream last night that was very much like the gnosis that you described," I stated hesitantly.

"Is that so," he said neglecting the road.

"Yes. It actually felt as though I was awake, but because of the events that took place, I have to conclude I was not awake."

"So you had a lucid dream?"

"I suppose so."

"And in this dream ya're met with Gnostic doctrine, eh?" he said with tempered speech.

"Yes, that's right."

"And now ya're all concerned because it seems coincidental that I was just talkin' 'bout the gnostic stuff?"

"Yes, it makes me a bit uncomfortable, but it was just a dream."

"Yeah, just a dream," he hesitated, "Ya're sure?"

I was startled, "What do you mean? Of course it was just a dream. It was just like a dream."

"Yeah, but last night I heard ya singin' in the livin' room. I found it strange, but 'ta each his or her own.' Then ya left till 'bout three in the AM."

"Epi," I pleaded in frustration, "please don't mess with my head. The last few days have been so confusing, I just can't take it anymore."

"I'm not fuckin' with ya. I was gonna ask ya 'bout it this mornin'. I remember it distinctly, unless I was also havin' one a them lucid dreams. Do ya want ta tell ol' Epi 'bout the dream? Ya know, I've been known as a profound interpreter a the activity a sleep."

Again I hesitated, then answered, "OK. I dreamt I was in a room that had boundless walls...or something like that. It was all blackness, like I was standing in a void."

"Were ya standin' on somethin', or were ya floatin'," Epi interrupted.

"I was standing on hard earth."

"I see. I see, very interesting," he said, as if making an important mental note of my answer.

"Well, a tall black figure, more like a shadow, I suppose, handed me an old book."

Epi interrupted again, "If he was a shadow, how did ya see 'im?"

"There was a candle floating above and behind him, which made a sort of a silhouette."

"Don't leave anything out, kid, I need everythin', every tidbit and action in order ta interpret the dream accurately. Will ya be truthful and exact?"

"Yes," I said obediently. "So, this man hands me a book. Then I woke up."

"Did he give the book ta ya or did ya take it from him?"

"He gave it to me."

"Did he place it in yar hands?"

"Yes."

"Was it real heavy?"

I was stunned, "Yes, it was."

"Did it then sorta float, so ya could bear its weight?"

"Yes, yes it did. How did you know?" I stated with excitement.

"Not uncommon, chile. Did ya read the book or open it or look inside at all?"

My excitement fled with his question. "No, that was the end of the dream. Then I woke up."

"Huh, that's interesting. I didn't expect that," he replied pulling gently on his beard.

"What do you think it means?" I asked.

"Well, it could mean a lot a shit, but I think it means ya need to... Wait, how does that have anything to do with gnosis?"

"Oh, the figure said he was from the Pleroma. I had never heard that word before."

"Well damn it, kid, you never said that the ol' specter talked?"

"That's all he said," I sharply stated.

"That makes a bit more sense. Well, my interpretation is that ya're hungry, spiritually hungry, and that it's a damn good thing ya've got a spiritually enlightened friend like Epi ta lead ya through the labyrinth...

"Oh shit! We're here."

The truck skid to a stop. A cloud of exhaust was the only sign of our former speed. We had escaped all traces of civilization and had barreled into the forest. The enormous trees stood like great and numerous supports upholding the sky. Their shade of green was nearly black, and their height and number allowed little light to penetrate the floor of the forest.   Only gnarled and aged ferns could suffer the darkness of the forest, no other shrub or bush could survive under the dark canopy.   The air had grown cooler with our elevation gain.   There was no sky now, only the black cover of limbs and needles.

"That's strange.   There ain't no snow yet."

Felling the Tree-O-Life

"Here we go, kid.   We're 'bout ta fell the Tree-O-Life," Epi shouted as he reached into the bed of his truck, "This's gonna take a while, so I hope yar up fer it."   He successfully struggled to pull the enormous chainsaw from the truck.   "This here's a McCulloch, maybe the most famous chainsaw in the fuckin' world.   It's taken the life a more *arbre gigantesque* in Oregon than any other implement a destruction.   This here's the first saw that truly took the place a the infamous 'misery whip'.   Yep, and this one's got an Oregon blade on 'er.   That's right, don't fuck with 'er, she's one mean and nasty bitch."   This chainsaw was truly a beast that had seen a great deal of work.   The blade was nearly six-feet long with savage looking teeth running along the bar.   The engine compartment was battered with scratches and dents, showing only trace remnants of its original yellow paint.   Without the blade, the contraption must have weighed at least fifty pounds.   Handle bars protruded from the housing, which, to the trees, probably looked more like devilish horns.   There was a handle at the tip of the singer testifying that this huge monstrosity was definitely a two man saw—Epi had brought me along for a reason.

"Ya know," Epi continued, "this here saw basically brought the London Bridge ta Arizona.   Yep, sure as shit, the bastard who brought this fuckin' tree scythe inta being used the money ta buy a bridge...   Ya what ta buy a bridge?" he exploded into laughter.

"Here, grab the bag, axe and gas can in the back, and help me with this saw; come on, Judas, we've gotta find ourselves some poor tree ta kill."

We made our way through the forest. Walking was difficult; ferns and dead limbs impeded our step. There was not a human being for miles. The pastoral chirping of sparrows glided on the soft wind.

"There we go!" Epi shouted. "That's what I'm lookin' fer, *picea sitchensis*, or, as the plebeians say, a Sitka Spruce. She's a goodie, ain't she." He smacked his oily hands together. Its top most branches loomed over one-hundred feet above us. The tree's diameter looked to be at least four feet across. The bark was gray and smooth. "These fuckers can get ta be up ta one-hundred and fifty-feet tall. I've seen 'em live fer almost a millennia. This one ain't that old, but they can be," Epi stated as he stared up at his victim.

He walked pensively around it three times, scanning the surroundings. Then he withdrew for his calculating meditation, "OK, I got it. Grab the gloves, goggles and earplugs from the bag; we want ta be safe. And look-e-here, when she goes down, she's really gonna go down, so get the fuck out a the way, or she'll give ya the buck a'a life time, OK?"

I nodded. "Is this legal?" I asked, feeling a bit paranoid.

"'Legal?' the chica asks!" Epi shouted, as if I had betrayed him. "What the fuck is legal, anywho? We's got work ta do, other wise I'd tell ya 'bout the 'Law'. Fuck the Law. Let's get cutting."

I submitted to his acrimony. We dawned our accoutrements and prepared for work. Epi strapped a thick leather belt with wedges in the pockets around his waist and hung a single-bladed axe from it. "Ya ready, I'm gonna give the beast life!" shouted Epi, in reference to the chainsaw. "She's gonna be pretty loud, especially till we get her in the tree."

He coiled his body around the saw and suddenly extending himself out, yanking the cord. The saw coughed, miss-fired and sputtered several times before erupting into a continuous howl. Even with my ear protection, I thought I would be deafened by the time we had toppled the spruce. I could feel the cacophony of the engine. Epi yelled something at me, but his efforts were entirely in vain, nothing could he heard over the firing of his saw. With one hand on the engine Epi, used the other hand in sweeping karate chops to illustrate the cuts we would be taking. I gripped the agitated stinger with both hands. Then we leaned into the tree. The sound of the motor evened out, although still deafening. The teeth of the saw ground into the bark and then in the white flesh. Wet, pulpy sawdust flew everywhere like snow; I could feel it in my lungs and in my eyes, despite the goggles. The flurry of sawdust infiltrated everything. The saw did not cut as much as it gouged its way through the trunk. First, we made a mouth in the side of the tree, which stretched less than a third of the way through. Then we battered shallow cuts on either side of the mouth. Finally, we plunged in for the big cut that was to topple the huge organism. My arms ached and convulsed under the strain of the machine. We took our time, frequently filling the saw up with oil and gasoline and packing the wound with wedges. Then, underneath the growling saw, I heard a snap, and felt the bar move. We continued to press the saw into the tree. Finally, Epi began pulling the saw out. We ran. First a sighing of cells being torn apart under their own weight, then a slicing gush of wind and snapping branches, which sounded like a hail of twenty-twos going off, preceding a relatively gentle swoop and anticlimactic thud to earth. I had expected an enormous impact from the great conifer hitting the ground, but it never came; the snapping limbs and a soft pillow of air cushioned its impact. A great wound of light had opened in the dark canopy of branches and needles where the tree had stood.

"Ya OK?" I heard Epi yell.

"Yes," I responded.

"The saw seems OK. I've lost 'em before," Epi screamed across the forest; the well-being of the machine was the furthest thing from my own mind.

We walked toward each other and met at the stump. A white cover of pulp and limbs blanketed the ground.

"What'd ya think a that shit, eh?" Epi proudly jeered with his the chainsaw over his shoulder. "Now that's some serious shit. Now we've gotta cut her up and load the best meat inta the truck. But before that, lets have some grub." Epi dusted off his jeans and wool shirt, then pulled out two hotdog sandwiches and a thermos of coffee from his coat.

As I munched on my meager feast, a heavy feeling of guilt crept over me. The tree was now dead, never again to stand like a titan in the forest. It would never be what it was. The great tower of life that had taken at least ten times my years to reach its tremendous height and girth was laid to waste in less than an hour.

Once we had consumed our meal, we set back to work. We used hatchets and axes to lob off the limbs from ten feet of the base of the tree; then we reverted back to the McCulloch, carving the tree into smaller, manageable sections. Before loading our booty into the truck, we used a special attachment for the saw to cut some of the sections into thick boards. Epi and I whittled that lumber down again and again in order to obtain what Epi called, "The best, most wasteful boards." This dissecting took most of the day.

By the time we had loaded the mere 100 pounds of wood into the truck and driven from the site, the moon hung high in the blackness of sky. Epi had spoken very little since lunch (a quite unusual feat for the garrulous luthier). He regained his affinity for words once we were on the highway. Epi spoke with a low, mockingly reverent voice, "Jeez, the stars on the backdrop a heaven're like flies on shit, there's so fuckin' many a'em." Epi always painted such a poetic vision of the world.

The drive back to the city took little perceptible time. The pickup's engine sighed easily under its burden as we traversed our way back down the Coast Range to the valley.

My limbs hung heavy with the work of the day. I felt the lactic acid inside my muscles burn with anaerobic heat. It had been a day of toil and a day of guilt. But, as we drove back home, the guilt was overcome by the strong aftertaste of fatigue.

"Ya look damn beat," Epi commented. "I sure did wear ya out, or was it the tree that did that?"

"Both," I responded.

"Ya know, there was two important trees in ol' Eden: the Tree a Knowledge and the Tree a Life."

"Yes, I know," I slurred tiredly.

"As I stated 'fore, we done just now fell the Tree a Life."

"Yeah, you have said that," I stated apathetically.

"Well, ya didn't notice that the ol' Tree a Life has got no fruit."

"Yeah, it was a spruce—no fruit—evergreen," I said, shifting in my seat to try to sleep.

"Ya see, the Tree a Life shoots straight up, straight up ta heaven; the trunk goes all the way from the ground ta the top, and the branches come right off a it. But the Tree a Knowledge, why, that's a pear tree (you know, I've seen it)," Epi looked over at me and dug his elbow into my ribs, "Don't go ta sleep on me, kiddo, this shit's important. As I was sayin', it's a pear tree, so that the trunk only goes part way up and then the limbs all branch from it from there. So ya got some big differences. First off, ya got a hard wood verses a softwood. (I reiteratin' here fer a purpose, it ain't like ol' Epi's marbles's scattered all over). Next, ya got the branches comin' off all in different directions. After that, ya got needles verses leaves, in other words, evergreen verses deciduous—different ways a collectin' light). Very importantly, ya got cones and fruit (i.e., different ways a fuckin')." He giggled. "Finally, ya got a huge tree, nearly touchin' heaven, as opposed ta the relatively short pear tree. Now I knows ya're usin' maple; it's very similar ta ol'pear, so don't be frettin'. But there's so many fuckin' differences 'tween life and knowledge, but ya don't care, 'cause ya're

100

basically crapped out, and I can start talkin' all kinds a mean an nasty shit 'bout ya," Epi jiggled the steering wheel to gain my attention.

"I heard you, 'lots of differences'," I acknowledged.

"Ya know, this shit flowin' from my mouth, it's some profound stuff. Ya shouldn't be sleepin', ya should be writin' it all down."

"I'm memorizing every word of it," I said sarcastically.

"Don't give me that shit, kiddo. Ya're so far from understandin' anythin', ya could be lookin' in a mirror and ya wouldn't recognize..." Epi stopped short of finishing his statement. "Go ta sleep. Sounds like ya're in need a it.

5.

Of Barbeliotes and BandSaws

I did not know what day it was—whether Tuesday or Wednesday, Saturday or Sunday. The numerical designation for the day of the month also eluded me. But, the cloud-filtered sunlight illuminating the lacquer and shellac surfaces of Epi's guitars was my only indication of temporal placement. I could guess that it was a November morning. I could guess the year, and I could presume the day within a week. I knew nothing except that I had dismembered the Tree of Life in the recent past. My mind was not functioning on a very lucid plane.

I found myself down at the café, feeling my empty stomach and my aching muscles. Eva served me a Mexican mocha, a French pastry and a wordless wink. I sat outside mechanically consuming my breakfast as I vacantly stared at the turning leaves. The golden colors of fall did not register in my head, the photons merely rebounded off of my retinas like images reflecting off of a mirror leaning discarded against a dumpster. I was in the haze of physical recuperation from felling the tree. At that moment, my mind sat passively against the world, yet my muscles shivered under even the coffee mug's weight—still spent and re-knitting, still fearing further labor. My whole being suffered with work's dull after-glow.

My body was focusing all of its energies towards biological repair. Mind, the function of cognition, took a back seat to the endeavor of recuperation. Thought and mental processing were superfluous, and all glucose and other nutrients found their way to tissues far from the brain. My eyes did not stray from their vacant gaze as formless and faceless apparitions passed by on the sidewalk. A persistent wind, pregnant with mild precipitation, blew through my clothes, yet my flesh failed to prickle at the cold. And Time passed nearly unperceived.

"Get the fuck in here," shouted Epi from his shop door. "I can use yar paws." He was covered in saw-dust; the white flakes were all over his apron and in his hair. "Damn, ya look like a zombie!" he chuckled. "Feels good ta get a bit a exercise, don't it?" he shouted with mocking jumpingjacks.

Consciousness trickled into my mind. I set down my empty coffee cup and saw the crumbs on my plate. I raised myself from the seat and stepped into Epi's shop with awkward stiffness.

"I did the rough milling without ya, the girls helped me," Epi said, brushing sawdust and wood chips out of his hair. "But the gals done run off, and I can use yar hands ta do some re-sawin'." Epi pointed to a stack of thick boards, virgin white. He picked one of them up and pointed, "This is some beautiful shit; ya see that tight grain, tight as a girl's never-been-plucked. What we've gotta do's cut it down and store 'em till they're good and age'd. We'll be able ta use 'em in a couple a years."

Epi threw me an apron—green and soiled. "Put 'er on." He then tossed goggles and ear plugs at me. "They'll do ya some good," he added.

The luthier pointed to his bandsaw, a tremendous machine whose green paint was beaten by use. "She's a Grizzly, and I ain't speakin' metaphorically, but she is a beast. Real new compared to all the other stuff in my shop. They calls her a Grizzly G1268 twenty-inch bandsaw. She's got a three-horsepower, two-twenty volt, fifteen amp, totally enclosed, fan cooled motor, steel frame, a magnetic switch, and rack-an-pinion adjustment—a fine wood-eater. She's got it, I'll tell ya." Epi spoke with apparent love for all of his tools. He seemed to possess an intimate relationship with them and great respect. "Now she ain't the biggest," he continued, "there're plenty bigger, but she's a goodie." He slapped the side of the machine with brute camaraderie.

"Now let me tell ya what I've done here already. The gals and yars truly here have quarter sawn what ya and the ol' fart ripped from nature," Epi explained. He grabbed my shoulder sternly, as if to ask me something of terrifying importance, "Ya remember what quarter sawin' means?" Epi's fingers dug into my shoulder until the silence was unbearable for him. His mind could no longer contain my speechless frown. "Goddamnit!" he yelled, his patience utterly evaporated. "Quarter, like cuttin' into four parts?" The question screeched out of him in a high-pitched supplication to my memory.

"When the lumber's cut perpendicularly to the grain?" I asked rhetorically.

"Yesss," Epi hissed with pleasure. "That's it. Ya just been fuckin' with the ol' man. And remember, it's wasteful as hell, but it makes stronger, more tone-facilitatin' boards. Ya see, it's a fuckuvalot better ta burn all this scrap and have all a this waste than ta've a shitty nothin' a'a sound. See, if ya use plain-sawn boards, all ya get's a dead tone no matter how 'alive' or how much voice the wood's got in 'er ol' fibers. Ya gotta quarter saw it. So fuck the waste, we're all goin' ta the same place anyway, and when I say 'we', I mean ya and everybodys else." Epi clapped his hands with enjoyment. "Now some folks don't cut the soundboards out; they split 'em with a froe—followin' the natural lines a the wood. But ya gotta plane and scrape it anyway, so that whole process don't make any sense ta me."

He preceded to show me how to operate the bandsaw and then sat back on the workbench, hunched over and swinging his legs like a child. "Shove that shit in yar ears, ya ain't no Odysseus, and there ain't no siren song a-comin'. We's gotta get ta work," Epi growled.

When Epi had said 'we', he had meant 'me'. I fed the wood into the bandsaw against a wooden fence that, Epi later explained, he had built especially for re-sawing (that is, cutting boards longitudinally). Even with the ear plugs firmly in place, the rattle of the Grizzly shook my eardrums. The boards quivered in my hands as I pressed them into the teeth. Epi continued to talk, although the bandsaw's noise and the earplugs fortified me against his words. I must assume that he knew this, for he was an intelligent (although eccentric) man. 'We' cut the boards into pieces a few inches thick, which, once they were dry and their moisture content stabilized in the shop, would be further cut and book matched.

Epi stood back, supervising with a cigarette hanging from his lips. Sawdust filled the shop. I finished cutting the boards, and Epi stacked them carefully on racks in the back of the shop.

"Good job, kiddo," Epi praised. "Ya done it like a pro. In a couple years, they'll make great soundboards. Now clean up the shop; we don't want no wet sawdust rustin' everythin' up."

I did as he asked.

With the large machine finally quiet, the cat appeared on the workbench. She began rolling on her back in wood shavings, exposing her belly to Epi's hand. He pet her underside gently, and the cat began to purr. "Ya don't like that loud sound, do ya, li'le one?" he cooed to the cat with the exaggerated tones of one who is speaking to an infant. "It's off now, baby. It's gonna be off fer the better part a the day." The tabby sat up and began licking herself.

"I could fuckin' tell that this here was a good ol' tree—nice tight grain and full a sound," Epi stated as he picked up one of the boards. "This's good shit. I've an ear fer seein' this kind a thing. I gave that tree a tap when we were out there in the forest. The branches rung like a xylophone. The whole fuckin' tree called out harmoniously, mostly in "G". Ya may not a been able ta hear the resonance, but ol' Epi sure could. It's got a good ol' voice inside—yes, yes, full a life." Epi held up one of the boards gingerly by its corner. He tapped as he brought it near my ear. I could hear a dull, but distinct ring. "Nice, eh?" Epi asked proudly. "Sounds nice, even before she's dry and cut thin." He nudged me in the ribs.

"Now glue the veneer onta the headstock and we'll get some grub." Epi handed me a piece of figured maple, sparkling with the illusion of depth. "This'll make the neck a hella'a lot stronger; them steel strings do a bit a work on the wood when they's at full tension."

I spread glue onto both the head of the guitar and the piece of maple. After evenly brushing the glue out, I clamped the thin piece to the head.

We walked over to the café. Zosimos was sitting at a table reading and mumbling to himself under the awning as the clouds sprinkled rain around his feet. He looked up from his book and greeted us, "Hello my friends. How you two fine people todays?"

"Just fine, ya ol' sphinx worshippin' sphincter," Epi replied caustically.

"Good to hear," Zosimos answered, ignoring the epithet. "You joins me for bite eat?"

"Sure!"

"You possess erudite way with language, my friend."

"Ya're jabberin' mighty fine, yarself," Epi continued, while he gave the Egyptian a fraternal squeeze. "I'm gonna grab us some grub. This pretender was pesterin' me yesterday 'bout gnosis. A diatribe on ol' Barbelo would sure do the trick ta shut the chile up." Epi entered the café.

"So, curious about Barbelo?" Zosimos asked. He began rubbing his hands together. His fat palms were dry and sounded like sandpaper on wood. "This very interest subject, something I have studied in extensiveness. It very important piece of Gnostic history and history of thoughts." His lips moved slowly over the words. "I see that too is piece of your life story, very important. You very interest in such topics. Do you know Gnostic means?"

"Epi has told me a little."

"Very good, this is good. You know anythings about Barbeliotes?"

I shook my head.

"There not tremendous literature concern these people. But I tell you funny story." Zosimos slurped and bit his words as if he was devouring a savory meal—his accent annihilating the meaning of his speech. "There young and devout Christian man of Third Century. His name was

Epiphanius. He went study in my country of birth with Desert Fathers. When he there, these beautiful young Egyptian girls came him in streets and persuade him to come to their religious ceremonies. They (how do you say it) bent the arm," Zosimos' whole body shook with laughter. "These lovely girls leads him to church, probably with beauty. He wrote what he witness that night. It his writing that testifies to rites of Barbelognostics. You know, he wrote of their orgiastic spiritualism. When poor man got to church, he and Barbeliotes ate sumptuous meal—very lot of food, very decadent and wonderful stuff. They ate and ate until bellies distended." Zosimos' thick tongue massaged his lips leaving a glimmering lacquer of saliva. "Once they very full of food, they threw clothes to ground and they had the sex—very much of it like beasts. They had the sex and they had the sex," Zosimos repeated with bulging eyes. "When men to ejaculate, they stop having the sex. Couples gathered men's fluids and held witness to heaven. 'This is pass-over, body of Christ,' they prayed. 'Our bodies have bathed in passion, Passion of Christ. This is our gift to God.' Then they ate it. Imagine, Epiphanius very disturbed by type of Christian worship. Boy's senses aroused and horrified by acts of carnal praise—very stimulated. He must have run out of church with confliction (he, a young man, full of juices, but sworn to church in Rome and dogma). But, of course, he stay to watch whole thing.

"Epiphanius wrote more, but I doubt he saw more. He got twenty-four Gnostics ex-communicating. This, all, near Alexandria. He wrote libel about people, says that they participate in ritual murder. You see, they not wish to perpetuate cycle of suffering—birthing. They thought this just continues Demiurge power over spirit. Instead, Epiphanius claims, they participate in ritual murder of newborns. As soon as child dropped from mother's womb, it be slaughtered and eaten. This, I doubt, took place—not good reasons, not consistent with spirit." Zosimos frowned as he spoke of this ritual murder taking place by a group with whom he somewhat identified. "These thing can not be correct. It is awful. Epiphanius would say anythings to dramatize and demonize 'heretics', spiritual rebels. He say newborns 'torn apart and duly prepared,' like rabbit or beast of forest.

I grimaced at the thought of 'duly preparing.' This seemed the worst sort of cannibalism—an infanticidal and incestuous cannibalism.

"He wrote things," Zosimos continued. He pulled a zip-lock bag of tobacco from his pocket and began rolling a cigarette. "These not bad peoples. They want to go to heaven and be part of Truth. They many type of Barbelognostics: Nicolaites, Zacchaeans, Stratiotici, Phibionites, Coddians, and, of course, Barbeliotes. To be Barbelognostic is believe there was female (sometimes male) power who lives in Ogdoad. She child of unknown father— most primal being. She slept with father and gave birth to Saboath. Saboath believed, or least said, he was only god. He created lot of henchmen to rule universe. Birth of Saboath and creation of archons disperses divine seed of light—this, glory of unknown father. Poor girl, Barbelo, saw she had done bad thing, so she gathers all of lights. She gathers lights by having the sex with archons. This, you see, is first act of salvation. So, Barbelognostics just performing myth of salvation. This sort of cult of woman—men finding savior in ascetic of female." Zosimos winked. "Only woman can gather spark, divine light, seed of light. This coitus of spirit—reclaiming—communion on most, how you say, visceral plane. But, most important, and most gnostical, it vehement denial of petty material world in they lived. Do you understanding?" his head tilted with question.

I nodded.

"This last part very deep thing. This part of philosophy I think true. Many good thing these people thought." Zosimos sipped his coffee. He lit his cigarette and it immediately went beyond his notice.

Epi stepped out of the café burdened with two plates of hamburgers and three cups of coffee. He had opened the door with his foot and was having difficulty closing the door without losing his balance. In his attempt at stabilizing himself and the meals, one of the burgers fell to the sidewalk with a substantial amount of coffee. "I don't give a hoot," he shouted, "that'll be mine." He set everything on the table, snatched the hamburger from the ground and took a gaping bite. "Tastes better with a little gravel and rain water," he mumbled with a full mouth.

"So," continued Epi after he swallowed the hardly chewed piece of meat, "ya told the youngster 'bout those constantly-fuckin', ritual-killin', daughter-rapin', cum-eatin', sonsabitches?"

"No," Zosimos said disdainfully, "I spoke Barbeliotes, wise Christian sect."

"Whatever," Epi spat, his language hindered by food.

"No," Zosimos retorted, "not, 'whatever'! This important. This very important distinction! You slander; you, who told me about them in first place—stupid carpenter."

Epi responded with a mocking high-pitched voice as he grabbed his ears, "I so sorry I offended ear. Please don't hurt me for utterings such sacrilegious drivel. I would never mean to offend."

They proceeded to argue. Zosimos became enraged and blood rushed to his face. He began hitting the table with his fists and shouting in his native tongue. Epi continued to speak with sarcasm. I announced, and was unheard, that I was going to take a walk in the park.

Reshit and the Oroboros

I walked off of the sidewalk and onto the street, then across into the park's wet grass. There were few people putting up with the monotonous drizzle. An old man was huddled over his soaked newspaper attempting to read the type as the rain gradually muddled the letters into one another. A skateboarder, dressed in the overlarge clothes of his generation, glided across the top of a park bench and landed confidently on the ground, only to grind painfully his palms across the concrete a few meters beyond.

I planted myself under a bronze statue. This figure of a forgotten city founder stood majestically: his eyes staring distantly toward progress, an arm outstretched toward the river, his shoulders bearing the epaulettes of pigeon dung (a symbol of fortitude despite modern disregard for the aged). Words in relief pressed into my back; it was his plaque reading: "Let this land be baptized in the waters of the Word." There was little indication of who this gentleman was, or why he stood in the middle of the park, only the word "Founder" was written after the quotation. Maybe it was the man who had once employed a Jewish servant who, in turn, owned a kabalistic cat. I rested my cheek against his pedestal. It seemed to draw the warmth from my face, although I was too tired to care. The wet ground began seeping into the seat of my pants; it too reclaimed more of my body heat.

As I was drawn toward sleep, voices slithered around from the other side of the statue, the voices of teenagers. "Come on, man, show us your tat," hissed one.

"Yeah, dude, we've been dyin' to see it," said a deeper voice.

"I guess," a third voice reluctantly moaned.

"Fuck, man, that's dope! What the fuck is it?"

"You wouldn't understand."

I slid my body down to the edge of the pedestal, attempting, successfully, not to be noticed. A boy was struggling to lift his heavy winter jacket. He pulled his jacket and shirt up to reveal Greek words newly tattooed on his back. The letters stood off his skin like the letters on the plaque indicating a recent scarring.

"Come on, tell us bro. What is it?"

"Well," he said as apathetically as possible in an attempt not to engage his cohorts, "it's Greek. It's the first paragraph of the *Book of John*, you know, in the Bible."

"Why the fuck did ya do that?"

"I dunno. I just felt like it."

"You're one fucked foo'," he said with a smile and then slugged his tattooed friend on the shoulder. "You're fuckin' loco. So what does it say, in American I mean?"

"Well, it says something like, 'In the beginning was the Word, and the Word was with God, and the Word was God...'"

"Word up, mothafucka!" one of the kids shouted with crossed eyes and a strange hand gesture.

The tattooed youth seemed displeased with his friend's mockery, "You guys have no idea ."

"Don't pay any attention to them," consoled a young lady with a large piece of metal imbedded in her nose. "They don't have half the brains you've got. They're all pigs anyways." She began massaging his shoulders.

"Really, dude, what's it mean?"

"It's the *Reshit*."

"Oh dawg," the two other boys began to howl with laughter. "The Re-shit? Like crappin' twice?

"Reshit is the word used in the Kabala to mean the Word and the Beginning."

"Fuck, dawg, your speakin' Greek to me." The boys began laughing hysterically again. The girl's shoulder rubs gained intensity as she sensed her boyfriend's dismay. The laughter subsided and the boys regained their composure; they seemed to have no problem ridiculing their friend, but they did not wish to alienate him completely. "Tell us more about the Reshit. I swear we won't laugh."

"It's like the snake that's eating its own tail, it's a circle, like incest or rebirth."

"It *is* like shittin' again, I mean if it's got its ass to its mouth—self enclosed," one of the boys said with a serious look.

"You're not that far from being right, but coming from you it sounds stupid." The boys allowed for this deprecating statement without retort.

"Ain't the Kabala like Jewish and the other is like Christian and shit?" asked one of the boys.

The tattooed youngster looked on at his friend with wide-eyed amazement, "Ah, yeah, that's right. But don't forget that Jesus was a Jew and so was John."

"I bet ya didn't know I knew what the Kabala was."

"No, I didn't think you did," answered the boy receiving the massage.

"Well, I knew this crazy-ass professor-dude that had this fine-ass daughter. She was one bomb breezy. You guys know, the guy that got his brains blown out?"

"Shit, he was a feak. You hear about what he was doing, who he was doing," one of the youths chuckled.

An awkward silence hung over the group as they looked down at the ground.

Unable to stomach the uncomfortable turn in which the conversation had taken, one of the boys evaded the silence with, "So bro, I'll lay down a bad-assed beat, and you read us one a your poems. Whatdaya think?"

"Sure."

One of the young men began to blow controlled breaths of air through his pursed lips; this process produced a sound similar to a drum, then intersperse hit-hat-like hisses. He held his hand over his mouth as he pumped the air, like a trumpet player using a mute. The boy had great control of this virtual drumset, both in tonal changes and in rhythm. The other boy proceeded to beat out a rhythm on the bottom of his skateboard, using knuckles and palm to alter the timbre. The separate beats created by the boys wove together into a tight rhythm section. It possessed an ambulatory pace, within its complex syncopations.

The tattooed youth pulled a piece of wadded paper from his jacket. He opened it up and began to read with the rhythm his friends had created. His voice did not hold the bold and overly confident gesticulation of an inner-city M.C. Instead, he sounded more like a long-dead English poet who is only read at the behest of tired school boards.

"The great passing of ecstasy
    When the lords of Time were marked
    With the howls of Rhyme
And meter bore noble quatrains
    With fiery and proud tongues:
    Promethean odes for powerful drums.
Yet a life of infinite pleasure can not be
    Sustained within iambic rivers
    Of song—nor can bodies maintain
The endless passions of the throng,
    For sleep overtakes the merriment of day
    As dreams cloak in darkness, a figment
Sun bearing away. But as for I
    Bleeding in the incandescent rays
    Of modern moons aloft,
I scribble out of tune on pages
    Wrought from ancient firs
    Struck down by course hands.
I watch your eyes, under soft lids
    Roll to and fro, captured
    By oscillating fancies of sleep.
And if I were a god would I
    Creep into your dreams to
    Gaze upon your mental streams."

"Dawg, that was some badass shit!"

"Thanks," he smiled humbly with eyes focused on the grass.

His girlfriend kissed him on the cheek, "You're so smart, that's why I love you. You don't pretend to be all hard like the retards around here." She looked at the other two boys, "I don't mean you guys."

"So are you guys really gonna leave tonight?" asked the boy who was beating on the skateboard.

"Yeah, we're gonna take off. I was able to put enough cash together for a couple of bus tickets. I'm tired of this place. It's just getting weird and scary. I know this place is in for some bad shit," the poet explained.

"He's my knight in shining armor. He's gonna take me away from all the crazies," the girl announced with her arms snaked around his neck.

"It's just too fuckin' weird. The language, the fires, I'm sick of it. We're gonna begin again."

Standing up excitedly, one of the young men shouted, "Then we've got a farewell party to throw! Let's get some Endo and some booze and go up to the park."

The band of teens got up and headed down the street. I, too, pushed myself off of the ground. Large patches of water showed where I had contacted the earth. Before leaving the feet of the Founder, I tapped on the statue with my knuckles. The statue rung out like a bell; this fellow was hollow.

A Holy Fool, A Whore and the Pearl

I walked back over to the café. My legs were heavy as if the rain water had seeped from the ground to give them additional weight. Epi still sat at the little table outside of Zoe's, but Zosimos had left, probably to dabble in his chemical philosophy. A man stood not far from Epi petting a dog. The dog reluctantly allowed the man to scratch its head and pat its back with a hand that appeared fixed—his fingers perpetually curved and joints rigid with hardship. The dog's tail jittered between its legs. He was an older man with a white beard and white hair straying from under his sweat-ringed fedora. This man stunk of homelessness',

114

bacteria breeding on his clothes. He wore a tan coat and tan pants, both ripped and patched and as abused as his flesh.

"Nice doggie," the man spoke quietly. "She has a lot to smell on me. Do you think she is a Pekinese?"

"'Looks like a mutt to ol' Epi," the luthier said, casually sipping his coffee.

"Oh, well so am I," the man smiled. "How are you two?" His eyebrows came together as he recognized me. "Did you ever find your mommy? Is that where you went for so long?" he asked me.

He must have sensed my confusion, and changed the subject. "Can I go pet Pistis?" he asked like a polite child.

"Get the fuck in there," ordered Epi. The man walked into the shop with a stiff gate and closed the door.

"He's a good man; 'been 'round here for years," Epi told me. "Get yarself a cup a joe, it'll do yar gut some good."

My stomach had been churning, although not from being empty. I felt *it* inside of me. *It* seemed to become more active as I looked upon and smelled the homeless man. I went inside and ordered a straight coffee and then rejoined the luthier. As I sat back down, the homeless man exited the shop.

"She is a very nice kitten. I scratched her behind the ears and she purred," said the man. He spoke with quiet precision—although the volume of his sentences trailed off asymptotically. "I like your cat very much, she is very kind. Can I play one of your guitars again?"

"Get the fuck in there and bring one out," demanded Epi.

The hobo brought out a classical guitar with brown and black rosewood stripes, the figure was so stunning and precise that it looked as if some one had painted it on. "This is a very nice one, Epi. You do a great job."

"Thank ya," Epi replied.

The homeless man laced his finger and extended his arms. A great crackling followed, sounding like frozen tree limbs snapping in a blizzard. His hands were suddenly transformed from stiff appendages to dexterous digits of harmony. He waved his hands over the strings, and great articulate chords reverberated from deep inside the instrument. The man played a few flamenco-like riffs at a blazing tempo and then stopped for Epi's approval.

"You've been practicing," Epi encouraged with a wink.

"Yes, mostly in my mind." He proceeded to play with easy articulation. The tones were absolutely clear and precise—almost staccato, yet relaxed in themselves.

"I like it," nodded the luthier. "It sounds like your brain ain't a bad place to be."

The music swayed in the wind and drizzle with the tempo of falling leaves. He did not play any note out of place. He did not confuse his tones in any chromatic scale or diminished. There was a major feel to it all. It was straightforward and honest music that was rendered with a gentle beauty.

"What's your name?" I asked abruptly.

. With easy, liquid eyes he stated, "Mani." He then look toward Epi, "I saw that you have some mother of pearl on your bench."

"Sure do."

"Do you remember the *Hymn of the Pearl*?" asked Mani.

"Sure do."

"Can I tell your friend the *Hymn of the Pearl?*"

"Sure can."

"Thank you. I really like this story. I think it has a lot of significance. It was written down a long time ago by the Apostle Thomas. I don't know who it was about, just a young prince who lived thousands of years ago. I can't tell it as it was originally written, because it wasn't written in the English language, but I think you will enjoy my story.

"A long time ago there was a young prince who lived with his father and mother, the king and queen. They were all very happy. They had many good things in their possession, and their people were very happy. The King and

116

Queen gave their son everything that he needed, including love. He was well cared for and wanted for nothing. The royal family then set their son, who they loved very much, out to Egypt. They gave him all that he needed to make the journey, but they took the royal robe of glory off his back. They had made this robe from love, and it was fitted especially for him. Before the prince left his family, they made a covenant with him and had him write it onto his heart." Mani pointed to his chest. "They did not want him to forget it. The covenant was written like this: 'Go to Egypt. There you will find the Pearl. It is in the middle of the sea. The Pearl is guarded by a serpent. Once you bring the Pearl back, you can then put on your robe of glory again. You will then be heir to the kingdom.'

The prince left for Egypt. He made the long journey to that country safely. The young prince went to an inn that was close to the serpent. He looked around the inn and felt like a stranger. To try to fit in with the people, he put on one of their robes. He still felt like a stranger, so he ate what they ate and drank their wine. He then forgot why he had come. He stayed at the inn for many months and became friends with the people. He partook of their customs and served their king. Their clothes were warm, their drink was intoxicating, and their food bore much weight. The prince fell asleep.

His parents knew that he had fallen asleep, and they wept for their child. The king and queen hatched a plan. They wrote a letter to their son with golden ink on paper of adamant. The letter said: 'Wake up and get up from the ground. You are in slavery right now, but you have the blood of kings in your veins. Remember who you are. Remember why you are there. Remember your robe of glory.' The letter floated on the wind and burst into word above the prince's sleeping body. When it became word the prince woke up, raised himself from the earth and remembered.

The prince went to the serpent. The prince put a spell on the serpent that made it sleep. He grabbed the Pearl. The prince stripped off his foreign robe and ran the entire way back to his kingdom. The loving words of the letter gave him strength to make the journey. He brought the Pearl back to his kingdom and put on his robe of glory. He had forgotten how beautiful his robe was. The prince looked at his robe, and it mirrored himself. He realized that he and the robe were two different things, but it held the same shape as his body. The robe radiated knowledge and begged him to sing. The prince sang. He sang of his robe of salvation and his love and his parent's love and the love of the King."

"Who's the sssssnake, kid," Epi hissed, laughing and slapping his knee.

Mani looked at me with honest eyes, "Did you like the *Hymn*?"

"Yes," I nodded. "Thank you for sharing it with me. And thank you for your beautiful music."

"You are very welcome."

"OK, OK. We've got some planks ta saw and some pearl ta plant," Epi interrupted. "Thanks, ol' boy," the luthier ended and took the guitar back into the shop. I followed him.

"'Time ta get back ta work," Epi instructed. Now ya've already done some bandsawin' today, but you've got lots more ta do 'fore I let ya sleep and forget it all." He handed me the soundboard that I had glued up two days before. "Get crackin'," he demanded. "Plane her down nice and even. Don't fuck up. Get down ta 'bout a tenth a'an inch. There's some dial calipers in that drawer." Epi then left behind the back door of the shop, behind his "muse".

I placed the boards on the bench. Before I had time to raise the plane, Epi's head appeared around the doorjamb, "Two things, look at the grain 'fore ya plane," he laughed at his unintended rhyme, "and plane down the back and sides too, ta 'bout an eighth a'an inch. Them's the tricky ones—gnarly grained bitch, them maples. *Adios!*" His head disappeared once again behind the door.

I labored with both plane and scraper for a few hours before I felt relatively satisfied with my work. Confidence with the hand plane and the scrapper filled me. I enjoyed the warmth generated by the scrapper against my thumbs and the effortless weight of planing.

Epi had impeccable timing; he entered from the front door of the shop as I dusted the final shavings from the boards. "Gettin' better," he affirmed. Epi held two cups of coffee in one hand and a half-smoked cigarette in the other. "Here's some java fer yar soul." He gave me one of the cups and set the other down on the bench. Epi began eyeing the sound board carefully. He picked the white board up and held it to the light. He ran his palm over its surface with a slow pass. Then, he held the board gingerly by its corner, about two inches from his ear and gave it a tap. His face was sent into contortions, "No good," he yelled, spitting his cigarette onto the ground. Epi quickly bent over to retrieve it from the scattered shavings. "It's got no tone." He threw the board onto the bench and began planing it. He took quick, steady passes, held it up again and tapped. "Much better," he approved. "This's got some voice ta it. She can sing.

"'Member how I was tellin' ya 'bout the ol' soundboard paradox, we'll call this soundboard paradox *redux*. So if she's thick, then she'll easily hold the weight a the strings, but she'll sound like shit 'cause she's gotta vibrate (that's how she pushes the air, and so doin', creates sound waves). But if she's too thin then she'll buckle under tension and time. When we glue the braces on, we'll have the same concern. Anywho, she's gotta be thin enough ta sing, but thick enough ta handle reality's hundred plus pounds a force. In other words, ethereal yet real. If this problem weren't enough, she's got to be in tune—sing right, not just loud and nice, but right" Epi took a sip of coffee. "So this here one sounds tolerable. She sings OK, and in G.

"Now, measure and scribe the hole and the rosette channel, route the rosette-ring, inlay the bitch with that purflin' material and some a that mop, route the truss rod channel in the neck, then ya can glue the heel block onta it," tossing me a cube of mahogany.

"What's mop?" I asked.

"Not mop, M. O. P., mother a pearl. I cut it for ya already. I got the radius' all ground nice and all. All ya's gotta just route the wood and glue 'er in. *Voilá*, ya're done." Epi clapped his hands together displacing the cigarette from his mouth, "Fuck!" He again bent to pick the smoke from the shaving before looking up, "I'm getting' senile, I tell ya.

"So while ya're doin' the inlay, think a Mani's story, I mean 'bout the Pearl. Just don't listen ta what he said 'bout serpents; there ain't nothin' wrong with a snake or two. It's just a metaphor." He smiled and nudged me in the ribs. Epi left out the front door.

I followed his commands. My hands worked awkwardly in an attempt to learn what they did not know. My joints felt the strain of new movement. I feared the small router. The process that he had explained took time and focus. The sun had suddenly disappeared and the street was quiet before I realized it was even twilight. The sunlight that cast a living shade on all of the wood, instruments and tools had vanished, leaving only the unnatural and dry hue of the florescent tubes. The light felt dirty, singed. My mouth felt of cotton.

The pieces of mother of pearl sparkled as if they held their own light. I found myself gazing unconsciously at their brilliant swirls of color. If I had a 'Pearl' I would not acknowledge it. The serpent must be untamable. The 'Pearl' must be too heavy. Sleep must be too deep. I glued the pearl with the purfling into the soundboard so that it haloed the sound hole. I smiled as I tapped the last piece home. It was good, even in the foul manmade light.

I continued through the laundry list that Epi had left for me, routing, cutting and gluing, improvising to make it all work.

As I finished wiping the glue away from the clamped heel block, Epi's "muse" caught my eye. I felt both attracted to her sensuality and repulsed by her explicit pose. My entrails moaned with the sordid pleasure of her body. Her eyes pierced me, unsettling the meditative focus that had been reached through work. She did not look through me, instead, she looked into me. Her eyes made her more complex. They did not ooze the same gross sensuality as her open cavity, but simultaneously radiated confidence and begged for understanding. My gaze was fixed on her, as if we were playing a game of who will blink first. I lost. But when my eyes refocused, I looked beyond the flowing tones of curving skin and saw the printed dots which made the image. I walked up to the poster and examined those tiny dots which, in themselves seemed of no consequence, but as a whole made the picture. I realized that each dot was a small nearly imperceptible letter. These were not symbols of the English alphabet, but of some other language. They appeared to be something like Greek letters, although some looked to be pictorial representations similar to hieroglyphs. I jumped as the door opened in my face, startled and embarrassed. It was Epi. I quickly stepped back to the bench.

"Didn't mean ta startle ya," the luthier smiled.

Pretending to have not caught me examining "Barbie", Epi examined my work and nodded to it in satisfaction.

He and I then cut the fret slots in the black ebony that would become the fingerboard. "These slots have ta be perfect," Epi explained, "otherwise it won't play in tune. Ya want it ta play in tune, right?" I agreed. "Ya see, the ear's gotta natural affinity fer certain tones based off a natural law. That's right, law—even Epi pays attention to some laws," he winked. "What we're cutting here is those mathematically occurin' intervals that sound good. No matter what ol' Epi says 'bout nothin', there is a deep relationship 'tween nature and soul, math and god. No matter what's ya says 'bout a mind-body dichotomy and shit, there's an intimate relationship 'tween mind and nature, even if she's sorta a fucked beast."

That night, as the sounds of the city ceased while the polis slept, Epi and I worked. I cut the fret slots with a special backsaw against a square, just where Epi showed me to cut. The glue had dried enough to cut and file a dovetail tenon in the heel block so that it may be attached to the guitar's body. We then placed the truss rod in the channel I had routed earlier, which would give the neck more integrity under the weight of the strings, and then glued the fretboard over it.

Epi showed me how to split the even-grained spruce blocks to form the braces. These braces were glued to the soundboard and back, giving the structure more strength without compromising too much elasticity. I enjoyed the splitting—the chisel effortlessly following the lines of grain. It was the ease of it all that appealed most, that it seemed to want to split. I thought that if I ever got proficient enough to read the grain, then I would never need to sharpen another blade, all I would have to do is see between the grain and place the tip of the iron there, then the grain would part for me. We shaped, then glued and clamped the braces and the bridge patch in place on both the spruce top and the maple back. Neither of us spoke a word.

The events of the day—the work, the spectacle and the words—were like a patchwork, yet I intuitively felt some commonality running through these seemingly disparate occurrences. The work of my hands and the sensuous data from people captivated my mind. I thought about the Barbelognostics and their erotic rites; the serpent and the pearl; the material constraints of sound; that inner-physical place that (if one can penetrate) splits wood fibers without force; the whorish, silent and wordy muse; the beginning word of the cosmos etched onto a child's back; the sleep of memory; the beautiful meditation of steel on wood; the law of ear and earth... There appeared to be a relationship between the physical and the metaphysical, between soul and action—a kinship between what is felt in the heart and occurs in the material world. On some level, these realms become compatible and apparent. I wanted to understand where this place was, where these two places of *is* meet. There must be some place between the dualism. My mind wondered to questions of song—a place where mind is captivated by abstract matter. My thoughts were groggy and dark—where's my robe?

Epi and I took the elevator to his apartment, the first time since the fiery night.

6.

The Verbose Messiah

The next day I awoke to a scene that was quickly becoming typical: Epi would wake me with a cup of coffee that always held a bitter grip on my tongue but comforted my stomach. As this awakening had become routine, following Epi's lead had also become something of a habit and, now, not out of the ordinary. I had become quite accustomed, within the few days we had been together, to the strange ramblings of this odd fellow. In fact, he had grown on me such that I felt directionless when his smell of sawdust and cigarettes was not in the air.

"I need ta tell ya somethin' important. Maybe I should a talked 'bout it sooner, but 'so it goes'," concern etched his face. "Ya know that guy down the block—the crazy fuck with all 'em street urchin's orbitin' him?" I shook my head, for I had never seen him. Epi continued, "Well, he's one freaky dude. That's ol' Agathon. Let me tell ya' the story.

"Here, sit down and have a cup a joe," he barked and pushed the cup of stale (nearing antique) smelling coffee into my hands. "You comfortable, 'cause this is gonna take a while. I want ya ta know the whole damn thing, 'cause I've got this feelin' that ya're gonna run inta 'im or one a 'em poor brainwashed bastards that hangs around 'im. This's how it goes," He spoke eagerly and rubbed his hands.

"He was this pretty nondescript guy who, for a livin', clipped the extra string off a embroidered name tags (like on work uniforms and stuff). He also published the translations he did a Coptic, Greek and Aramaic texts. Neither a these endeavors made him much cash, but I heard he did sorta have a name fer himself as a translator a ancient esoteric documents. Anywho, he kept pretty much ta himself. He'd

124

hang out at Zoe's café, down there, and listen ta other people's conversations. The crazy fucker's ears'd really perk up when kids from the University'd start jabberin'. Oh boy, it was like his ears were glued ta their tongues. Ya could see his fixed stare at their lips as the names 'Hegel' or 'Lucretius' or 'Godel' were uttered. This bastard was a funny kind a voyeur." Epi reached into his pocket for a cigarette. Fumbling with his lighter, he sucked hard on it, puckering his lip and bulging his eyes as he inhaled.

"Anyway," the words mingled with the smoke as he talked, "this hombre was a silent intellectual since Hector was a pup. I caught a glimpse inta his apartment years ago, and it was nothing but stacks, towers, mountains a ol' moldy books. I've no fuckin' clue how the guy moved 'round in there, even ta get ta the John ta take a shit, it was so crammed with literature. (Ya know, I never looked behind the books)," Epi hissed with glee. "Nobody knows his history, at least 'fore 1950, not even the ol' timers. It's like he just appeared one day out a the blue. He looked ta be 'bout seventy ever since he moved inta that slumlord's wet dream over yonder. Shit britches does have a sense a humor, even if it's been repressed fer centuries. He's worn that same holey sweatshirt fer the past decade. 'Fore all the letters peeled off," Epi chuckled and pointed to his chest, nearly burning himself. "It was a joke, somethin' 'bout readin' a book inside a dog. It's some quotation from Marx, and I don't mean Karl the Commie. I've heard Tie, ya know Tiresias, the clarinet player, joke about how that must be his sort a abyss, I mean livin' in the dog's entrails: dark and caustic."

Epi scratched his head with the hand holding his smoke. He continued with a renewed vigor, "The guy's loony. He was loony then, and now he's utterly consumed with madness. Cause ya see, I haven't gotten ta the truly fucked part a this whole thing. A few years ago, he started ta butt inta conversations at Zoe's. And everybody would sorta humor him, especially since he didn't do it all that often. But he'd become a battleship when people'd naïvely discuss language, his guns'd blaze. Oh my God! One time I was sittin' there readin' some shit, sippin' some java, right? And these two kids start talkin' about the Gospel *According ta John*. Anyway, they must've both been takin' Greek 101 or some shit 'cause they were spoutin' 'bout *Logos*. Ya know, 'the Word'. Anywho, Agathon declares war and verbally pummels these two frigates. Nothin' was stoppin' him. With every shot, he blasted smolderin' holes inta their understandin's."

He slapped his knee with pleasure and continued, "Whatever. After that day, everythin' changed. Agie spoke less and less, it's almost like words were heavy on his tongue, till nothin' was comin' out a his pie hole, nothin' at all, he hardly even breathed. Come ta find out, he was gettin' so wrapped up in linguistics and all that etymology a words stuff, that he couldn't find meanin' in any verbal or written communication 'tall. I guess he was obsessed, ta put it mildly, with *knowing* exactly what he was sayin' and hearin' and bein' understood perfectly. That's whatcha get fer over thinkin', ya go a bit looney. Ya see, Fuck-Head wanted ta use only the words he understood absolutely on their deepest levels, ta their most primordial roots. Ya know, ya could be usin' a word or phrase and have no idea where it comes from or what it means. Like," he snickered covering his mouth, "like the word faggot. In jolly ol' England, it meant a 'bundle a sticks' like kindlin' or a cancer stick. Well, they fancied burnin' queers at the stake. Them homos were such a source a light and warmth that they just started callin' them faggots." Epi cackled so loudly that the tenants above him began stomping on the floor in protest. He paid no attention and continued his monologue. "I mean no offence, a course." He winked.

"At that time, Fuck-Pants was walkin' round with all kinds a dictionaries and lexicons, some in English, others in Sanskrit or Arabic, even Aramaic, Hebrew, Phoenician and Doric Greek. Dude was fucked. He'd sit in that damn coffeehouse and pour o'er his books. He musta been luggin' 'round over a hundred pounds a paper wherever he went.

126

That's probably why he walks around all stooped over like God bent the speechless moron in half fer tryin' ta know too much.

"Then," Epi clapped his hands, "he stopped talking all together. He just shut up and there was nothin'. Agie was completely silent. Some a the homeless kids'd tease him, tryin' ta get him pissed off and talk, but it never worked. He finally cloistered himself in that cell a books. I don't think he even ate, never venturin' out fer groceries. He lived dead in his tomb. He spent nearly a year in that sepulcher. Some folks thought he'd died, but nobody seemed ta care enough ta find out if he still had a pulse. There was no stench, so nobody bothered. And then, poof, like the Son a God resurrected, comin' back from liberating hell (and he did, I'll get ta that part), he was seen runnin' naked along the waterfront. It was enough fer a sane man ta blow chunks, kiddo. There's nothin' worse than seein' a naked ol' man, bent and twisted, skippin' with his transparent flesh hangin' off a his body. Ugh, and guess what, the crazy fucker was singin', not hummin' or whistlin' or yodelin', but singin' *words*. Or at least sort a."

Epi's cigarette had burnt to the butt. He glared at it disapprovingly and tossed it out the window. Pistis had finished her breakfast and settled on the old luthier's lap. Epi stroked her fur as he continued. "Ya've gotta understand," he mumbled with a new cigarette already in his mouth. "Understand what he'd been doin' while in exile from humanity. Well, he'd become so immobilized with the paradoxes an disappointments a language, that he decided ta start anew. Ya see, he couldn't possibly trace the genealogies a words back ta their original sources, if they had any. It'd be like tryin' ta understand infinity. He'd either hit a dead end, or the etymology kept goin' and goin'. So he created his own language, a 'rational' language. That day, as he was a-hoppin' and a-skippin', he was like Adam runnin' through the Garden namin' all the beasts. Nobody stopped him, not even the cops. He exuded power through his namin', as he pointed and sang. Agie was drunk with it all. He was a free spirit with the impunity a Baachus. Then a bunch a homeless waifs joined him, perceivin' an opportunity fer some revelry. They all stripped past their knickers (we're talkin' lads *and* lasses, wink-wink). And paraded 'round with him and echoin' his twisted namin' song. The whole city seemed ta fill with it, that unstoppable song, as the herd danced their way through the streets. There musta been a hundred a 'em. The onlookers just stared with their jaws open down ta their kicks. It was crazy. I'll never forget that sight. And neither'll this poor city. The face a the Rose is forever changed, chile.

"Since then, the great unwashed have been his minions. Some call it a cult, others, bastards who are close ta the street life, call it the *New Truth*. The gutter trash claim that one must cleanse oneself from the ol' grime a past languages and get baptized in the new lingua. These plebeians espouse ta the belief that from Agathon's new form a communiqué they're able ta contemplate the universe free a corruptions. Some say it's the only pure language. Others state that it's the language a God, others still the, Devil. Whatever it is or is not, the ol' pseudo-prophet has an entourage a over two-hundred and climbin' every day. It's a sort a subterranean army a the Word. They live by their own laws and traditions. They only speak this language. This evil speech's more than just words; it's a whole culture, separate and isolated from all else. These guys've been transformed inta birds a prey, from being the rats and roaches. They've found their place in the cosmos, no doubt. They're still livin' off a everybody else, but they're not eatin' garbage anymore. They have that rigorous code a thieves and fanatics. This band a parasitic youth comprise the largest, most powerful and bloodthirsty element a this city. Perhaps the best organized and disciplined too. He's even getting middleclass folks now!" Epi began coughing and throwing ashes everywhere as he flailed his arms.

He composed himself. His jaundiced eyes burned as he spoke his warning, "Stay away from 'em. They'll either suck ya in, in which case ya mise-well sign yar soul over, or they'll crush ya like a snail.

"Ya can't know everythin'," Epi stressed, leaning forward in his chair to close the gap between us. "He's pushin' too far and he don't respect the sublime. Ya can't run from what is inexpressible. There was a time when he'd collaborate on projects a translation with professors from the University, but now he's just in an unnatural world of his own creatin', the King a the Nada."

He got up from the oak chair and entered the kitchen. The cat jumped off his lap and followed him in hopes of more food. When he reappeared, he had a full cup of coffee and a less vexed look. "I'm gonna go down ta the shop." He left the apartment, and he also left some more clothes for me to put on. The blue jeans and wool shirt fit well, but the diatribe did not sit well with my stomach.

Vapid Distemper

My abdomen ached. Somehow, Epi's words hinted at my past. The parasite riled, feasted. My being, once again, seemed only to exist for the devil within me; I was merely a meal—a feast for another organism, this was my *rason de etre*. My muscle and sinew, my bone and skin, brain and liver, all had the same final cause, of a most morbid nature. As I contemplated my fate, I began envisioning my insignificance. The tangled branches of my ancestors rose up like a great twisting tree, all faceless limbs, and I was a shrunken bud on a withered branch. These limbs, sprouting and dying, traced themselves back years and centuries and millennia. Fifty thousand years, back to the first man, the Aleph of humanity. This lone progenitor, who, for all of his children, remains nameless to history's muse. How many millions of individuals rose out of his primordial seed? I am the nothing within the lineage. I am the faceless and nameless child of History, who does not see my own past, who is blinded and deafened by my own ignorance, being eaten alive.

I had made my way down to the coffee shop. Neither Zosimos nor Glaucon sat at the sheltered table; I was alone. Shriveled leaves, those who had escaped, for the moment, the wetness, danced in the November wind, whispering their unknown language as if to try to calm my thoughts. Fall filled the morning breeze and filled my nostrils with stillness. Solitary contemplation had never soothed me; I had a tendency to lie to myself and forget that which can not be forgotten. I played a hideous game with myself, a game that meant self-imposed asylum from self. Nowhere could I call home, for the beast now captivated my every move, stripping the lining of my stomach with razor teeth, then making its way to my pancreas and liver, leaving the heart and lungs for its last course, so as not to kill its host and home before ascending to maturity through my trachea. This was life, under the gentle whistling branches of the trees.

The Tree of Life, could I climb it to its top and look down at all that lived before—this One of All, the true endower of the curse? Could I tackle it with spikes and belt, inch my way up its spire? This tree, which represented the whole of breathing animals, the amoeba and the kangaroo. Is even the leviathan part of this hooded tree? Would I pass its ominous branch, or would the god of wrath force me to fall, plummeting to the base and losing all of my breath under death's bony hand? Life held not the fire of love, but captivated only the fire of destruction and annihilation. The God of wrath, I am like you—in your wrathful image. I too would spite Job just for a bet. I too would purge the world of my own creation just to see them drown. I too would sprinkle tuberculosis into children's lungs merely to watch them suffocate on their own fluids; I would do it too, but I do not possess the power. I too would create in order to breathe pain into my creations. I would tell my creatures to be moral and violate my own law. I would allow my desire of destruction to pass judgment on every being. I would watch the suffering. I would never sleep in order to revel in my own malignant play. This is boredom's antithesis, the creation and destruction of things. This is the antidote of self-suffering—to destroy.

And for this, I rest, I sleep, and pass judgment on myself. My contradictions have risen to the surface and I no longer possess trust for myself. The hatred of the world, the hatred of the self, this is the yellow hallway that capture the hallucination. I set it on the shelf, for I will dye it the color of life and call it good. God cannot judge me, for he and I are the same, father and child and holy mother. I will not worship the divine, for in the divine is the great tragedy, the great fuck-up, the creation of pain and evil and the Nothing. Through life comes the redemption of what should never have needed redeeming. This is the Holy Error, this is the divine plan of disease, incest, war, disastrous accident. I am my father's child, wrapped in the swaddling cloth of wrath and alienation. Where is my mother?

Who dares cross the mind from whom I am spawn? Who bleats under the stony moon of patricide? Who will hunger at my jealous ocean, unfathomable to mind, for mind can never reach itself? The unconscious wells up like the river Lathe and drowns all that was, it washes with jealousy as its tool. But did I create this river for myself? Did I bid it to flow into mind before I was through? I long to forget that I am the cause of my mother slamming the door. It all repeats itself—the fateful circle of action. Yet I tried to stop it, or did I? She fled out of fear.

...And, within the puss of anger and confusion, I stand before the tree with a jealous saw. My blade quivers with eagerness to down that which is my father and my mother and sister, that which has nurtured me and called me child. This is the end of that tree; this is my fire and my sword and my severing wrath.

I pull the cord of ending, the saw glows hot with negation, it beats from within, it pulses, and its darkness eats through the bark, the bark of Life, the first protector of the World Spirit. I am your end, through me you will die, and *your death with be an endless nothing, never to grow and live again. History will end with you. I drive the saw deeper, penetrating the pulpy cells that pumped with life. The white entrails of the tree scream for forgiveness, but a divine heart hears not their pleads. I am your host of hosts, in me you will feel no more sorrow, for in me history dies as if never born. All will forget. I will cauterize your life so that it will never tower toward heaven again. I kiss the Tree of Life as I plunge the blade deeper and deeper into the dark heartwood. In me you will die as the enormous monstrosity topples to the ground, aching under its own weight. I, too, topple with its tallest branches—the lamb of wrath and penultimate bud...*

A Bending Will

I lifted the coffee cup to my lips without the aid of vision, for the world was full of darkness; my eyes were open but sightless. I could feel the dim rays of the fall sun against my cheek. I felt the warmth of the coffee bitterly run down my throat. It dragged me away from the sightless words. I had dreamt of words as I sat outside of the café. My mind was suffocated in a lightless blanket of the past. Now, there were no longer feelings associated with these words, only the concrete words themselves. I only remembered long words and short words, but all existed without context—only loose and lonely words, as though someone cut a page out of a novel and threw the pieces on the wind. None of the ideas associated with those words held meaning. Whether I forced them into fragmentation or whether they parted on their own accord is for the reader to decide.

I found myself in Epi's shop. Time had continued to flow as the words formed their bonds and then were loosed. The sturdy and scarred workbench stood at my conscious periphery, slowly gaining ground from the un-remembering. Then the weight of a chisel presented itself in my hand. The presentment of the shop overpowered memory's disruption with the finale of Epi's voice, "Ya're like a fuckin' zombie!" When one is locked in a black prison of memory, one is always like a 'fuckin' zombie.' "Ya done cut out the head and drilled the holes fer the tuners, ya done cut the tail and head blocks, ya done some whitlin' on the neck itself and her heel, cut out the back and top and done a whole lota sandin'—followin' orders like ya was some soulless mothafucka." Epi spoke only a few inches from my face. It was probably his breath more than his volume that had brought me to the present, for it held the toxic odors of centuries old cigarettes, burnt coffee and gum disease. "Thank the devil, ya're alive. Now I was thinkin' I'd have ta make a fuss and bring down my exorcism kit from the apartment, shit.

"Now I showed ya how: bend those sides, shape those braces (not too much and not too little), glue the blocks on, and inlay the headstock. Git goin', I'll be back in a bit." Epi left the shop. As he slammed the door, the poster of his wordy muse quivered with the shock. I followed all of his orders.

A steel pipe was being held horizontally by a clamp on the bench. A propane torch was rapidly heating the pipe. Two long buckets of water held a maple slat in each. An aluminum template of the guitar's form lay on the bench. Everything was ready for bending. I swept my fingers through the water and flicked them at the pipe. The water droplets stood on the pipe for a nearly imperceptible moment before vaporizing; the pipe was at the correct temperature. I drew one of the sides from the bucket and brushed the water from it. I studied the grain, then, feeling satisfied with my knowledge, I put it to the pipe. Water boiled inside the wood, although not rapidly, but steadily and evenly. I applied pressure and set it against the form before subjecting it again to the iron. So doing with my will, I bent the sides. I fashioned them to my liking. They submitted. They did not split or crack, as flamed maple is prone. They submitted and I took pleasure in the act of torturing them into shape. I do not wish to give the impression that this task was easy; it was not. It took several trials before the desired shapes were met; applying heat, checking for shape and reapply. The wood rebelled even under the considerable stress of heat and water, but it eventually submitted. If the planks had bent quickly and dutifully into their form, I would not have taken such pleasure in their transformation (it would have been no conquest—but it was). Things that bend easily seldom hold much value. If a woman easily gives herself to you, you will rarely call her back. This is no insight.

To bend wood is an obvious force of will over the material universe. This act is quite unlike carving the braces. The braces are airy straight-grained spruce. One places a sharp chisel between the wood fibers rather than forcing them. There is pleasure in the ease and cleanliness of the process, but it's not the act of brutish will. Instead, the spruce carves itself, there is no fight, only falling away as if the wood had decided on its own to take a different shape. There is muscle to the bending, there is obvious force, not a tremendous amount, but it is present. There is also water and fire. The process may sound more like something out of a chemistry book than woodworking. There is the breaking down of the cellular structure. The cells are tortured and ordered to submit. One uses a bit of practical alchemy to break the spirit of the wood. I accomplished my task.

I was focused on my craft. Several times that day I lit cigarettes that were entirely neglected until they became ash—so was I caught up in the art. I have described this state as meditation, but dwelling upon the subject further, I have realized that there may be different types. My type of meditation, cutting and bending and fashioning, collapses time and space on each other, always leaves me with a slightly dusty feeling. Like the electric lights in the shop beaming their artificial rays, they were blanketed with a tan layer of sawdust, I too never felt clean. I felt dirty after my artificing meditations. I felt like dust had penetrated me.

134

Like Epi's Buddha, I felt full of exterior particles. This, in itself, may not be negative. Sometimes a layer of grime adds value to a work of art, giving it the aura of authenticity and age. Who wants a pristine antique—they are usually forgeries.

That day I bent the sides to the template and immobilized their shape with cam-clamps. I glued the heel and tail blocks. I even inlayed the thin mother of pearl symbol that Epi had cut out for me. It was tiny and fragile. I placed it in the middle of the headstock. It was an exaggerated symbol of the planet Mercury: a circle with two horns on top and a cross at the bottom. The cross, however, had been dramatized and looked more like arms and legs. The whole appeared to be a little devil dancing, rendered in the silvery-white pearl. Epi always took pleasure showing his rye sense of humor.

I felt better than when I had begun. I had forgotten the words and felt empowered by the force of my will. All went well in the shop—things appearing to turn out as I wished. My stomach had not bothered me.

Pistis lay curled on the bench. She gave little notice to my actions. She seemed apathetic to my deeds. Likewise, I paid her no attention, since I was so compelled by the struggle of forceful creation. I had done so much today.

Eva and the Silent Song

I no longer used clocks; I had transcended the mundane idea of time pieces. At this point in my journey, it was difficult for me to determine whether weeks, days, or hours elapsed while I dreamt and fought with myself. Time seems to contract and expand with the presence of sleep, waking and what I usually experienced; one can never judge with accuracy and confidence the number of orbits of the clock's hands in the waking world and even less accurately when asleep. Clocks held no value for me, since my estimation of time was an internal one. I hoped to abolish Time altogether, and with it History. What better way to accomplish this than to sleep. I realized that even trapped in the worst of lucid nightmares, I preferred to sleep than engage with the world of wakefulness (although I seemed to be doing something inbetween). There is an ease of action in sleep, even when eluding a nocturnal demon or sinking hopelessly in soporific quicksand, than the work of being awake. The nature of action, within a dream, takes on a different character than the actions of "real" life. This difference is the element of work and effect; when one attempts to cause an effect in a dream, there is no logical or temporal consequence, but in waking life, the works of one's hands follow him or her into the future. One is bound to his or her actions while one is awake, but in sleep, cause, effect and accountability do not exist, instead, events transpire without intelligible connection, and then, usually, erase themselves as the dreamer is buoyed up to the surface. It is the act of erasing that I longed for most; an art that I was slowing developing.

I was back at the café. The table shifted as I set the cup down. It was warped from dampness and age. The wooden legs bowed out in disfigurement. The tabletop was concave and its varnish was pealing to reveal weathered gray maple, unlike the sections that were still white and protected. I felt the slosh of the strong pressed coffee warming my stomach. The cell phone, which I had unconsciously brought in my pocket, dug into my thigh, a reminder that there was much more than this moment.

I watched as a man, with a bulging jaw and wearing a blue jogging suit, tied his Labrador to a "no parking" sign. A little girl, newly comfortable with speech, walked up to the dog. She had been walking around outside of the coffee shop as her mother sipped and read inside. This small one talked to everyone who passed by without looking at their faces.

"Is this your dog?" she asked confidently and without reserve.

136

"Yes ma'am, he sure is."

"Can I pet him?" she continued, not waiting for an answer.

"Yep, he's a nice dog."

As she patted the dog with splayed fingers, a hope shot through my mind. I wished that some fiend, in my chivalrous presence, would snatch this child in a horrible and viscious abduction. I would then rescue the girl from the devilish maw of her villain and restore her to her mother's thankful bosom. I would humbly allow the mother and all the other grateful citizens to lavish remarks of heroism and selflessness on me for my most noble deed. The mother would then invite her daughter's savior to dinner, but I would refuse, remarking that 'I have done what any other decent human being would have done.' I would conclude, 'I must be going now, I am just thankful that the little angel is safe.' Walking away with my head held high and full of the virtue, I would escape back to my solitude.

"He has pretty hair," the girl remarked.

"Yes, he has a pretty coat."

"A coat?" she shouted with glee. "He's not wearing a coat, you silly man." Being mocked by a child sent the man into the café. The girl began showing others her tricycle that was parked on the sidewalk and drawing upon phrases filched from parents, phrases that always sound odd, and reveling, coming out of a child's mouth, like "god damn it" or "The President is freakin' incompetent."

Then she approached me. Standing in front of me with fingers entwined behind her back she asked, "Can you help me put on my helmet?" Her words came with no introduction. I had never seen this child before, who was now addressing me as she would address a familiar pre-school teacher. I was taken aback by her forwardness, wanting to ask her if she had been taught not to talk with strangers. I fumbled with the chin strap while trying to keep my distance from this direct little girl. Once the helmet, with decals of cartoon daisies and kitty cats, was securely fastened, she scampered off to try to persuade her mother from her cup of coffee.

Eva stepped from the café, face puckered and sheltering a flame in an attempt to light a cigarette. I was paralyzed by her presence. Once the cigarette had a glowing cherry, she sent a friendly grin in my direction and walked over to me. She screeched a chair across the cement to my table. "How are you?"

I stammered and finally spit out, "Well... I am well."

"That's good," she nodded.

"How are you, Eva?" I asked awkwardly.

"Working, you know," she continued nodding. "Zoe can be such a bitch."

"I haven't met her yet."

"No?" she asked with a skeptical look, "I thought she must have poured that coffee for you, because I didn't."

"Oh, I hadn't realized that was Zoe."

Rolling her eyes in an exasperated circle she said, "That was Zoe. I think every employee hates their boss, no matter how nice she is. But Zoe is so inconsistent, one minute she's great, asking me if I need time off or if there is anything she can do to help, and then all of a sudden she's on the war path, and nothing is good enough for her. Sometimes I even wish she'd be pissed off all the time, then I'd know what to expect. And then... Oh, I've got to be boring you talking about my measly little problems. I'm sorry."

"No, don't apologize, I want to hear about your... I mean, I'm a good listener. I don't mind at all," fidgeting in my seat. Silence followed. I reached into my pocket and pulled out a cigarette. Eva immediately grabbed her lighter to assist me in my dirty habit. "Thank you. That was very kind."

"If you don't mind me saying, you talk sort of funny," she replied grinning.

"Oh, I apologize," being caught off guard.

"No, no, no, don't apologize, I'm just saying. I think it's sort of cute," she chuckled. A thin crease appeared on

138

her upper lip as she laughed. "Yeah, don't apologize. You shouldn't have to apologize for who you are."

Again, silence grew between the words. Eva looked at the trees and the church and the few people walking in the park with her wide, luminous eyes, jerking them around with bird-like motion. Her delicate fingers parted her hair into tendrils only to have it collect again. "So how are you feeling? I mean, you seem sort of distant or something, I mean, from everybody else, like you've got something on your mind that you can't let out," she pried.

Her comment took little insight, but, nonetheless, it struck me. "Oh! I guess…You see… Well…" I stuttered, "I've been a bit under the weather, as of late. My stomach has been bothering me, and I've been having disturbing dreams."

Her aspect became serious, and she leaned toward me with concern and intimacy. "I'm so sorry to hear that. Health problems? Well, you know, I have some experience with that, I mean, I'm OK, but I am totally into alternative medicine and stuff like that. The mind and body are so connected." She nodded her head. "Of course you have stomach problems and nightmares."

She reached for my hand. I repelled a reflex to recoil from her touch. Her thin but strong fingers began massaging my palm. Her touch was heavenly. My whole arm relaxed, sending soothing waves though my whole body. She kneaded the mound of my thumb and stretched back my fingers causing relieving pain in my wrist. "Everything is connected. The soul and body and mind and all that stuff is really one thing. Modern medicine denies this, but your spiritual, psychological and physical health are all dependent on each other. Really, we shouldn't distinguish those three ideas; they're all the same thing. We just distinguish all of them because we don't really understand it all." She was now rubbing each section of each finger as she spoke. Blood flooded my loins with sensual pleasure.

"You know, I'm going to a party tonight where there'll be a couple of people who know a lot about this stuff. They're really smart. Maybe you could come with me and talk to them. They're totally cool. You'll really like them." She set my hand back on the table and picked her cigarette out of the ashtray. She drew on the cigarette. Smoke wreathed her head as she exhaled.

"I'd like that," I stated eagerly, less to talk with her gurus than to spend time with her.

"Great! They're totally cool. But," she said changing her countenance to warning and lowering her voice, "don't tell Epi about it. Just tell him we're on a date or something. He can be so close-minded. He doesn't trust these people at all. You know, Epi's sort of... I guess 'Old School' or something."

"Sure, I'll tell him we're on a date," I smiled devilishly at the idea.

"Don't get me wrong," Eva continued. My heart sunk with those words, but then rebounded as she elaborated, "I really like Epi and think he's a really smart guy, but he's kind of conservative, in a funny kind of way. You know, he's been so generous to you, but he's kind of weird, in a neat way." She tried hard to be diplomatic. I wanted to add that Epi was generous, but in a manner that was completely on his terms, and he must suffer from some type of mental instability.

"I don't know what I would do without Epi's help and guidance," I interjected.

"He really is sort of the guide of the crossroads. I don't mean to know what's going on in your life, but people do talk," she reported cautiously.

"What do you mean," I asked calmly, trying to leave paranoia out of my voice.

"Oh, I really don't know. Everybody says you're sort of reserved, and you've got this problem, like you did something bad in another life, but that you're a really great person." Eva was guarded and flicking her nearly spent cigarette too often.

"I see."

"I don't want you to think that everybody talks behind your back, but people are worried about you. I don't know why, but I'm worried about you. I mean, I worry about every being on this earth, but for some reason I'm especially worried about you. You may not know it, but Epi cares about you and wants you to get better."

"Wow, I didn't know I was the focus of so much concern."

"Well, there's some type of connection going on. I believe that all people are connected spiritually, but some people have a stronger tie that goes beyond this life and this apparent sphere of reality. I think that fate has a hand in all of our lives, a fate that transcends this life and moment. Epi and Tie have talked about how you're part of some kind of song that's being written or that you're writing. I don't know, I just overheard them say something about a song and a divine tragedy. You really shouldn't listen to me; what do I know, anyway." She snuffed out her cigarette and got up.

"I've got to get back to work, or Zoe'll bite my head off. She's in one of her moods. I'm off in a couple of hours, and then you can walk with me to my place. I'll drive you to the party. You'll really like these people. They are so smart." She returned through the doors of the café. My eyes followed her short journey back to the door, watching the swagger of her hips.

I too stood up, but walked over to Epi's workshop. Opening the door, I saw Epi hold a spruce soundboard to his ear and yelling, "Be off with you, you two dirty bitches!" A smile creased his face as his two youthful assistants stumbled through the door of the "Muse". Epi turned his attention from the girls to me as I walked toward him.

"Those tricksters," he said laughing, "they're just as bad as their old man. Come'er, I've got somethin' to show ya. Get your ass over here, this is important shit." He waved his hand urgently to his bench. "This here's the top of a guitar. Now, even before ya put the strings on, ya gotta tune the fucker, like we did yours." He held the thin piece of spruce between his thumb and middle fingers, and with his other hand, tapped it gingerly near his ear. His eyes bulged as he listened to the wood's response. "That's the shit, I'm tellin' ya. It's perfect, better than yars. The song is really loud. Get closer. Listen ta this."

He held the board to my ear and tapped. I heard a mellow ring to the wood. "Ya hear it? Ya have ta hear it; its all right there, every note that'll ever come through the sound hole, all right there," he said excitedly. "Now take it. Be careful, mind ya. It ain't easy ta make one a these suckers so fuckin' perfect." He held it out to me. I reluctantly took it from his hands, worried that it would be harmed in my clumsy hands.

"OK, now set it on the bench," he ordered. I did as he asked. Then I waited for some trick or divinely foolish comment. "Ya hear it now?" he giddily inquired. I shook my head. "Damn it kid, it's still there. Don't ya hear it! Shit, ya've gotta ways to go, I'll tell ya. It's right there. It's louder 'an hell." He spat furiously as he spoke. "Damn it, it's still there, but it's silent. It's the silent song. It's prayer and hymn and communion. This's profound shit. Listen ta it. It ain't easy ta whittle this kind a shit. No, not easy at all. It's taken me millennia ta figure this shit out. I figured it out. I'm the inventor a this shit. Everybody's tryin' ta perfect this shit, tunin' whole thin ta F sharp or the braces ta C. Nobody else does it like me; I'm the one that has the formula. And now ya're standin' there sayin' ya can't hear it. It's louder than hell. This's deep shit, chica. Ya should be writin' all a this down."

Suddenly Epi's visage changed from angry disgust to bellied amusement. He slapped me on the arm laughing. "I'm sorry; I'm just fuckin' with ya. Ol' Epi loves ta fuck with folks. Now, ya walked in here with somethin' on yar mind. Spill the beans, what's up."

Regaining myself, I answered, "I've got a date."

"No shit, a date!" he howled. "Good fuckin' fer ya. That's cute. Ya deserve it. Maybe it'll take yar panties out a'a knot." He slid a cigarette out of the pack on his bench and lit it. "So this is the fuckin' two-thousands, so I'm not gonna specify gender. Fuck catagories and concepts! So, who is the lucky human who ya gotta date with and puttin' that shit-eatin' grin on yar face?"

"It's Eva."

"No shit. Well, I lost that bet. She's a damn fine girl. Nice girl, good lookin' and quick, ta boot. Oh yeah. Well, good fuckin' far ya. Where ya gonna take that fine lady?"

"I don't know," I lied, "maybe a walk in the park."

"How fuckin' romantic. Ya'll have ta tell me if she gives it up on the first date." He nudged me with his elbow and winked.

Remembrances of the Pleroma

"By the way," the old luthier said, "Your sides are ready fer gluin' kerfing."

"No, I bent them this morning, they can't be ready yet," I disagreed.

"That ol' Epi's got all kinds a tricks up his sleeve," he answered smiling. "Ya want ta know what kinda pixy dust the stinky ol' man sprinkled on yar sides?"

I nodded. Epi pulled a hairdryer from under the bench and jeered. "Now I don't want nobody playin' 'round with this kinda powerful magic. So don't ya be tryin' this shit at home, not even NASA scientists could pull this one off."

Amused by the idea that Epi had blow-dried the wood with a pink hairdryer that was probably manufactured in the nineteen sixties, I observed, "I didn't see that in your tome of lutherie."

"No, and ya ain't gonna find it there neither. Some times, kiddo, ya gotta think outside the tome-ba," he snared. "Get it? Like tome, but its tomb." He clapped his hands with enjoyment of his joke. "Now, ya gotta get gluin' or you'll be late for the encounter with little miss sweetie pants."

I set to work. With Epi's guidance I glued the mahogany kerfing to the striped maple sides, only on the parts that would receive the soundboard, and then used spring-action clothes pins to clamp them. Then I filed the little pearl devil, whom I had inlaid dancing on the headstock, so that he lay flush with the wood. Pistis sniffed the inlay, shot her hind leg up in the air with toes splayed and then began licking her anus. Epi saw this and commented, "That's a good sign, she don't do that for just any kinda work. She approves a yar geeter."

I smiled at Epi, dusted myself off and went up to prepare for the date. My mind was full of the evening's possibilities. I felt my stomach soar with anxious butterflies. And I didn't have much time. A shower, which included a sawdust removal, was the first order of business. I brushed my hair and teeth, and then set out to find something appropriate to wear. Epi, as I had discovered, owned one dress shirt, that I borrowed. It fit well and looked tolerably good on me. I found one pair of jeans on Epi's floor that were both unstained and clean (a garment quite unlike anything else in his apartment). My jacket was the last item, unfortunately it was a bit dirty. I shook it out well and was on my way. I was nervous, but ready for a night out.

Zosimos was sitting in front of the café rolling a cigarette when I got down there. "My friend, come sit with me," he beckoned with his fat, ringed hand. "I something to talk with you. I been think about Gnosis you asked. This very serious and confuse things."

I sat down next to him, thinking that there would be no better place at which to wait for Eva.

As if Zosimos had not originally seen me, he almost jumped from his seat saying, "Oh, you look very nice. Is a special occasion?"

"No," I lied.

"You look nice. Is Epi's shirt, or you buy it?"

"It's Epi's."

"I don't believe," Zosimos joked.

He took a sip of coffee and continued to fill his rolling paper with tobacco as he spoke, "I been thinking. I have been thinking about your Gnosis. From thinking I have been about Barbelo. You must understand, because I not remember how well I explained all of before. But Barbelo, she is not simple individual. No," he nearly shouted. Catching himself he continued, "She very complex and changing figure in Gnostic cosmogonies. She been not she. Often she bisexual figure, both Mother Goddess and Heavenly Father. She also been Sophia character. Sophia, as know, means wisdom in Greek."

Zosimos slid his thick, wet tongue across the rolling paper and placed the cigarette between his lips. He proceeded to light match after match, only for them all to be blown out by the wind as soon as he struck them. I finally withdrew my lighter and ignited the cigarette for him. "Thank you," he said in his mumbling English. "I saying she often seen as figure who errors by create Demiurge (individual who create material world). Barbelo's error seen as passionate act. In many of story she sleeps with heavenly father, this how she impregnated. This part of her passionately errors, this sometimes called Achamoth, lower Sophia, or Sophia of Death. There a lot of names, because there a lot of culture writing similar thing, but I will wait.

"So Barbelo violates unity of herself. She perfect whole, but she errors and creates Demiurge. Oops." Zosimos made a sound as if imitating a lawn mower, which I took to be laughter. "Little lady now perceived in two ways, like all women: one the mother of all, the other whore. One can create number of dualistic trait from idea, honored and despised etc. Interesting thing, Sophia, in Jewish wisdom literature, identified with Torah, which law. So there many thing going on here, and one read things in many different way. Jews, as you see, have seen Wisdom (Sophia) and Law as saving knowledge—this what redeems.

"Other tradition speak of other thing. Valentinus thought Sophia fell, and for her be saved (and rest of world) a new aeon was created, that Christ and Holy Spirit (aeons always come in pair)." Zosimos chuckled and sipped his coffee. His cigarette had gone out, and, before he could reach for his matches, I assisted him with my lighter; I could not take the frustration of his eternal match-lighting. "Thank you. Other think Christ born from Sophia through her remembrance of where she came from. Some of stories Christ leaves her, and she give birth to other child, Demiurge. Some think when Christ left Sophia, he left only lower Sophia, so he must come back and redeem her.

"There many story, many variation. They all interesting and most look something like truth. There very few account of Barbelo written by one who believed. There some, but most retelling by Church fathers, who considered people heretics. But as prophet become heretic, soon he become saint martyr and then, after few more year, he become another heretic or merely historical figure. Story and word have traveled globe. Become part of one tradition and another, take on different property and lose other. They take shape through time and through different language. They have their roots everywhere: Hinduism, Hellenistic Greece, Egypt, Iranian Zorasterism, Judaism, and Christianity, to name only few. It mingling and forgetting, melding and falling away. So as word sung in hymn or written in psalm, it change and evolve (not necessarily making better)." Zosimos gave me a fleshy wink. "But it change. And even now, the word coming from my mouth are mingling with understanding of your soul, becoming bit different. The song continue. It like jazz musician playing variation on theme. He add some syncopation here, play it in minor key there, so song evolve. Always improvising—this is Man.

"You could read some of people wrote these thing. If interested, read *Three Steles of Seth, Apocryphone of John* or what Irenaeus wrote—very good thing, very interesting. But reading only part," Zosimos spoke more methodically, "Gnosis about experience. The story is story and life is life."

Perhaps I should have listened to Zosimos' story of Barbelo more closely, but I hardly heard any of it, so captured by my anticipation. Doubts raced through my mind. I worried that Eva may not be thinking of it as a date-date, instead she would be seeing this as merely a night out with an acquaintance. Was I reading too much into what she had said, adding meaning propelled by my own hopes. In my disorganized state, I could do no one any good at all. Even then, the parasite living in my entrails was over taking me with its writhing, finding a meal of butterflies that lingered there.

Zosimos sensed my agitation and my inattention. "I going," he groaned as he pushed himself from his chair. "I some businesses to attend. I hope information helpful?"

"Yes, yes it was. Thank you."

"Don't mention. But you come to my house. I cook you wonderful foods and play Scriabin. You very much like it, I know. You bring your friend too," he smiled and waddled to his mini-van. Piles of notebooks and boxes of all types of junk were stacked in the back. He waved and drove away.

Two men in black suites approached me. They were both stocky and balding, white men in their late forties. They needed not tell me their occupation, it was obvious; their cheap suits and self-importance gave them away—cops. "Excuse us, but we are looking for a Mr. Eepee..." the man paused, looking at a small notebook in hopes that it might help him with pronunciation.

I pointed to Epi's sign.

"Thank you. Do you know if he's in."

I nodded. Both men walked into the shop. I noticed the bulges in their jackets. They walked with their arms slightly rounded and distant from the sides of their bodies, as if to look bigger than they already were. My hands shook with nerves. I hoped that Eva would soon be ready to go.

Leap of Faith

Anxiously, I waited for Eva. Even in this chilly weather, I could feel sweat bead on my temples. Then she emerged from Zoe's, no longer wearing the green apron of her profession—streaked by espresso shadows left by her fingers. Her face possessed the same merry smile I had seen earlier, and her eyes shone with the glimmer of her intoxicating spirit. She seemed to be my opposite in so many ways: full of optimism and mirth, compassion and buoyancy, innocence and depth. I stretched my elbow to her dramatically so as not to give her a piece of my self, hoping that her delicate fingers would slide through the V of my arm.

"Have you been waiting long?"

"Oh no."

"Let's go to my place so I can freshen up before the party. You can see some of my paintings before we go!" she chirped enthusiastically as she slid her arm through mine and pushed her hair back from her eyes with her other hand. "I hope you like them. I have a lot of fun painting."

"I look forward to seeing them," I replied stiltedly.

We walked a few blocks, Eva speaking with excitement about her paintings and her dreams of supporting herself through art; I nodded and inhaled her proximity. I longed for the skin of my forearm to meet the flesh of hers; only a few layers of clothes prevented the fruition of this fantasy.

As I was wrapped in the thought of a union of flesh, I caught the sounds of shouting. The Sibyls were standing on a rooftop, yelling like carnival barkers to the pedestrians below. Their howls were of the marketing variety, as if they were attempting to sell 'veg-o-matics' from four stories up. One of them held a megaphone to her lips producing shrill catcalls to those of us below, while the other half of the duo was doing handstands on the ledge of the roof, gravity pulling her coat to reveal her naked midriff and pierced navel.

148

"Step right up and get your vacant, soulless hands on the truth. This is a one-time offer that no reasonable person could refuse. And let me tell you how much this modern time saver—this revolutionary product—this harbinger of the new millennium—this epiphany of cataclysmic proportions will cost you. But wait, for this limited time— and by that I mean while my beautiful assistant and I (and ain't she gorgeous folks) are perched on this rooftop—this limited time you can choose your poison from any of our tremendous and terribly useful parting gifts. Don't be fooled by shoddy imitations; this is the genuine, no-nonsense product that your friends and loved ones have been gossiping about. Be the first person to try the new and improved version of what many intelligent shoppers have counted on for years. Even researchers at our nation's finest universities have sworn by this amazing laborsaving product. Don't delay on what will change your life and the lives of your loved ones forever. This product is not in stores. You must act now, because our inventory is limited. And let me tell you the price. I know you are hanging on the edge of your seat, but let me tell you this first. This product has a full lifetime guarantee, it is fully refundable with proof of purchase, and if you are not fully satisfied with this product, you can bring it back risk free and we will... what's this... we'll double your money! Yes folks, you heard correctly; if you are not completely satisfied with your purchase, we will *double your money*. And if, for some strange impossible reason, you can find a product more efficient or more durable, you can return your product for, what? Double your money.

"We offer this amazing promise, because my lovely associate and I are entirely confident no one can match the integrity and ingenuity of design or the awesome savings that this investment will pass along to you and your family. And now to the price. What do you think that an item I have just described to you could cost? I am sure numbers with several zeros at the end are racing though your minds. But let me tell you this, the price is much less than thousands. But now you are thinking, 'It has to cost hundreds, anything that saves me time and energy, anything of such superb quality and craftsmanship has to cost hundreds.' But I have to tell you... You'd be wrong. We have cut costs, but not on materials or workmanship. This product is produced in the (and I'm damn proud of this one, ladies and gentlemen) the U. S. of A. That's right, you heard correctly, this divinity of the modern age, in which we are all so lucky to be, comes to you from America. And I'd like to add, God bless America, whichever god you choose to believe (we're pluralists, people). So step right up and read my lips, because you're not going to believe what I have to say. Not only is this the most modern and timeless product; not only is it backed by scientists and engineers; not only will it save you, your friends, loved ones, and the community tons of time and energy; not only will everyone around you envy you for your good sense; not only is it backed by a life-time-double-your-money-back-guarantee; but (and I'm just now getting to the good part) it is free. No folks, you don't need to clean your ears, you heard correctly. This amazing invention is free to you. So step right up and claim yours today.

"All my beautiful assistant and I ask of you is that you *step right up*. There are no shipping and handling charges. This product is absolutely free, zilch, nothing, nada, no money whatsoever. So *step right up*! This small act of will on your part will make you the laborsaving envy of all your friends and neighbors. This offer will not last forever, and this can not be purchased in stores, including Wal-Mart and Groucho's Tattoo Palace. This exclusive offer will last for only a short time (or at least until my voice fails me). You must not wait. Space is limited. And please, only one per customer. The time is running out for you to take advantage of this tremendous opportunity. Don't wait. Operators are standing by to take your order for this revolutionary, this timeless, this time saving—laborsaving, this amazing, this fabulous technology of the new millennium. Act now, our stock is limited. If you act in the next half-an-hour, you will receive, absolutely free, your choice, a set of stake knives or three feet of hemp rope. Please, for your own sake and the well-being of your children, do not pass up this amazing, limited time offer.

"You sir," the Sibyl pointed at a stooping, middle-aged whiteman in a worn suit, "you in the beige coat, you seem disheartened, beat down by the world. It looks like lady-luck has not knocked at your door in some time. This product is what will change everything forever. Not only will people turn their heads when they see you, but no longer will you have to trudge behind others in the rat race. This is your ticket sir."

The man looked up at the gleeful girls. He probably saw that their youthful bodies could possess a temporary anodyne for his pain.

"This product is designed for one and all. You may think, 'They can't possibly have something that will change *my* life.' But that is where you'd be incorrect. We do. Let me say it again: we do. You will never see things the same way again. I see, sir, that you are not persuaded by my testimony, but you will suffer because of it. I am offering what you need most, what you cannot possibly pass up, because you are the type of man that will try it on his own, the type of pitiful, wretched, ugly, wining, individual that will try it without the assistance and wisdom of my beautiful partner and myself. You are the type that will write a sympathy-seeking note. You are the type who will leave messages on revolted ex-lovers' answering machines. You are that type that will only ingest half a bottle of painkillers, driving away any integrity that is left, for you will succeed only in driving people further away, removing any traces of respect that people may have for you or you have for yourself. It will be only another half-hearted cry for help that social workers are paid to pretend matter at all.

"You sir, step right up. Take that minute amount of self-respect you have left, gather it together and get it over with. Why haven't you killed yourself already? No one else knows why you haven't slid the blade down your wrists, or why you haven't felt the noose around your neck or known the cold excitement of the nectar of death running down your throat or sensed the pleasure of gunmetal against your skull or felt the wind of time flow through your hair as you plummet for six stories."

At these words, the man pointed his middle finger at the girls and walked away while looking at the ground.

"Yes sir, why haven't you killed yourself, you nasty little loveless man, the feces of the Universe, the decomposing refuse of the world, the most spineless-ennui-filled-rotting-putrid-smelly-angst-ridden-servile-masturbating-cock-sucking-piece-of-shit we've ever seen.

"Step right up and jump. Do something noble for a change. Take charge of your miserable little life. Make a mark on the city, if only on the sidewalk. Have some balls, man. Don't allow yourself to be a wretched servant to god (whichever god, it matters not). Don't allow the laws of man to stop you from taking your life into your hands. Be the director of your own fate. This could be the only action in your life that you have complete control over. This is your time to become king of your fate, to mock the abyss and god and the mayor and the president of the USA and the Dali Lama and the Supreme Soviet (you just think he's not around anymore). Man 'Fell' once. This time you can JUMP! Take the power that is within you. You have nothing to loose and everything to gain. Wake up and smell the coffee, you are a ghost walking through a circus of semblences. Ask yourself, what is the meaning of life? To serve God? To love your neighbor who steals your newspaper? To not covet your neighbor's wife (the one with the great ass)? To be a clerk in a miserable stock room all day and get home, heat up your left over soup and watch sit-coms until you pass out and wake up to do it all over again? There is only one answer: *step right up*!"

"Those crazy girls," laughed Eva. Her comment brought distance between us, as if I was looking at her through the wrong end of a pair of binoculars. I was shocked at the Sibyls' display. Or could it be an honest attempt to persuade this poor man to fling himself from the top of the building?

"Those girls are always so playful," Eva continued. Eva had no idea that I had drawn away from her. I felt anticipation in my stomach. I also felt tortured that those girls might turn their attention to my plight and begin speaking the truth. *Do not turn your jabs and coachings in my direction; I could take you up on your offer—buy your 'product'.*

The two girls continued to taunt the pedestrians and sell their wares from atop the building as we walked toward Eva's apartment. My imagination continued to look out from the top of that building, looking out over the city with contempt and horror. Yes, my blood rushed faster and heart took up a more rapid rhythm in bliss, as I saw the windows of the adjacent building speed upward toward the sky.

The Unwrapping Party

I walked with Eva, carrying her dyspeptic comments resentfully. She, being a naive but insightful girl, sensed my relational indigestion, and our amorously timid conversation completely lost tempo. Uncomfortable with this turn of events, I attempted to resurrect our dialogue, "So, were you born here, or are you a transplant like so many others?"

"Well, I'm originally from East County, but I've lived in town since college."

"That is remarkable, most young people that live here seem to come from the East Coast or Midwest," I stated dryly.

"I've noticed that too. You're from these parts aren't you?"

I jumped over a puddle, pretending to lose track of the conversation. "It will be nice to see your paintings. I think that one's art is a truer reflection of his or her person than one's manner of speech or dress." As I spoke, the breeze changed, sending her scent straight to my senses; her lovely smell of jasmine soap, coffee and youthful sweat began sapping my disgust for her comments. I seemed to smell her feminine sex, clean and powerful. The siege on my reason was soon over, and I had once again fallen prey to my sensual infatuation with this barista. Unaware, I closed the distance between our bodies as we walked toward her apartment.

"Did you study art in college?"

"Oh, I've been studying art my whole life. I think that everybody is an artist as soon as they are born. Little children are all artists, interpreting their hopes and fears with crayon. It's great to look at their art: thick confident lines, jagged unsure scribbles, stick figures with asymmetrical heads—it's all great. I'd love to be an elementary school teacher.

"I'm gonna try to get into the teaching program soon. I love kids; they're so honest and sensitive. But people gradually loose the ability to make art as they get older, especially when they get shitty jobs at coffee shops. As we realize ourselves, our art goes bad, gets muddied with our self-consciousness. That's why I like Jack Kerouac. I mean, he's not a painter, but he is all about flow. Sort of like a jazz musician. I mean, you can't think too much about it; you've just got to tap into your heart, or whatever, and let the paint or notes or words flow through you. Start being too critical, and you dam it all up; the muse hits the highway."

Our locked arms grew tighter. Eva's elevating smile reappeared as though the short tension between us had never been. And, for me, the strain and doubt was relegated to distant memory.

"You have an amazing spirit," escaped my mouth.

"Well thank you," she said, drawing the other hand around my elbow. "You're not too bad yourself. A bit glum and mysterious, but cute and smart." She winked and then poked my belly playfully.

"So, here we are, my humble abode." She pointed to a three-story apartment building done in red brick with white sash windows. It was simple but overflowing with character. Each room had a wrought iron balcony with potted flowers brown with the season. "What do you think?"

"I like it. It seems very you."

"I'll take that as a compliment. I think it's cozy and cute."

We entered and went into her studio apartment on the second floor. She had obviously painted the walls—each shouted a different primary color. The room was awash in bright spectra and warmed by the well-worn oak flooring. A futon, hinting the contours of her form, lay in the corner. An easel collaged with bright residual paint stood in the middle of the room. Black and white charcoal sketches, etudes of nudes, hung with large canvases of fighting colors on the walls (all of which hung meticulously level). A screen stood next to the bed, cubist cats with triangle ears gazed from its surface acrimoniously. Tubes of paint, sticks of charcoal and assorted artist supplies sat in transparent plastic drawers in a wheeled stand next to the easel. The soothing smell of jasmine filled the room with an underlying hint of turpentine. My nostrils were elated with *her* scent. The aroma of her surrounded me, and I was consumed by her.

"What do you think?" She asked with excitement.

"I love it. It looks very much like a great-souled artist creates in this space," I joked.

"Oh, you silly. What do you really think?"

"It is a very warm and colorful space. I love the way it smells."

She grabbed a long, black dress and an orange sweater and hid behind the cat screen. "Thanks. It's nice of you to say. I really like bright colors; I guess you think I'm sort of childish, but I don't ever want to grow up," she giggled.

My mind wandered behind the jeering cats with square pupils, contemplating the mystery of Eva's youthful body.

"What do you think of my pictures?"

I forced myself to turn to the pictures on the wall and away from my carnal imagination. An oil painting of naked Adam and Eve became my forced object of concentration. The pair was depicted in flamboyant strokes and smooth cylindrical appendages. They embraced with closed eyes. A feather-winged serpent was woven around them and drawing them toward the moon. It was impossible to determine whether the serpent was crushing them or lifting them to some divine realm. The earth below the couple held withered twigs of trees and dead animals. A half-eaten pear lay on the ground. It was difficult, however, to determine which was Adam and which Eve; both looked androgynous and the serpent's body covered much of theirs.

"Is this a picture of the Fall?" I asked.

Eva poked her brilliant eyes over the screen. "Sort of, but no. I mean, it is Adam and Eve, but I think they're being raised up, instead of *falling*. I like to think of eating the *forbidden fruit* as the first Holy Communion. They ate of knowledge, and then they drank of themselves." Eva began changing again. "The Bible is so uptight and so against *knowing* your fellow being and so against life and experience. And experience, for me, *is* knowledge.

"My parents were *really* Catholic; my mom would have taken us to church everyday if it weren't for her working so much. I really loved the stories and the ritual, but I hated all the uptight guilt…But you haven't answered my question; what do you think of them?"

"This one is quite erotic and frightening simultaneously, but it calls to me, as if I need to look at it."

"Wow, that's one of the coolest things anybody's said about my work."

"It pulls one into the picture. There are many elements tugging at your eyes at the same time, everything, in fact, but Adam and Eve."

"Well thanks.

"I'm ready. Let's blow this popsicle stand." She reappeared from behind the screen wearing a black dress that accentuated the feminine taper of hips to waist, and was slipping her ams into her sweater. "I'll grab my coat and keys and we're off." She stumbled eagerly to grab her keys from their hook on the easel, her thick-soled shoes provoking imbalance. "Oops. I need to slow down!"

We walked behind the building to her car, a faded orange 1975 Volkswagen Bug, dented, scraped and dinged. "This is *Oránge*," she said, using the French pronunciation. "It's my great little car. She's sort of rough, but she's seen a lot of road, more than me," Eva stated proudly, as she unlocked my door first. "I think she was originally red, but she's faded to orange. I like that better anyway. Now get in and let's go to the party!" The engine revved with tinny taps. She sped the little car down the street.

She drove us through the city and over the river to the eastside of town. Our journey to the party took less than twenty minutes. If we had been traveling at the rate set by the municipal government it may have taken us forty-five minutes, but Eva, as she explained, is not one whose actions and desires are dictated merely by signs and the will of the community. And I agreed, she is a free spirit bound only by her own mirth and passions.

Our destination was a Queen Anne 'painted lady' on the brow of a hill; her gingerbread woodwork and narrow stained glass windows were striking. The house could be categorized as a mansion, encapsulating at least seven bedrooms, and the property of the establishment was huge compared to the lots surrounding it. A dense expanse of 1950s ranch houses had encroached right up to its elaborate iron fence, causing it to look out of place. Trees and bushes surrounded the home, sheltering it from eyes and light. Cars were parked tightly up and down the street.

Eva explained that the house was owned by a wealthy physician who spent most of his present time studying the religions and remedies of the past in an attempt to synchronize spirit and body to optimize the health of his patients. She spoke enthusiastically of his practice and ideas with endearment of his persona. I subdued a tinge of jealousy as she talked of his intelligence and generosity.

She called him Dr. Simon M. Turpis. "I don't know him real well, and I've never been to one of his *parties*, but everybody talks about how enlightened he is. And he gave me a $10 tip. I met him last week at an art opening I was catering; that's when he invited me to the party. He said he could tell, just from talking to me, that I was 'discovering the mysteries.' Maybe he was just flattering me, but there's no harm in going to the party, do you think?" Of course I thought she was processing the conversation through vanity facilitated by a dirty old man, but I did not voice my opinion.

Dr. Turpis greeted us at the door. He had managed to fit his sphere-like body into a tuxedo. "Greetings friends!" He announced as we entered his home. His baldhead, stained with liver spots, gleamed in the light. He possessed an apple-sized goiter on the left side of is neck, and his skin held a yellow hue. "Welcome to my home and the temple to Man. This is my beautiful wife Helen," he spoke emphasizing every syllable and was pointing to a frail woman in a white dress who appeared to be half his age. She was not a particularly pretty woman; instead, she looked to be quite used up for her years, bony and gaunt. Helen failed to make eye contact, merely limply raising her hand as salutation of our presence. "She is my Athene Moon, my heavenly wisdom and the mother of the Universe." Turning to Helen he continued affectionately, "What would I do without you, dear?" Her only acknowledgment of his praise was mechanically taking a swig of brandy. "Please friends and fellow searchers, take your coats off and talk to your fellow humans. The rites will begin in a few minutes. I suspect they will be a splendid balm for your souls. Have a drink, eat, interact with everyone! Be joyous!" He lowered his voice and pointed, "The alms safe is next to the sideboard in the dining room. Thank you for coming and be merry and enlightened."

Even Eva seemed a bit stunned by his histrionic reception and his wife's hyperborean salutation. The addition of the 'alms safe' was also disturbing for a spiritual man and a man of apparent means. "Maybe he's excited about the party, trying to be a good host and his collection is for the needy. Maybe this is a fundraiser?" Eva attempted to rationalize.

Over a hundred people were milling around the house, a homogeneous bunch of upper-middle class baby-booming professionals. Many were decked out in their most spiritual attire. Most had streaked gray hair conservatively cropped or pulled back in post-hippie ponytails. Some wore expensive "vintage" dresses or suits, others wore black turtlenecks reminiscent of the fashion of their "Beat" longings, still others held to the Pacific fad of blue jeans with a sports jacket (attempting to sympathize with their middle-age success mingled with casual 60's freedom). There was an air of spiritual importance in all of their conversations—a ting of their own self-proclaimed individualistic wisdom. Their conversations whirled around us as we walked through the crowd in search of drinks to numb our sense of misplacement. Bits of their dialogues filtered through the loud hum of initiates. Names like Alice Bailey, George Trevelyan and Gerald Gardener were thrown from one individual to another. Many spoke of their gurus or yoga instructors. Some talked coldly of regaining their inner child. The phrases like 'mother goddess', 'morphic resonance' and 'new paradigm' were flung throughout the room. Names like Thoreau and Starhawk were used in the same sentences. One ex-yippie eagerly joked about Shirley MacLaine's attempt at dynamiting a mountain in New Mexico, another crossed himself when mentioning messianic UFOs, and a third ecstatically described three of his past lives in which he was a much worshipped cat pharaoh, an alcoholic assistant of Gutenburg (who continually misplaced the type in the first few sentences of Matthew's Gospel), and one of Ben Franklin's whores in Paris (a not improbable assumption considering his use of makeup). A woman wearing beads and a silver pentacle was giving a stump-speech on the 'revival of the ancient matriarchate.' Inner experience drenched every conversation. A vicious verbal altercation raged between Mayan and Ptolemaic astrology that nearly reached the point of tears when it became personal. Guests traded the business cards of their herbalists, hypnotherapists, tarot readers, séancists, polarisists, acupuncturists, aromatherapists, naturopaths, shamen, and psychics. All of these people melded the antique, the pastiche, the esoteric, and the occult with a modern secularized individualist approach. This was American spirituality encapsulated at a dinner party: garrulous diatribes of the self, chakra aplombs and Zen meditative narcissisms, all of them searching for an holistic miracle that would elevate their souls to that of immortals.

Eva's eyes were wide, not with her characteristic infatuation with life, but with sensory overload. She tugged at my sleeve and asked, "Do you know what *paleopathology* means?"

I jumped at the opportunity to demonstrate my knowledge of language. "My Greek is quite rusty," I stated humbly, "but *paleo* comes from the word *palios,* meaning ancient. And *pathos* means suffering. So I suppose it means the study of ancient suffering, in the forensic sense, I imagine. Why, who was talking about that?" Eva pointed timidly at a man in a black cape and long gray sideburns. A crowd of guests surrounded him hanging on his every word. "He looks like a magician. I wonder what Dr. Turpis has in store for us?"

Eva and I got a couple of drinks and a plate of organic humus and sat together under the stairwell. Eventually, we were able to tune the other guests out, which resulted in a bubble of intimacy within the chatter of the party. Eva held my hand as she talked about her paintings and asked me about how I expressed myself artistically. I attempted to ridicule the idiosyncrasies of the other guests, but my jabs fell on unsympathetic ears; Eva had similar ideas concerning spirituality, but was only taken aback by the shear number and volume of people in the room and Dr. Turpis' frightening greeting.

Eva began to voice her doubts about her own spirituality and her personal 'dead-ends', including a failed attempt to quite smoking through hypnosis. "The hypnotherapist was really scary, not in an obvious 'monster' kind of way, but in his overly calm manner and monotone voice. I think I could of said, 'sometimes I feel like loading an Uzi and shooting a bunch of people from the bank tower,' and his response would be, 'Well Eva, that is very interesting. Would you like to change the way you feel?' And when he would try to put me under, he would say, 'Just enjoy...enjoy...Use your comfort tool...You are feeling soooo comfortable and relaxed... Just enjoy...enjoy...' It was really creepy and funny at the same time."

As Eva shared her story, her body slowly slid into mine. I worried about my hand perspiring against hers. I wondered if my breath stunk. I felt the anxiety and excitement of our proximity and forgot about all the mad post-Enlightenment, neo-Vedanta, crystal healing, transpersonal, pop psychological, Gaia worshipping conversations in the room. Now her jasmine aroma carried with it the languid weight of whisky. She massaged my hands as we sat in the cozy corner. We sipped our dark liquor and fell continually closer together through our tipsy interplay. I laughed at her silly jokes and she at my plastic faces. The world was us, the heat of our bodies and our warm breath co-mingling to create the present. After an hour or so, it mattered little what she or I said, the joy and sensuality of our interactions gained being in itself.

We had not noticed that the table in the dining room had been cleared of its edibles and the chandeliers had been turned down to a faint glow, nor had we sensed the quiet in the halls of the old estate and the tense anticipation heavy on the patrons. Dr. Turpis stepped with methodical solemnity into the spacious dining room. He wore a white smock, much like a choir member, although the black tuxedo could still be seen underneath his sacramental garments. A line of acolytes followed and then made a semi-circle behind him after he found his place behind the dinning room table. Then, more white-smocked helpers wheeled out what looked to be a stiff human form underneath a black cotton sheet.

They proceeded to lift it onto the table, and then they exited the room. The party was hushed.

"Friends," bellowed Turpis, arms raised high in the air. "I have the great pleasure tonight of having so many guests, all of whom are my friends, brothers, sisters—celestial kin. For those who do not know me well, I am Dr. Simon M. Turpis. Some of you may know me from my practice, others through my writings, still others through the slander that has been spoken of me. I am like you, a searcher for a higher truth. I am like you, cutting through the illusions of this world in order to *know*. I am like you, who, by standard definition, are human beings. And I have a gift for all of you. It is a gift of knowledge, for I have witnessed the Truth through direct experience. Do not hate those who call me a sorcerer and those that call my wife whore, instead, pity them. Pity their ignorance. Kiss them, and perhaps you shall free them from their bonds of becoming. Hug them, and perhaps you shall rouse them from slumber. Tell them the Truth, and perhaps you shall open their hearts to the Stranger. I am here, not because Jehovah has willed it, but because he can't stop me. Nor does he possess the omnipotence to stop you from knowing the Truth."

Sweat was beading down Turpis' forehead as he spoke. His voice quaked with religious zeal and revolutionary intensity. "Listen to the words of Jehovah. Is he a god of compassion or love? Obviously not. He is a god of wrath and jealousy. He is sadistic—vindictive and evil. Yes, don't be afraid to hear it. You too feel it in every ounce of your being. There will be no lightning bolts from above, for, although he is tyrannical, he can not hurt us, because we hold the truth. And above the truth is the spirit that burns in all of us. It is the divine fire that was not created by Jehovah. Yes, he created matter, but he did not create the pneuma. He cannot extinguish this light. He can try, and has tried, but he cannot put it out. Even Jehovah's choleric temper can not blow out the pneumatic flame. No!" Turpis pounded the table. "He can not. Brothers and sisters of Light, do not be deceived. Don't accept this matter or space that surrounds us, suffocates us with suffering. Deny the cosmic swindle, for you have the power to do so through knowledge. Listen to me!"

Turpis' wife was standing at his side. She was also dressed in a white smock, but did not possess the same passionate affect that her larger half had. Instead, she was focused on pushing back her cuticles. Helen appeared to be the only person in the room not concentrating on the pleonasm at hand.

"Every man, woman and child can return to the Divine. Just because we are estranged from it now, does not mean that heaven will not welcome us with love, nor does it mean that the Stranger does not care immensely for us. To think this way would be defeatist. He loves us, for we are part of him, a part of himself that was stolen through the swindle—the cosmic tragedy in which we find ourselves. Do not be disheartened; we will assimilate back with the true god, for I have seen it.

"I wish to show you all something that testifies to the Truth." The doctor flipped the sheet off of the table, revealing a mummy. The remains were wrapped in dark brown cotton strips the width of a hand. The bitter, dusty smell of the corpse released itself on all of the guests. "This is one culture's attempt to go back home. This is the spiritless tomb of one of our brethren. He attempted to save his body in hopes of eternal life. He tried to halt the process of decay, and, instead, we have the shriveled prison in which this man walked while he lived. There is nothing here but a semblance of a man. Do you see him walking about or speaking with his fellow spirits. No. Before us is a spiritless shell, just like the illusion of all things material."

Turpis, with the help of his attendants, began unwrapping the mummy. First, they removed bands that circled from the bottoms of the feet to the top of the head. The material was not dislodged easily, being brittle and retaining some of its adhesive strength. Then they unfurled diagonally and obliquely until they met a layer held down with a black resin. Oddly, what looked to be a moistureless onion had been bound under the mummy's foot. Turpis threw this into the crowd without thought.

"What is your name, Sir?" shouted the doctor, holding his face close to the mummy's. "Is no one home? That is because he is merely matter. Matter, which is nothing but a falsity." Turpis dug his fatty fingers into the skull of the mummy and brought out an enamel eyeball. "What is this? Can you use this to see the Truth? Poor misguided man, this is good for nothing. It can not see the truth, for it is made of matter." He then bellowed to the audience, "Do not allow yourselves to be like this man, this shell, this tomb, this prison, this nothing. You are not just matter; you are the divine fire of the One. You are not empty like this corpse, whose abdomen is filled only with rags and incense." An acolyte stuck his hand into an incision made below the mummy's left armpit and began pulling out wads of pulverized herbs. He then raised the matter to the crowd in order to illustrate the doctor's point. "Behold this attempt to vanquish decay, to cease becoming, to stop decomposition.

"But I will tell you, friends of the Truth, let Time and Space and Matter and Energy and our fathers and mothers and friends and children and everything that we once held dear and clung to as if it held meaning decompose into what it is—nothing; all that is seen and felt is a vicious plot to keep us from returning home. This is not our world. We are aliens in a place that mocks us. We should feel lucky to live in a dream where moisture facilitates the decay of matter— where the rain hastens the process of the decomposition of the illusion. Everything here rots, thank god. We will not be cursed with attempting to preserve our penitentiary.

"We are here tonight to re-establish and remember the primary trans-cosmic order. It is a new age for us. We will cast the trivial sins of our forefathers into the fire of Truth. They will burn. We, scattered embers of the One, will mock the laws of man and the laws of Jehovah. We will melt the tablets of Sinai in the blaze of our Truth. We will start the reassembly of the union with the reassembly of ourselves. We will overcome the unnatural stratifications imposed by the 'Creator' by breaking down the petty concepts of 'I' and 'you'. For there are no such things. There are no categories 'male' or 'female', nor 'husband' or 'wife'. There is only spirit. And all spirit is destined for unification. So, my brothers and sisters, in the presence of our former bodies," he moaned, pointing to the shriveled cadaver, "begin the re-fusion with each other. There is only one true force in the universe, and that is the force of love. Love attracts us toward each other in an attempt to rectify the evil separation caused by Jehovah. Unite! Make Love!" and at that moment he grabbed his stone-faced wife and kissed her.

As Dr. Turpis' assistants began de-smocking, the majority of the guests began looking around the room quizzically. Most hesitated from shedding their garments until a few enthusiastic guests took the lead. Once a few had disrobed, the herd followed with frenzied enthusiasm. Surprisingly, only a few guests snuck out without taking part in the middle-aged orgy. Sport coats and evening dresses were thrown into the air. Panties and trousers, blue jeans and starched shirts were tossed on the surface of the white tempest. Their pale skin sagged. Knobby muscle-less men stuck their tongues down the throats of stretch-marked wives. Sagging breasts, hairy moles, varicose veins, platinum heads, arthritic limbs pounded a-rhythmically together. Shrill laughter and harrowing moans filled the room.

Enveloped in this baby-boomer debauch, Eva turned to me laughing. "They are having such a good time. I hope no one gets hurt. Let's leave them to their fun," she gleamed without judgment.

The rotting coitus, however, disgusted me. "Yes, let's get out of here before the police come."

"Oh you, loosen up; they're just having a good time. Listen to them laugh, they're like kids again," Eva responded to my dismay.

We made our way through the genital ocean and out the door. As we slipped into the car, we noticed a group of kids starring into the long windows of the house. They drank from a paper bag they were passing and made obnoxious jokes that were not out of context. Eva started the bug, and we drove back to her apartment.

Questions and an Assumption

Eva dashed through town, her inhibitions suppressed by alcohol and the evening's esoteric excitement. She was full of giddiness. She had had a fair amount to drink, especially for her light frame, and was not a regular drinker; it showed. The featherweight car screeched around corners and bounded into the air as it hit any type of meager elevation of road. She controlled the automobile with surprising ability, as if it was following her as she moved, rather than carrying her by its own fuel. The small car seemed to radiate from her like a nimbus. We arrived, fortunate enough to survive the journey back to her apartment. Her excitement and my own fermented blood set aside my usual self-censorship. We skipped through the halls of her building hand-in-hand like little children. I was not thinking. I was free for those moments. The bitters and self-loathing of my predicament evaporated in the heat of Eva's presence. As she fumbled for her room keys, she pecked a kiss on my cheek. Blood rushed to my face. She pulled me inside with the full jest of her body, leaning with diagonal merriment.

She pushed me from the shoulders, down onto the futon and ran to the kitchen. Eva walked out with two beers and a bottle of water, smiling and ruddy-cheeked. "We've got to stay hydrated, or else we'll have headaches in the morning," she said handing me the water. She plopped down on the futon and lightly bit my shoulder amusing herself.

166

"So," she stated friskily, "while I was in the kitchen, I was thinking: I don't really know that much about you. Don't get me wrong," she said, popping the caps off of the beers, "I really like you. I want you to be my friend, but I want to know more about you. What makes you tick? Who were your parents? Do you have brothers or sisters? What led you into my life? How did you get to this wet, wet city? What are your thoughts on God? Do you pray or meditate? Do you sing while you take a shower? Do you play a musical instrument?" She stopped, appearing to wait for an answer to all these questions. Then she burst into laughter. As she did, I gazed into her earthy Yucatan eyes. I thought that I could see into the first primal space beyond the chaos. Her eyes possessed a purity of color that led me to feelings of serenity and a soft joy.

"So talk, cutie. Tell me something about yourself, maybe a story from your childhood."

"O.K.," I stalled while reaching back to my memory and finding most of the inventory locked up. "Here's something. I was dyslexic as a kid, which made reading nearly impossible. My teachers were often frustrated with my performance in school. One day I was scared to go out with the other kids on recess, so I hid in the coat closest. While I was hiding, I overheard a discussion between my teacher and one of her peers. I don't remember the entire conversation, but they referred to me as 'Paint-Chips'. 'I don't know what we're going to do with Paint-Chips. The child can't read or write and won't even talk to any of the other children.' At the time (I was only in the second grade) I didn't know exactly what it meant, but I intuitively knew that it was not an honorable epithet."

Eva exploded in laughter. "Oh, you poor baby. What an awful teacher. That woman should have her teaching license revoked," Eva consoled me by rubbing my back; I allowed it. "Poor you. So, can you read well now?"

"Of course. By the fourth grade, some part of my mind had just clicked and turned all of the letters around, but before that occurred, I felt a great deal of stress in school because of my inability to read at grade level." I was not afraid to soak up some of Eva's sympathy; her warm hands relaxed every muscle in my shoulders.

"It sure is a funny and awful story. See, that's great, you're talking about yourself. That's what I like to hear…

"Oh gosh! We totally forgot to ask anybody at the party about your stomach. Shoot! Does it still hurt?" She interrupted herself.

"Not so much. I haven't been thinking about it. I suppose there has been enough excitement tonight that I am quite diverted from the pain," then I added with a smile, "even with that churning drive back—in *Oránge*."

"Oh you. I was, I mean I am a little tipsy, but I drive just fine," she defended and gave me another peck on the cheek to show her acceptance of my teasing.

"So, another question: where were you born?" This question was posed with one brow overly raised, as though she was a condescending shrink with foreknowledge of the answer. She sat with her knobby knees together, lower legs splayed out and her toes pointing toward each other. Her shoulders slumped in and she held her beer with the tips of her fingers.

"I suppose this is where my stories become more complex," I disclosed. "You must understand (and I hope that my statements don't push you away, for they are the complete truth) I have tremendous difficulty recalling anything that took place before a week ago."

She stared at me with the same "therapeutic" visage for a moment, then, my words suddenly hit her. "Oh, shit! Are you serious?"

"Yes."

"Oh, my god! Its like amnesia."

"Yes, I suppose it is, but not really."

"Oh my god, what do you remember? What do you think happened?" animated.

"I don't know."

"You're not just pulling my leg, are you?" standing up.

"No."

"Shit."

"Yes, shit," I affirmed solemnly.

"Have you tried to retrace your steps?"

"No."

"What is the first thing that you remember?" she whispered sitting back down.

"Thinking about memory."

"That's weird. What's the next thing you remember?"

"Epi and the gang playing music in the street," I lied.

"You don't remember how you got there?"

"No."

"Jesus, what are we gonna do? I mean, this is serious stuff. There could be people looking for you. Maybe you have a family that wants to know where you are."

"I doubt it," I said stoically.

"Is there anything that you had on you that could be used as a clue, like a driver's license?"

"I had a cell phone," I confessed, regretting the words immediately.

"Oh my god! Have you checked to see if there are any messages on it, or have you called the phone company to find out if it's yours?"

"No."

"What's wrong with you? Why haven't you checked, maybe you could figure out what's going on?" she said dismayed.

"I don't think I want to know what's going on. I'm not sure if it's really amnesia," I confided. "I know that I know. I am certain that I have within me the history of my life, but it is locked away. As I think about the past, I often stumble upon bits of history, but I don't want to unlock it. I don't think I want any of it."

My resigned confession interposed distance between our bodies. "I'm really confused. None of this makes sense," she frowned.

"Do you want me to leave? I should have told you before."

Eva tugged at her hair, trying to spur an answer, "I don't think so. I mean, no. But I really think you've got to figure this out and not be so passive. This is incredible. Have you talked to Epi? Don't you want to know who you are? He knew you from before, right?"

"I am reluctant. And, I think, I am better off not knowing."

"I don't get you. I mean, you sit there so calm, and we were skipping and laughing, and the whole time you don't know anything and don't want to know. It's hard for me to understand. You've got to know more than you're letting on. You've got to."

"I swear to you, Eva, I am not lying," and as I said this, my stomach churned painfully.

I began thinking about Plato's Noble Lie. What was I doing? What was I keeping from myself? Have I created an ignoble lie? The truth, dear reader, is for you to exhume. I am giving you a shovel and showing you a place to dig, but do you have the strength to separate the earth from itself? I did not. There are two principles that live inside of me; they contradict each other. I both wished to bury history and reveal it, but at that time, I had done neither one completely. The Noble Lie alleviates confusion over men's relationship with each other and seals their divine social and spiritual origins. It makes life easier and, hopefully, more meaningful. To whom am I lying and to what extent. I no longer possessed the faculties to differentiate the true from the false. What do you believe, insightful reader? What do you hear in my words? Can you cast the first stone? Are you any better than I?

Eva was puzzled and frustrated. She lit a cigarette and began her diatribe, "I just don't understand you. You say that you're 'better off', but how could you be? Do you think you've saved yourself? Do you think that you, by denying the past, are somehow re-born—have escaped from yourself? I've never heard of the redemptive characteristics of denial. Redemption can come from faith, grace, knowledge or works, but you're seeking sanctuary in forgetting—through burying the past. I don't get it. You're not doing anything. As far as I can tell, you're seeking salvation through apathy. Who are you? You're like the mummy on the table; do you really want to be that empty?" She finished and lit a cigarette.

Her opprobrious words fell hard on my ears, yet I still sought for a conniving way through them, "Yes, you're right. I am running from myself. I can't deny it. No, I don't want to remember what I've forgotten. I would prefer to sleep the rest of my days than engage my fears. But I have to confess; I didn't feel empty tonight. I was with you, and your presence has always filled me with a joyful anxiety. And, I hope you won't think that I am petty or narcissistic, but I have been harboring a question in reference to my emptiness. I have felt empty, yet at the same time full of the fear of past things and the fear that you will not want to be with me in the present. So my question is this: what do you see inside of me that compels you to massage my hands? Because there must be something there that I haven't seen. Please tell me, am I truly as vacuous as I fear?" I pled, still distant from the real topic and hoping that she may accept the diversion.

"I don't know how to reply," she spoke with smoke wafting out of her mouth. "I don't know who you are, but maybe I sensed the whole time that you didn't either. Maybe I was attracted to that. Maybe I was attracted to your uniqueness. Maybe I was enamored with the idea of your silence; even in a group, you seemed alone. Maybe I wanted to *fix* it or learn from it. Did I want to be silent with you—alone with you? You are a stranger, and it was easy to pity you. I sort of saw myself in your solitude." She washed her hands over her face, fighting sleep and confusion. "There is something inside you that is beautiful and horrible at the same time. You speak rigidly, but move like a child—with an awkward grace, or like a ghost who hasn't really realized that it's a ghost."

I looked into her deep eyes, overcome by what my parrying question had created. She trapped me. I took her hand gently and stroked her honest fingers. She allowed me this act of tenderness.

"I look at my lovely ghost," she smiled comfortably, "and I want to touch you and make you real. I want to kiss you and call you my friend and lover. But I don't know if I could ever trust your stilted words. And then I think to myself, maybe it doesn't matter." She kissed my hand, sending warm waves through my arm. "Other people have made assumptions, as you have. And for one person, their assumption brought a woman into heaven, body and soul. Maybe your assumption will too."

I found myself trembling slightly, overwhelmed by her words and caress. She was beautiful and free. She was an honest and tender spirit who did not deserve the depravity of a person like me. And yet, every cell in my body desired her love. Every corpuscle of my being longed for the salvation of her embrace. I wanted to be baptized in her grace. Did she hear sincerity in my words that I did not? I, too, began to believe what I had said.

She relaxed her eyelids as I ran my fingers through her hair. Then, taking the risk—my heart palpitating with anxious pleasure—I pressed my lips to hers. She accepted. We laid back; the silence of the night shrouded our bodies. We found congruence. I felt the faith of her lips. I felt the providence of her thighs and breasts. The night fell away in the cathartic rhythm of our bodies pressed together. I was not empty, not that night. When a couple truly makes love, both partners are fully engaged in the present—neither is thinking about past or future. Time melts into the carnal moment. There was nothing so strong as to draw my mind from that sensuous present; it was like a dream—action followed action without the separating force of thought or consequence. In the morning I looked at her sleeping body curled in the blankets of our evening's desire, and I was not sure whether I would forget the nocturnal pleasures or remember them for the rest of my life. Perhaps I should check the cell phone; recognize the past in order to incinerate it and bury its ashes. This fiery emancipation from history could usher in a new life, with Eva.

Aposematic Messages

As I left Eva's apartment, the iridescence of the alarm clock read 4:30a.m. The sky was still hung over with night. I vowed to dig, at least a bit, into the past; I could always bury whatever smelled of rot (at least I thought I could).

There was no one in the streets. Only a few windows were illuminated. The street lamps lit the night only to reveal my actions and annoy the sleeping transients. The sky was unusually cloudless and the wind was bitterly cold.

I beeped the cell phone on. It took a moment to gain consciousness from its long sleep. Then it was ready—six messages. I pressed 'listen to messages.' A gruff voice, full of static distance, began barking, "How long does he say it will take? Tell him that our clients are on a schedule. I bet he's some weird-ass little man. Give me a call as soon as you get this message. Tell me if you think I should give him a call to get his ass in gear, or will that scare him? I know he's touchy, so let me know."

Next message, same voice: "What the hell's going on up there? You haven't called me back. What the hell's taking so long with this fucking thing? It's not like he has to translate all of the codex, just verify authenticity so our clients can sell the fucking thing. Time is money, and if you want your bonus, you'll hurry him up. Call me immediately."

The following message: "Where the fuck did you go; did you drop off the face of the fucking earth? This is our biggest client; we can't loose them. Call me ASAP."

Next: "OK, stop fucking around. I heard about the fire. What the fuck is going on. I need information. You didn't leave them with him did you? You need to call me. We're in deep shit, and I won't let this take me down. The insurance company is breathing down my neck. They want to see the book. You know they don't fuck around. I can't hold them off anymore. You better fucking give me a call. Give me a fucking call."

Message five: "You better be dead or in a coma, because I'm calling the cops. Your ass is mine. You'll never work again. Call me if you know what's good for you."

The last message, the voice became cool: "You can't hide forever. Now the insurance company is on your ass. I turned it over to them, and I called the cops, they're very interested; they think that you were the one. You better start looking over your shoulder, friend. It isn't my problem anymore. Take it easy." That was it.

My inebriated afterglow of Eva disappeared. Reality set its jaw. I prayed for an apoplectic solitude, but to no avail. An undeniable plot was forming, for they had been called. They were probably here already. They could be watching me now. And I didn't know what they looked like. The past would torture me. Perhaps I could run further and deny my fate?

My lighter took three failed attempts before my cigarette ignited. It tasted acerbic in the chilly morning breeze. The air was dry and withering. I dropped the phone and shattered it with the heel of my boot. Then I kicked the pieces into the street as if to try to negate what I had heard. I walked to Epi's shop. The light was on.

To whom am I writing this? Is it for myself or some other entity? These words objectify my consciousness. Why do I want some type of objectification? I don't know. I am filling my deeds, thoughts, feelings, perceptions and lies with ink. I have set the pen to my ignoble lusts and dyspeptic fears, and yet, I cower from myself. This work of the pen does not massage soothing ointment into wounds of self-reflection; instead, I am creating my own vehicle of pain. This is my literary apparatus of torture—a recounting of the myth. And, as you read the black ink letters, measurable and well formed, you will admire their objectivity—their size and density. Then, perhaps, their form will manifest into your own subjective experience, as you let them seep silently off of your mental tongue and into your mind's eye. Thus, they may become part of your present vicarious subjectivity, after which, you may forget that I made love with Eva, or you may forget the name of the Doctor. You may ask yourself, 'What was the author's name?' or 'Why did I waste my time with that memoir?' You will receive no answer, because time has already taken it from you. But, if nothing else, I hope you have the opportunity to judge my absurd illusion—fill it with your criticism.

A plot seems to be taking shape. It explodes above the waves, soon to sink back under the swells of the present. How many plots have you forgotten? Where did they go? What elements of your own personal plot have been forgotten in the secret prisons of your mind. A person of rational character will admit that there is only one plot in life—the journey toward death. Here, death is the only objective reality, whether your mother denied you love or you slept through three divorces matter nothing—there is only death when you arrive at the end. But I speak falsely of subjective and objective reality (please do not trust me). I cannot differentiate the two concepts. I see only the torture of expression—an ink-riddled myth. You are reading the sum of my forgetting and the sum of my spiritual impotence. Here, in these words, I present to you my sanctuary of sloth, i.e., the words themselves. Does your life have an apocrypha?

I watched Epi silently. He stood over his wood, wearing his bathrobe, scratching his chin and sipping from a cup. His ankles were white and thin, brown wild hair grew thinly from them. I did not enter the shop...

To Eat a Book on the Seventh Day

I sat on a stump, my clothes were wet with the morning dew as though I had been sitting there all night. A valley stretched before me, carpeted with conifers. The trees sparked red and gold with the rays of the ascending morning sun. Larks and sparrows chirped around me. The wind blew lightly through the bows of the spruces and the arms of the ferns. I watched reverently as the silky colors of the trees changed through time's prism.

Then a hand descended from the clouds, and a voice asked me to eat. I extended my tongue and closed my eyes. I swallowed. The pages of the book irritated my esophagus. The words churned in my stomach with dark and lamenting swells. My intestines digested testament. Spiritual vertigo filled my belly. The misconceived epiphany bent my body in pain. I attempted to regurgitate the book, but without success. When I opened my eyes, the hand had disappeared into the ether. The voice thundered disapprovingly, and I wept for my error.

The trees began to shake, and their veil of red sunlight turned into flames ignited within the branches. A conflagration took the place of the pastoral scene, tremendous waves of smoke and heat belched from the forest and assaulted my skin. The fire and the exploding trees lost their color and their heat. The crackling of the burning forest died away as gray clouds covered the earth, only to part and reveal a new scene.

I forgot the book, as I stared at the monochrome village before me. The streets were of black cobblestone and the houses were timber-framed, waddle-gray; the whole looked like a rendering in chiaroscuro. The slate roofs glistened with rainwater and not a sound could be heard. Rain silently fell onto the rustic buildings. Shingles were missing and a shutter hung diagonally from a single hinge. The only motion came from the rain. Space filled the substance of buildings and street until there was only space. Windows and doors became the vacuum of space itself. Walls and cloud evaporated into infinity. There was no horizon, no delineation between here and there, sky or earth.

Only a shadow advancing toward me gave a sense of distance and becoming. The black figure approached, although never gave way to concrete from. It was diffused around the edges, merely hanging like a stain in the white void. Within this infinity without definition, I felt claustrophobia's squeeze. My throat constricted. A thought crept into my brain: this was my hell, and I would be statically confronting this formless demon for eternity. This was the place of infinite absence. I would continually search for its eyes, hoping, at one moment, that I would find them and, at another moment, worried that I would.

7.

It was not one of those dreams that startle the mind awake. Instead, guitars and books calmly bled into the vacuum, as I scanned the room for my abstract devil. Finally, my bladder, stretched tight with the remnants of the evening's drinking, forced me to full consciousness. I had slept in my clothes, deciding there was little need to change them. Epi's white shirt bore the wrinkles of an eventful evening. I walked down to his shop, and we began to work. I had no concept of how long I had slept.

He assisted me in leveling the kerfing and gluing the the sides onto the soundboard. We set the work board aside, cam-clamps sticking straight up immobilizing the body.

Epi noted, "Ya know, ya shouldn't be workin' at all."

"Why is that?"

"Well this here is yar seventh day; it's a day a rest. But," he added, "ya ain't got the pleasure ta stop, 'cause ya ain't done creatin'." He slapped me on the back. "Get the fuck outa here and get some coffee, ya look like shit. Ya can tell me all 'bout the date later."

I passively tried to remember the days since the fire. My fingers unconsciously began counting through seven. I had been there seven days. When would I rest?

Zosimos sat outside of the café under the awning, sheltered from the smattering of precipitation around him. I waved at him and entered. Eva was not working; it was her day of rest. I was thankful, worried about any sober reflections from the date. A gravelly female voice came from the back room, "Grab your own damn cup of coffee, I'm busy."

I sat next to the alchemist.

"How you, my friend?" mumbled Zosimos.

"I am doing well."

With a smile he asked, "And your date, how did go?"

"I think it went well," I answered dryly.

"So it *was* date," Zosimos laughed. "Oh, youth, this wonderful thing, though *Corpus* may disagree."

Not knowing what he was talking about, I merely said, "Yes, it probably would."

"So you know *Corpus Hermeticum*? This very good. Everyone should know *Corpus*, especially if person both questions about Gnosis and works with Epi." Zosimos sipped his coffee, understanding well that I had no idea what he was talking about. He winked as he set his cup onto the warped table.

"Maybe I misunderstood what you meant by *Corpus*," I sighed giving into the Egyptian.

"Maybe did, maybe didn't. It work of Thoth, who is Hermes. Hermeticism has similarities to Gnosticism, but it also sharply different." He removed the clear plastic bag of tobacco from his pocket. "Books speak of mysterious knowledge. Books probably written in second century AD. They very interesting books. They talk about origin of world and nature of soul—very interesting. Later, people mingling *Corpus'* philosophy with sciences, Paracelsus did. This became alchemy." Zosimos spoke frankly of this, as if it was only a recapitulation of what I already knew.

He removed a pinch of brown tobacco from his bag and laid it into a rolling paper. His overly large fingers began molding the tobacco into the paper. His hands seemed inadequate for the task, being too fat to dexterously shape the dried leaves. "*Corpus* speak of knowledge, but does not deny world to extent Gnostisism. The body not prison, as is for Gnostic, but one does shed body when one finally transcend world. You can see, then, their difference." The wind increased and blew the majority of the tobacco out of the unfinished cigarette. Zosimos mumbled what were probably Arabic obscenities and started the process over.

"Both school of thought hope through knowledge, man (or at least soul) is restore to its original greatness. Good example of their similarities is snake. Do you know caduceus is?"

His question startled me, not because of its content, but because I had not been listening. "What? Caduceus— we talked about that, like on your hat."

"Oh yes, we did. But caduceus also what Hermes carry—wand with two snakes wrapped around it and wings on top. Like in medicine. It signify knowledge." Zosimos had finally rolled a decent cigarette. I swiftly lit it for him in order to remain unperturbed by anymore feats of his incompetence. "Snake, or serpent, it wise beast. Who Eve meet in Tree of Knowledge?"

"The serpent?"

"Yes! That correct. For Gnosticism and Hermeticism, serpent is savior. Very interesting, no?"

"Yes," I answered.

I drank my coffee and watched the Sibyls. They were flirting with three teen-aged boys across the street. They twirled their hair around their fingers with their heads cocked to one side as if to play coy. The boys were making big, masculine gestures with their hands, vying for the ladies' attention. The girls then began rubbing their hands on one of the boys and playing with his hair. The other two were visibly jealous of this attention. The boys began arguing and poking one another. Finally the girls slipped away as the boys threw punches and wrestled to the ground. They skipped down the street hand-in-hand as if nothing had happened, giggling like innocents. The girls waved provocatively at Zosimos and me, then entered Epi's shop.

Zosimos had also seen the actions of the Sibyls, although it did not offend him, as it did me. "They such lovely girl, don't think?" he asked.

"They are quite something," I hedged. Changing the subject, I commented about some graffiti on the church, "I've been seeing that type of graffiti all over the city."

"Yes, tags by minions of Archons," Zosimos said matter-of-factly. "They all over. I do not understand them. You know street kids write name on everything in way that those uninitiated not understand. This nothing new. Secret language been around long before you and me." I re-lit his cigarette for him. "One must communicate, but sometimes wishes to communicate only few. These want all to see, but not understand—wanting only few understanding. They want to wonder at script, study fluidity and mystery, but also feel powerless in face of lawless of placement." Zosimos laughed, unaffected by the focus of the conversation. I felt a sense of foreboding from these related scripts all over the city, on churches and mosques, bookstores and police stations, strip clubs and firehouses.

Conductor of the World

Glaucon and a friend of his joined Zosimos and me outside. Glaucon seemed somewhat distant from the conversation. His eyes were red and his face puffy, as if he had been crying for hours. He was chain-smoking and talking with this man I had not met. I came to understand that this fellow was Glaucon's comrade of letters; they wrote and discussed writing together. This man spoke eagerly of their projects and projected ideas concerning the nature of the universe. The new man was roughly my age, shyly creeping to thirty. He talked as though he had traversed the entire globe and knew of all of nature's and heaven's mysteries, in fact, arrogance permeated all of his words. Glaucon appeared continually drawn to people who could "explain" the workings of the cosmos; he perpetually sought guides, being too unsure of himself to venture anywhere on his own, including anywhere intellectually or spiritually.

Glaucon introduced the man as, "My writing companion, Jake."

As Jake sat down, Zosmios found an excuse to leave his presence, "I must leaving; it time feed my cat."

"I didn't know you had a cat," stated the naive Glaucon. Zosimos' only response was to drive off in his minivan.

I sat back down at the table after retrieving more coffee and listened to very little of their conversation, at first. Instead, my attention was caught by motion, rather than my static friends: the red slickers and yellow umbrellas across the street; the nyloned legs of young women running back to work from their lunch breaks; the chattering wheel of a shopping cart that a wino called home; the bicyclist in black, rain-soaked spandex; and a woman with thick, exposed calves streaked with green veins, getting into a truck. All of this motion won my attention. The movement itself captivated mystery. The ebb and flow of the city: running home to begin an elaborate dinner for loved ones, clutching the cherished bag of Christmas cards to be dispersed to friends and family, the heavy sighs of exhaustion ambling through the streets in contemplation of who will be the next lover, the thin legs of a college freshman hurrying to make it to class because her car was being suspended in a greasy shop, a purple drum bobbing on a back, and all these items and images somehow making up the whole. The parts, somehow, seemed greater than the whole. Perhaps, because I could not see the whole. I paid little heed to Glaucon fidgeting with a napkin.

The voices slithered into my ear. "It's about a chick that you, I mean the reader, doesn't really trust," Jake described to Glaucon. "I mean, she's not despicable, she has redeeming qualities, but the reader can't trust her. She's not one of these untarnished heroines, she's more like most people; she will stretch the truth just to please herself, and she is constantly hiding, even from himself. She gives everyone, including the reader, a limited view of herself. It is precisely this limit, this spiritual barrier, that the protagonist must overcome. But when I use the pronoun 'she', I don't use it in the book; the character isn't a-sexual (far from it), but she is not identified with a gender. She's sort of a hermaphrodite or bisexual, like many archetypal figures." Jake explained with excited gestures of hand.

"That sounds really interesting, Jake. How did you come up with it?" Glaucon asked sycophantically, lacking his usual genuineness.

"Well, I guess I'm a friggin' genius—I don't know," Jake retorted caustically. "But I do like the idea, if I do say so myself."

Taken aback by Jake's response, Glaucon scratched his head and changed the topic, "I've been thinking about adding a divine conductor to my novel."

"A what?"

"A divine conductor. I really like music. In fact, I've been playing with Zosimos and Epi…"

"You've been playing with Epi, that asshole? He's fuckin' nuts! You should really stay away from him; he's so condescending. He's so bullish, don't you think?" Jake interrupted. People that are similar in verbose pride never seem to like each other. "The guy's a freak? What do you see in him?"

Timidly, Glaucon defended his band-mate, and in the process, was brought temporarily out of his funk, "He's a nice guy, and a great musician. He is kind of weird sometimes, but he's more eccentric than nuts. I wouldn't call him nuts."

"Well, I don't like him one bit."

"He's sort of 'in-your-face', I can see that, but he's a nice guy."

"Yeah, he's in-your-face and down-your-throat. God, he thinks he knows everything," Jake said angrily, as if being confronted by Epi in the moment.

"You've just got to get used to him, and I think you might like him."

"No way, he's too arrogant and loud. I hate people that think they know everything."

"Well, anyway, I've been playing in this band, and I've been thinking about how it works, I mean how we take solos and how it comes together. You know Ralph Ellison was a trumpet player. That's what he studied in college…"

"Yeah, I've heard that, go on," Jake interjected.

"Well, he wrote about music a lot. He said when you're playing music, you've all got to play in the same rhythm and key, but you can take it pretty far, especially in your solos. But if you take it too far, the whole thing will shatter. So there is this tension; everybody wants their solos to standout and dazzle the audience, but if you stretch it too far, it won't be a song anymore, it will only be selfish notes that don't have a connection to one another," Glaucon proposed to his friend. "I think he's right on. It's allegorical."

"I like that. That's really good," affirmed Jake, "Ellison said that? I have some ideas you might want to think about. The whole idea of music is pregnant with symbolism. I think it was Schopenhauer who said that music is the most abstract, and therefore, sublime form of art. Because of this, it is the form of art which most closely represents the Will Itself."

"That's great, can I use that in my story?"

"Sure, everybody loves Schopenhauer," Jake said through a smile.

Glaucon continued to describe his idea: "So when you're playing jazz in an improv group, you are all playing by the same basic rules, if you break those rules, then the whole thing falls apart. So, it's like there is this divine, unseen conductor who has come to Sinai and given you these rules. People sometimes break them, but when they do, it usually sounds like crap."

"Like Phillip Glass?" Jake interjected.

"Yeah, sort of like him and all the avant-garde guys. There's no 'divine' conductor, because they have left the rules behind. I suppose that the rules are like the Will Itself, like you said. They may seem like abstract rules, but (the beauty of it is) you can see them in physics; music is all about ratios. This is what makes them divine. But this is real life, so there are some compensation factors in all of it, and some commas too, like in writing," Glaucon laughed, the only one who got his joke.

"How are you going to work the 'divine conductor' into your story of the road-trip Moby Dick?" Jake asked. "Is your leviathan going to be singing and dancing and Ahab going to get a-tonal on everybody? (By the way, I hate commas)."

"No," Glaucon retorted, "No, there's no dancing. I haven't worked all the ideas out, but music has to be in my novel. In the novel, I get to be the divine conductor, or at least a grand conductor. It's my world. But like in music, if you start breaking too many rules, it all starts to fall apart."

"That is the great thing about writing, it is your world," Jake agreed. "That's what I like about it. I love the language and style, bringing different ideas into juxtaposition and messing with the characters. It's always cathartic."

"I like the idea that I'm the grand conductor." Glaucon stooped to sip his coffee from the table, his long neck giraffed awkwardly. "So, when can I read what you have so far?"

"Oh, it's not ready yet. Soon, though, I should have a completed draft," Jake responded, averting eye contact.

My attention to their frivolous discussion was broken by a girl walking toward me, or, to be more exact, walking in my direction. She strode with slim oscillating hips; as her torso moved to, her bosom moved fro. She could not be more that twenty-five. Her black hair was bound back tight against her head and then burst free into a ponytail, swaying sensuously with the harmonic motion of her gait. Her breasts seemed imprisoned in her blouse, ready to burst in escape. This, not my companion's familiar talk, was my love for the coffeehouse; it is the stability of desire, the vicarious penetration of eyeball that makes the coffee sweet and palatable—these women walking or jogging or bicycling by me. They, unknowingly, rub rouge on their cheekbones for my sake. It is for my pleasure that they wear flowing dresses or tight slacks revealing the seam of panties. I watch, then seep through the hem of their skirts or between the zipper teeth to engage the pink mound of nipple or journey into the forest of their sex. My only fear is to be caught in my voyeur's art. Perhaps I may look up too quickly or avert my eyes too suddenly; acting natural is everything. So, I yawn; I portray ease and apathy. I affix my mask of ennui, but I savagely consume the fertile objects—these egoless forms of sexuality. She looks at herself in Epi's shop windows. She does not look at him; instead, she sees the semblance of herself in the old rippled glass. Her pink-nailed fingers swiped the bangs from in front of her eyes. She resumed her focused pace and drifts past me.

Their meaningless discussion crept back in my ear. Jake was on a diatribe. "Fiction writing, like most other forms of art, is an act of narcissism. This is unarguable. The writer is opening up his soul to the reader in the hopes that the reader will embrace it. Some say that the writer writes for the act itself. I scoff at this assertion. I agree that writing is an outlet and a force with which to be reckoned in itself, but behind it all is the shadow of public approval. Without the eyes of the reader, there would be no great works, for there would be little impetus to polish any work. The writer would jot down his primitive thoughts, and that would be that, there would be no flawless work that the author painstakingly combed of imperfections. Yes," Jake stated with conviction, "the true writer writes for publication. The true writer screams to the public, 'Love me, as I deserve to be loved. Validate my divine soul!' This is why he scribbles. It is narcissism and self-love. He feels that all others should place him on a pedestal, as he feels he deserves." Jake took a sip of coffee and then continued. "In fact, I read books only to fish for material. I talk with eccentrics only in the hope that their mad conversations will spur a great novel or play. I sleep with women only in the search for a muse of letters. I do not seek the admiration of one pitiful human being. Through writing I may fuck everything: man, woman, child and dog. All of them become my lovers when they sop up my words. I live to be revered, not to write for its own sake. I would make a poor

186

Buddhist; I cannot wash the dishes to wash the dishes. I do nothing for its own sake. My writing is an act of narcissistic pleasure—the public is my mirror of self-love."

Glaucon frowned at his friend's words, "I don't want to offend you, but you seem to be saying two different things. On the one hand…"

"You just can't understand," Jake interrupted, "you can not possibly possess my spiritual perspective. I have talked with many people and read many books. This is the truth, you may attempt to frame it another way, but it would be false."

Glaucon recoiled at this reaction and apologized.

"You must see, the writer knows in his heart that he holds the key for humanity—that his thoughts are worthy of the people's love. This is the narcissism. He knows that through his words the people will come to know themselves better. It is the writer's vanity that allows others to see themselves, but this is a byproduct of his vanity." Jake paused to watch a young female ass in blue jeans bob across the park.

"This is how worlds are created, through vanity and ego. This is why America is such a poor breeding ground for readers; everyone has the notion of equality. No one will step out of the way for another, because they are all deluded by the idea of equality, both intellectual and spiritual. No one will split a spine in the hope that this author has created a world far better and more divine than the one that he or she already perceives or knows. If a writer is truly great, that writer will be branded with the iron of elitism. What, god damn it, is wrong with elitism. Some men are more intelligent and more right thinking than others. Some men have the power of insight, while others will always lurk in the shadows and beat their wives out of self-hatred. This is life, my friend. Only people like us can see that."

Jake screeched his chair back nearly tipping over in his seat. "Great talk, but I have to get back to work. By the way, I want to offer my condolences; it is a pity what happened to your friend. I fear that the Archons had something to do with it. They are the antitheses of everything I believe in; they hope to negate the greatness of the Word. Well, I'll see you tomorrow." He left without acknowledging my presence, as if I was not. Glaucon's expression reverted back to melancholia with the reference to his friend.

"Glaucon," I asked quietly, my tongue feeling unaccustomed to speech, "what did he mean about your friend?"

I could see a great lump appear in his throat, as if all of the previous conversation was only a diversion. He choked the answer out, "Oh, almost a week ago a friend of mine died in an apartment fire. He didn't deserve what he got."

"I'm sorry to hear about that," I said with my stomach doing cartwheels. "I heard about the fire that broke out a few blocks away, but I had no idea that a man died." The gruesome picture of the splayed, obese body dominated my mind.

"At least his daughter was saved. Some phantom brought her out before the building completely went up in smoke," his voice quivered.

I looked sideways, "Oh really, I hadn't heard about that either."

"In fact, I'm going to the hospital now to visit her. I was sort of like a brother to her. Mr. Bythos was a professor of mine in college, he often invited me to dinner. For the last few years, both he and his daughter have been like family to me. I don't think they're going to have a funeral, but if they did, I would probably be the only one to go. He didn't have too many friends. He was sort of a recluse for the last couple of years since he left the university. I know his wife left him a long time ago. I don't know how many kids he has, but I think he's got at least one other daughter, but he and Sophia always kept pretty tight-lipped about the family. Something happened, but I don't know what. There were a lot of rumors, but who listens to them?" Glaucon gazed into his mug. "Do you want to come with me to the hospital. I'd appreciate your company, and Sophia, well, you won't surprise her, she's still in a coma."

"Yes, I'd like to go," I mumble, unable to either summon any feasible excuse from my guilt or repress a morbid longing.

"Let's go then," Glaucon stated, pushing himself from the table. "I sure appreciate your coming with me. I know it's probably awkward for you, but I hate going in there by myself. But remember, she's in the intensive care ward, so they'll ask what your relation to her is. Just tell them that you're a sibling of hers, from out of town. That's only half of a lie, right; you're from out of town." A half-hearted smile winced across his face as he tried to make light of his suffering. We began to walk down the street.

"Did you know that the police came to talk with me?" Glaucon asked.

"No, why did they do that? Do they think you killed him?"

Glaucon glared at me, "No. But they did ask me some strange questions. Like whether he owned a shotgun, and if I knew what project he was working on before he died. They also asked if I had met the messenger that had brought some codex to authenticate. I didn't. Cops always make me nervous; I felt guilty, even though I hadn't done anything wrong." Glaucon blew his nose and wiped his eyes with his sleeve. "They also asked if I knew where the rest of his family was. He never kept family portraits around. You know, I couldn't answer any of their questions. I think they'll get more information from Epi, he was a close friend of Mr. Bythos, until about twenty-five years ago, but I don't know what happened."

We walked past the Old Church. The clouds were painted on the sky with dynamic, full stokes of black and gray—their appearance foretold a story of continued precipitation. The rain is always cleansing, and I prayed it would wash me away from myself. The organ and the rain were kindred spirits, as the tempo of the rain's natural beat gained, and the organist practiced at her usual time. The groans of the pipes studied themselves and looked inward, exposing sound and breath. The rain pattered against the black sidewalks and ran down the red glow of crucifixion in glass. The breathing organ played with the rain, compensating the other—filling the space between the drops of sound. I liked the rain and the organ. They transported me from myself, at least temporarily. One is allowed a diversion, swept up with rain and thundering pipes of sound, riding up ten-note chords, full like the billowing clouds pregnant with precipitation. It is the mundane that drives us to misery, late for a meeting with the boss, a zipper stuck and unmovable, breaking a favorite mug, imprisoned behind the flashing gates of a railroad crossing and one sees no train, a tiny stain on a white shirt, the natural death of a loved one. These mundane things are no different than those which, we are told, hold more weight: lying, being lied to, compelled into unjustifiable deeds, foul and unconscious actions, being torn unnaturally from what is cherished.

Drummers in tie-dyed shirts and bell-bottomed pants sat in the park in a circle, oblivious of the elements. They played with the organist, without her knowing. They swayed their rhythm to the omnipresent voice of the great instrument—pounding bongos, tinny snares, and a raucous kettle drum that someone had wheeled all the way from the college. The homeless kids in soaked sweatshirts tapped on bottles and a wino beat out a cacophonous melody on his shopping cart like a xylophone; all had a kinship of intent. Even Glaucon participated in the rhythm, nervously flicking a fingernail against his thumbnail—joining the rain and percussionists and thickly layered organ chords. In this moment in time, the whole exploded beyond its parts, and, it seemed, Glaucon's divine conductor ruled over them all.

The Walk

We set out under the gray skies; skies faintly permeated by anemic light, and we drew distance from the music. The wetness of the season penetrated every microscopic orifice of our clothes. Mists blanketed the city and clung to my coat; droplets beading, gathering and then running down blue valleys of Gore-Tex, then falling to the ground. The rain was ubiquitous; it infiltrated my mood, allowing an environment for mold to grow on my bones. As we walked west, that long walk over the freeway and up to the foot of the hills, coffee sloshed in my stomach testifying to my body's vacuity. I was empty—even my flesh was pruned with the presence of water. And under the damp midday oppression, our goal was the girl—the lovely, frightening girl whose beauty and tragedy is my misfortune. If it were not for me, she would be dead—perhaps buried, her ashes, her scalded flesh given back to the footstool of earth. She lives. She breathes, and this comatose sleep is my doing. Yes, I was the one who crept up the stairs and plucked her from the consuming fames. I bear the responsibility, for it was History itself—that bitch goddess— who compelled the deed, who filled my legs with motion, who saved my lungs from heat and pushed my will in a ghastly direction. Yes, I will face her. My brutish endeavor has made that angel my responsibility. I should have let her lay, to be incinerated, therefore relinquished from suffering any more. But this was not the case; I interfered with fate, for I was pushed by the past, by memory. The distinction of memory and history serves little consequence; they live symbiotically—living together in their existence by mind. I loved that poor girl.

We walked on in silence. The tribal beats of the drummers and the lofty organ moans were behind us; we were left only with the cars splashing through puddles, groans of diesel buses and the persistent tapping of rain on the gutters and overhangs. Glaucon was trapped by thoughts concerning his "sister", and I had hid behind my mask. People strolled past us as we made our way to the hospital. A woman in a slick red coat walked past us with her toddler son following her. The boy pounded the sidewalk with his awkward and heavy steps. His back was arched and his belly was extended and round. The child's arms were constantly crooked like chick's wings flailing for balance. Every step was an act of war on gravity—determination welled up in order to keep up with his ever-distancing mother. He was at least a year from making motion a habitually unconscious act. This child was gathering experience in order to step fluidly some day, but for this moment, he traveled as though falling after every rise of the foot (helping to validate Straus' thoughts). Each small shoe struck the pavement with flat and conscious success. In these cases, like the child, will must be present, otherwise inertia forces one's bodily mass into stasis.

I could no longer bear the silence, "When did you start playing the bass?"

"Oh... I guess it was when I was in high school, before that I played the guitar and the violin. Yes," he recounted, slowly emerging from his concerned thoughts of his friend, "my mother made me learn the violin when I was in kindergarten. She really wanted me to be the next Iztak Pearlman, but I hated it (at least at that time). Later, after I had been playing for a few years, I would get home from school before she and my father returned from work. I would shuffle the papers on my music stand, set the metronome to a new beat and move the stool so that it looked like I had practiced. I hated carrying that instrument around. Then, in middle school, I began playing the guitar. That was a much 'cooler' instrument. The guitar I practiced. I still play the guitar quite a bit, but now, everybody needs a bass player, so I get a lot more gigs with the bass."

I sensed that he was trailing back to the thoughts of his "sister", so I asked, "Have you always favored jazz as a style of music?"

"Oh no," Glaucon denied. "What got me hooked on jazz was my experience in the high school jazz band. Oh yeah, I began practicing my ass off just to keep up with…what was his name? He was a drummer, but he could play anything. He was a naturally gifted musician, and I was always jealous of his talent. He had 'it', and I hated him for it. But jazz and blues began eating me alive in high school. I stopped doing homework and just played. I practiced scales and chord progressions all night. I would slide the needle on to albums of Muddy Waters or Joe Pass and spend hours listening to the same lick over and over again, just trying to get it right. Sometimes I would slam my fist into the speaker, frustrated with the thought that I didn't have what it took to be a real musician. I guess that's how it goes."

Glaucon stopped talking as we made our way across the freeway overpass. The speeding vehicles spewed toxic clouds of sulfur and carbon monoxide from beneath us. Passing trucks and cars raged, sending constant tremors through the overpass and, in turn, through our legs. A small man in ragged clothes and with a gnarled black beard lay passed out on the bridge. His arms lay palms up and stretched perpendicularly from his sides, and his tongue flapped lazily in his open mouth. We stepped over him cautiously and soon found ourselves past the torrent of freeway noise.

As if our silence had been only a long rest of several measures, Glaucon began right from where he had left, "But there is a problem with jazz and blues; they eat you. Blind Boy Fuller, a great blues and ragtime guitarist, died in his early thirties. On his deathbed he blamed the blues for his illness. He called his sickness 'heavenly retribution' for playing that type of music. When I first read that, I thought it was pretty silly. It seems like a lot of people have sudden religious conversions on their deathbed just because they are scared of the unknown, but lately I think I am feeling what he meant. Maybe it's just because I am starting to become competent, but regardless, I feel the sickness in my chest.

That's why I'm having Epi build me a classical guitar and a violin. I can't take playing jazz or blues anymore. I can feel it in my chest, like it's squeezing the air out of my lungs like a boa constrictor does. That type of music relies too heavily on air and soul. I can't do it anymore. I need a music that is written rather than improvised, like classical music. Jazz and blues are also too bound up with a layer of emotional devotion that no other type of music necessitates." Glaucon pushed on his chest as if feeling the pressure just thinking about the music.

I tried to funnel the conversation in a slightly different direction, "So Epi is going to make you a guitar and violin. I didn't know he made violins."

"Sure he does. That's what he started making. Well, I guess he started out making lutes, but no one is buying lutes. He's really good, maybe the best. Epi has won tons of awards for his guitars, lutes, banjos, violins, and everything else. If it has strings, he will build it, and he will build it best. It's as though the instruments that he makes come with a spirit all their own. He can take a piece of wood and channel breath into it. He has this power to endow the instrument itself with song. I don't know how he does it, but it's as if all the air molecules around the instrument open up and flow with music when you strum one of his guitars. Maybe his hands exude a divine sweat. Whatever it is, he is the best luthier I've ever met."

A disheveled man with gray stubble on his checks walked toward us. He trudged slumped over a shopping cart as if it was a walker. The cart rattled reluctantly over the cement sidewalk. "Hey, you all have some change; I want to get drunk tonight?" the tramp bellowed unabashedly. Glaucon pulled a few nickels and dimes from his pocket and allowed them to fall into the bum's course paws, not wanting to make physical contact with him. "I appreciate it. I really do," the transient spoke, eyeing the money. He looked up quickly and asked Glaucon, "Sir, wouldn't you gallantly spare a cigarette for this tired gentleman?" Glaucon pulled a cigarette from his coat pocket and handed it over. "Well thank you very much. I truly appreciate your tokens of humanity. Because of your generosity, I will stretch my legs over to the mayor's abode tonight in the wee hours of the morning. I will proceed to rap sternly on her door." He bent over the shopping cart and began miming his clenched fist, pounding, his eyes bulging at each soundless thud. "When Ms. Doggs comes to the door in her satin nightie, I will take my left thumb and index finger to her red nose and squeeze. I will do this tonight in your good name, for you have helped another human being, a man who loves humanity. I would give you a kiss," he said edging closer to Glaucon, "but I'm not done with all my TB meds."

The homeless man's face contorted with laughter and snot shot from his nose involuntarily. He resumed talking without wiping his nose, "You are a true humanitarian, unlike that pip-squeak Orgien who's been informing for the cops. Orgien's in with that scary language gang, but he plays both sides in order to hedge his bets. He's gotten my friend Mani in lock-up; he's been vocalizing malicious lies. He is not a man of integrity like me. I don't know what is worse: a rat, a pig or one of those Archons? I don't know." He spat on the ground in disgust, most of the saliva, however, failed to capture enough force to leave his lips, and, instead hung from his lower lip before finding a home on his yellow slicker. "I hate them all.

"You see this cart," he said rattling his vehicle, "this is the only one you've seen in this area, right?" It was not, but we nodded anyway.

"Do you know why?" His abnormally large eyes bulged at us in question. "It is because I own this cart," he said illuminated with pride. "I own it, it's mine. I have the receipt. The cops have locked everybody else up for theft, and it's because those street kids and the Archons, who never even used carts, have made it worse for every decent bum out here. The cops are cracking down on everybody, just because those kids are causing trouble. They receive their orders from the Honorable Mayor Doggs. The Archons, the snitches and the pigs are all beating down on us good homeless folk. It used to be that righteous street people, like myself, could borrow a shopping cart and sleep in a doorway. Not now, by God, not now. Homeless gentlemen like myself play an important, mind you, a necessary role in the complex society in which we live: we recycle the cans and bottles that the bourgeoisies throw from their cars, we keep an eye on the sky in order that it does not fall on the city and kill everyone, we talk to ourselves and yell at people who can't be seen so that normies get some exercise crossing to the other side of the street, we are receptacles of society's pity and disgust (choose your poison), we allow those with real beds to reframe their lives when they see us, and, most importantly, we unburden you of that annoying spare change that jingles in your pockets. But we are being persecuted by Ms. Doggs and her storm troopers. The cause of her crackdown is the Archons' mad terror." He had worked himself into an agitated state. His thick fingers gripped the handle bar of the creaking cart and shook it with anger.

"I'm sorry good gentle-people. It seems as though my good nature has been overtaken by coarseness," he said regaining his composure. "I will be off. Please give Epi my best and Godspeed to you both. Oh, might I be obliged another cigarette?" Glaucon handed the old man another cigarette. The cart then creaked by us.

"He knows Epi?" I asked Glaucon.

"I guess. Epi knows everyone. I've seen that guy before, but I've never talked to him. I guess he's seen us hanging out with Epi... He is so proud of his cart. That's sort of neat."

"I've met Mani. He was a very sweet man. It's unfortunate that he's in jail," I expressed. I truly felt a sense of loss, as when one hears the news that an acquaintance's child had died—confused and sorry but not grieving.

"Oh yeah, he's the real quiet guy who likes to pet Epi's cat."

"That's right. It's really a shame; I hope he gets out soon. Everybody's reacting to these kids. The worst is really coming out in people."

We were getting closer to the hospital. The proximity of which sent my stomach into spasms, and I buckled over.

"Sister"

The hospital building stood from barren earth like a great windowless sepulcher. It was a red brick structure built in the 1950's. Its grid of mortar was perfect in its geometry. The ground around the building held no grass or shrubs or even bark dust, only dirt vacant of topsoil, so dense that rain merely pooled rather than sunk into the ground. The sidewalks surrounding the structure of healing were meticulously clean, without debris or cracks.

We entered the building silently and ascended to the intensive care unit. The doors of the ward were locked. A sign hung above a speaker reading, "Press button for access." Glaucon pressed the button, and a guttural female voice asked, "Who are you here to visit?" He answered. "Relationship to patient?" the voice questioned. Glaucon lied into the intercom as he had done in the past, "She's my sister." I followed suit. The doors swung open.

A young nurse led us to the bed. Her youth and petite stature did not match her hoary voice. She walked with a jarring limp; her whole body shook as she made her way down the hall. A purple scar creased her face from her eyebrow to her lower lip. "Here she is," the nurse announced apathetically. She was an ugly human being in both appearance and spirit—too bitter for her age.

"Has there been any progress?" inquired Glaucon.

"No," the nurse replied, "not since you were here yesterday." She hobbled away to her desk and began filling out paperwork. She may have been a pretty girl before whatever deforming circumstances took place. But even her eyes possessed the ugliness of her mutilation—cold and vacant.

"Thank you," Glaucon said anxiously to the absent nurse.

The girl I had saved was beautiful. She still held a sensual intoxication, even though she lay in a coma and was being supported by machines. Her hair framed her thin face in fertile brown waves. Her skin was immaculate and pure. The muscles of her neck gracefully came to a warm hollow and then stretched into her delicate clavicle. She wore a sterile light-blue gown. Her nostrils and lips were harassed by tubes. Halos of darkness circled her eyes. She appeared serene, yet under the surface of her flesh there lay an unresolved tension of muscles. I did not touch her; touching her would have filled the past with a reality that I could not bear. To make contact with the comatose child would have been like breathing life into a corpse. Instead, my fingertips asymptotically traced the tendons of her hand and the organic path of veins bulging around her curved fingers. Her nails were elegantly rounded and narrow; gentle parallel lines were etched in them as if they had been manufactured on a conveyor belt. This hand was pale, but its knobby joints were red, pushing themselves from the membrane of skin. The hollows of her hand reminded me of the cadaverous and bony appendages seen on the mummy. It seemed not to be the hand of a beautiful girl, but the claw of a corpse. But I was not the one to judge the difference between life and death; I who had dreams in my waking life, who refused my own living name, who stood silently watching the fatality of incinerated truth. Her chest rose and fell with the motions of life, but machines compelled her breath.

Glaucon brought her right hand to his lips, her fingers curling with unconscious rest. He kissed each digit, leaving only the thumb unrequited.

I watched him cry and felt the stony expression on my own face. It was the visage of necessary distance. There lay, between the girl and me, a microscopic distance of ether that held light years of space-time. I refused to straighten this tangled and compressed distance, even though my fingers hovered only nanometers above her corpuscular form.

"Sister," wept Glaucon, "who did this? Who killed our father? Was it the Archons? Who is to blame? I miss you so much." He was a blubbering fool; his face was streaked with tears, and his mouth was contorted in anguish. I forced myself to hear his words and see his lugubrations through the lens of melodrama. I covered my mouth from laughter and forced a cough in its place—all a political disguise. In order to shield my heart, I envisioned grabbing the breast of some tight-shirted woman in the coffee shop or pulling on the wet beard of a hippie park drummer. I embraced mental distraction to protect myself from my own malnourished heart, not allowing myself the privileged curse of what I wanted to feel, for this would be History's recognition. I would not allow it, not the search and not the acknowledgement. The refusal of the past prevailed. Would the gathering of the past yield blood soaked hands, horrendous victimization? I would not touch her. The truth of history lay in a coma.

I left the ICU. Glaucon seemed not to notice my exit. I stood in the hallway biting into the meat of my hand. The swelling and disjointed pain eased my mind. I giggled nervously at my ridiculous situation. The iron taste of my blood oozed onto my tongue. As I glanced down the hallway, I glimpsed a figure duck around the corner. Had I been followed? What little of the figure I had seen sparked some kind of recognition. It was that abstract type of familiarity where one isn't sure that one knows the object from life or from a dream. I recalled the ghost I had seen after the fire, this was a similar feeling. Was I being paranoid or rightfully anxious? The darting figure could have easily been a nurse, doctor or patient. Maybe it was an insurance agent researching a claim or a grieving widow leaving the room of her former spouse. I had little evidence, except for the foul churning of my stomach.

I sat down in a stiff-backed chair to wait for my friend.

Child of Light

The antiseptic stench of the hospital had gone away. A soft glow radiated from my pores, but there was nothing around me to illuminate; my surroundings were vacuous and infinite. I looked down at my flesh: my immature belly, twig like arms of white purity, my thighs free of the impressions of muscle or exertion, my naked breast without form, and my whole body unbounded by the maturity of hair or scar. My body looked to be that of a little girl in the pasture of pre-lapsarian innocence. I traced, with angelic fingers, my rib cage and small, loose nipples. I breathed in the light that radiated from own body. I kissed my milky shoulder with my pink lips. I sang three notes in joy of myself. Solace filled my lungs and dissipated through every cell of my being. My examination of my new body continued; I was enamored by its purity and luminescence. I tickled the pink cushions of my feet. I squinted and looked at myself through the blur of my radiance. I squeezed my cheeks to experience the exuberance of discomfort. I ran across the vacuum that was my world, surveying my own light—the light that radiated forever into the continuum of infinite space. I was myself and no other; no other being or thing existed but my body and my light. This was the pastoral nothing, full of empty space, endlessly framing my purity.

Then I had a revelation; I was alone with the Nothing, suspended in its darkness, which I could not even see, for all I could see was myself and my light. I wept, and my tears sparkled with my light, but gave me no hope. They fell from my cheeks and descended through that which was not. I sat down to examine my situation. What at first had seemed to be a heaven of myself, now felt like a hell of solipsism. The nothing and I were the all. I was a prisoner trapped within a cell without limits. I shouted to the

Nothing, but not even my own voice echoed back in response, although it, too, was framed forever in the void.

"Nothing," I shouted, "will you come to me? Will you be my friend? I am so lonely." My shrill words were consumed by the Nothing. "Come talk with me. I want to talk to you," I said, bringing my knees into my chest. I shivered with sorrow. "Come play with me!" I shouted, as my sorrow boiled into anger. "Come talk to me right now, I demand it!" But even my wrath failed to return from the infinite abyss. My eyes stung with tears. "Who has placed me here? Who has played such a joke? What foul person could do such a thing? I don't understand!" I bellowed, receiving no reply.

Words held no power or meaning in this place. I trembled with myself, and my light had no place because space was infinitely great and infinitely minute—there was no place of reference but my thin, pale body and my great confusion. So I spoke to my light and my confusion, "Will you be my friend?" But from my light and my confusion there was nothing, because they were me.

I ripped at my hair in vexation. My hands came away with long brown strands tangled around my fingers. I threw these clumps up and forced myself onto the Nothing, making it flow through myself and become part of me and called it father, for the Nothing was all that I knew. Then I slept, and in my sleep I did not dream. My mind was filled with the darkness and not being conscious. It was the sleep of death. My mind had become a tomb where my light did not penetrate. I became the darkness as I slept and knew nothing else. The absence of light and self was so powerful that my mind and soul cease to exist. So powerful was this darkness, which no question of "I" or "it" or "other" or even "darkness" existed. Only the profundity and absence, without verb or being, lay sprawled across the universe.

And then I opened my eyes and beheld my distended belly. I retched with sickness. I cried. Guilt and sin fought inside my body—the body that had been so pure and innocent, the body that I had loved. My womb ached with the horror of conception. What I had created through accident, loneliness and self-love was Error—the great tragedy. I recognized this immediately. I had become wretched, and in this wretchedness, I attempted to hide myself, but my light continued to permeate and mingle with the Nothing.

In my shame and sin, a tree began to sprout from my belly. Pain slowly filled my body as branches spread through the Nothing. This tree grew from my belly smattered with my blood. It smelled of oranges and iron. As it filled space, I lay watching in disgust at what I was bringing forth—this great growing tragedy. I tried to apologize, but there was no one to apologize to. I wept and pleaded for my old body that was pure and free of the corruptions of my deeds. My face grew red from my sobs; my breasts grew large and round with knowing; my hips widened in excruciating pain, but my light continued to illuminate my mistake and misery. I yelled for help, knowing that no one would rescue me. I dug my teeth into the palm of my hand in an attempt to alleviate the pain of my error. "This is Life!" I screamed through the nothing and through the boughs, now plentiful with bloodstained fruit. "This is Error! This is my error, which I hate."

The tree continued to grow and fill with fruit. It continued to tear through the walls of my womb, its caustic bark smote with my blood. Then the tree ignited; it glowed yellow and red with heat and fire. The fruit exploded like bombs. The flames ravaged my skin and singed my hair. I shrieked in terror at my creation. "Stop! Stop! Leave me," I ordered. And then, wrapped in the Nothing, who was my father and my husband, my victim, in the full light of myself, I grabbed the trunk, my fingers rigid and bleeding with fire; I ripped the flaming tree from my womb and threw it far into the Nothing. I ran away so that when it grew old it would not remember my face or remember that it had a mother. This bastard child of incest would think that it is self-begotten, and I would, forever and forever, keep my back to it, because the shame of my deeds will haunt me throughout eternity. I will become barren and build a hermitage of light and conceal myself from the Nothing, whom I desecrated, and my son, whom I hate.

Then I slept.

8.

Street Urchins

I awoke what felt like fifty thousand years later in the white waiting room surrounded by the stench of disease, iodine and bleach of the hospital.

"You were really out," said Glaucon emphatically. He towered above me with an outstretched hand. His eyes were glossy with tears and the flesh around his eyes was red with grief. "Let's get out of here. I'm tired of this place."

We left the sterility of the hospital and found our sanctuary in the traffic and fall's dampness. The city had grown dark during our visit; it was twilight, but the oppression of cloud brought the night prematurely. Workers sat in rows behind the wheels of their cars awaiting permission from stoplights to resume their journeys home. Others weaved through traffic on slim bicycles. Still others stepped with focus, shrouded in coats or vinyl parkas, swinging cases full of the papers of the day. All of this hustle, while the scant remaining fingers of light pulled themselves beyond cloud and horizon. The city's lights glowed with the disappearance of veiled sun. The street lamps, vehicle headlights, illuminated shop windows. The yellow eyes of office buildings glowed in the half-darkness of the wet twilight. The workers scurried, or attempted to do so, in this dying limbo between day and night. And Glaucon and I walked with sad reserve through the watery streets of this once great port city. The impatient haste of those around us possessed a soothing characteristic compared to the sedated silence of the intensive care ward. This was a walk of therapy—a reencounter with life and energy.

We found ourselves walking behind two street urchins. They strutted as if unconscious of everyone else around them, talking with large hand gestures, overly loud and taking up most of the sidewalk. Their pants looked to be more like jean skirts, the bottoms of which were brown and wet from dragging on the sidewalks and they periodically pulled on their belts so that their pants would not fall beyond their buttocks.

"That's bomb, dog!" one with a black stocking cap pulled all the way to the back of his neck blurted out. "He's a fuckin' savage dog, a fuckin' savage. The fuckin' Archons won't give up. I bet they were down with Tu Pac. Fuckin' savages, dog! So they're gonna blow it fuckin' up! Damn, that's gonna be some fuckin' punk, dog. They're gonna fuckin' bitch slap the city. Shit!" The young man thrust his fist into his hand with a *smack,* quickly grabbing the waist of his oversized pants before they fell to his ankles.

"That's right, fool. Fuck the city up the ass, mother-fucker, punk those bitches!" The other added with enthusiasm. "Nothin' stoppin' the Archons. No bitches gettin' in the Archons' way!"

"Dog, can you talk that shit like them yet?" asked the youth in the stocking cap.

"No, fool, that's some fucked up shit. I only knows a few of them fucked up words."

"Shit dog, that's some fucked up way they talk, damn."

"I'm learnin'. The real bad mother-fuckers are the only ones that talk that shit, the other fools speak English."

"Damn, bitch, did those crazy fuckers ever get the book back? They find that shit before lightin' the shit up, dog?"

"No, fool. They still lookin' for the bitch messenger, I know. They don't know where the fuck that punk-ass bitch is hiding. But I don't think they know what the messenger looks like. Fuck knows why they lit that shit up without findin' the book first. Archons took a chance, but they're all pissed cause they don't know if they burned the shit."

"Why the fuck the Archons want with some fuckin' beat-to-shit old book? What the fuck they gonna do with that shit, dog?"

"Fuck me? How I'm spose to know, fool. I just bring the fools lunch now and then, deliver packages. I ain't nobody big, fool," he said lowering his voice out of humility. Quickly he changed his affect and, trying to impress his friend, said, "Bitch, lets go get sparked. I know where we can get the best shit—blow your fuckin' head off, fool."

I looked over to Glaucon, his face was contorted with rage at what he heard. His whole body was tensed like a huge spring. He walked without moving his arms and his fingers were rigid like claws. His eyes beamed at the back of the youths' heads. A premonition of events flooded my appendages. I would follow Glaucon's lead without thought, although I did not feel the same rage that surged through his heart.

We trailed the urchins as they led us through the maze of streets. They continued to shout and laugh, but I only heard garbled and frenetic talk. The boys continued into Chinatown, past inebriated winos and boarded up facades. As the youths turned into an old brick hotel whose windows were cloaked in plywood sheets, Glaucon's claws clenched to white knuckled fists. We followed them through the hallways, which reeked of the ammonia of urine and the dense oppression of mold and trash. Garbage littered the corridors: blackened beer cans crumpled and pierced into pipes, discarded bags, molding cardboard boxes, newspapers (from months prior) laying in the present, and other rotting debris. We passed a woman sleeping under what was once the front desk; saliva dripped from her open mouth and from her torn and soiled red dress protruded white limbs emaciated to the bone. This was the womb of oblivion; the world of nine-to-five hurry seemed thousands of miles away.

We watched the boys step over the woman, open a heavy door at the end of the hallway and descend down a flight of stairs. Glaucon followed them, and I followed Glaucon. The stairs leading into the basement creaked with our weight, sending chills through my flesh. Soft amber light from a string of filament bulbs dangling above us, leading our way down to the underworld. The rantings of the children echoed through the stairway, "Shit dog! I've never been to this place. Fuck, how far down does this place go?"

"Fuck, this bitch goes down to the center of the earth!"

The light did not allow us to see the kids nor could they see us, and their laughter and self-absorption cloaked the sound of our presence. Glaucon advanced faster, careless of our concealment. He was consumed with vengeance. We were in a foreign place far from the comfort and camaraderie of the coffee shop. Regardless of the risk, I followed my friend down the steps like his shadow. I followed as I followed Epi the night of the fire, compelled without thought; there was nothing else to do, no other options seemed to exist. We must have descended at least four subterranean stories, the staircase twisting ninety degrees every twenty steps in its descent down.

"Dawg, Dawg, wait up. Let me light a smoke." We heard the click of a lighter within the silence. Glaucon's heavy treading did not cease. "Dawg," the hushed voice floated up, "do you hear that, dude?"

"Fuck yeah!"

"Who the fuck is that, dawg?"

"Shut the fuck up, fool!"

Glaucon increased his pace. As he thrust his weight on the treads, he began to speak. His voice was deep with judgment and anger. "Your words have condemned you," Glaucon bellowed, each step sending greater and greater shock waves through the wooden staircase. "You have dug a grave for yourself." Glaucon's coat was open and full of the wind of his descent.

The boys stood on the landing framed by a dark tunnel. These children, naive white boys from the suburbs, runaways, confused, embraced a culture and life far from their origins, now lay in the path of fate. I, too, saw the furies of fate circle around the actions of that moment, their screeching sank fist into jaw, and blood spattered the ancient rock corridors. And I stood and watched.

Glaucon loosed a shrill cry. The boy with the stocking cap trembled wide-eyed at the unrestrained Glaucon as the other boy ran for his life. The boy threw up his hands to shield his pockmarked and pale face, but Glaucon's fists hailed down with anger. His punches were without skill or grace, but were filled with savage power. The boy screamed sharply under the pummeling fists. He did not attempt to fight back; his arms buckled to Glaucon's punishment. The urchin, lost soul, condemned, sank to the ground, collapsing completely under the barbarisms of Glaucon's boot. As Glaucon kicked, shattering rib and ripping tendons, the boy expired a slow and windy breath. Glaucon stopped. The other boy had ran down the blackness of the hallway.

Glaucon's fury had been spent; then, recognition of his deeds infused his face. Tears welled up in his eyes, and he dropped to his knees. He stroked the hair of the motionless boy, the cap long beaten off. Glaucon's own blood from the seams of his knuckles mingled with the boy's.

"What have I done?" Glaucon wailed. "What did you do? What did you to do deserve this? You did not kill my family. What have I done?" he wept as he stroked the boy's head. "You have done nothing, only talked my blood into anger. You did not know that I loved them. You did not know that I called them family, that he took me in and taught me. You didn't know that I was behind you, listening to your words. You're a child, a boy. You ran away from home. When was the last time you talked with your mother? Did her boyfriend beat you? Did he burn your forearms with cigarettes? Did they drink and berate you? Were you confused and ran away thinking that the streets would teach you to be a man?" Tears stretched down Glaucon's puffy face, dripping from his cheeks onto the boy's blood-matted hair. The boy's face was swelling with inflammation, his nose a bloody mash, contusions gushing from his cheekbones and eyebrows.

Glaucon paused, leaning further over the body of the suffering young man and touched his lips to one of the boy's temples with eyes gently shut. Then, whispering into the boy's blood-soaked ear, "Please forgive me. Please forgive me. It was just talk, the exuberance of adolescence. Just talk." Glaucon raised the body from the muddy ground and trudged back up the stairs, the boy's head hanging limp, exposing his neck to the warm yellow light. I stood watching Glaucon, with the motionless body of his vengeance in his arms, struggle up the staircase. I stood and listened to the slow rhythmic *thud* of each boot hit a step and the high-pitched moan of the tread and stringers under the summation of their weight like a tragic ballad. Then, after several minutes, the tonic of door slamming ended the dirge.

I was left in the dungeon. The masonry around me was slick with dampness. Mud seeped through the black rocks that composed the walls and ceiling. Large timbers framed the corridor every ten or so feet; gashes and splits adorned the old structural members. Little could be seen down the hallway, for light bulbs only hung above the staircase. I could hear the squealing of rodents and a soft gnawing through the darkness. My body did not move; no motivation captured me. I did not go back up to street-level with Glaucon, instead, I stood staring into the darkness. The abyss that trailed in front of me possessed a mesmerizing characteristic, as though it held me in a trance. Without the momentum of Epi or Glaucon or any other, I stood vacant of direction, captured by the inertial forces of the vacuum of myself. My focus was not on the light reflecting off the wet stones, the slurry in which my boots were stuck, the residual creaking of the stairs, or the sulfuric stench in the air, but on the darkness that lay before me.

The blackness' grip on me was broken by the slamming of the door at the top of the stairs. I felt the light breeze that the door charged through the change in pressure between the upper and lower worlds. The soft wind stood the hairs on the back of my neck on end. I attempted to gaze up the shaft that enclosed the stairway, but to no avail, I only saw a shadow wind evenly around the stairwell. My mind was seized with irrational thoughts that this shade was the same as the specter in the hospital and the figure in the street after the fire. This mad conclusion hung with me, until the shadow edged around the last banister. Fear overtook me, and I began sprinting into the darkness. Through the eyes in the back of my skull, the figure took on shape: a black trench coat and a black hat, a faceless entity captured within, and the aura of a reckoning hovering above the spirit. I pumped my arms for more speed. Mud flew from my feet. My heart bruised my ribcage with its frantic beating as I sped deeper and deeper into the darkness of the tunnel.

The Cave of Semblances

I sprinted as though my life depended on eluding the specter. Through my blindness and speed, I tripped over an invisible object; my whole body came crashing into the muddy earth. Frantically, I regained my footing and sped further into the cave, scrapping my knuckles against the walls and stumbling several times until, out of breath and endurance waning, I looked over my shoulder—down the path of my flight—to see nothing at all; absolute blackness shrouded sight. I had no idea where I was. In what type of catacombs had I found myself? Why would such things exist under a city? I had been running for several minutes, which suggested that these subterranean passages stretched for miles. I continued through the darkness, now walking due to fatigue and following my hand against the walls. My fingers scouted, feeling the cold irregular forms of the masonry, then the ancient timbers supporting the earth, streets and foundations above, finally they touched open air. There was a T in the passageway. As I continued to walk and explore, I found that this tunnel was only a segment of a vast network of twists and turns, doorways and steps. I had been lucky during my sprint of fear not to have run into a wall or a door. As I walked, I felt the weight of exertion seep into my muscles. My pace grew heavy. My fingertips became raw from the texture of the walls, and I stopped to regain my strength. Water glugged through unseen pipes above. A distant door slammed shut. Rumbling voices, captured behind stone, met my ears softly. Then singing penetrated the darkness and a thin bead of light appeared from around the sharp edge of a corner.

I walked cautiously toward the faint radiance. My knees ached from my blind fall. The perspiration on my forehead mixed with the dripping water of the ceiling. I wearily edged my eye around the corner, fearing that someone or thing would see me, and I would be reveled. My pupils took a moment to adjust to the glow, having been unaccustomed to use. As I made my way around the corner, the earth under my feet gave way. The few feet that I fell felt like a plummet of several minutes and miles; silence prevailed as the light was enveloped in the mire of sludge. Water surrounded me. I had fallen into a pool of refuse and decay. The path of these subterranean catacombs, in which I had found myself and fled from my faceless demon, had receded to a watery womb. I felt the slippery chunks of half-matter in its decomposing state, in a limbo between life and death, floating restlessly against my skin. This, my baptism in the primordial slime of life, the beginning and the end— the darkness of rotting material—the feces and urine—the excrement of the living process. I was bathed in the pre-moral swamp—the bacterial pit from which our ancestors walked millennia ago. And I floated beyond gravity's power, no longer trapped by time or reason. My body melted into the buoyancy of silence, hovering in the strange illusion of my fall. A motionless peace gripped my soul. Inertia crept into my veins through the substance surrounding me. Oxygen seemed unnecessary in this womb. Soothing echoes from the outside world danced on my skin. This noiseless sanctuary of sensation mocked the heavy world of mass and volume. I was suspended in the belly of the world, yet the world was not me. I had been alienated from the world that had been alien to me. I melted into the silence. The silence protested the reflection of what is. And in this hyper-world, without sound, I found it easy to deny History. The demarcations of Time decayed with the matter around me. Ignorance laughed at itself, made love to itself in silence. Simon and Helen skipped hand-in-hand denying the world. It was silence that conquered the earth, not Alexander or Xerxes, for they were wraiths in a world of semblances. And I floated beyond the illusion.

Suddenly, the waters of solace filled with sound: screams from beyond the masonry, crashes and thuds, the low chanting of foreign voices, and all of the world descending at once through the lightless fluid. I gasped for breath, shaken from my trance. Like a newborn, taken to the house of God for its baptism—confused and crying out, renouncing the frigid water to which it is subjected, immersed into the suffocating waters of the earthly present and stripped of trust for its parents at allowing this immersion into what takes breath—I dogpaddled, panted and thrashed through the rancid liquid. Flailing for terrestrial stability, I grabbed at the invisible earth with chaotic splashing. The stench of the waters filled my nostrils—bitter and overpowering. Trying to keep the abortive waters from my lungs, I coughed unconsciously for air. Struggling, my fingers dug into brick walls and pushed my body onto muddy floors. My hair was plastered to my forehead. My clothes were heavy with its mass; the foul liquid oozed from my clothes as I moved on the ground. I caught my breath and freed my arms from underneath my body. My eyes were full of the nasty fluid, and the thin line of light was blurred and mixed with the darkness. I rolled to my back. Staring upward into the blackness, I felt my lungs inflate and deflate with large rapid movements. My lips quivered. I spat up black water. I gasped, clutching my throat as if my hands could help supply more oxygen. Slowly, as my chest stopped fighting for air, the chanting filtered back into my ears. I sat up. The water within my clothes groaned with motion. *There must be a geometry to confusion.* I pushed myself to standing. My limbs ached remembering the sudden trauma of my fall. I coughed more and tried to wipe the sour taste of decay from my mouth with my saturated sleeve.

I limped around the corner and found that the light was down two more turns in the passageway and emanated from under a plank door, but the darkness had made this dim glow seem like a far greater illumination. The chanting was louder and monotonous; no longer did the sound gain ringing depth from the echoing of the tunnels. The voices droned in predictable rhythm. Some of the voices were male, others female. I guessed that there were twenty souls behind the door chanting in unison. The words meant nothing to me. These vacant syllables sounded like no language I had ever heard, but were most closely related to the unintelligible sounds that infants utter as they make attempts at language. Drenched in vowels, with an occasional click of the tongue, the chorus continued. I feared the noises that the door would make if I attempted to open it, so I put my head to the ground in the hope that I may see this odd choir. I cared little about the mud crawling into my ear or on my cheek, in fact, the sound seemed to travel with a more profound depth through the slime of the earth; no longer was the chanting as hollow and cold, but carried the deep tones of the city with it. The monotone voices mingled with the elements of the city: the fire, water, air, earth, and spirit of a million humans, and all of their creations and energies. It was as though there was another voice, or perhaps not a single voice but an overarching collective voice of the city itself, chanting beyond the meaningless words of the people on the other side of the door.

From that vantage point, my eyes took in the odd sight of the chanters. They lay shackled. I could see only a few of the apparent initiates. Rusted chains immobilized their bodies. They lay on their bellies with their chins on the stone floor, their eyes wide and unfocused on the wall before them. A woman behind them sat at a slide projector, sending distorted images on the coarse surface of the wall. They chanted with her as a collective. Their voices were like one voice. A frog appeared on the wall, the image was contorted over the grid of bricks and mortar. Then a water buffalo glowed. Next a pigeon appeared. The whole time the gazers chanted, appearing to name the projected shadows. To what form of madness were these prisoners being subjected? Still, the chanting continued: "Naaagiiiillaaansaantooo… Boooooootooocaaalnaaaa… Eeeeeeenouuuuuuuuteeeeeeee…" There were nearly thirty of these people, although it was difficult to tell their exact number from my perspective. It looked like a type of cinema of the absurd—one part visual and the other a harmony of audience participation; what utter madness. Some looked to be children no older than five or six, others were easily retirement-age with gray hair and wrinkles, most, however, were in their teens or early twenties. They dressed in an assortment of attires, traversing the entire socio-economic spectrum; some wore silk suits and others torn white T-shirts, some blue oil-stained overalls and others expensive sweaters. More reflections of life appeared on the screen as the prisoners stared beyond them: a white dairy cow in a field of green grass, an apartment building (that looked familiar to me), a white hen pecking at an eye, an open book whose pages statically held flames. "Aaaaaaaroooooooooneeee… Bouuuuuupeeeeeeezeeeeeet… Quiiiiiiiiiiiiliiiiiiiiiiiipooooooo…," they continued.

I regained my feet and walked back down the passage. I felt the urge to kick in the door and yell, "Fools! Be free and look at real objects! Are you prisoners or some strange cult, initiates in some modern conspiracy? Have you forgotten what is real?" I got up and felt my way along the walls, stepping carefully, testing the floor for stability. I did not wish to take any more plunges that day, nor could I stomach the chanting of pedagogical imprisonment.

214

To Have Never Been Born

I continued carefully through the blackness. Wooden doors, brick and mortar, fir beams, and cast iron pipes found themselves under my blind fingertips. I had resolved that I would live in this underworld for the rest of my days, for each moment brought a greater feeling of comfort with these nether regions. Here I could live purely as an observer, without the tribulations of action or the persecutions of the past. I could gaze underneath doors, through fissures in the brick, or just be in the solitude of darkness. In this realm, I could lose my shape and matter and embrace the panacea of darkness.

I don't know how long I spent wandering through the entrails of the city without thinking about anything but my simple, blind traveling—minutes or hours, I don't know—but the serenity of the lightless world suddenly halted when I heard human voices again. A thin shaft of light stopped my beautifully meaningless passage. It was an intruder in my region of darkness. A hole in the brick, the size of a pinky's breadth, was the source of the intrusion. I looked through the hole and saw a woman with bouffant gray hair and wearing a skirtsuit. She was reading to a group of six.

The woman's nasally voice educated the crowd from the piece of paper in her hand, "This is the beginning of our journey through the city's infamous Shanghai Tunnels. It is believed that the digging of these tunnels began in 1855 for the sole purpose of the white slave trade. Although their use reached its most productively horrific in the 1880's, their continued use through the years by bandits, crimps, bootleggers and blackmarketeers continues to this day. We have just descended from the city's oldest currently standing bar, whose past is as checkered as the tile of its beautifully remodeled bathroom. After the tour, please take the time to patronize the Old Town Pub, you may run into the wandering spirits of sailors and fur traders while you eat the finest steak in town." The tour guide never averted her eyes from her script. "Over here," she pointed 20 degrees to a set of rusted iron bars, "is where many a newly stolen soul sat before being placed on a ship bound for China. These shackles," she held up a pair of twisted pieces of chain, "once could have held the ankles of a sixteen year old girl bound for an overseas brothel where her freedom and innocence would have soon been a lost memory."

The tourists flashed cameras at the archeological items and pointed and covered their mouths in exaggerated horror. "Why would a humanbeing commit such amoral deeds: greed. One could fetch a handsome sum for a strong back for a Pacific ship or the untouched loins of a soon-to-be prostitute. This was the wild Pacific Northwest where the laws of the United States had not yet reached. This city was run by lumbermen, trappers, boatwrights, escapees, pimps, speculators and lost souls of the frontier.

"This was not a city for the squeamish or faint of heart. No one knows for how many miles these tunnels stretch; during modern construction and renovation projects, builders are still finding elements of this complex web of human suffering under floorboards and behind walls. These tunnels have never found a purpose for good, only for the evil machinations of the human imagination. Please be aware, there are ghosts of the departed, those souls who died during their incarceration here. This place is haunted. Please follow me..." she abruptly stopped her monologue when a moan issued from the walls followed swiftly by the rattling of metal. The tourists gasped in bewilderment, and some clutching their comrades. "Please follow me to what we now call the Cellar of Anguish, where it is reported the pirate, rapist, murderer, black-market merchant and Shanghai aficionado Pas Anar cut the ears off of..." she resumed and led her herd to another area.

I walked further down the corridors, hoping not to run into another group. My short musings on having found a solitary world of my own, where I had to only watch and wander, were shattered by the interruption of the tour group. I could not do it, it was too much to even watch. Now, I had to leave. The shock of more flash bulbs, promotional jargon

216

and inflated history I could not bear. They were worse than confronting my own demons.

Suddenly from behind me: "They're sure funny."

I turned to find a fat tatterdemalion of a man lying on the ground. "You know, you're blocking my light," he snorted. "I'm trying to read here."

If he had been there when I had approached the arrow of light in the wall, I would have seen him.

"You look confused, but you're still blocking the light. I'm reading important shit," he drawled his words and pointed to his book. "I'm educating myself," he burped; he stank of whisky. From his slow speech and his slumping gestures he was obviously drunk. A string of rusted chains lay beside him—he had obviously been the source of the tour group's fear. "Sweetie, I need my light; I'm trying to read. And it isn't a bad book either. He's got it half-right, but why take all the time to jot it down, what a waste?" He began smacking the book's cover, which was disengaging from the pages—a few pages became dislodged and fell into the puddle in which this man lounged. The cover read, A Short History of Decay. "You, miss or sir, would be better served to have the ears of an ass, than to stand in my light." I stepped from the beam and noticed the man's enormously carbuncled nose.

"Thank you, thank you very much. For your luminous gift, I will tell you a story, because, from your looks, you could use it. You are half way there—halfway," he let out a startling belch and continued. "Now this story comes from an extremely reliable source a few thousand years old. It has been said (and you may have heard this one before, because it is quite antique, but still very revelant—especially for your dogged looks)...It has been said that there were two farm boys from Iowa or someplace, Cleobis and Bito. They were big, strong boys who were prosperous enough for their wants and had gained prestige in winning all the pie eating and calf roping contests in their county. Now, their mother was set on going to the county fair in her brand new carriage that her boys had bought her with all their honestly-come-by wealth, but the horses would not come in from the fields. The brothers feared their mother would be late for the evening's festivities if they were to spend any more time trying to gather the beasts, so they harnessed themselves to the carriage and pulled her under their own tremendous strength. They made it to the fair, over ten miles. People were excited; men came up to the boys with hard slap-on-the-back type of praise and the women rained the boys' mother with accolades for having such great kids. Everybody was happy. The mother was so proud of her sons that she knelt down to Jesus in prayer. She prayed that Jesus would bestow on her Cleobis and Bito the highest blessing that human beings could attain. The boys, while their mother was praying, fell asleep in the center of the fair and never woke up. Later that year, as a triumphant memorial of the loving strength shown to a mother, a statue of the boys was erected in the county seat." The drunken man blew his nose on his sleeve and continued, "It is said that they were the second happiest humans to ever live. So, sweetie, what do you think of my story?"

"It's a bit dark."

"Well sure, but it's the dead-ass truth. Doesn't everybody prefer meaningless joy and naïve glories, than to rot away with the knowledge that life is the walls of the abyss, and death is the nothing inside?"

"I suppose so."

"Well then, there you are." He removed a flask from his pocket and drained it with his head flung back. "Yes, sweetie, that's right. There are two worlds that the spirit dwells in: the life world and the death world. Where are you?" I did not respond. He adjusted himself on the ground and pointed up to me, "Look at yourself. When you get out of this darkness, go look at yourself in the mirror. Even in this meager light, I can see the bags under your eyes, the perpetually hanging lower lip, your windburned soul. You are like a shade who hasn't had a good taste of Lethe. Why else would you still be down here?"

"I don't know."

"One time I was drunk (well, saying 'one time' is not accurate, I'm always a tad tipsy) and I had lost sight of my companions in the forest. During this time a king came upon me asking what, for man, was the most desirable of all things. I will tell you what I told him." The bum stopped for a moment in recollection, his watery eyes staring blankly at the ceiling. "Yes, I remember! I told him that it was to have never been born." He laughed hysterically.

I could only think of what the startled tourists made of his cavernous howls.

"Then I said, 'Second best is for you to soon die.' What do you think of that? Oh it doesn't matter. You'll keep going. You'll keep agonizing over yourself." He put his fists under his chin and mocked, "Poor me. I can't run anymore. I can't take any more illness of soul, no more memory demons, no more of Nero's genius, no more nothing. Oh, poor me, I'm so tired, can't I sleep forever. Don't let me ever wake up."

He cackled at his own parody, then resumed his normal slurred speech, "Many thousands of years ago I had a revelation. This was before I found the bounty of the vine as pleasing as I do now. I was eating this fantastically beautiful young lady's pussy, when I tasted death. I had bronchitis at the time, and her wet sumptuousness and my disease paired to a foul tang. The revelation hit me that death does not come from the external, but is inside; it's with you all the time, like a dormant virus. There is no salvation, only death. That's as good as it gets—stupid Christians, Jews and Muslims. So, if you take nothing from this conversation, sweetie, wish for an immediate end to this world or just give up all your bitching and moaning. This will all sound familiar soon.

"Do be a doll and fetch me some more libations for Dionysus. Then go talk to Epi about clearing this whole thing up. What you're playing is just crap. Get it over with. He has the message. Stop talking to me, he'll be a little more warm and cuddly about the whole thing. Tell him 'Hi' from Sil!" He ended with a rumbling belch.

I walked quickly from the tunnel-drunk and hurried to get out of the darkness. My stomach screeched with pain, nearly buckling me to the ground several times. The agonizing spasms from my gut thundered like torturing bolts throughout my body. I needed to get to the upper regions. I needed to get to the fresh air of the city. I felt a spiritual neurasthenia—running, holding my entrails from falling onto the ground with one arm, while scanning the darkness with the other. The sharp odors of the sewer and acridity of the wino stung my senses. My eyes felt raw. My shoulders and knees were beaten from the blind contact of brick wall and abrasive floor. The hopelessness of being stuck eternally in this miasmic tomb crept into my heart. Racing, I scrambled up a pitch-black staircase, slammed through a door, stumbled over a heap of junk, and into a strange room.

The room was filled with the warm smell of freshly cut wood and cigarette smoke. Light framed a door at the end of the room. I could see a desk covered in books and a toilet in the middle of the room. Woodworking tools were strewn everywhere. Large pieces of paper with drafting sketches of guitars hung from the walls; their corners were torn and curled. I knew where I was, although I had never been here before. Then I noticed a shotgun leaning in the corner. I opened the door and found myself in Epi's shop. The luthier was not there. I closed the door where the 'muse' was posted, noticing that the lock was lying on the workbench.

I went up to Epi's apartment. Sleep came upon me and I dreamt. I had dreamt of being chased through the hazy nocturnal streets of the unconscious by a band of runny-nosed children asking to use my soul as a means to draw their hopscotch grid.

9.

Anodyne of Action

Upon waking, I intuited that this was my last dream and my last sleep. Never again would I slumber under the tolls of slothful pictures and events. I would never again possess the luxury of "living" in the monosyllabic world of my own world, no matter how anxiety ridden or depraved it may be. A tyrannical fate is ever-present in a dream; it's a thing you cannot fight, one must give up, and through this relinquishing, one finds peace even in the nightmare. Dreams are dominated by a personal fate dictated beyond the laws of reason, science or cause and effect. Slumbering fate captivates the dreamer in inactivity. The plots of dreams evaporate and condense with chaotic fury. What is the dreamer to do? Nothing. There is not even a semblance of control or power within my dreams, even though I have been told that their stories unfold within my own head. This feeling of powerlessness takes on a comforting role for the dreamer; there is nothing to do, nothing to think about, only to be bombarded by specters, zombies, horrific acts of imagination, sensual perversities and the like, but decision has no place in a dream.

I have felt it is always better to be dreaming of the worst tortures rather than to be awake during the most blissful experiences. I have longed to slip into a soporific coma where night terrors toss my psyche until I die, rather than trudge with decision and intent through the valley of wakefulness. Yet, this solace would never be afforded to me again. I was confident that the rest of my "living" days would be dedicated to insomnia. I would be a somnambulist who cannot sleep—forced to act. This waking world is one ruled by a fate who compels will and action, who forces these endeavors, but who takes no counsel from them. This is the world of Oedipus; he who was intelligent and, for the most part, well intentioned, but could not see the furies dictating the will of the bitch. Oh, Oedipus, man of great deeds, brought down by the tyrannical Bitch. She allowed you to pretend, act, contemplate nobility and play in a world of illusory empowerment, for nothing. In a dream, the whole territory is illusion, there are no pretexts that one can *do* anything, because there is no time to think, only reactions of the moment compel the movement of the appendages and the beating of the heart; it is entirely subjective and nothing else. I wanted to weep for my lost world, where I had been a content servant of sleep.

Woe to the man who has to make choices and contemplate his existence. Woe to the insomniac whose days are taken up with lucid trepidations. Now the pollution of Time and Light would contaminate my thoughts forever— one long day with conscious rhythms without borders of darkness. This would be my agony. In a dream, there is no time or light, only shadows of being breathing unaware of the nothing that surrounds. I wanted to fall back into the repose of sleep, but my eyelids would not have it. When awake, one can not will sleep; she must come to you, seducing your own consciousness from itself and breaking Time free of mind. Why do infants fight sleep?

The Sibyls ran out of Epi's bedroom giggling, obviously part of one of Epi's Bacchanals. They wore only their camouflage coats. Smoke and the rancid vapors of liquor poured from the room. The girls blew me mischievous kisses, flipped the backs of their coats up in a display of a double "moon" and sped out of the apartment in a cloud of laughter. Epi then walked out of the bedroom wearing a green bathrobe.

"Lookin' at yar sore mug I can only think a one thing: there ain't nothin' worse ta see than a blues singer on Prozac." He shuffled around the kitchen out of sight before emerging with a plate of cold fried chicken. It looked to be soggy from being in the refrigerator. Who knows where he had gotten it.

"Them's two special little twats, let me tell ya," he said prouly as he sat down without modesty. "I'm sure glad they came my way. Not only are they damn good little helpers in the shop, but they keep Epi young and full a life," he praised, his mouth half full of the cold fowl. "So tell me, what the fuck's wrong with ya? Them cops talk ta ya yet?" I shrugged my shoulders not wishing to allow Epi the opportunity to pass judgement on my trepidations. "Ya're so fuckin' closed mouth," he ridiculed. "Ya probably think that some fucker cares. *Hello!* Nobody gives a shit! Ya need ta get off yar ass and do somethin'. Journey out inta the world and fuck it all. There ya go; ya need a piece a ass. A young shit like ya needs some fuckin', let me tell ya."

Fatty oil glistened on his lips and gristle from the carcass stuck from his teeth as he spoke. His fingers dug into the skin and muscle of the bird, separating it from the bone and then he threw the rest into his mouth with a flick of the wrist. Thankfully, he finally crossed his legs.

"Anyway, get off yar ass and get some, it'll do ya some good." He bit into a bone and attempted to slurp the marrow out without success. "Ya know, there's too damn many folks that just sit on their asses all day thinkin' 'bout what a shit-hole they've found themselves in. And when these plebeians-a-self-pity try ta have a conversation with ya, ya gotta go kick their asses. That's what they needs, a good ass woopin'. Kick 'em inta tomorrow. They *think*, and that's it. They don't *do* a damn thing. They think themselves inta an abyss. Now, I'm not sayin' that there ain't an abyss, but fuck it! Fuck thinkin'! Fuck reason! It's all shit anyhow. Ya find a man who's done some thinkin' 'bout the meanin' a life, and ya either gotta fanatic on yar hands or a depressed shit-fer-brains that has yet ta take his own life. Ya hear me? What ya need is action! Just fuckin' *do* somethin'. Dialogue's fer saps and midwives. Just go fuck and get off a yar ass. Go kill somebody fer all I care, at least ya'ld be doin' somethin'. Don't worry 'bout life; if it ain't there at the end a the day, ya won't be the none worse fer wear. Fuckers like Freud tried ta bury men early, shoutin' curses 'bout the unconscious and what not. Fuck him! Don't worry 'bout that kind a corruption, just go get laid. Ol' sissy pants Socrates hollerin' 'bout the Good and virtue and knowledge. That shit's never done nobody any favors. Fuck it. Good thin' they killed that cocksucker, ta bad they didn't do it sooner.

"Let me tell ya somethin': ya'll die and decompose and become the shit fer either an animal or bacteria, but whatever the case, ya'll become shit. But let me tell ya, ya won't fuckin' care, 'cause ya'll be fuckin' dead—fuckin' dead, I say." Epi was now using a half-gnawed drumstick as a pedagogical tool, waving it in the air to highlight his words, during which chunks of fat and skin would fly off onto the piles of domestic refuse. "Don't waste yar fuckin' time tryin' ta find meanin'; I've been ta all the corners a the earth and heavens; I've been the messenger a the gods; I've been ta hell and the Nothin' and everyplace in-between; I've shared a joint with Satchmo and watery wine with Thales; I've seen lambs strip the bones a tigers; I've fed the birds a Osiris, and there ain't nothin', no argument, sight or action that reveals the meaning a this shitty sphere a phlegm. So what do I say: go get laid. Consume yarself through consumption! Go get drunk. Go play yar guitar. Go fuck till ya can fuck no more. Do what the fuck ya like, but 'bove all, consume yarself in the dark fires a this horrendous life.

"Whatever ya do, don't think. Did the barbarians think 'bout the meanin' a life when they were rapin' and pillagin' Rome: no way Jose. Were they sippin' tea and readin' Polybius' history a the Roman Empire, askin' themselves what was the *real* or *historical* reason fer Rome's demise, fuck no. No, they were a fuckin' and a lootin' and doin' a whole bunch a mean and nasty shit. There's only one Roman emperor that I've any respect fer, ol' Nero. He was one fucked motherfucker. Dude had some balls and a mean ass sense a humor. Now, he produced a sequel that was better 'an the original, 'cause it was more malicious." Epi wiped his mouth with the sleeve of his robe.

"Speakin' a food, fuck chefs. Fuck 'em, fuck 'em, fuck 'em. And fuck those proverbial shmucks who think they're all high and mighty when they go ta some Frog restaurant and get some sautéed savory shit that costs 'em an arm and a leg, and they start debatin' 'bout wine. One must eat, but eat ta fuck. Sure, I like suckin' down grub as much as the next fella, but gimme food ta eat, not food that one's ta peruse. That's decadence. That's shit. Kill the chefs and their patrons. Fuck 'em all. Don't get swallowed by your food. Go eat. Go fuck. And if ya've time, get back ta the first curse. Do ya think the barbarians sat 'round sayin', 'Thor, this is the most delectable dish we've come across in our raping and pillaging of Rome. Perhaps my wife Olga will find this recipe of subtle ingredients much to her liking.' Fuck no. Chefs are fer those who're already dead. My point is, don't get dragged inta the shit that doesn't consume ya. That kind a decadent shit'll lead ta despair and petty crap. If there's no meanin', no truth, burn yarself up! Desiccate doubt and ennui with action."

Epi was a coach—a piss poor coach. His team would be drunken savages fucking through the night, sodomizing their opponents and their loved ones at the same time. But, his lecture was sufficient to get my body out of bed, although my spirit was still hiding under the covers.

The cat jumped onto Epi's lap and began nibbling at the remains of his food. Epi stroked her coat lovingly, losing the fever of his speech, "So what the fuck are ya gonna do?"

"I'm going to head down to Eva's and get a cup of coffee," I whined.

"Ya mean Zoe's, ya dog?" Epi smiled, catching me in a slip. "Oops," he giggled.

If I was to be awake for the rest of my days, then I should consume myself in this dark fire, burn myself up in the petulance of my fellow man. Apathy needed to be annihilated. Within the mythos of action, perhaps I could cauterize memory and history with thoughtless action.

Perhaps I could beat myself back into the slumber of the void through debauchery. Did I have it in me?

Homeopathic Asceticism

Epi's words began ringing louder and louder in my brain. Their tempo quickened. Their truth rebounded and redoubled until corrupt material asked—begged for—its own destruction. The spark had been tossed on my tinder-dry spirit: exhaust life, ignite melancholy, inflame doubt, incinerate illusion, torch tragedy, set ablaze accountability and morality. My entrails burned with delight. The pyrotechnics of action would soon turn my world into ash. Flames of action would decimate all temporal dismay. And even within this bonfire of ego, I would start small; I would burn the sexual plenum rather than consume an entire life. The best place to begin the inferno was in the loins.

I rushed from the apartment to street level, skipping stairs and slamming doors. The tempo accelerated as I left the apartment and bounded chaotically to Zoe's. Jumping over the counter, I grabbed Eva, spilling coffee mugs and displacing silverware. I dragged her stunned body to the kitchen. Patrons stood shocked and dismayed at my incensed affect and focused display of savagery. Eva trembled slightly, not out of fear, but out of erotic sublimation. Her eyes sparkled with elated passivity. Her chest heaved with the moment's lustful anticipation. I took her. She pretended to protest weakly. The buttons of her blouse shot off onto the stainless steel counter tops and ricocheted off the tile walls.

"Stop," she slurred as I lifted her skirt. "Please stop," she asked politely with head rolling back and eyes loosely engaged. "You'll hurt me," she pleaded hollowly—passively.

"Everything is permitted," I whispered.

Her fingertips dug into my shoulders. I grabbed the hollow of one of her checks with my thumb and stretched my fingers around her neck; her mouth was forced open. My lips moved over hers. Her body sighed with defeated pleasure, falling limply into mine. My fingers slid behind her underwear, finding an erect clit. They massaged the hard organ softly and deliberately until entering her wet vaginal passage. My fingers sternly and methodically rubbed and caressed, quivering then stopping only to resume the tease. I twisted her nipple; tremors of pleasure further aroused her flesh until I could feel her tense inner spasms. A long slow breath eased from her mouth into mine; I sucked it into my lungs, my fire glowing brighter with her added spirit. I, too, was overcome with the swelling primal crescendos deep within my body. My arms held her from slipping away. Her sweat bled through my shirt.

I was spent. All the luminous flame was gone; now, we stood in the kitchen among the coffee grounds, the grill, the pots and pans, the blender and cooler—all the material items that had been invisible under clouds of lustful smoke. The world filled with color as I held her tense body. Her contractions slowed—then stopped.

"That was startling, but amazing. I've never come that fast before," she said sleepily, as if slowly leaving a trance. Strength began filling her appendages, and I no longer felt the need to support the weight of her body. "It was so sudden and direct; I really liked that... I bet everybody that wants a refill is pissed, though."

I was dismayed at the world's sudden conversion back to the mundane, but I lacked the strength to attempt another coupe. She now stood under her own power and pecked a kiss on my lips before straightening her clothes. "I'm gonna have to put my sweater on, 'cause this blouse is history. Maybe I can sew the buttons back on. I should really get back out there; can you find all the buttons and put them in that bowl over there. You're sure a passionate one; I like that," she said nonchalantly. "Good thing Zoe is out, otherwise I'd sure be in trouble. Get a cup of coffee.

Somebody should be here in a few minutes, and I'll hang out with you on my break. You're a cutie, little tiger," Eva stated casually as she walked out of the kitchen after putting on her sweater, fixing her hair and reassembling her bra.

I sat on the kitchen counter; my fiery demeanor had consumed itself. I was realizing I had not the stomach for long bouts of debauchery, let alone mayhem. My spirit was devastated by the idea that I did not possess the endurance for sustained consumption; my infernos were more like the fires set by girl scouts that are soon extinguished by their watchful mothers. I hesitantly picked up all of the buttons. Most had fallen on the counter, but I found a few behind pans and glasses.

As I exited the kitchen, Eva slid a cup of coffee to me without eye contact. She was busily making up for lost time, apologizing for the delay in several orders, mixing mochas and grinding beans. Some of the patrons were visibly upset with our escapade, others were chuckling behind their hands.

I resigned myself to waiting for her shift relief. I sat outside in the light drizzle, smoking and sipping coffee. There was almost no breeze. The smoke from my cigarette loomed over itself like a cobra's hood then swirled and dispersed into the air. I tapped the ashtray. Coffee grounds floated in my milky-brown mixture. A crow squawked as if to remind me that I too was a scavenger. People strutted by without glancing. Someone two blocks away whistled for her dog.

An abrupt commotion came from the lutherie shop. Epi's voice rang out despite the closed door and sealed windows, "Fuck ya, ya little bitch. Don't fuck with Epi. Get yar stinkin' questions out a here. Don't go fuckin' 'round with the dead... Yes, I knew him, and let me tell ya what, I know exactly what happened, but I'm not gonna tell yar sorry ass a damn thing, 'cause ya're a nosy, shit eatin', sphincter suckin' little sonbitch. Yar punk-ass-corporate-insurin'-weasley-question-askin'-cock-suckin'-psuedo-carin'-fuck-franchising dick is *not* gonna get a word from me. Go back home. Yar book is gone. Ya're never gonna see it again. Forget we ever had this conversation, go pay yar client and get off a my fuckin' property!" A few moments later Epi began howling again, "Fuck yar reward. Fuck yarself. It'd be more productive ta shove a broomstick up yar asshole and fall down a flight a stairs than ta harass me with yar insolence. Ya want ta know somthin', I took the book that night; I fuckin' wrote it! He deserved what he got! Pow, right in the kisser. I dealt with the cops, I can deal with your sorry-ass. Whatchya gonna do, fight me fer it? Ya'll never see it again!"

I heard a crash. Then, a tall blonde haired man in a silk suit and trench coat scurried out of the shop. He carried an umbrella, which meant he was not from around these parts. Epi, still in his bathrobe, soon followed holding a battered guitar. He looked at me, flames still in his eyes from the melee. "This was a damn good blues box, too," he shouted in reference to the guitar. "It just needed some lacquer—the fuckin' prick..." The suited-man failed to look back as he hurried down the sidewalk and behind a building, the entire time clutching his forearm in pain.

Quickly deescalating himself, Epi walked toward me and asked, "So, you didn't..." He caught a whiff of something and proceeded to sniff around me. He took long stiff snorts, as if sucking pasta through his nose. *"Pardon moi,* ya did take ol' Epi's advice. Ya nasty little whore. Was it that sweetie-pie in there," he hounded, pointing to Eva through the glass. I blushed my confession. "Way ta go. That was damn fast. She's a hottie—nice piece a ass." He struck my shoulder with approval. "She looks damn satisfied, too. Look at 'er slingin' those drinks with that shit-eatin' grin. Good fuckin' fer ya." A smile passed beyond my defenses.

Epi hoisted the battered guitar onto his shoulder, and his expression fell back to seriousness, "Don't talk ta that fuck shyster. He's no good. Say no more. If ya see him again, either run the other way or kick his fuckin' ass. Don't talk ta the cops neither—they don't mean ya no good, and they still haven't recognized ya."

"OK. What did he want?"

"Nothin' decent or even voluptuously immoral. He's an insurance agent—a parasite, a capitalist cock-biter. He's no good. Fuck 'im!"

The door to Epi's shop had stuck open after the wrathful encounter. The kabalistic feline peered around the door as if to see if Epi was all right. She inquired with a loving "meow". Epi turned around. "The sphincter licker is gone now, baby. It's OK. I'm OK too. Let's go back inside. I need a fuckin' cigarette," Epi consoled. He and his cat re-entered the shop and set back to work.

After another cup of coffee and two cigarettes, the shift relief had arrived and Eva exited Zoe's. "You're the sexiest little beast ever," she cooed.

"Thanks."

"You were wild. I've never done anything that spontaneous before, and with everybody in the café. I should have been embarrassed, but I'm sort of proud. I can still smell it all over me, and I think the customers can too. Its pretty sexy," Eva remarked, grinning through the smoke. She inhaled hard on her cigarette, her mind retreading our lustful ground. "It was fast. I didn't know what was going on. It was like you swooped over me and ravished every cell of my body. I didn't have time to think. It was great. At first I was sort of scared and aroused at the same time, but then it was like I had no choice, and I really got into it. It was really cool." She ran her fingers through my hair.

"Gimme your hand." I laid my hand on the table passively. She picked it up and brought it to her nose. "It still smells like me. You're so sexy." Her bright eyes were filled with solace. Her sentiment, for some perverse reason, caused my throat to choke-up, as if I was nearing tears. "Oh gosh, I've got to get back; the new girl really has no idea what to do. I think I've left her alone too long already. I'll see you after work, right?" I nodded. "You dirty bitch," she growled playfully before disappearing into the cafe.

I felt a tear streak down my face and burn coldly as the wind picked up.

Metempsychosis of Burial

Epi's hand poked out of his shop door and beckoned me inside. My joints creaked as I rose from my seat. Zosimos had joined me shortly after the interlude between Epi and the insurance man. Zosimos and I drank our coffees together while he told me about his grandmother's Welsh castle. As was always the case when Zosimos is my interlocutor, I only understood fifty percent of his words. From what I could gather from his macerated speech, his brother was currently renting out the fortress to a Hollywood production company for a pretty sum. Zosimos liked to visit the castle of his forefathers, but it cost too much to maintain the facility in the winter; its primary source of heat in the winter months is its many fireplaces, and its only source of insulation is its four-foot thick walls. It had fallen into disrepair over a hundred years ago when the family vacated the premises, only to visit it a few times a decade. I had no idea about how an Egyptian would have come by a castle in Wales. My world had gotten quite ridiculous.

I followed Epi's call into the shop. Pistis lay curled on the workbench in a pile of ringlets of shavings. Epi was talking to the Sibyls, who were noticeably excited. "This thing can be fun," Epi told the bouncing ladies, "but be careful. I don't want ta be bailin' anybody out a jail tanight. Just remember: calm, cool and collected. Now ya've the times and places. Get the fuck out a here, ya nasty little twats." He slapped them both on their butts like an overly concerned coach. The girls grazed my chest with their gay fingers as they ran out the door.

"God damn it, they're good girls," Epi praised, as his voracious eyes followed their young bodies out. "So," he said to me, "I have a project, but ya have time to glue the back onta yar geeter. We've gotta give the gals a good headstart."

The previous day Epi had cut the sides down, leveled them, glued kerfing to the joints that would receive the back and chiseled some of it away to make room for the braces. We spread glue on the kerfing and bound the back to the carcass by wrapping long pieces of rubber around the whole body. "Ya gotta wrapper 'er up like a mummy," Epi explained, "so that she knows the darkness. Once she's come back from Hades, she can really sing!" He informed me that the rubber, used here to mummify my creation, was merely made of bicycle inner tubes that had been cut longitudinally and then tied together. "I was usin' car and truck innertube, but they don't make wheels like that no more, excepting on a few big rigs," Epi barked.

Once we had sufficiently wrapped the dead, Epi was back to previous business, "That should give 'em time. Grab that box and the weapon, and come out ta my truck." The weapon he was referring to was the instrument used in warding off the insurance agent. I gathered them both and took them to the truck. Epi met me outside with a shovel, and we left together.

Once we were on the freeway headed south, Epi began talking. "Insurance, what a stupid idea. Ain't nothin' stupider than the idea a risk management. If fate's gonna kick yar ass, its gonna kick it." Epi tuned the radio to a country music station that was playing a Woody Guthrie marathon and then revved the truck to ninety miles an hour.

Woody's tinny voice crackled through the speaker, singing *The Worried Man Blues.*

"Woody's great," bellowed Epi, smacking the steering wheel. "Ya know, this cat has it all right. There ain't any risk managers hangin' 'round him, and I don't mean 'cause he dead. No, he was ridin' the rails and pickin' fights; he embraced the chaos a life, and ya can't blame 'im fer takin' those government commissions or havin' a son who only wrote one decent song."

"What song is that?" I asked.

"Why, a course the *Motorcycle Song*," Epi said matter-of-factly. "But anyway, we need ta have a heart-to-heart talk. I can't bear seein' ya waste away like this; I mean it's great that ya did the dirty, but then yar just rottin' away with Zosimos like that. He's ol', it's OK fer him ta sit on his ass all day swillin' joe. The hombre's retired and a little batty. But ya're young. And if nothin' else, watchin' ya's givin' me an ulcer." Epi threw a cigarette into his mouth. It jittered under the motion of the truck, making it difficult for him to light it; the cigarette's tip eluded the lighter's flame for several minutes until the tip burst into combustion. "So, what's yar fuckin' problem?" He glared at me.

"I don't know."

"Fuck ya. Ya do too know," Epi shouted.

"Not really."

"OK, OK. If ya're gonna be like that, then I just tell ya what we're doin'. I've got the girls breakin' inta a car. They're not exactly stealin' it. Ya see, the owner a the car beat it up pretty good one night after spending several hours with Jim Beam. It ain't a real nice car, but it sounds pretty good on paper. He had it insured pretty good, but not good enough ta pay far the repairs, so he asked me ta get rid a the damn thing so he could get a nice sum a change from the risk managers." Epi cackled, the cigarette flew out of his mouth, landing on his leg. The truck vibrated as its tires ran over the outer lane border.

"Fuck me!" Epi howled, as he placed the cigarette back in his mouth. "Jesus fucking Christ! I hate that. Any-who, so the girls're takin' his car while his wife's shoppin'. Now, she don't know we're gonna steal it (I mean, help my friend), so that the whole scenario's more authentic. Then, we're gonna bury the fuckin' thin'." Epi released a chortle, very pleased with himself. "Ya gotta understand (and this applies ta yar shit too) some times in a person's life, he or she must bury elements a the past. Sometimes ya even gotta bury the future, but that's fer another lecture. Some things, most things—I should say—'re born ta be buried. The great unwashed can't handle everythin'. They want a break fer some shit, even if they don't know it. Mediocrity's where ya'll find most a the happy people. It takes some slight a the hand fer anybody ta be happy. So, we're goin' out ta hide the evidence: that guitar, the car and the box. Ain't nothin' like the nympholepsy of the graveyard." He laughed, slapping his singed pant leg.

"Let me let ya in on a little secret." He pulled my collar toward him as if someone else could be listening. There's this super cool idea in many religions called *metempsychosis*. I bet ya didn't think ol' Epi knew such big fuckin' words, but I've read and written many book and lived fer thousands a years. Metempsychosis, in its most distilled state, 's the migration a souls. Most folks use the term when they're talkin' 'bout the soul's journey after death inta another body. Now this's a fabulous idea, but its crap— crap, crap, crap. Their idea a what occurs after death may be crap, but it don't mean that the word ain't any good." Epi spit out the window, however much of it sprayed back at us.

"Ya ever hear a the Riddle a the Sphinx?" I nodded. "That's what I'm talkin' 'bout." He patted me on the back.

"I don't quite understand your connection," I hesitated.

"Shit, folks undergo metempsychosis every day. When ya were born, ya were shriveled, squishy and purple (all babies is purple when they pop out). When ya're young, ya're all horny, lanky and all ya want ta do is piss yar folks off. Older folks only worry 'bout the taxman and their next bowel movement. There's constant change: four legs in the mornin', two legs durin' the day and three at dark. Now, fer an adolescent boy, maybe it would be more accurate ta say three legs at ten forty-five." Again, Epi pummeled his leg with enthusiasm. "People change. People forget. People purposefully bury shit so that they can change. Now remember, some change's easier than others types. Ya get my meaning a metempsychosis?"

"Yes."

"So what does it have ta do with ya?"

"I'm going to bury myself."

"Good, but don't do it literally; ya amuse me."

"OK."

"I think its pretty cool that there's all this invisible music shootin' through the atmosphere," Epi interjected, pointing to the radio."

"I agree."

"Ya're sure one fucked up kid. Ya act like a pregnant chick."

"I suppose."

The sky was growing darker. The blood of twilight could be seen on the clouds like a sacrifice of thanks for the day. I was not sure which part of myself I needed to bury, or if I should bury the whole thing. Nor did I know what 'bury' means in reference to my life. Asphyxiation via earth had its appealing elements, but a portion of myself rebelled against the idea of absolute physical annihilation—and there was Eva. Since the apartment fire, certain new elements had been created—metempsychosis had worked its magic without my realizing it, although only partially. I had begun building a new history—migrating, although much of the past was still soaked into my being. Regret is dependent on history. As a mathematical equation, history equals action over time multiplied by memory. Perhaps regret equals emotional disturbance over history.

Epi pulled onto a farm road as the sky was growing black. He stopped the truck in the middle of a spacious construction site. Heavy machinery and mounds of earth were scattered over the area. "I've got a buddy who's the foreman a this landscapin' job. This's gonna be a big State garden. They're gonna be puttin' pho-Greek statues right on top a our burial site—hopefully a statue a Mercury," he spouted with glee. He hopped into a CAT and began removing earth.

Soon, the burning of an engine could be heard over the rumble of the earthmover; a red '99 Ford Mustang skidded into the site with the Sibyls in the front seats. The entire front end of the car was crumpled. Although the car ran fairly well, the extent of the body damage would classify it as 'totaled'. I was sure the frame had been bent and an abrasive grinding sound could be heard even without the transmission engaged. And what was worse, the loud beats of hip-hop pounded from the car.

"Can we bury it with the radio on?" one of the Sibyls pleaded as she exited the car.

"Sure, why the fuck not," Epi answered from behind the controls of the Caterpillar. The girls slapped a hi-five and jumped giddily up and down. "Throw the shit in the car," Epi hollered to me. I placed the guitar and the cardboard box into the Mustang. "Is it in neutral?" he asked the girls.

"Yesssss it is, daddy," they squealed in unison.

"That's fuckin' cute, ain't it," Epi said to me.

He finished the hole and we all pushed the car in. Epi filled the hole and compacted the earth. Even so, a large mound was left. "What'll they find under the foot a ol' Mercurius?" Epi laughed. "Some things should be buried only fer a time, then their magnificent presence should be released in their full luminous splendor… That's the easiest clam I've ever made." Even with all of the dirt, the hum of the radio emanated from the mound.

"Maybe that radio thin' wasn't such a good idea," Epi stated, "Oh well. Let's get the fuck out a here, I need a cup a coffee."

"Oh no, we brought you a thermos, but we left it in the car," replied the Sibyls.

Epi squeezed their asses and, in a fatherly voice, "Ya're the best kids anybody could ever have." They kissed him with puckered lips, and we crowded into the truck.

Epi found it somewhat difficult to shift the truck with the number of people in the cab, but we managed to drive back to the apartment despite the encumbrance. There was little conversation, only ear battering and monotonous techomusic. The girls tried to dance to the beats, but their dancing was no more than trapped fidgeting. Epi even attempted to smoke while in the truck. His attempt merely burned one of the girls. He apologized profusely and licked her wound. She seemed to enjoy the tongue contact.

236

When we arrived, Eva was sitting and talking with Zosimos. She jumped up and embraced me. "Baby," she said, "I'm going to get some groceries. Do you want to meet me at my place after that?"

"I would love that."

"See ya there... Oh, don't eat anything, I'll fix you dinner. Toodles." She waved and skipped down the street.

Zosimos waved to the empty seat with his thick hand, "Sit, have coffee. Wait for beautiful girl. She is treasure."

"Yes, she is," I responded.

"What you do with Epi?"

"Bury stuff."

"So what you bury?" Zosimos asked.

"A car."

"Yes, yes, but what *you* bury?"

"Nothing."

"You buried nothing? That quite impressive, good for you," he grinned through his flesh.

"No, I mean I didn't bury anything of my own," I clarified. "When I said nothing, I didn't mean the Nothing," I joked.

"That too bad. There nothing better to bury than Nothing." He smiled. "You know what say metaphysics is?" I shook my head. "Thoughts concerning void," he answered, "blood on hands of Lady Macbeth, tone of madman's lament, handshake with Thoth.

"So you did not bury anything?"

"No."

"Why no?"

"I'm not sure what I should bury and how."

"Go talk to Tie. If don't know, he will. You see, must look at thing before bury it. Hold it in hand and drop it in hole. This how bury something. Then can cover it dirt. Tie see. He not see present well, because he not have eyes, but he see well into past and little into future."

Obsequious Finiting

Eva and I ate dinner together. She cooked. I washed the dishes, cleaning the orange-colored oils and thin basil leaves off the pans and smelling the fish oil and peanut sauce mingling with the sweet soap. She had cooked an Asian noodle dish. It was hot and refreshing, leaving a slight burning sensation in the mouth. I continued to feel the flames of our meal on my tongue, even after she began to paint, and I began walking to Epi's shop. The meal smoldered for hours.

Epi and the Sibyls were unloading boards from the pickup into a storage area behind the shop. I had never seen inside this shed. The room was dark and musty. This was where the freshly cut wood dried, often times for years. The sides of this long shed were of shiplap, the green paint peeling and flaking off with age. On many of the boards Epi or the girls applied paint to the ends, and sometimes, on the more exotic species, wax. This was to dissuade the boards from cracking as they dried. Vacant spider webs hung between the rafters—it being too dark and isolated for even spiders to find comfort and food. The area was like a tomb from where, some day, the boards would see the light again, but for now they had to cure in the darkness until their day of rebirth.

While the strange family filled the storage room with new material, I worked on my guitar. There was little else to do for one trying not to recover the past. I unwrapped the body of the guitar from the bands of black rubber and proceeded to route the guitar's body to accept the end gaft as well as the purfling and binding. Then I carefully glued them into the vacancies I had routed out and taped them to dry. This process took some time; I measured and re-measured, cut and re-cut the rabbet until the depth was perfect. I used a laminate trimmer initially, but detailed the work with a chisel. I set the guitar aside to dry.

The plastic binding both frames the guitar and protects the edges from abuse—it adds aesthetic integrity to the whole, giving the wood body a clear division from the objects of the world rather than hanging in the atmosphere without border—melting ambiguously into the rest of the world. The gluing of the binding and purfling separates the guitar and the world into subject and object, like a Kantian soliloquy; yet the melody will, ironically, diffuse the world's order with sound. Without a binding, the spruce and maple would also mingle in deceptive play, the observer would be unsure of where one wood ends and the other begins.

I immobilized the neck in the vise. Epi's fretting hammer hung above his bench. It was originally designed for autobody work. The hammer's face was large and round, slightly convex. The handle felt satisfying in the hand—well balanced and polished with sweat. I set it near the neck. Then I cut twenty-two pieces of fret wire, each about three inches long. They sparked under the yellow illumination of the shop. With my index finger I ran a bead of white glue down the spine of the wire and then set it into one of the ebony fingerboard's fret slots. Dead and straight blows were the requirement—the hammer should not bounce. I drove the spine of the wire into the dense wood. It is to take about four or five whacks of the hammer to properly seat the frets without distorting them; I often took eight to ten thwacks to seat them completely. They were, eventually, all set in the black fretboard, and I wiped the glue away with a damp cloth.

The carcass was beginning to look like a guitar and the neck was looking like a neck. I was admiring my work when I felt that someone was watching me. It was not uncommon for a pedestrian to glance into the shop windows, but it was a rare occurrence for someone to stare and examine the contents of the shop. A feeling of examining eyes bristled the hairs on the back of my neck. I anxiously looked over my shoulder; there was nothing. I took this for my own paranoia and began reading Epi's tome. My fingers grazed over the ink renderings of fingerboards and heel blocks. All the illustrations were done with a delicate hand; fine lines weaved in and out of each other creating harmoniously balanced diagrams. These pictures looked like something out of Leonardo DiVinci's notebooks—like pieces of art in themselves.

The hum of metal slowly being worn by a fine stone hung over my reading; Epi stood silently honing some chisels. I did not have to wait long until the glue of the binding had dried. Once Epi gave me a jeering 'thumbs up', I began scraping the binding flush to the wood. This was a most pleasurable task; the plastic gave way easily to the metal scraper.

Once the binding was leveled, I came to one of the most crucial tasks of the entire guitar-building process, setting the neck. I cut the dovetail with a backsaw and cleaned up the mortise with a chisel. I had to ensure an exact fit according to the nuances of the body and the proposed angle of the strings. It took hours, even with the luthier's guidance. "If you fuck that joint up, ya mise well throw the whole thing in the fire," Epi encouraged. Not only must the joint be perfectly snug (for the only glue used in this process goes on the fretboard only, not in the dovetail joint), but the joint is made of compound angles requiring a specific height and angle at which to sit. Complications can easily occur, so I breathed deeply and called upon my patience. Not only must the mortise be cut, but then I needed to pare away wood from the dovetailed tenon on the neck, check for fit, and chisel some more.

Epi sensed my trepidation. "This's 'bout life," he testified. "'Bout yar hands fillin' with knowin'. Ya can read 'bout it and ya can talk 'bout it, but ya gotta do it even if ya're gonna fuck it up. The hands gotta learn fer themselves."

It took some time and focus, but I managed to create a snug joint. The invisible line from the plateau of the neck to the potential saddle appeared to be at the correct angle. If the neck and the body do not meet at the correct angle, then the entire playability of the guitar is compromised. The mind is a beautiful place for geometry, but the world is a piss-poor place for geometry's implementation. I would wait to glue the neck on until I had finished lacquering both the body and the neck.

After some final carving of the neck, it was on to finiting—the process of preparing the wood for finish. First I scraped the instrument. Afterwards I sanded with successive grits of paper until I reached 320 grit. Again, I took my time, meticulously erasing blemishes caused in production. I removed any traces of glue seepage, nicks and dents. And throughout this process, I worried. Epi had left on some enigmatic errand, leaving the shop vacant but for the finiting. The world was quiet. Traffic had ceased. No light filtered into the shop, causing the windows to be only a reflection of what was taking place inside. Only the gentle scuff of low-grit paper on wood filled the room with sound. The easy sounds of finiting seemed to exist independently of the action—self-begotten rather than the work of my hands. The two phenomena, sound and action, transpired aeons from each other, yet came together in this place. The guitar was coming to a close—finality of becoming was nearing. I felt silent distance creep in between the joints of my life, like the space between poorly sawn dovetails. Would the instrument play in tune? Would the neck succumb to the tension of the stings and collapse in my hands? Would the finish suck in the light, being dull and dead? Would the action be too high? Would the strings buzz angrily against the frets? Would its voice be hollow and dry, unlistenable by the world?

Doing good work is not solely dependant on the material's compliance. Some degree of uncertainty dwells within the wood's fibers, but far more uncertainty resides in the hand and mind of the artificer. There is the obvious shortcomings of the physical ability of the creator—his or her skills with a chisel and a saw, but the great task is balancing knowledge with the self. A novice of any art learns through trial and error, many frustrated stomping-aways from the craft. The greatest ability of the novice is to overcome uncertainty. I do not mean getting rid of the uncertain nature of creation, but being able to cope well with the inherent force of what is not known. No matter how much one reads or asks about a certain task, there are always things that surface without one's foreknowledge. Certainty does not come from knowing everything, from omnipotence, for this is never a realistic state of being. Uncertainty paired with pride is an ugly beast, whose growling distemper has shattered many soundboards. Doubt always lingers in the creator's mind. One must accept doubt without it stifling all energies. Yet, perhaps hubris is even more dangerous.

Ideally, one works without hope of product, for then the frustrations of doubt and uncertainty vanish. This state would be a mental place of meditation in the moment— distancing one's self from the outcome, yet *doing* entirely in the present. Sadly, this was not my state of mind. I, instead, worried. I vexed over every detail, which often hindered me from going on. Or, the fear rushed me headlong into hurrying through before something was done adequately. In my state of anxiety, my mind was not with the work. I continually looked over my shoulder and examined my shadow. I stared at my own reflection in the window, attempting to see who was looking at me. I allowed distraction inside my mind. I wanted the product, less for the process. I was dogged by my potentially fruitless efforts. These trepidations dominated my mind—all the potential error and pointless striving. Vanity overpowered the endeavor. I sanded obsequiously.

I taped-off the fingerboard and wiped the wood with tack cloth. Then I brushed on a thin coat of sanding sealer, feathering the liquid over the wood, on both the body and the neck. The grain exploded from the surface. The smell of the substance, however, was overbearing. I felt that I was not breathing air but a toxic substance. I walked out into the cool air of the evening coughing, and then I lit a cigarette. The fumes of the sealer had followed me even outside; I felt their weight in my clothes and tasted them in my mouth.

Finishing, for the craftsman, does not mean that one is done. Instead, it means that one is not done, only nearing the point where he or she thinks is to be ended. This word is an oxymoron, for to finish is to complete, yet the progressive tense undermines the word's very definition. Finishing, then, is the process of approaching the end. I ask the reader, what would not fit this definition except for being ended (i.e., death), for all that is being, is approaching the end. I thought about death as I tasted the sealer that persisted in my mouth and clung to my lungs.

Would I ever finish this guitar: brushing on the lacquer, polishing, making and installing the bridge, gluing the neck on, leveling and polishing the frets, carving and setting up the nut and saddle, installing tuners and strings, intonating it? What am I going to do with this thing if I ever finish?

Melancholia

The organist pressed not the organ keys. The street kids cynically joked not in the park. The hippies beat not their drums. The suits and laborers had arrived home already, for their presence graced not the wet sidewalks. I sipped my coffee, feeling the strain of my belly—that constant reminder that something unholy continued to dwell within me. The time was probably nearing ten o'clock. The city was quiet; only rain's soft tickling of concrete skin could be heard.

I could see Glaucon walking toward me from blocks away, the sidewalk was otherwise vacant. He conducted himself with the slump of a beaten man—his shoulders falling in, his head hung low, his feet scrapping the concrete with every step. His hair was matted and disheveled. When he sat beside me, I could tell that he had not bathed in days. He looked at me hollowly.

"You're a mess, Glaucon," I observed quietly.

"Yes, I am."

"Have you eaten anything?"

"What?"

"Have you eaten anything?" I repeated.

"Oh…no, I haven't, I don't think," Glaucon mumbled, slowly withdrawing from his stupor. "I haven't done much except walk and think, since I beat that poor kid. I did get a phone call from work. A friend told me that a cop or something is looking for me again. I don't care. I'll…" he stopped in mid-sentence. A clear presence overtook the mists of his eyes, "I found out that he's dead. I killed him. He was seventeen years old."

"Jesus, what are you going to do?"

"I don't know. I can't think of anything else but my guilt." Glaucon pulled a cigarette from his pocket and lit it. He held it without smoking it.

"Let me get you a cup of coffee," I stated, not knowing how to address this situation, "Zoe's isn't closed quite yet."

"Thanks."

I retrieved the coffee. Glaucon sipped from the mug, but appeared to be lost somewhere else. "You know, one can have contempt for the laws and conventions of man, but you have to be dead in order to be free from the feelings of guilt," Glaucon explained absently. "I used to toy with the idea that the laws were only around to protect people from other people, and to a certain extent that is right, but what I didn't realize is that they also try to protect one from one's self. There are some people who'll tell you that breaking the law means nothing, that the law is a man-made contrivance that is created to maintain the status quo. What they fail to express is that the laws are a reflection of our potential guilt." Glaucon sipped his coffee and looked up. "Do you see what I'm saying?" I nodded sympathetically. "Someone would have to have no emotional connection with anyone else to be able to live beyond the law. There is a law in our guts the shape of an hammer. It beats us when we commit acts of spiritual treason. It does not matter whether there is a god or not, we can't run from ourselves, because our emotions will always catch up to us. People try to rationalize the world. They use reason to deny the existence of will. They say that free will is a joke, that the world is not knowable, that we're surrounded by void and darkness. The world is an illusion!" he shouted. "It doesn't matter if the world is an illusion, because my gut is disintegrating; I'm coming apart. If the world is a great joke, or if we, as conscious beings, can only perceive subjectively, then our emotions are the dictators of law. My actions have violated my own law..." He threw his cigarette into the street.

"Did you know that in Greek the word for law, *nomos*, can be translated as song?" Glaucon continued.

"No, I did not."

"It's true. They are both things dependent on harmony. There is no despair in polyphony. There are also no tri-tones in polyphony. It used to be illegal to play tri-tones; they were considered to be sounds of the devil. Most people don't like the sound of tri-tones, but what dictates that? Their guts tell them that it sounds like shit. Even in modern music you'll only use them in passing to something less caustic to the ears. A composer can't stray too far from the rules. If one does, it all falls apart. One has to respect the *Nomos* of the self—and the *Nomos* of the World.

"I would love to have the constitution that could radically reject this shitty world, but I don't. While I am conscious, I will be eaten by regret, guilt, despair, hopelessness, anger, jealousy, melancholy—all of it. I would love to be suspended in a vacuum without thought or feeling, but that is not the case." Glaucon paused to light another cigarette that he would soon neglect.

"People commit suicide for a lot of different reasons, I suppose. Some kill themselves by accident. They want people to see them and pity them—lavish them with attention. I mean, ambulances come and they get to talk to doctors and shrinks. Some go too far by accident—a few too many pills or a bit too deep. Others want attention too, but they want it in the afterlife. They write eloquent and moving suicide notes. Also, they often do away with themselves in some grand manner that they hope people will remember and talk about. They commit suicide to move people. It is often a big 'fuck-you' or 'I told you so'. Others kill themselves for similar but more abstract reasons, often opting for a less dramatic and visible approach. They may blow their brains out with a shotgun, but, instead of doing it at the transit mall, they'll do it in the forest. These people want to be dead in order to mock god. Still others just want silence. They want to silence the world. They want to go back to before they were born. They want a stillness of being. I can respect these last people." He took a shallow puff on the cigarette. "These people are calm, they don't leave notes, nor are they angry or guilty; they're just tired. Then, there are the people who have no other choice. This is Brutus or Cato. They have no other option. The world is already gone, and it is better to take your own life while there is still a semblance of will rather than allow others to do it for you. However you look at it, suicide is a way to right a wrong. I wish I could be indifferent."

"Do you want to come over tonight? Eva would love to see you," I gingerly asked.

"No, no. I can't."

"Come on. You have nothing better to do. I won't take a refusal," I pitifully demanded.

"No, I'm not going to go," Glaucon affirmed.

Jake appeared from behind me. He sat down between us and quickly started spouting angrily, "Did you hear? They've started burning bookstores. They hit three last night. It pisses me off. They think they're the only ones with valid words. I hate them, even when I can't get published. I sent some work out, what if it was in print. The fuckers!

"Fuck, you look like warmed over puke. What's wrong with you," he asked, finally noticing Glaucon's face.

"Nothing. I just haven't had much sleep," he stated wearily.

"These crazy street kids are burning everything. First that apartment, and now the Word. They're trying to burn the Word. Stupid fucks. I hate fanatics.

"Anyway, I'm on a roll with my play. The characters are talking about the plot structure itself. They're saying things like, 'Everybody wants a crooked ending, an ending that twists itself around to the beginning, something that forces the audience to reconsider everything they've seen and heard, like, what is that movie?' and 'Don't let them take anything for granted. Have them ask themselves what the difference is between a comedy and a tragedy,' and 'Don't count anyone happy until she's dead.' Isn't that good shit? I think I'm really on to something. I'm talking about a surprise ending in the play itself. Everybody likes those endings that make you look back and have one of those 'oh shit' kind of moments, where everything looks totally different than what they thought." Jake began to tap the table with nervous excitement. "It's like the process of life. That's why people like those endings so much. Everybody's been sitting at a café and, without realizing it, put salt instead of sugar in their coffee. They think their coffee is sweet, but when they taste it, it's salty. This is life. One day you think that you've got life all figured out, but, *pow*, the tables are suddenly turned. We're amused with the process of re-looking—re-examining, because this is what we are forced to do every day. 'What the fuck was I thinking at twenty-five?' It's the horror of our own actions—things committed in ignorance. There's a sick pleasure in looking back at our own naïve offenses and seeing them in a context of greater perspective.

"But maybe, even more like life, the play won't really end at all. I'll just leave it open and the audience can guess for themselves what actually happened.

"Well, I'm going to grab a cup of coffee and get back to writing. I hope you feel better Glaucon, you're usually so starry-eyed, I miss it." Jake slapped Glaucon on the back saying, "They should make a bumper sticker that says, 'Do a good deed, shoot a street kid.'" Jake went inside, grabbed a cup of coffee and left.

Without any farewell, Glaucon stood from his seat and resumed his melancholy peripatetic. I also left the café.

It was a short walk over to Eva's apartment. I was not looking forward to it. During Glaucon's lucubration, I had developed a headache. His words applied to my plight also, although history was lucid for him. Glaucon did not suffer from abstract guilt; instead, his guilt was smeared clear and cold all over his hands. Would he turn himself into the authorities, kill himself or allow the act to burn itself out? Time's hollow musings would be the testament. There was a band of pressure all around my skull and a sharp pain running down my neck. My entrails, also, emanated a dull pang throughout my body, like usual.

To Sleep

Eva was staring at a blank canvas when I walked into her apartment. We went to bed with endearing kisses. The lights then went off and Eva fell to sleep quickly. I, however, could not compel sleep upon myself. I lay staring up at the ceiling. My body ached for slumber to fill my eyelids with its heavy substance, but to no avail. I got up to go to the bathroom several times before I decided to take a walk. Quietly, I crept out the door.

The streets were calm; the lamplight coruscated from the wet surface of the blacktop. I was one of the few who was awake in the city—one of the special people witnessing the moment. One could almost hear the collective snoring of the hippies, the winos, the suits, the street kids, the invalids, the clergy, the plumbers and carpenters, the legislators, the activists, the window washers, the cops, the dog catchers, the potheads—everyone but the speed freaks, poets and myself. There is probably a twelve-step group for insomniacs. This group must meet at 3:30 AM. All of the participants hold one personal characteristic collectively, metaphysical anemia. The IA meetings would have people stand up saying, "Hi, my name is Bill, and I'm an Existentialist." The group would answer lethargically,

"Welcome Bill, try to sleep." Perhaps going to one of these meetings and listening to the drivel would be the cure for any sleepless night.

I thought of domestic tranquility. Perhaps I could work for Epi and live with Eva. Eva and I appeared to compliment each other well. My mind wandered to nights of cooking dinner and taking warm showers together, massaging her thin shoulders, staring into her voluptuous eyes, and watching her throw paint onto canvas. I could build musical instruments and have coffee with my new friends. The scene was especially pastoral, but my stomach began rumbling dysthimicly.

As I headed through the park blocks to see if Epi was whittling away in his workshop yet, I heard a clarinet waft through the breeze. Tie was standing on top of The Hotel Pronoia lavishing Phrygian tones upon the deserted streets. The notes descended to the asphalt gracefully.

I entered the building and climbed the stairs to the roof. The wind blew cleansingly over my body. There was a purity of height up there, away from the miasma of the street. My feeling of being part of the wakeful elect intensified with the altitude. Tie stopped playing and turned to me, "Hello. Can't sleep?"

"No. Please don't stop playing, it is beautiful and calming."

"Thank you, but you have come for a reason," Tie stated acutely. "You desire something I won't give you."

"What do you mean?"

"You wish to ask me about the history you know," Tie condescended.

"I just came up to listen to you play," I defended.

"Don't bullshit me. I don't like to be bullshitted. But if we must play, then let us proceed. Go ahead, ask me any question, even one that's not in your heart."

"How did I get here?"

"You walked."

"No, I mean to this city."

"You flew."

"What kind of plane?"

"A Boeing 727."

"Next to whom did I sit?"

"Mrs. Margery N. Thomson, who showed you pictures of her seventeen year-old twins in their footfall uniforms. She is very proud of them. Mrs. Thompson was returning from a 'No-Husbands-Allowed' vacation with her book group," Tie remarked. Getting into the game, he crossed his arms with the clarinet clutched in-between.

It was difficult to look into his eyes, even though I knew he was blind. There are some people with whom you are reluctant to make eye contact, because you find that they are physically or emotionally threatening.

"Where was I born?" I smiled.

"Just off of Interstate Avenue," He pointed northeast.

"How old is Epi?"

"Older than you and I put together, although the guy looks great for his age," Tie smiled.

"Do I having siblings?" I heard a tremor in my own voice.

"Yes, two."

"Where did the codex come from," I asked, getting more to the point.

"It was found in Southern Iraq during the Gulf War. An American GI stumbled upon it after an ancient statue was destroyed in the air assault. The Mandeans had placed it there hundreds of years before, but had forgotten about it. Before it was taken to Iraq, it had been in Syria, Alexandria, Athens, and Egyptian Thebes. It journeyed through the centuries compiling additional pages en route to today."

"Did I start the apartment fire?" I shook as I asked.

"Yes and no."

"Did I kill the doctor?" my throat nearly closed as I asked.

"The Stranger is dead."

"Do you know what I truly remember, and what I can't recall?"

"You are like the fools who think Oedipus had not the slightest idea of his origins. He knew the prophesy. You disregard Oedipus' intelligence, demonstrated by the riddle. You never ask why Oedipus is not concerned by the simultaneous death of the king and the slaying of the rich man at the crossroads. For such an intelligent and concerned man, he showed a great deal of recklessness and suppressed insight."

I pushed, "Tell me who killed the doctor."

"He had sinned through his neglect and his actions, as you have too."

"Don't be coy with me," I chided.

"Don't bother yourself with the past; the past won't do you any good. You have no kingdom to save from the plague," Tie disclosed fiercely.

I raged, "You need to tell me what is going on."

"I don't *need* to tell you anything. You are acting like a child. Pull yourself together and get on with life. The insurance men don't recognize you, and the police are glad the doctor is dead due to crimes he commited that the police could never prove," Tie bellowed. "I refuse to fill in the pieces, they will cause nothing but misery to you and others."

"You will tell me who set the fire, and who killed that man."

"You need to leave now. You need to go downstairs and learn Epi's trade; the first-curse is also the first-blessing after sin. Go, make love to Eva. Drown yourself in life's pleasures and its mundane rituals. Live in the present where there is no memory. Sing and make music, they will fill your fecund deficiencies. This is my petition to your health. Allow forgetting—the boon of man—to take the place of your agitation. If you follow this prescription, you will know sleep. Do not pursue the past. I, more than anyone, know that a lucid past is the greatest curse. There is no reason to study history's tragedy." Then, Tie put the clarinet back to his lips and began playing high-register arpeggios.

The notes squealed in my ears. My blood boiled. I wanted to push him from the roof, onto the hard concrete below. He was blind, therefore he could not see me coming. He would defend himself poorly. Nor could he see the present. The present was my ally. He turned his back to me as he panned his body with the music. The sounds possessed angry intensity.

"You will tell me who killed him!" I shouted. Tie played louder. "You will tell me, you blind son of a bitch." Tie's music gained further volume. I grabbed his robe. The music stopped.

"If you do that, your past and future will come to a crashing head. Do you want to know who pulled the trigger? I will tell you, but maybe the murder is nothing compared to the other sins? I will take great pleasure in putting into words what you know and fear. I will fill the scene with life, describing every detail in such malignant shades of truth that they will never escape you. You will rile in horror at your most unnatural birth, that every subsequent moment of your life will be spent imbedded in the atrocity. You will never know sleep again, because your eyes will be pinned open with knowledge."

During that sleepless night—as the city dreamt peacefully, as Epi pushed a hand plane gently across a board creating translucent curls of wood, as Eva sighed under the happiness of pleasant dreams, as Glaucon lay unconscious on Zosimos' floor with an empty bottle, as Zosimos dreamt of his Welsh castle—the wraiths of history tormented my ears. I did not push Tie off of Pronoia. I did not scream or cry. I walked away slowly, stoically, without a sound. Silence seemed the only choice.

Secret Defilement

I expelled myself, an expulsion more profound than I had ever undertaken. I found myself ontologically self-excommunicated from the world and man and cosmos. I walked. The acridity of Tie's words eternally burned the pictures of history into my brain. Present did not exist, instead the bold etching of the past dominated every sense. The world reeked with the sulfur of incest and the muriat of murder. My eyes would not possess the present, nor ears hear the moment—both consumed with the alembic of bygones. I walked through the city, but I can not relate where I went. My body traversed the metropolis for hours or days, I cannot recall. This apparatus called self burned in chemical visions of what I did and what was done to me and the sin of my birth. I hated myself, and I hated the Stranger.

I know, only from the accounts of others, that I was led back to Eva's apartment, where I laid in the throes of a mortal fever. My penitentiary of blind visions mutated into delirious abstractions. Madness pissed into the ambrosial waters of sacrament. Archons fed me vapid words with their incendiaries. Theosophical torches scalded my flesh. A frenzied group of children sang songs of embryonic torture. Fires bloomed across metaphysical cityscapes. These prophecies did not come in the form of dream or sleep or any type of unconscious ramblings, but from a hyperconscious realm. This world of past and future, transcending the present, glowed brighter than the tangible café or Epi or Eva. It was a world holding more being.

Then, the wandering thoughts of my illness took on a more dialectic character. My waking coma began:

Any modern thinking person, not the bitch of religious brainwashing or cock-sucker of blind indoctrination, knows—feels—seethes with the presentment that beyond the Earth and stars, there is nothing. This nothing is the most profound nothing: no god or devil or angels or pleromic light, Nothing. So, this great tragedy of our senses rots in its own feces and urine. The creative imagination suffering and extolling the abyss of emotion. The illusion—the swindle of self—this is our fate, to be washed, finally, in death's nothing. Better to be Nothing's temporary semblance, than a malicious deity's cunt. Oh, to love the sadist, this is madness.

Give me the blissful Nothing after years of sorrow rather than the harrowing Love of the Son. Let me embrace the comedy of my suffering and the tragedy of my mother's loins. I will the myth of self and the laughter of my solipsism. I understand the soterology of lonely cunt. I worship the gnosis back upon itself. I shun the carnal Father, as the shot speckled dove plummets to my feet. Sing your song of eschatology—sing it while masturbating in the shower. Historical Truth is the fetid void. I am your slave. I sacrifice Nomos on the altar—slitting her milky throat from ear to ear and ravishimg her quivering body.

...Hello, who do I see in the sphincter of my room. Yes, these are fever sweats. I am cowering from myself, does that bother you. Are you my father or virginal mother? No? I see, you are the policeman looking for the murderer. Was it patricide you asked? Well, your investigations have begun. What is the term for killing one's uncle? Do you have the celestial evidence? No, No, you're not the policeman; you must be the risk manager? Yes, is that right, no matter. You play the flute with the devil. Your codices are gone. Epi knows. He took them from the father, you see, he wrote them, he is ten thousand years old. Do you remember him? I care not to remember, but I am happily cursed with Life, yes this fever is Life, or is it too much coffee. Yes, my stomach pains me. It's not the coffee and it is. I am a slut. I am the abomination of myself. My narcissism extends to my defilement and that of others. I long to be burned. Where is Barbelo? Gone to lunch? No, she's fucking Epi? That is very interesting. Have your books been burnt? No, no, I buried them. You must ask the messenger...Oh, not me, the psychopomp. Yes, Yes, ask him. My stomach—upset with paternal indigestion. You have

beautiful blond hair; may I run my fingers through it? Paradoxes smell like orange and jasmine.

Eva's a fine one, firm little ass. She reminds me of my sisters. Does that bother you? Risk is a beautiful thing, like Eva's ass and her taut nipples—spectacular nubs of brown understatement, quite delectable. Risk, you sound like the devil. Yes, the devil, humbly your servant. It is a pleasure to finally make your acquaintance. Do you prefer Mr. Devil or just plain Lucifer? May I create my own universe, because this one has caused my entrails great agitation? I don't like it at all. No, that is unfortunate. So, may I scrawl a haiku in the blood of the Archons? May I paint sonnets with feces? Would you allow me to etch iambs with a shotgun? My lyricism, you see, is dependent on those barbaric deeds of creativity. I am a poet of cannibalistic rhyme. I slit throats with the troche's sharp edge and hang men with hexameter. You may be familiar with my work, like the ravishment of the muse and the consumption of her festering hole. Oh, I apologize; this is your job, but dualism seems so petty and pastiche.

Sir, you are like the fire inspector, asking me questions. How do you inspect fire? Is there truth in the red and yellow heat? Combustion is a very interesting subject— it is an inspiring and creative reaction. Fire—the rhapsody of the abyss—fatal liturgy of flame. I see. Yes, it is quite hot in here. You are the sly one. Can I call you Meph? No, too familiar, I apologize. I can hardly move here, would you be a gracious fellow and ignite my cigarette. Good man, thank you very much. You are a very thoughtful fellow to do such a kindness to an invalid of spirit. Incendiaries are much more palatable than the history of decomposition.

Is that music? I love music. You crazy girls. What did you say? 'He's pregnant, or is her dick hard?' Always the pranksters. Ladies, your fingers wander. Ouch. I am not the whore you are looking for. Today is over. The music...arpeggios of decay, trills of despair, fatality of minor ascension, modulation of madness, tonic nothingness, chromatic infinity, alienated octaves, staccatos of sickness. I hear it.

Epi, is that you? Are you playing the guitar, deity of medicine and word? Do you remember Thoth? Thrice what? I have not miscarried hope. There is much left to do, you are right. Oh, your wintry ninths, your choleric mixolydian... Why are you here, and so concerned? Yes, I understand. Why would you take such an interest in me if I were not dead?

Elevator Music

Epi, have you ever had dinner with Death? I think most people have, but few people have realized it. Is Eva there? Does she speak of taking me to the hospital? She seems quite concerned that this fever will not break without taking me with it. You both talk as if I can not hear you. Yes, I am sick. Yes, there is more to the story. Sickness has no equal, nor, like guilt's petulance, it does exist outside of matter or time.

I need a cup of coffee in which to gaze—into its black eye. I need a cigarette so that I may bitterly suck on its lip. You may dream peacefully of ambrosia intoxication while I cough green phlegm from my lungs. Today's clouds hover while my throat stings with bacterial strife. The cars and trucks of our industrial heritage clank and spit over the pavement as a molasses of illness drains from my nose. Clerks type the symbols of communication on proverbial cathodes while disease fills my muscles with its refuse.

I remember, I remember; a cigarette can begin the process of speculation. Its thick smoke irreverently tickling the organism's throat toward the question. The answer oscillates from 'sickness' to 'too many cigarettes.' But eventually, in every case, the evidence of ominous and foul taste can not be denied. It is the taste of illness—that burning throat, the sinuses are obese with infection, nasal tissue are swollen and pregnant with bacteria, the green and golden fluid drips into one's lungs—those bladders of breath becoming a microbial womb. Oh, those insomnial hackings are tethered to the weary diaphragm. Soon, the sickness stifles the lungs. Oxygen flow to the brain becomes a trickle suffocating thought. The world, for the infected, revolves in a cloud of bastardized images. A cough travels through the chakras from anus to crown, and life is slowly spent. A sneeze becomes a soterological event—twenty seconds of messianic relief. Oh, to play in that emerald sea of ailment, where the malignant goop holds hearing hostage, and one hears only the beating of the heart and wheezing of the chest. One becomes of bathysphere of self. The frailty of the body highlights solipsistic thoughts; the world becomes the self, as in a dream. Each ache and pain of the body debunks the outer world. Where is the penicillin for the soul?

I hear you talking, but I can not quite make it out. Epi is against the hospital, self-righteous hacks, eh? But Eva fears the worst. Epi, you are a healer, are you not? You invented medicine, why do you hate your Hippocratic followers? Ah yes, times have changed. And they will change further. Memory is a creative force, a geometric illusion, something true and beautiful and yet lacking any reality. To remember is to sculpt and paint with the past's implements. And I know and remember life, thanks to a bit of persuading by Tie. I know and remember it with the presence of decay. How will my memory be preserved: hung in formaldehyde or on canvas, on an anonymous death certificate or etched on a marble stone, maybe in the neurons of a friend soon to be buried deep in the ground or in the zodiac's twinklings, perhaps on the side of a city bus or written in a police report. You see, life is ninety-percent prepositions, those elements of language that tie it all together. Verbs, nouns and what not are highly overrated.

As the last thing I do, maybe I should publish a new translation of <u>Crime and Punishment</u>, in which I will leave out all of the adjectives, participles, articles, nouns, adverbs, punctuation, and verbs, leaving only the prepositions. This *would be a great feat of art and a tremendous swan song for all those who are left on earth. People would testify to my brilliance, as they sip their coffee and confer with their friends. This masterpiece would represent the relationships themselves—placement transcending place. What do you think, Epi? Do you like the idea? I think it is brilliant. I hate pronouns; they boil everything down to categories. He, she, it, I, whatever—all bunk generalities. What do you think Epi?*

No, Nietzsche could not dance, not a step. No rhythm in that white boy, but his Greek was better than god's. He was a fumbler. How could he dance, he died before Jazz was born. Poor man, he never knew Satchmo or Bessie. My mind is pushed into this peripatetic by my disease. Oh, this neurasthenia of spirit, it is my fault. I fear it. I know it. Time's fecundity spins the clock's hands, presses our organ's functioning and facilitates our decomposition. There is no rhythm without Time, that cock-sucking drummer of the world. But Time depends on place for its harrowing ring to be heard. Time requires vectors of being. Although we can't see it, there is a future beat—that celestial hi-hat of necessity tapping beyond this moment.

What will come of the present? What will the future look like? Eva, how wide will your aging hips grow? How far will your now pert breasts sink to the floor? I can see it: you and I sitting below the apple bows, both of us holding the hand of the other, yet both minds distant and slow— scattered from the presentment of sitting. Do you remember my cracked lips on that first evening, when place and Time were present but not recognized? This, when love was not an abstraction of brain but the juices of the moment. I do not remember that first embrace. I do not recall first running my fingers through your hair. I can not gather that first penetration of your warmth when love pulsed primordially through our corporeal beings. Sitting under the apple boughs, pleasure upon pleasure has faded into today. Each important moment of spontaneous absorption has passed into the past, leaving only the semblance of love—the

258

routine kisses of a 'couple'. Yes, I will chop the vegetables while you heat the skillet. We will dine at six in front of the local news. I will pat your thigh out of obligation, and you will massage my hands reluctantly. For you and I are no longer together, as we sit under those future fruits. We are ghosts for each other. What emotion that is left dwells in creative memory and the calculus of suffering. The beast of change hangs like the apples over us. Neither wishes to take on that burden, for we are apathetic to life. We would prefer the cool domestic mutterings during dinner to the ravagings of the beast.

    And then back to illness. This is life, the present of my present. Life is best felt through sickness, that wandering sickness of the soul where every movement of the finger begs life to cease. Yes, this is life, a fine meal of pork and scallions with the devil. He takes enormous bites of meat without fork or knife. The dinner clings to his whiskers as he demands more. I enjoy watching him eat. I wish I could eat as he does. He cares little for taste or texture; he merely devours and takes pleasure in the destruction. He is not tepid but boiling with energies. I want him to fuck me and leave my stricken corpse draped on the staircase. He will not remember any of it, for eternity is too full with pleasures. Maybe I will watch him ravish Eva through the peephole of mind. She is a scandalous whore, I imagine, and will enjoy the thumping marvelously. And within this fever of mind, I must ask, how long is the devil's cock? Does his prolific nature stem from a three-inch rod, bathing in Freudian overcompensation, or does he have a judicious foot-long monstrosity that splits his victims with passion?

    Hades is a wonderful dancer, I suppose. After dinner he arcs in diabolic circles of lyricism. His body sashays fluidly in steamy step.

    Epi, have you convinced Eva not to take me to the hospital? Yes, my forehead is very damp with sweat. No sir, I can't breath, not at all. But my mind is quite awake. Yes, my eyes are shut tight. It makes no difference. I am quite alive, or maybe not. Perhaps this is death. It is difficult to determine. Eva would be sobbing, I think. Maybe she would be relieved. I would be. Your voices are going silent. The fluid in my ears compels silence. Are you two speaking? Oh, it makes no difference.

He is back, that figure with the codex. He has returned from the darkness. I fear him not. He makes me laugh, all of his pomp and premonition. Did I burp? Excuse me sir, whether you are god or devil, I do not know, but you seem very noble, in an ethereal way. His ominous silhouette holds another document from my past. Oh, maybe it is my memory? It is another codex. It is very ancient, bound in goatskin and etched with important looking symbols of a celestial nature. Why is geometry so important? Plato sure thought so. And Euclid, the guy loved it. I am drunk with sickness. I love it. I am untouchable—inebriated with infection. Life, yes, life is over there, far away. So, how are you, Mr. Shadow? Are you doing well today? I hope so. You know, Mr. Shadow, Barbelo is a bitch, a cunt, the procurer of horror upon horror, and a whiny slut. You seem not to listen. Oh, I see, you want me to read the book. I've got your meaning. Give it here. It is very pretty. Who wrote it? Yes, I know. It is in the hand of a friend. I sure like the Orphites. They seem like a lively bunch, although a bit too raucous for my tastes, with all of that debauchery. Nice paper, is it made of papyrus, the finest from the Egyptian Delta? Yes I remember, it has all been explained. Yes, my life has taken an ironic turn, I mean, the translator and all. Who would have thought? And his death, or should I say murder, to be more exact, very tongue-in-cheek. Yes sir, I will open the codex. Oh, gosh, is this sheet music? I thought these books were much older than that. This could be the oldest written music ever found. This is quite a find, no wonder they've released the hounds. I suppose I am in big trouble. Everyone is looking for me. So this, that I have in my hands, is the Song Itself? I knew it all along. The Archons and the insurance man would both love to get their fingers around this little book. I wonder if Epi can play this music? I would imagine he could; you know, he is a man of *many and diverse talents. It looks to be a very simple song. I am glad that I have committed it to memory, for I buried the music—I mean the requiem.*

Mr. Shadow, I feel like Ivan, I would like to pose a question for you, for you appear to be a wise and very old being; what will become of me? Will I survive this little bout with ill-formed memory or will I perish? Well, I suppose there are more pages, which must mean Hermes will not soon lead me to the river. You know, Sir, I hope to drink from the river soon, for I am tired. My stomach aches with life and guilt. My head beats with all that I remember. The future, too, seems pregnant with vicissitudes—it's as if I can hear a Russian chorus, like elevator music behind all of my thoughts and actions. Yes, it is also called musak. Horrible, horrible stuff, that type of music.

Is that Epi playing his guitar? I thought I heard him earlier. Epi, your tones are like a balm on my wounds. The notes are beautiful. Is this song called Atmos? *If not, it should be. It is filling my lungs. You are a great messenger and healer. How could I have ever doubted you? You are funny, old man. You make me laugh…*

Felling Knowledge

Am I one of the heroic knowers—one of the angelic innocents or the spiteful idiots? Oh, it is much too late for innocence. All has been seen. The gun has been cocked and fired, now hidden in the labyrinth's beginning. The question remains only of heroes and simpletons. I am overtaken with myself. I am bathed in my own subjectivity—trapped and free. Thomas Aquinas ballooned with death—a ravenous overeater, insipid and brilliant, who could not carry a tune. He would have enjoyed the volumeless harpsichord, with its passionless, tinny tone. I would like to rave of homilies and hedgehogs. I hope to write of pantheonic sphincters kissing in the dark. I wish I had the lyrical bent. I wish I could live in noble innocence, preaching a gospel of feces and hope. But hope has died. Her beauty withers with her flesh, as she slouches over a Bloody Mary. Who is to sing? The primordial church looms like a Sudanese Karaoke bar on the Sunset Strip.

Are you tired? I hear your voices. I hear Epi's lute. You are quite good, old man. And my name, do you remember it? Cioran died of Alzheimer's—the goddess of irony gave him his wish. Oh, my stomach shivers with pain. My lungs seize under their own weight. To forget the body... I am dead and yet, not quite. The tree! Epi, throw me your chainsaw. It is a wondrous piece of art, although one is not immediately struck with its subtlety (nothing subtle is ever 'striking' at first sight), it begins, with long contemplation, a sublime aura. It is both phallic and ferocious, and yet, it holds feminine buoyancy. It is a very erotic tool. Thank you. I see the tree. Its limbs hold greater diameter than my waist by ten fold! The sky bleeds through the gnarled branches that are grafted back upon themselves. Oh, the bright gray sky of earth, how I hate you! Tree, you are bare of leaves; they have all fallen to the ground, as soon will your body. Mankind plummeted from grace, so too will your tremendous collection of cells crash to the ground. She's full of gas and ready to go. Pull the cord. The engine whines. Very good. Do away with gloves, for let my fingers and palms blister with knowledge's demise. Do away with goggles, for let my eyes sting—be blinded—with the chips and flying pulp of knowing. Do away with bodily protection all together, so that I may suffer awakening's negation. The bar grinds into the trunk. Wet and white debris engorges the air around us. My arms ache with negation. My body vibrates with the blade. No need for wedges of formality, this is a brutish cut straight into the beast. No stopping. The sharp teeth of chain devour the wood. Straight through! My limbs shake violently with fury. Hee haw, mother-fucker! Father-fucker! Fuck you! Yes, I will leave this forest of discontent with only a few pounds of wood. I will burn the rest—tons and tons of your body. All I need is two thin boards whose stripes oscillate perpendicularly to the tight grain.   Oh, the magnanimous ripples of figure are like fire to the eye— captivating attention and touch.   The boards, soon to be flat, will inspire reflective depth-conveying optical deceit.   How beautiful.   Your body will soon lay on my bench, four boards only an eighth of an inch thick.   Your vicious trunk will be a pile of glowing embers on the forest floor.

What will I do?   I will plane your boards with iron.   I will scrape them with iron.   I will heat an iron pipe to sizzling and shape your knowing entrails.   Your deciduous knowledge will be formed into bust, waist and hips; they will be the sides and back of my instrument.   They will reflect light in gorgeous ribbons.   I will laugh as I fashion you to my whim.   But I will always remember, I can only take you so far before you splinter.   I must admit, Nature has placed restraints on my will.   There exist certain laws that even I must not violate without fracturing repercussions... So, as the process of your redemption continues, I will brace your back with the tree of life.   Will you resent that?   No matter. You need a new type of integrity, for everything decays, but this will prolong the ultimate end of your days.   Then, I will weld the tree of life on your front so that you may only look back.   I will weld it with hide glue in order that you are always reminded of the stallion's spirit.   You will only reflect song off of yourself, and this reflection will pass through life.

I am not bitter, only mad.   Metal wires will be strung over life.   You will reflect their voice, their tonal oscillations. Yes, metal full of fire and song.   From them, you will reverberate the Meta-song.   I am sorry, but you have no choice in the matter.   This does not mean I am not empathetic.   No, I will protect you.   Your glorious exterior will receive several coats of shellac.   Do you know what shellac is?   The lac bug excretes it.   Oh yes, I will cover you with shit, but you will partake in something beautiful and greater than yourself.   You, knowledge, life, fire, and feces will be my instruments of song.   And not just any song, no, the Song Itself!   Are you excited?   Yes, you will be stripped of most of yourself—the vast majority of yourself will be consumed by flame, all of your branches—but you will be able to sing! Your boards will become a vehicle of voice. You should feel lucky; the strings apply more tension over life than over knowledge. Are you happy? You should be.

Epi, is that you? Would you care to help with felling this great maple? No. Then I will do it myself. You have shown me before. I love this saw. It is so powerful. It puffs smoke and howls as it digs into the tree's flesh. What a powerful odor. The fumes, smoke and sawdust infiltrate my lungs. I am coughing with joy. Pour me a glass of wine! Oh, the song, spinning out of wood and fire. You lead to the pleromal vacuum.

I miss you, mother. You who was suspended outside of memory. This is your song crashing to the forest floor and wreathed with the chainsaw's wailing. Your song spins through the fallen limbs, around my naked fingers and through the air. It is not a song of righteousness or fear but of the members of life and knowledge.

Epi, at the foot of my bed? Did you hear the branches snap? Your guitar sounds so sweet. The notes weave around my body. I feel lighter, as though the weight of my material body has been infused with levity. My nostrils are clear. My throat is free of strife. My lungs—the thick sludge that clung to them has evaporated. My arms and legs are no longer stiff with toxins. I am cured. Is this the song you transcribed thousands of years ago in some strange Egyptian cave? When did you first hear it? Or did you write it yourself? Music is something that must be experienced to be heard. One must allow the tones into the bone and muscle in order to know its harmony. So many sit passively hoping that the Song will come to them. But now, as I lay smothering in death, I can hear *it. Yes, I can hear it with my fingertips. I can hear it with sternum and biceps. I can hear the melodic truth with my rib cage and heart. Or am I mad? Have I lost all sense of the world? I hope I have. I hope I never recover...*

10.

Epi sat at the edge of the futon strumming a guitar. Eva stood wide-eyed behind him, her checks red and puffy with tears. "The chile's eyes are fuckin' open!" Epi shouted.

"Alive?" I asked, my head feeling foggy and my limbs gaining their earthly weight.

"If you were still alive, would I take this much interest in ya?" Epi howled with laughter. Eva grimaced with his comment. "Do ya remember yar name yet?" Epi asked.

"Yes."

Reprieve and Rapture

"I told ya that ya'd build a geeter," Epi stated just before he slammed the door. The air in the room was sucked out as he left. A woody thump and a cacophony of open strings sounded from the hallway. "Shit!" Epi blurted, hitting the guitar on the doorframe. Eva chuckled at Epi's accident. "I hear ya'll in there, it ain't that fuckin' funny," he bleated. "Don't forget, I'm the one that saved your ass. Ya should be fuckin' thankin' ol' Epi." His voice trailed off as he walked down the hallway.

Eva sat on the futon with her fingers on my forehead. "I'm so glad you're awake. Your fever just broke. I was so worried," she spoke softly, as though if her voice rose anymore, some dark force would catch her words and blow the fever back into my lungs. Her fingers felt cool and soothing. She swept them from my brow down across my cheek and off of my chin. "Epi told me I had nothing to fear," Eva sniffled. "What would I do without you? I thought about *us* the whole time that you were sick. I even tried to paint your picture so that if I lost you, I would still be able to remember what you looked like and who you were. But the whole thing made me even more upset—more sad and angry. The whole time I felt like I was painting a portrait of a dead person. I stared and stared at your face: the thin wrinkle on your forehead, the curve of your nose, the outline of your cheeks, the pale colors of your complexion flaming evenly into each other, the wisps of your hair laying motionless and flat on the pillow, your pink lips—dry and starting to crack with the cold, and your eyes—always half open and rolling back and forth with fever." She kissed me on my temples.

"Your skin was so hot. I only touched it once. You were burning up. I thought I might burn myself if I touched it again. I was scared—scared of what was inside of you. I wanted to take you to the hospital, but Epi wouldn't let me. He said you had to burn inside—part of you had to be incinerated, die. I don't know what he said, I'm just glad you're OK. He forced the telephone from me when I went to call for an ambulance. I was so angry and scared I hit him. I was so upset."

I picked her hand up and began stroking her fingers.

"Do you want some soup or something? You haven't eaten anything for a long time," she asked. I nodded. Eva stood from the bed, drawing her skirt in out of habit as she got up. She walked to the kitchen wiping her eyes.

"I tried going to work for a couple of days, but I was so upset I accidentally broke mugs and was short with the customers," she continued from the kitchen. "Zoe finally sent me home, because I was driving people away." I heard the scraping sound of a can opener tearing into metal and the copper clank of a pot being set on the stove.

"The world is just going crazy," she elaborated. "That gang of kids has been setting things on fire. There are police officers everywhere. Those street kids even tried to burn Epi's shop, but his girls drove them away. I don't know what those kids want. They're just crazy."

The room held utter disorder. Cups and dishes were scattered over the floor. Paintbrushes were strewn

266

everywhere. Clothes were piled in the corners. A glass of beads rested overturned, most of its contents defused throughout the room. An oil painting lay on the floor; green and gold snakes wove a frame around the central motif. It had been a portrait, but, before the paint could dry, a hand had swept through—five finger streaks of paint running together were all that were left of the visage.

She walked out of the kitchen with the bowl of soup. Steam wafted from the rim. The room filled with the savory odor of onions and garlic. "I hope chicken noodle is OK," she apologized. "It's all I have, but Epi got you to eat it. You must be full of noodles and chickens." Eva chuckled nervously, "I'm so glad you're OK. Epi sat with you for over two days. I don't think he slept a wink. You know, he really cares about you. I was even a little jealous. He even got you to eat. I couldn't. There's something special and scary about Epi. He played the guitar for you, he said that it would make you better."

She handed the bowl to me. The sides of the bowl were warm. I cupped them in my hands and blew some of the heat off of the surface. "Thank you, baby," I cooed. I began slurping the broth down in full gulps. "This is great," I muttered through glossy lips.

Eva felt my forehead again and announced the results, "Oh, your temperature has gone way down. I can feel it. Epi saved your life. That song was so strange, like nothing I've ever heard before. It was sort of like really old music, but sometimes it didn't even seem like music, more like talking. He called it the 'Shadow of the Song.' I don't know. It both made me a little uncomfortable and put me to sleep at the same time. I'm not describing it well. Epi said that you brought it back to him, whatever that means. He talked about how he owed it to you to play it. Epi said that it would make you better—calling it a remembering. I guess it did help you." She tucked the comforter around my body. "He said something else weird, I guess he always says weird stuff, but this made no sense. He said that you had built that guitar. Epi rambled about two trees. It was kind of funny. I didn't know you were done with your guitar. He always speaks with so much confidence, but everything he says is kind of nuts," she rambled.

"I haven't finished it, but Epi doesn't care much for the concept of Time."

Her eyes began welling up with tears, "I'm so glad you're OK. I was so worried that I'd lose my other half as soon as I'd found you. Now I can shower you with kisses and love you forever." Her red cheeks elevated into a grin, and her watery eyes reflected my own image. Stray black hairs dangled from her head like an earthly halo.

"You're beautiful and good," I told her. "How long have I been with the fever?"

"I don't know. Time sort of disintegrated. Less than a week, though."

"How's Glaucon?"

"Not well," her grin evaporated. "I'm worried about him. He's been wandering around like a crazy man. Sometimes he'll sit at the coffee shop, but not often. He even smoked inside. When I told him he couldn't do that, he didn't seem to notice me. It was like he was in another world. He came to visit you. Glaucon just sat on the futon and mumbled things at you, like he was talking to himself. He kept talking to you in the third person. He's not well at all. He picked up one of my paintbrushes and tapped it constantly on the floor. He even took it with him. I mean, I don't care about the brush, but it goes to show that he's really unconscious." Eva took the empty soup bowl back to the kitchen. "He kept talking about some street kid he beat up. That didn't sound like the Glaucon I know, who's so meek and generous. He also talked about his friend who is in a coma. This is what really scared me; he said something about you as a witness. Then he'd talk about 'pulling the plug.' That got me so worried, I almost called the police. I just want everything to go back to normal."

She burrowed her face into my neck. Her warm sent of jasmine and soap elated my nostrils. I wanted to comfort her. I held her tightly and rocked our bodies back and forth.

Her confusion concerning the world's events and her joy of my recovery gave me strength. Arrogantly, I thought I could be her protector. I would defend her from the madness of the world. My arm would shield her from tribulation. It would give my life meaning. My stomach tingled with affection for this lovely girl. Why did she care so much? How does her heart deflect the cynicism of the world? What did she see in me? Eva possessed an enormous wealth of compassion and creative beauty. That night I saw beyond her material comeliness and into the illuminating grace of her soul. She worked for Life. She worked in Providence. She represented the world with flashing depth and colorful symbol. She spoke with innocent levity and passion. Her inner spark mocked her corpuscular beauty. There were countless girls that possessed a similar pulchritude of face and body, but none that could compare in spirit.

"I love you," I whispered into her hair. Her chest began heaving with sobs.

"I love you too," Eva moaned into my shoulder, "I love you so much." She looked up. Her face was streaked with tears. I kissed her; her lips tasted salty and wonderful.

"I'm sorry I've been so far away," I squeezed out through the emotional constriction of my throat. "I'm sorry for everything. I will be here for you." Tears clouded my eyes. I did not attempt to hold them back, for they held honesty and truth, things that were foreign and good.

I held her tightly that night, as tightly as I could. I would not let her go. I longed that our souls would touch, to mingle and mix. I hoped to become part of her, taking part in her inner life. Our arms flexed with the pressure of our desires. Our oneness cloaked us from the world. Joy was our subject, all else disappeared into non-being. The singularity of *us*—the ecstatic presence of being—stood beyond language's petty representations. Time and History evaporated in the flames of our embrace. I sighed within the tears. I had found a place that took no part in geographical encumbrances or spatial malaise. The unison of our breath was the only sound in the room—the only tempo of being.

Living Witness

I slept dreamlessly. Either Tie did not see well into the future, or he had spoken in metaphor, or I had died.

We woke late in the day. All physical symptoms of my malady had vanished. The sun's rays penetrated the white filter of clouds, casting a cool and luminous light into the apartment. I cooked bacon, then eggs in the sizzling grease, and finally toast as Eva reined in the entropy of the apartment. Smiles, mild jokes and tender affection filled the morning. Once the air was filled with the odor of food and all was put in its designated place, we relaxed on the balcony—huddled together under a brightly knit blanket. We laughed good-naturedly about our eclectic friends; Eva spoke about obtaining a cat—perhaps a tabby from the Humane Society; I recounted to her my vision of the tree and speculated as to whether Epi would take me as a fulltime apprentice (and start paying me). That morning I lived in the Life Cosmos. The conversation meandered to renting a larger apartment, then to saving in order to buy a house, along with other mundane domestic hopes. Every cell of my body brimmed over with invigorating possibilities. I paid no heed to the shade of unfinished business in the corner of my mind. The light of that day was too full of love and sparkling life to give any attention to the powers of darkness. Eva and I even joked about ceasing our dirty habit of smoking.

The following three days beamed with joy. I spent the daylight hours finishing my guitar with Epi: applying, sanding and polishing the lacquer; gluing the neck to the body; gluing the bridge; fitting the nut and saddle; attaching the tuners and strings; and playing the guitar. Epi's shop became, for me, a home of tranquility—a temple of silent meditation. Even the Sibyls grew fondly in my heart; their merry ways shed light on free-spirited action, sublime compassion and aplomb joy. Once the sun set below the West Hills and Eva and I rejoined each other, time enclosed around the *us*. We strolled through the neighborhood chatting of a future life, hand-in-hand, like giddy honeymooners. I would massage her shoulders and she my callusing hands. A pastoral contentment hung over us. Our affinity had become a protective barrier from the elements of darkness. No vacuous and profound philosophical questions were promulgated through nihilistic lips, instead life was pregnant with affectionate solace. Even Zosimos spoke only of happy memories of his grandmother's unconditional love and the joy of running through his ancestral home as a boy.

The only concern that infiltrated the levity of my life was of Glaucon's well-being. I did not see him until the third day after my fever broke. Jake told us that Glaucon had been seen wandering along the river's east bank—under the freeway by decaying warehouses. Rumors told of Glaucon living under overpasses and in city parks. I began searching for him, talking to homeless men and women concerning my friend's whereabouts. Soon, I started losing my newly regained sleep over Glaucon's madness. I knew that I had played an important role in his mad drama. I realized that I must visit Sophia. She tied Glaucon and I together—we were a triumvirate of pain, and it would be through her that I could reconcile with him and History. I felt compelled to ask her forgiveness; it was my fault she lay comatose in the sterility of a hospital bed. I also knew, however, that in all likelihood she would not answer my request.

I rode the trolley to the hospital, passing a group of kids in oversized pants agilely kicking a hacky-sack, a gray-haired woman persistently pushing a walker down the side-walk, a homeless teen tapping out complicated rhythms on the bottom of an empty five-gallon detergent bucket, a toddler running awkwardly with outstretched arms to her mother and a prostitute clutching her threadbare coat tightly around herself in the cold rain. The orange streetcar was little faster than walking—stopping every other block to pick up others who avoided walking in the rain. A couple stepped onto the vehicle, a head of lettuce and other vegetables peeking over the brim of their bags. They sat holding hands and smiling with fat red cheeks. Across from them sat a young man dressed all in black: black slacks, black turtleneck, black wool coat—his face veiled by long black bangs and a book by Heidegger. Giggling in the back sat two middle school girls in matching pink rain slickers; they spoke only in rhyme and excited kicks into the open air. Coughing at the front sat a frizzy-haired woman biting into her nails.

I exited the trolley and sat on the front steps of the hospital in order to collect my thoughts and smoke a cigarette. As I sat thinking, Glaucon limped over to me from across the street. A pervasive aroma of sweat and urine reeked from his body. His hair had grown into a mangy mass. His beard hairs stood in twisted disarray. Webs of red veins clung to his eyes. His pupils were dilated with mad intent. "Are you ready?" he asked frankly, looking straight through me. I nodded affirmation. We stepped into the hospital.

Neither of us spoke or looked at the other, until we had entered her room. She lay in the hospice ward, in a room with three other dying patients. The stench of iodine and chlorine overwhelmed the senses. The hospital was waiting for her to die. Machines perpetuated the functions of her body out of habit. I did not know whether the apparatuses did all of the work of keeping her alive or if some primitive part of her brain continued to send crucial messages to her organs. The machines hummed and 'beeped' with electric determination. Her chest seemed to rise and fall mechanically. Bags of clear solution dripped nutrients into her atrophied veins. Her skin was translucent; one could see the green rivers of blood trickle underneath. Hollows gaped where cheeks should have been. Her closed eyes rested below cavities of skull. I gazed upon this tomb of bone and flesh—this that I had once called 'sister'.

Glaucon looked at me with a stony face and articulted "You will be my witness. I need someone to testify." I nodded solemnly, although I did not know exactly what he meant. He removed the mechanism that was listening to her heart and placed it over his own. The machine seemed not to know the difference between the body of the dying girl and Glaucon's. Then he unplugged the machines, except for the heart monitor. Each cord popped from the socket. Glaucon placed his fingers over the girl's jugular checking for a pulse. He put his ear to her hollow chest to listen for life. After a few minutes, Glaucon, tears heavy in his eyes, turned to me and whispered, "Feel. She's dead." He took my hand. His nails were black with living in the street. The wrinkles of his skin were accentuated with dirt. He placed my hand on her neck. I felt no indication of blood flow—not even a shallow movement of life. A low-pitched groan reverberated from Glaucon. He clenched his eyes shut.

Glaucon's anguish had summoned a nurse. The nurse waddled urgently into the room. "Out of the way! Out of the way!" She pushed me from the bedside. I grabbed Glaucon by his coat and pulled. "Get out of here," the nurse shouted. "Leave before I have to call the cops. I know what you two've done. Now scram!" I dragged Glaucon from the room as the nurse continued, "If you two don't leave now, I'll remember your faces. Then you'll be in a whole lot-a messiness."

I pulled my friend towards the door in order to escape the police and the hospital authorities. But, standing at the threshold, I looked at the corpse and pleaded, "Please forgive me."

The nurse turned from the body and consoled, "Somebody had to do it, sugar. At least you is family."

I felt no obligation to humor man's law and be judged for what we had just done. I led Glaucon out of the hospital and down several blocks in order to evade any pursuers.

Glaucon fell to his knees and began pummeling his fists against the sidewalk. "What, what, what is going on," he raved through clenched teeth. "Why is this happening? Why!"

I put my hand on his shoulder. He batted it away.

"Everything was fine before you arrived," he hollered. "I want it to end—everything to stop." He stood and faced me. "Make it stop. Can you live with it?" his bitter breath accosted my senses, and his penetrating eyes forced me to turn away. Then, he left.

Striving Beyond Ogdoad

I wanted to help Glaucon, but knew not how. Madness had consumed him. The tragedy of the apartment fire coupled with his action under the street had singed his reason. His condemning eyes continued to burn in my memory. What was I supposed to do? Did he know the truth of that evening? Had I betrayed him? The fire of thought was charring what I had built with Eva. I was left with doubt and despair. There was a passionate righteousness to my sin, which he may have been unaware. I tried to rationalize what I did or the role I played in the murder. Confusion still reigned; had I severed the snake who eats his own tail?

"Why was Prometheus punished?" bellowed a voice from across the street. It came from a boy, who obviously called the street his home. I have wondered why so many homeless youth have made this wet city their residence. Was it decent social services, cheap illicit substances or was it that this town is some spiritual Mecca for those who have no place? The boy's face was red with the cold. Every inch of his clothing was torn or stained by material deficit. He held his meager profession in front of his body—a black electric guitar, chipped and scraped by the elements and continuous use. A small battery operated amplifier had been duct taped to his cowboy hat (like an exaggerated Hasidic prayer box). The boy wore sunglasses even though daylight had long been replaced by the phosphorous illumination of streetlights.

"Why, Why, Why was he punished?" the boy screamed to people rushing by him, the by passers trying to escape his esoteric song. He seemed not to strum the guitar, but rather beat the instrument. Remarkably loud and distorted tones oozed from the small amp. "Why? Was it good? Was it right? To tether the dude that gave us light?" The street child shook his head, and the amplifier followed to the pounding rhythm of his music. "Knowledge, ain't she a bitch. And Time ain't just an itch. Yeah, yeah, yeah..." he continued.

I made my way to him and placed a dollar in the boy's decaying guitar case. He smiled.

"Who could have known that knowledge is just a bone...er..." he explained under the thrashing chords, "What was Pro thinkin', or was he just dinkin'? Bind that fucker, 'cause he made us all suckers. We'd be better off, to have our minds all soft... and mushyyyyy, yeah, yeah, yeah." The urchin began to yodel. It had been some time since my ears had been graced by yodeling. It was awful. "I'd rather be a plant, or an elephant, than to be a dude, with knowledge too rude. Fire ain't so great, nor to tempt fate, but gimme a gun, and I'll kill everyone, yeah, yeah, yeah. I got a grip of fire, but I'm still in all this mire. So fuck the police, and gimme release, yeah, yeah, yeah..."

Upon closer examination of this punk-rock minstrel, I realized that he may not be a he. This street child could also be a flat-chested girl. The child's shoulders were thin and without muscle, its neck was taut with veins and tendons— not a trace of excess, its fingers griped the guitar's neck in long ambiguous talons, and its chin and cheeks bore not a trace of hair. This was a clean-shaven boy, a sinewy girl or a pre-pubescent musician. But the confidence of this figure betrayed its age; it held itself with sure composure, although a bit out of tune.

The androgynous bard's song came to an end with a frenetic barrage of feedback, produced by it holding the guitar above its head next to the amplifier. Pulsing waves of electronic screeching emulated from the child's head aggravating my ears. "Embrace the abyss. Embrace the abyss," it screamed. "I love sympathetic resonance!!!"

The minstrel then began a new song, one a bit less caustic to the ears. The instrument's tones were softer and rounder. The notes were thick, although still distorted and unclean. It chanted its words in front of the backdrop of chords,

> The winter moon rises with the lugubrious tide. Gravity upon gravity bellows from matter and time. Oh Time—Cronos—you ate your children. Why do we worship you so? Why do we supplicate with clocks and watches? You were a bad father. Time to History to Time and infinity fucks it all. And my thoughts wither into themselves, the harvest moon a memory. Petulant eyes of dreaming conscience, hollowed in their sockets, they see neither the angels of future's passing nor the quill of past light. Knowledge of soul and self drifts upon waves of moony might—droops under hymns of steel's cold flush. Meaning wanes between memory's jests and its pale turpitude. Profound doubt…Profound…doubt of self and world vacant of love's thick lips. Oh, harrowed elan in song's bitter maze and lustful memory's a-tonal whip. The horror of action's bleeding curtains shielding life's dry spite. And if tigers of melancholy would eat alive the hearts of politic man, then my eyes would fill with happy tears, and resentment of life would give way. For in horror's apocalypse, I pray, to bury malevolent Life. I sing the song destruction and pound the drum of piss. The body protonic—the murder's end—sublimity and fusion: anguish in the tepid feats of petty soliloquy. I drool and spit on harangue of life.

Eschatology beaming plenty of lifeless matter lying—acting in the drama of non-being. Raise a toast to immediate cataclysm—to end the rapture NADA. A coitus of epiphany and blood—this menstruation of fear. For I walk upon the moon's feminine shadow, across hips of seductive death whose cliffs of pleasure sink to the cush of abdomen, then nipple summit, to finally coast to auricular despair. Cotton swabs and lunch pails draw no lateral derision, nor scrumptious ass or plasma torch beckon twists of contemplation. But dilated heart on love's black eye and the endless hum of freeway traffic evaporate the course of polyphony. Can your ear elate to lunar furrows? Does your cilia prick-up under Calliope's warmth? Can you sing Life from Jupiter's pores? Or is your thumb's delight the veil of muscular lightless contractions? You and I are done with this—gamma rays and baby's breath—polychords and grammarians—you and I curse through vapid lips, you and I are the foreign born. Shelly could not sing, nor Byron play, nor Colridge dance on air. Atmosphere thin and lax reckoned with oedipal flair. Moonlight coughs and wheezes. Words grow weary of themselves. Your sister's thighs grow cold and dead. Narcissism sanctifies your bones. A cigarette glows in shadow's diversion. Dark halls erect memory's burden—stony black of celestial plight. A silver dollar buys beer at twilight. A naturalist moans at Neptune's tears and commercials of bulimic lust sell nihilistic dreams. But the pregnant mind pleads for midwife, thoughts of spastic pain. Go baptize in urinal and fetid cisterns. To you a greeting card of white light burns disgust and apathy—the symbols known and sublime.   Anarchy's redoubling mirth resounds the mushroom cloud's bloom—cities' flattened passions.   To be in Providence's gaze, then cold shoulders of grassy haze; I am your lover; I am your spark; I sing the body of fear. Through lacerations of mind and ulcers of spirit the dread of life peers.   Defoliate your dreams and pluck nightmares from the trees.   Let the moon reflect your thoughts, for in your bedroom stands the spirit to haunt remembrance and loin. Ejaculate soft hormonal chants—spit the body from the soul. Orphite rites on monadic curse snakes redemption and rebirth.   Long red rays of hermetic casts will harbor pubescent regrets.   Tempests of urban unrest and fiery reflections bleed from the cards. You and I will defile the moon, leaving her sore and dumb.   You and I will witness her death—pungent and callous seeming.   A corpse will sing the solace of night—pulling the tide toward apogee. Zenith of sun in rice fields will hum your song of bitter toil. Work is to work is to work is to breathe in a vacuum of meaning, then divert the mind with self-abuse.   Sing in vacuous space the silence of your intellect and the barbarism of your deeds. In what sense can ravished moonlight cleanse? In what sense do your words wash ignominy from your base soul?   You and I are tired of this.   You and I will dance in the wind.   You and I will joke of ovum bloom and parish within the transcendental conflict.   For you and I are tempered in confusion and polished with self-disgust. But you and I share not the center of the words or patricide's humbling light.   Go publish your woes to archonal eyes—promulgate fading history on city winds, for reckoning writes words of truth on their caloric skins...

The child beat on the already abused instrument. A string snapped, yet the youth continued to batter tone from the guitar. Thick chords of refracted sound filled the sparse street. The night had grown empty of people; everyone was at home, except for those who did not have one. Eva was probably concerned with my whereabouts, but I could not yet face her. I could feel that resolution would come tonight—a reckoning with both the living and the dead. The musical youth bobbed its amplifier-head to the self-produced music. I could only imagine that its eyes were shut tight from the lack of audience. It must have been playing for me and no one else—somehow a mirror of my own confused thoughts. I placed a five-dollar bill in the case and left.

"Thank you," spoke the youth in appreciation, "It's all for you, you know. Epi has provided and Eva has loved."

Frightened by the words, I hurried from the scene. I slipped on a curb due to my haste, bludgeoning my knee. Regaining my balance, I thought of the dead girl, of Glaucon's unstable mind, of my precious Eva, of the mysterious and crass luthier, of Zosimos—fat with his ideas, and I thought of the book, the one that I brought to this city. Knowledge is a fickle bitch; she is merely information, not a call to action. Action marches from another direction altogether. Sometimes, however, waiting in the right place is the most profitable course.

The world went dark as strong fingers trapped my appendages...

Hebdomadal Abduction

When I think about the concepts of Heaven and Hell, certain questions always drift to consciousness's surface: Do you really think that Life is a metaphor for something else? Do you really believe there is a metaphysics of suffering? And when these questions have floated upon my mind sufficiently, I usually laugh out loud, even if I am alone. These questions bobbed upon my thoughts as the many fingers of my entrapment dug into my body. I felt every digit's strength press and immobilize my material freedom. The pain of their force echoed through my body, but I laughed like a drunken stoic.

I could not see the stars, for the night had grown absolutely black. A canvas bag of some sort had been placed over my head. My abduction was absolute—my abduction by absolute night. Within this lightless kidnapping, I looked back upon my struggles and pleasures, abstracting from them hovering thoughts. The hands of my captors could not shackle the flight of my mind.

I thought: *Can one excavate meaning from Life's pandemonium? Some aesthetes, the monks and nuns of world-denouncing, call the world an illusion, a falsity or an evil. They retreat into their desert cloisters (or behind blossoming careers in advertising). This is the life of solitude and silence. These people hope to live as far from material experience and the lusts as possible. Although a human made of blood and bone can only emancipate him or herself from the bodily temperaments via death or walking with God, these world-denouncers come closer than most to the negation of desire. I raise my glass to those who begun severing the umbilical of material relationships. Good for those lads and lasses who have found for themselves solace in solitude. That clean arid desert air benefits many people. There are others, often spoken of as less wise or revered, who embrace all that is sensually and emotionally elating. These folks often burn out quickly, their souls a tinder of passion and zeal. Sometimes one can find these people with embers still glowing at age fifty, usually because they have switched, at some point, to a less combustible means of living—often attending twelve-step meetings rather than the more caloric bacchanals of their youth. If, however, the fire of youth has not been suppressed some, then the entire organism is calcified before age thirty. These fiery spirits ignite life with sensual extravagance, yet are self-consumed prematurely. Then there are those lukewarm souls who live between the extremities. Their lives are neither the tremendous fiery columns nor the slow burning coals of monastics. Instead, they burn evenly. Their daily toils are unaccustomed to conflagrations, yet their weekends sometimes possess the short surface-scalding passions of gasoline. Every once in awhile their own flames are whipped up by the external winds of life's tragedies and elations, but only in times of the occasional tempests.*

Where, then, goes a Napoleon, a Ziggy Stardust, a Hume, or a Galileo in these categories of combustion? Where does my life fit in the classification of heat? Which life is better, the dizzying flames of cataclysm or the embers still burning in the stove for breakfast? One could generate numerous other divisions of combustion—differing forms of fire: flames of narcissistic passions, coals of meekness, blazes of humanitarian zeal, fearful embers of doubt, and more. All would be metaphoric half-truths. I tend to be jealous of the fanatic's confident actions. Where as the pessimist's tedious nihilism is not to my liking (but more to my constitution). I hate backgammon, even though Hume makes so much sense. Intuition rebel from him. My ears dilate with the chromatic rapture of Coltrane and the haunting tones of Palistrina. The adolescent angst of ELF members always amuses me. I hold respect for the self-restraint of Epictitus' broken limb, but care not for his scribbling. I laugh at Diogene's marketplace antics, but would find a more intimate place for my own self-pleasure. I, I, I, and them, them, them—the only division. Oh, what if self could melt into the bonfire of macrocosm? To quote Hamlet, "Words, Words, Words..." Kant was a twit,

Heidegger a Nazi, Pascal a holy fool, and Hegel an esoteric bore. Line them up in front of the firing squad, for they give me nothing. At least Socrates possessed wit and never wrote, otherwise he would be joining his colleagues.

The abstract fingers carried me. I could feel the rain bleed through the canvas sack to my eyebrows and cheeks. The revving engines of cars and trucks sped by. I even heard a voice quietly ask a silent interlocutor if the police should be called. The light drizzle tapped upon the sidewalk and overhangs. I could hear my gaolers' rhythmic breath. There were four of them. They did not speak. Their scents mixed through the bag on my head—tangy body odors of rose perfume and musk. There was at least one woman in the bunch. I sensed the unpitying sharpness of her feminine fingers and the sensual bitterness of her breath.

I was trapped, although I was not scared. With my liberty compromised, I had time to think and be. My mind wandered further: *What is the Universal? Surly not Life or Being, for some things are not, and those things which are so very different. Life holds so many variations of itself. Death, perhaps, is the only universal. No one, however, can speak with experiential knowledge of Death's essence. If one does speak of the shape and structure of Death, they are called 'fool' or 'liar'. Those few who have sallied through the catacombs of death are all dead: Orpheus, Dante, Jesus, Odysseus, etc.—mythic men who did not experience death even while on holiday in Hades. These are not men who hold the testimony of nothing within their lungs. Neither words nor thought captivate the true sublimity of Death, for how does one express the Nothing? Thought, something that is not a universal, can not do justice to that which is a universal. There are some dirty old dead men who have attempted to raise thoughts to universals. Some harangue over a priori concepts that never change, which are unconditioned. Geometry is a beautiful idea, sketching breadthless length on mind's template, but only dolts conceive these figures as participating in anything called*

Life.   These fetching ghosts of geometry are bits lost in fettered minds.

So, one is begged toward the Unconditional, with all of its pomp and grandeur.   I am very much conditioned. There are so many 'ifs' in my head that my whole being is a hypothesis.   Yet the Nothing is unconditional.   There are no 'if' statements hedging the Nothing.   And what is the Nothing if not infinite?   To say that the Nothing is infinite is merely expressing the Nothing's formlessness.   One can not capture it, as I have been captured.   One can not build with bricks or words around the Nothing, which is synonymous with Death. Even reporting of its boundless nature is speaking falsely of its pervasive nature.   One possesses no pure means of conveying ideas of the Nothing.   The closest experiences that one may have to simulate the unfathomable Nothing are dreamless sleep and music.   Music, of all the arts, participates least in form, and the form that it does have is the most abstract and primally moving—moving toward the Nothing.   But music moves asymptotically toward the Nothing, never actually reaching it (there are laws to music- a nomos).   I speak of asymptotes; I mean them only figuratively.   So you see the problem of these words; everything to man is an illusory metaphor.   Words are so inadequate—impudent—as is thought, to capture the Truth.

Coming back to mud and happiness, one clearly sees that the infinite negates both happiness and tragedy.   Our greatest accomplishments pale when hailed by the infinite. History itself suffocates under the seas of infinity.   Its bloated and dead carcass floats up to the surface now and then in order for us to witness its absurdity.   Time and place are eroded by the infinite, therefore borders of human history and personal events wash away—cleansed away and baptized in her negating waters.   But let us pose a hypothetical (i.e., a conditional statement); if the cosmos is not infinite (and so contracts upon itself there by creating borders), then would you smile—feel better—that History has a chance?   Would the suffocation of the Universe make you happy and content?   It would give the fanatics their

Armageddon. Does cosmic death send religious chills down your spine? Let me add some small piece; all would still be suspended in the Nothing, both beginning and end. So what do petty inconveniences matter? What matters the horrors of my actions, for they will pass into the Nothing? What matters your traffic-jam agitation or burnt-toast hassle? What matters the egregises of murder, rape and lie in a world without unconditioned History? I emphatically shout: EVERYTHING. I am conditional and limited in the now—even my metaphysics.

I worry about myself, although in a somewhat perverse manner. The dark-fire of emotion and strife sear my consciousness. This is undeniable. I want and love and sink and hate. I may be bounded by the Nothing, but I am not merely nothing. The cacophony of internalization pounds my being. This is the height of my mortality. I seethe with life—the conditioned. I have embraced the great tragedy—Life, the great error of being. Even as Scipio was suspended within the perfection of the heavens, he could not take his eyes off of the game being played on Earth. And laughing at the absurdity of this place, I will shout, quoting the philosopher, "This is the best of all possible worlds," for this is the only possible world, mine.

My ears could hear the defiance of plaster walls and a wooden floor. Hollow thumps of my captors' boots against the boards penetrated my ears. My head hit a doorframe. "Can I have a cigarette?" I asked politely. An elbow struck my ribs as reply. Into the echoes of a stairwell I was escorted. The sounds of breath and footfalls reverberated in an acoustic spiral around me. Several turns upward did we wind, at least nine stories. My biceps ached with the strain of the fingers. I felt welts rise flooding with blood on my head. I coughed and smelled my own foul breath, captured within the canvas. It had been a considerable amount of time since I last ate, and my breath stank of it. My tongue was dry and swollen, for I had not drank anything in hours, except for smoke.

This abduction was not done in the style of insurance men, nor were my captors common street rabble or mere hoodlums, for these people were well disciplined in silence. There was a professional air to these people, yet the police or FBI had no reason to bring me bound and cloaked into a musty apartment building. Demons would have chosen a more torturous and spectacular show for my imprisonment. The only other possible group that might have found value in my captivity were the Archons, those mad, focused human beings attempting to promulgate their language to the great unwashed. Only the Archons would be so crude and structured in their kidnapping. They finally had me, I realized. Men and women of the new language now possessed infinitesimal me. I grew a bit anxious after gaining a more concrete idea of my predicament. Then, I absurdly hummed Mr. Parker's *Ornithology,* frequently straying from the appropriate tones. What else was there to do? The Holy Spirit would have appreciated it, and even my stomach felt at ease.

The Song Itself

I heard the metal clamor of a hatch open, then the cold pressure of the night spin around my body. My captors pushed me up a ladder and through the building's roof. The wind possessed more power here than on the firmness of the ground (that had its protection of trees and buildings). The zephyr that had been predominant below was a powerful wind full of icy chill at this unimpeded elevation. My clothes whipped in a frenzy. The darkness was filled with sirens and shouts—a clamor of terror had begun. Frozen hands snatched my wrists and bound them with rope behind my back. An anonymous entity kicked my legs from under me, and I crashed unbalanced on to a bench.

Then, these fingers that had stolen my liberty, slowly summoned my vision by removing the darkness. With the shackles of vision removed, I gazed upon a crew of fanatics—these, the Archons and the Demiurge himself. I was the hostage and supposed supplicant of their present will. The Archons were all dressed in black coats and pants that blended in with the night. A few wore dark stocking caps, another wore a dented bowler, and two wore no headgear at all. They were a mixture of humanity: women and men of all heights, ages and races. They all stared at me with furrowed contempt. Agathon sat at the center of his forces wearing only a sweatshirt that bore the incomprehensible traces of a slogan whose letters had peeled off or disintegrated through numerous washings. He was an old man with hollow cheeks and azure eyes. His eyes glowed with self-assured focus. His thin wisps of white hair shivered in the wind. I recognized him as my father's collaborator. I recalled delivering him my father's essays, but didn't remember ever seeing them together.

I began laughing. Nothing is serious anymore. My stomach hurt with the laughter. My eyes watered at the sight of them. One of the Archons, a short, obese Asian woman, walked over to my bench and slapped me across the face with the back of her hand, then retreated to her former place in the formation. This did not stop my discordant laughter, in fact, I was overwhelmed with levity. My gut ached with the absurdity of the situation.

I regained my composure and asked for a cigarette, "They're in my breast pocket," I added. Agathon nodded. The same lady stepped forward and retrieved the cigarette. She stuck it in my mouth and lit it. I had been hoping that they would remove the rope from my hands, but they did not. Instead, I had not the pleasure of holding the implement of my addiction. Smoking without the use of one's hands takes much of the satisfaction out of the endeavor. Not only does one lack the ritual of drawing the narrow cylinder to and from the mouth, but one has the annoying burden of smoke wafting into the eyes and nose. Luckily, the wind spared my senses this harassment.

"Hello," I chuckled.

The Demiurge smiled. He pointed to a tall, gangly Archon. "Hello," the Archon gesticulated.

"I will not be so obtuse as to ask why I am here, for I presume to know. But I have not decided whether I will tell you or not," I said.

Agathon kept his grin, despite my insolence. He spoke mildly in his esoteric language. His translator communicated, "You have knowledge of the whereabouts of the codex. You must tell us where it is." The translator sterilely announced the words, failing to capture Agathon's gentile intonation.

"Why?" I asked.

Agathon spoke in the foreign tongue, and his man translated, "For two reasons. First, if you don't, we will kill you, your lady friend and Epi. Secondly, you would be standing in the way of History. We, beginning in this great city, are embarking on a journey to elevate man back to his rightful place. We are incinerating the debilitating words that have kept mankind from reaching its true potential. I am sure you hear screams of the old language tonight, this is our day of conflagration. This city's outdated institutions are being set ablaze: City Hall, churches, bookstores, synagogues, mosques, police stations, libraries, everything which would attempt to hold the institutions of false speech. Today is the day of fire that will burn from this city the decay of an old, false, manipulative language that hampers thought and reason."

"You fools," I announced, "you speak about History, but you mock her. By attempting to root out the language, you fail to appreciate the complexities of History. You have created for yourselves a mere contrivance—a technical language. 'Reason' and 'Truth'—you are on a children's crusade. These 'outdated' words you speak of are our ancestral lineage of meaning, for better or worse, no matter how twisted, corrupted or corrupting. They are mysterious and pregnant and so ubiquitous and cherished that only mass extermination of the speakers or a millennial long strangulation could kill them. The destruction of living language is a denial of History and Spirit, for within the ring of verbal and written symbol is the clamor of human becoming and decay. Do not vainly try to deny man of all of his deeds, despairs, thoughts and deaths. Besides, language is innate in man. The content of all languages is the same, stemming from our communication instincts and not dependent on vocabulary, word order, declensions, etc. Changing the way we talk or write will not fundamentally change how we reason and think.

"And you," I pointed to Agathon, "you sit there grinning at all this madness. Where is your violin, Emperor?"

Agathon was unmoved and spoke quietly.

"You try to mock your superiors, but you mock your yourself instead," the tall fellow interpreted. "I will not take the bait; I am not interested in your ignorance nor do I have the stomach for debating in this incestuous language. To the point, holy fool, tell us your story. Lead us to the codex. Where is the miserable book?"

The old man rocked back and forth with anticipation.

"I will not breathe this tale to you," I stated dryly.

"We did not ask for your recounting, we demand it."

Fires and plumes of smoke were rising from the city's floor. A ghastly red and yellow aura reflected from the clouds, the colorful haze of combustion. Whining emergency vehicles could be heard through the wet night air. The screams of citizens resounded through the manmade chaos of language's attempted incineration.

"Although you may disagree with our goals, we need the manuscript. The masses could draw a false messianic message from the codex. The polis is very taken with the ancient and esoteric. The book has inspired others. We need to destroy it, or our project could be slowed.

"You have little hold on History—you who is so conditioned to untruth. To scold us concerning History and language is absurd. You sit there in your angst and falsehood, speaking a suicidal language, reprimanding us— the enlightened leaders of the new world. There is fire in the air, and soon you will be added to the blaze for your insolence!" shouted Agathon's mouthpiece.

The Demiurge stood up arthritically. Looking directly into my eyes, he walked toward me. His visage was peaceful with a thin smile and heavy eyelids. He raised a finger to the sky and said, "I will sink to your level, for just a moment. I will communicate in the ancestral language, the same language that was forced upon me by my forefathers. You are an infinitesimal barbarian. You speak without knowledge of the new language. It has not seeped into your brain and become part of your being. It will be the greatest boon to man! You are the nocturnal fool—the insomniac who violates all laws of man and nature. I know who you are. Like your father and mother, you harbor only the horrific banality of your own emotional tremors—nothing more. You are that lonely child of the nothing, whose words have manipulated, raped and enslaved. You are a whore of History—an indentured prostitute of irrational pleasure and false trembling. Go ahead; do yourself that great entertainment of recounting. Sift your tale through the sieve of lie, then give me the codex or confirm its destruction." When Agathon finished, he stumbled back to his seat. He smiled at me and, with a gesture of his hand, summoned me to speak.

"I will tell you," I mumbled past my cigarette, "all that you want to hear. I will begin with the events of my life and end with your music. The gathering of history into words is not pleasant for me, but I will do it for you.

"The story may be a blessing or a curse, but it is my story—my illuminations and my darkness. But first, please unfetter my hands; if I am to speak of my life, I must have at least the semblance of freedom," I requested.

The Archon who slapped me came forward. She drew a six-inch hunting knife from her belt and slid it across the rope. I stretched with my renewed physical liberty. My shoulders, still sore from my abduction, popped as I stretched. "Thank you," I said. Then, as I twisted my neck for release, I noticed that Epi's kabalistic feline sat behind me. She winked and extended her paws and back in a long comfortable arch. The hairs on her back stood up as she did this. Then, she sat back down, a peaceful witness of the evening's coming story.

"As light both reflects off of the back of my hand and is entombed in my wrinkles and pores, so too is my story a mirroring and capture. I am not of heroic stock caught in tragic nobility. No, my story is neither great nor tragic; it is merely human. What you will hear are the words of an escapee and a messenger. Yes, I was born of this city, but from this city I ran, as my mother did after my birth.

"Who am I: a liar, a story teller, a sibling, a child, a murderer, a messenger, a being full of doubt and confusion? I answer yes to all. I am the one who dwells in the absurd and sings the ebb and flow of emotional discord. Tonight is not only a night of fire and tall tales, but also a night of cathartic song. A song built upon over millennia, like the music and libretto that you wish to find. You will hear the doxology..."

I told them my story. I explained who my father was and how I sprang from the first Sophia's loins. I reported how I was entrusted to deliver the codex to a well known scholar, who was also my uncle. I painted the picture, with words, of my plotting and my forgetting. I spoke around the cycle of unnatural love and its consequential flight, so common in my family. I lied only through omission; my words held truth. Finally, I spoke of the codex. I had buried it in a horse, but its song could not be trapped. At the time of the burial, I both knew and knew not what I was doing. It is difficult to explain paradoxes of the soul—they just are, like when you love and destroy simultaneously.

When I had finished my monologue, tears hung in the eyes of the fat, prone-to-slapping Archon. Others, too, had been somewhat moved by my story. That I had both killed and saved, that I had both defiled and been defiled—I pushed my humanity upon the group. The story held sobering truths that made sense within the deeds. They knew that my father was to translate part of and authenticate the codex for auction, but that I witnessed my sister's death was news. They learned who had wielded the shotgun. They found out that I had only recently learned who my mother was. They took pity upon me. I explained my dream of Sophia Pistis, and I cried.

The Archons no longer held the desire to witness my demise. Maybe I was too dirty in their eyes to be touched, much like Cane. For a moment, they seemed uninterested in the civic, commercial and residential property being incinerated around us. The perspective of all of us had changed significantly while on that tenth story roof. Then, in the midst of the madness—the vain cataclysm of language, the burning psalm, I sang the Song Itself. It was the salvation through Nothing. I had seen the hands who have written the notes of silence. This song is the eschatology of self and world, it is the dark fire. The Song swept through the city streets, into the souls of every citizen with a resounding silence. It quenched the a-tonal flutterings of Time and Space. The entire city, for that momentless moment, stood beyond error and beyond infinity. Everything was not, all at once. Every spirit, collectively and individually was filled with Nothing's pleasure. In that moment, the city brimmed over with clarifying darkness— this, the great cathartic melody, the Hymn of Life. It was a great celestial death—the greatest blessing and the greatest horror. That night evaporated under the unheard tones of the Song I had read in a dream and in the texts that I brought back to my homeland. And once in my homeland, I painted the walls of my father's house with blood and passionate righteousness.

I, who was cast into memory's dark fire and walked with the psychopomp, am now not what I was. Memory has scorched my cheeks; I am guilty, but I see little truth in either the Law or Reason. I see truth only in the Song—that baptismal in the formless and contradictory. Every being who felt the Song soon woke from his or her cathartic stupor of life. None of them remember what took place; none could gather the events of the cleansing. They had died prematurely that night, and what is there to remember of the Nothing. But each person was left a small, absurd shard within themselves of that primeval place beyond error, doubt, Truth, Law, knowledge, joy, melancholy, and everything else. Within them still shines that purifying darkness of the Stranger. The Stranger is our ancestor whom we must forgive as we forgive ourselves, he who neglected us and committed the greatest sin.

Epilogue

I have written my testimony of life and death. It is my inky shroud of words. The pages of my history will be scattered in the winds. If some lost and deranged soul chooses to spend life gathering all the pages back together, I hope he or she finds meaning in the act. I never intended that these words be collected, and, hopefully, they will not suffer that fate. Instead, I hope that the individual pages float on cloud's breath into diverse hands, and there find a place out of context in the absurd. For in absurdity, revelation is born and meaning ignited. Besides, I can't stay serious for very long.

Whence back in a world of Time and Space, the reader may ask, 'What happened next to our narrator?' Did I escape the Archons' clutches, to go on to living blissfully with the beautiful Eva? Or did I, after promulgating the tones of the Nothing, jump from the roof's heights—take the Leap? If the latter was the case, perhaps, as I fell to my death, I took Agathon with me. Or, was I such an ethereal blessing to man that, like Oedipus, I disappeared within the Fury's embrace? Maybe I donned the garments of the messenger himself, building instruments in basements with a Hebrew cat. Perhaps I gave birth to my stomach pains. You guess the lie, for my words are fading into dream…

Comments, accolades, reprimands?
TheSongItself.net

www.ingramcontent.com/pod-product-compliance
Lightning Source LLC
Chambersburg PA
CBHW031102260626
47172CB00001B/175